CW00555269

House of Lost Secrets

L. J. Hutton

Published by Wylfheort Books 2020

Copyright

The Necklace
The Western Coast of Greece c.AD 135

Sofia reverently placed the necklace into the hands of the statue of Hecate and stepped backwards, bowing as she went. Kneeling on the cool mosaic floor of the small shrine, she began to pray,

"Lady, I give thanks for your watching over me during my confinement." She knew her voice was catching with emotion, but struggled on. "I give thanks to you for the safe delivery of my daughter, and for preventing the arrival of the doctor my husband sent. I know now that had he come, neither I nor my sweet little Guilia would be here now."

She had no worries about the slave who stood behind her, back beyond the covering of the shrine, hearing her words. Had it not been for the help from her and the other women of the household, none of this would have been possible. It had been Hecate, Sofia was sure, who had sent the ash-blonde slave from Britannia her way, and without the girl's tantalising fairness and her willingness to seduce the doctor on Sofia's behalf, she would never have known the truth.

With a sad sigh, Sofia looked up into the serene face of the goddess' statue. "Six daughters I have born him before this one, yet my husband thinks nothing of me unless I can give him a son. And now I have nearly died in trying once more to satisfy his demands. Hecate please hear my plea: let him go away! I do not ask for his life. I just want him to go far enough away that I will be past my childbearing years by the time he returns. I have fulfilled my wifely duties many times over, and if the gods have not seen fit to send me a son, then who am I to continue to seek what is denied me? I love every one of my daughters – I could not love them more. They are more than enough for me. So please, I bring you the offering of this necklace in thanks, but also in supplication so that I may have no need to call upon your protection in childbirth again. Hecate, please watch over my home and my family."

Sofia leaned forward and placed a kiss on the sandalled foot of the statute.

"Ceridwen, your arm, please," she said as she turned from the shrine, the effort having already tired her.

The young British slave immediately came forward and put a strong arm around her mistress, holding the other out for her to grasp.

"Come mistress, let me take you back as far as the tree," she said gently, referring to an ancient olive tree – which had a bench piled with cushions beneath it, already prepared and waiting for Sofia to rest on. They saw the familiar figure of old Yia-yia bustling out with fresh fruit juice in a cup for her mistress, and Sophia knew she'd be in for an affectionate scolding. Yia-yia must have a proper name, she knew, but she had been Sofia's nurse when she was a child, and nurse to her younger sisters too, and 'Yia-yia' (Nanna) was all she had ever been known by.

The warm afternoon sun of the Greek autumn warmed Sofia as she rested, and she allowed herself to be pampered by her two faithful servants. This had been her family's home for centuries, and if the long, low white villa was not exactly to the tastes of the Romans who now ruled Greece, it was to hers. She felt safe here. Safe and protected. Thank the gods her husband had been just an ambitious young officer who needed her family's name and lands, or else she might have been in Rome – or at least somewhere else far from home – when this had happened. But Tiberius needed someone present at the estate to ensure it remained his, and so she had been allowed to stay.

He had rightly assumed that the estate workers' loyalty to the original family would mean that Sofia would have no trouble from them. What he hadn't been so astute about was in his affairs with other women, forgetting that even if Sofia didn't travel very far afield, word would be brought to her by those same loyal workers. So now Sofia knew that he was besotted with the raven-haired slave who had come in Emperor Hadrian's entourage from Egypt, and that that same girl now had a belly nearly as big as her own had been only days before. But unlike Sofia, this girl came with no money or land, so Tiberius wanted his wife conveniently dead so that he could keep all her family lands, but take a new wife – a wife he was absolutely convinced was carrying the desperately wanted son.

Luckily for Sofia, Tiberius had paid the doctor who attended all the resident Roman families in the area a handsome sum to attend to her confinement to ensure that she did not survive the birth. But a male doctor in attendance was so unexpected that the women in the household had immediately become suspicious. Yia-yia was the one who ought to have attended to Sofia. This was women's work, not a man's. And so when the doctor had come to examine Sofia a month or so back, all full of meaningless platitudes but little help, Yia-yia had taken charge of the matter.

She and Ceridwen had terrible trouble understanding one another most of the time, the British girl's native singsong language being unintelligible to the entire household, but Yia-yia spoke only Greek, so they didn't even have a common tongue in Latin. However this time they were united in purpose, and suddenly they went from being enemies to allies. Yia-yia had tempted the doctor to remain in the house overnight, had plied him with food laced with aphrodisiacs, and then Ceridwen had seduced him. And as the lithe young woman had pinned the doctor to the bed and ridden him like one of the horses from the stable she handled with such ease, she had also pumped him for information – for one of the things Ceridwen had was the intelligence to have picked up Latin easily, and if she couldn't speak to Yia-yia, she could definitely speak to the man.

Come the morning the doctor left feeling smug, having had his pleasures and having forgotten all he had told in the heat of the moment the night before. Ceridwen hadn't forgotten, though. During the remainder of the night, in a hurried conference in the kitchen after Ceridwen had left the doctor sleeping off his excesses, the women had decided he must be rendered incapable of assisting at the delivery.

"We need him to break an arm or something," Lamia the cook declared. "Nothing drastic, just enough so that Yia-yia will be the one actually touching Mistress!"

"Wicked man!" Penelope, the housekeeper spat. "And not just him, either! The master! What is he thinking?"

Ceridwen had snorted at that point, saying in her rough Latin, "He not thinking, Penelope, his cock ruling his brain! That woman he bringed back from the south, she have him by the balls."

Someone translated that for Yia-yia, who also spat and made the sign to ward off evil. "It was a bad day that man ever came here," she growled. "Thank Hecate all my younger doves all got good Greek boys for husbands!

They may be only farmers' wives now, but they're safe. My poor Sofia, though, what's to become of her?"

Lamia looked out of the window to the yard. "I think Hermes' time has come," she had said, referring to the elderly cockerel who had to be kept separate from the new cockerel they had just acquired. "Come on, no time like the present. It's a new moon. Let's take Hermes up to the shrine."

Lamia, Penelope and Yia-yia went out into the yard, grabbed the protesting Hermes, and walked the short way across the grove which formed the immediate space around the house to where the shrine lay. While Ceridwen stood well back, but observing carefully, the three older women made their obeisance to Hecate, and then with a swift blow, Lamia took Hermes' head off. To Ceridwen, the ritual made no sense, although she understood full well what animal sacrifices were, and why they were made. What she wasn't expecting was to see the ethereal shape of a graceful woman rise above the three kneeling on the earth, just before the shrine's mosaic floor began. Clearly here in their own world these eastern goddesses were a power to be recognised, but there was something familiar to her as well – this was a goddess who embodied the Maiden, the Mother, and the Crone, and those she knew very well from her homeland. So she called upon the Matronae softly in her own tongue, and believed that in their own ways both she and these Greek women were asking for help from the same goddess.

With the sacrifice made, they had all gone back inside and gone to bed, but Ceridwen was sure enough of horses to ensure that a burr was under the doctor's saddle when he rode off. What none of them expected was the following afternoon to be told that the doctor's horse had thrown him, and that the doctor had broken his neck and died. That was rather more than they had hoped for.

"Serves him right," Yia-yia said without sympathy, as they told Sofia what they had discovered. "He would have killed you with less thought than we gave Hermes last night!"

And so when Sofia had been safely delivered of her seventh daughter, she had felt compelled to take a beautiful necklace up to the shrine and offer it to Hecate. It was a lovely thing, with cabochons of polished, pale agate capped at either end with circles of garnets. In between the longer beads were spacers made of amethyst, and in the centre of it was a large garnet set within a larger circle of creamy agate. Tiberius had forbidden Sofia to wear it when they entertained, calling it old-fashioned and un-Roman, but although Sofia didn't particularly enjoy wearing it, it had belonged to women in her family for generations and it seemed fitting now to hand it on to the goddess. For Hecate was the guardian of the home and the family, as well as of women throughout their lives, and this old villa sat at the junction of three ways, which was also regarded as Hecate's space. Therefore Hecate was not just her guardian, but the guardian of this house too, and Sofia wanted to be sure that she continued to watch for them, so that the actions of her servants did not rebound badly on them all.

Yet Hecate must have been appeased, for only a few months later the message came that Tiberius had found favour with the emperor – he was to go with a message from Rome to Ceridwen's home island of Britannia. Whether he was pleased with the posting was harder to tell. Sofia presumed he must think that he would go and then return covered with glory, but Ceridwen was far more scathing.

"You wait 'til he gets there, Mistress! He won't know what hit him! He be too cold to be dipping his cock then! That wall he talk about is in far north of my land, and once he get there they not likely to let him just wander back!"

And so it proved to be. The months and then the years rolled by, Sofia and her daughters flourished, and Tiberius was never heard of again. Meanwhile the necklace was always kept by a shrine to Hecate, and was handed down through the generations.

Chapter 1
The modern day

Cleo was just arranging the large Grecian statue in her tiny hall, when the doorbell ringing right above her made jump nearly out of her skin. Before she could even turn to the door, the letterbox flapped open and her friend Angie's voice said,

"Good grief! Sorry about that! I heard you squeak. I thought you'd be upstairs."

Opening the door, Cleo gestured her to come in.

"So this is the new place," Angie said with little enthusiasm. "A bit on the pokey side compared to your old flat, isn't it?"

"Come on up and I'll put the kettle on and tell you the tale." Actually Cleo was more than glad to have an excuse to stop hauling boxes around, and Angie was always good company. Some folk found Angie's blunt honesty a bit too much, but Cleo found it refreshing.

"So what went wrong with the old place?" Angie asked, as they squeezed past a pile of boxes to get into the lounge with their mugs of tea, and collapsed onto the sheet-covered sofa. "I bet it was that shit Rachel, wasn't it?"

"Got it in one! Oh Angie, what a mess! She's really gone and done it this time."

Angie looked with concern at Cleo. Rachel was Cleo's slightly older stepsister and the bane of her existence, not helped by Cleo's mum being utterly smitten with her husband's trashily-glamorous daughter, compared to whom Cleo seemed dull in her mother's eyes. There had been several unpleasant incidents in the past, but given the way Cleo was reacting this time, something seriously bad had happened. "Go on then, tell me, and then I'll tell you my news."

Cleo gave her a grateful smile. "Well we both know how many times Rachel has ended up on my doorstep over the years, and how many brushes with the law she's had. And you've heard me ranting enough times to know how frustrating I find it to have Mum on the phone from Spain telling me to go and bail the wretch out from one magistrates' court or another. But I really thought that the last time I moved and only gave Mum my mobile number, that we'd put a stop to her actually coming to where I live."

"Oh no!" Angie felt her heart sinking. The trouble with Rachel wasn't just that she'd been spoilt rotten by her father, but the fact that she spent half her time shoving every substance known to man up her nose, and the other half thieving to pay for her habits – albeit primarily from people she knew, who she thought in some bizarre way ought to support her addictions. Combined with that were the kind of looks which she could and did use to manipulate men, and often to the distress of another woman. Consequently she was not a pleasant person to have around, and Angie remembered clearly Cleo's relief at having finally found a way to get around her contacting her in person.

Now Cleo was nodding. "I can't believe how stupid some people can be! I mean, I told Mum about how she'd forced me to move because she broke into my previous flat before the one I've just left, but you know, I don't think Mum ever really believed me. Every time we've spoken on the phone she's asked me if the police have found the burglars! Like we don't both know that it was Rachel!"

"Sadly, I don't think she wants to see how bad she is," Angie tried to console her friend by saying, but by the way Cleo was shaking her head she knew that worse was to come.

"It's not just that, Angie. It's the fact that Mum hasn't the faintest understanding of how unbearable she made my life. She's flatly refused to even listen to me telling her of how many complaints I had about Rachel turning up stoned out of her mind and disturbing my neighbours. Or the complaints I had from the owners of the previous block of flats I was in, followed up by threats of action against *me*." Cleo brushed a tear from her cheek. "I was so happy in my last old flat, which I moved into to get away from all of her chaos the previous time. That lovely big garden I could get out into from my French window, and then finding my lovely big statue under that tangle of ivy. I would happily have stayed there forever."

"So what went wrong? How on earth did she track you if she didn't even have a landline phone to trace?"

"My own stupidity!" Cleo said bitterly. "I told Mum that I'd rented a broom cupboard of an office in Malvern so that I could keep my files safely locked up – you know, on the off-chance that Rachel would break in again, but never really expecting her to. It never occurred to me that she was pumping me for information when she kept asking me if I was okay financially. 'What are you going to do if you need to change your car?' she asked me, and like a fool I said, 'oh the old Ford has a few more years left in it.' I just thought she was thinking I'd taken on too much with buying my own flat and renting an office. It never occurred to me that all of this information was getting handed on to Rachel!"

"Oh crap!"

"Yes! So having realised that I had an office right in the centre of Malvern, and was still driving the old Fiesta I'd had back when she'd been a more regular 'visitor', all Rachel had to do was lurk around and watch for me. She must have been searching Worcester high and low for me, you know, which was what gave me that year or so's grace. But Malvern isn't that big, and once she knew I'd come this way it can't have been hard for her. ...Well there I was at home, and suddenly the bitch walked in through the French window! Bold as brass! Just walked in!"

"Fucking hell!" Angie was appalled. Rachel was what might best be described as Junoesque, and once inside there was no way someone of Cleo's petite size would physically get her out. "So what did you do?"

"I threatened her with the fire poker. Told her I'd break every bone in her body if she didn't get out!"

"And did it work?"

Cleo gave a sour chuckle. "Actually it did! She was sufficiently out of it to take me seriously that time, but she went threatening that she'd be back – and she came."

"Oh no!"

"Yep, rolled up at three in the morning throwing stones through my windows. Thank heavens I was on the ground floor – I shudder to think of the damage she'd have done if she'd had to throw them higher. She could have wrecked so many other flats! Luckily my neighbour called the police and they came around and arrested her, and because it wasn't me making the complaint, the charges stuck. Would you believe it, I was very late home because I'd been up to Birmingham for a conference? So I wasn't there when it all kicked off.

"But, oh Angie, I had my mum on the phone screaming her head off at me. She called me all of the bitches under the sun! Told me that I must withdraw the charges immediately, and then when I told her that I couldn't do that because it wasn't me who had made them, she completely lost it. She called me a liar and started screaming about how she didn't know how I could be her daughter when I was so cold and heartless."

Angie dumped her mug on the floor and immediately wrapped her arms around Cleo. "Oh, hon', I'm so sorry! Oh God, that must have hurt so much!"

"It did. I'm so upset about it even now. I couldn't believe that she would set herself so against me. It's like I was the step-child, not Rachel."

"So what happened?"

Cleo disentangled herself from her friend and found the box of tissues to blow her nose. "Well I realised that there was nothing to be gained by moving instantly. There was going to be a court hearing at the very least, and so my address was going to come up. But I decided that the moment it was over and done with I was going to move. So I started packing straight away. I knew it might take a while to sell the flat, so I started looking for somewhere to rent. I got rid of the office and initially packed everything into the flat – there's no way I could afford my mortgage, the rent on that, *and* another place, not even for six or nine months! Then I found this place. It's as cheap as chips because it's surrounded by social housing, but I've only taken it for six months. So my old place is now totally empty and on the market, maybe even with an offer coming, the office is gone, and there's nothing left that would lead here. Until then it's me and endless boxes wedged into here. By the end of her sentence, hopefully I'll have sold my place, and then I can start again somewhere new."

Angie forced a smile. "Well I'm glad about that, at least." She gestured at the dingy chocolate brown paint on the lounge walls. "It's going to take an awful lot of magnolia to cover that up! But if you're not stopping than

I suppose you can cope with it."

Cleo managed a genuine smile at Angie's disgust. In truth it wasn't far off her own, and it certainly explained why the flat had been empty for so long, and the landlord being willing to take such a low rent. "I know, the landlord said much the same …they did have a bit of a thing about it! It's on the hall and the kitchen, and the bathroom too! And I don't feel compelled to do much about it. If I was staying it would be different, but it's serving a purpose – nothing more. And I think the landlord's been thinking of how much it's going to cost him to redecorate the whole place and was glad to find someone who'd take it as it was.

"But what really hurts, Angie, is that I've had to cut all contact with my mum. I just can't trust her anymore. And I can't bear having those stilted conversations where I'm watching every word I say to her, which were what we were having even before all this blew up. I'd rather not speak to her at all than that. But what cuts so deep is that she told me that she doesn't want me anymore after Rachel got six months inside. She told me that Rachel had told her that she got my address off Imogen, but Imogen didn't have my address, only my phone number and the landline was ex-directory anyway. So that was a pack of lies."

"I still wouldn't be giving Imogen your new number, though," warned Angie.

"No I won't. But then we've been getting further apart anyway since she became so chummy with that weird Goth, Kimberley."

"Is that the one who told Imogen you were into Devil worship because of your statue?"

"That's her. Not that she'd know fact from fiction! She's another one whose view of the world comes out of a pill bottle or strange tobacco. I tried to explain that Hecate isn't a vampire-like Dark Goddess at all, but a perfectly respectable Greco-Roman goddess who protects women, house and waysides, but she wasn't having any of it. And I'm sure that Rachel has worked her charm on Imogen as far as possible – she always could turn it on when she wanted – but there was a limit to what Imogen could ever have told her, and she certainly couldn't have traced me from it. Imogen didn't know about the office for a start, only that I'd moved out of Worcester and that was why she hadn't seen much of me. So the sad truth is that it could only have been Mum who betrayed me."

Angie shook her head in dismay. "So when you texted me and said you had a new mobile number, I'm guessing that your mum didn't get that one as well?"

"No. I still have a note of her numbers, but she has no way of contacting me. If I feel the need to speak to her, I'll just use a public phone, but I can't see that happening for a long time. The old phone got recycled and the sim card went on the fire as a last act in the old flat. My beloved old car got sent to auction, and I've temporarily got that hire car which is outside. I know I'm still more or less in Malvern, but I'm in a part I never had any associations with before, and by the time Rachel gets out, I'll hopefully have moved on again."

Angie was appalled. "What an awful thing to have to do just because of your family! But what about your business? How will your clients get hold of you?"

"Oh that was the easiest part, strangely enough. My post is being held for me at the main post office, so I'm still getting that, and most of my work comes from contacts who use my email or website. Luckily my business name is nothing which Rachel would have the wit to connect to me, and anyway I don't advertise. Virtually all of my work these days comes from referrals."

Angie sighed with relief. "Good! ...Well I was going to tell you my news and then ask you a favour, but by the sounds of it, it might be more of a mutual thing than I ever expected!"

Cleo was suddenly curious. It was out of character for Angie to ask for any sort of favour – it was uphill work just getting her to accept presents. "Okay, now you've got me. What favour?"

But Angie grinned and wagged a finger. "Well first you have to have the news! James is gone!"

Cleo let out a whoop of delight and high-fived with Angie. James was Angie's husband, but why and how the nice lad she'd married had turned into the pompous and arrogant bullyboy he was these days was a mystery. Both James and Angie worked as estate agents, but the competitive edge to the job hadn't twisted Angie.

"How are the kids taking it?" Cleo asked, suddenly anxious as she remembered how James had had a knack of twisting things when he spoke to little Charlie and Alice, so that they saw their mum as the bad guy every time.

Now Angie's face broke into a broad grin. "The bastard shit his nest! You remember Houdini the Rabbit?"

"How could I forget? He's the only rabbit I've ever met who's that big!"

"Well those huge paws of his dug him right out of the garden." Angie sighed sadly. "The daft thing went and made a run for the main road and got squashed. But James made the big mistake of gloating about it to the kids. They were heartbroken, of course, but not only did he make some very nasty comments at the time, he just wouldn't let it rest whenever they got upset."

Cleo could feel the relief wash over her. "So they've seen him in his true colours! Thank heavens for that!"

"Oh yes! And they're the ones who turned to me and said that they didn't want to live with daddy anymore. 'Daddy's nasty!' Alice said to me, and Charlie actually won't talk to James at all. So at the moment all three of us are in Mum's tiny holiday cottage. Thank heavens we've got another couple of months before the first bookings start for the new season, so I've got a bit of grace time-wise. If we haven't found somewhere by then we'll all have to squash into Mum's for a bit."

Now she gave Cleo a grin. "But the thing is, I've got a strange commission."

"Strange? How 'strange'?" Angie had long since moved away from the estate agent firm where James was a senior partner, and now worked for an agent who specialised in large country houses and the larger commercial deals, such as whole farms. "I can't imagine many of your clients having a 'Rachel' lurking around."

Angie shook her head. "No it's odder than that. We've been asked to sell an amazing old place out Bromyard way – which of course is nothing out of the ordinary for us. But the woman who's selling has made a rather peculiar stipulation – we only get the contract if we can find someone to investigate the history of the house."

Cleo blinked. "Good grief, that is odd! Why? What does she think she'll get from that?"

Angie shrugged. "Well apparently there was some tale her late husband used to tell her about something hidden in the past. He'd never say what, but this woman… honestly, Cleo, she'd show a crab a thing or two when it comes to being grasping! Not content with the fact that the house is going to fetch way over one and a half million as it is, she thinks that if she can attach an important history to the place, then she'll get even more for it. What we can't get through to her is that the place she's seen which is on the market for a lot more is actually owned by the National Trust, and will be on a long lease to whoever buys it. She just sees this grand house and thinks hers ought to fetch the same! In truth, while hers is a very nice Grade II listed Georgian house, it's not in the same league as the NT one; but she thinks if she can give her house as good a history – or even better, some fame – then it will go into the same price range.

"She can't see that architecturally the other one is far superior; and she wouldn't want any of the national charities involved anyway, especially not if it meant them telling her what could, or couldn't, be done with the house. She wants to sell it on her terms in every way. The thing is, she's already shown our two main rivals the door because they told her that it won't make a scrap of difference to the value, and if we don't play ball, she'll go to one of the London agents and keep going until she gets someone who does it her way."

"But surely your company isn't that desperate for the commission?" Cleo asked, having a momentary twinge of worry that Angie's job might be rocky.

"*They* aren't," Angie replied, "but *I* am! If I can pull this one off, my share of the commission will mean that I can buy a cottage I've seen! Or rather, I can put down such a big lump sum that the mortgage will be manageable on my salary by the time our divorce comes through, and I get my half of the family house. It'll be the first really big job I've brought in to the company – the bosses have only let me loose on it because they were so repelled by the client! But if I prove my worth, then they can't keep giving me the leftovers. Up until now I've had only the smallest jobs which have come in, but the partners and my senior, Ellie, have all at some point actually brought business in rather than just waiting for it to appear. So I'm trailing way behind them until I can do something like that. And that affects my commission percentages on other jobs, too, so I really need this to work out."

Cleo was beginning to get an inkling of where this was going. "Well that's great, but I assume you want me to do this investigating for her?" And then as Angie began to nod, protested, "But Angie, I'm a genealogist! I trace people, not houses!"

"I know, but hear me out!" Angie pleaded. "It's not so much the house itself but the people who were there who she thinks will make it interesting. I must admit I was going to come to you on bended knee to beg you to take this, but seeing you here like this, I think there's a hook which might just make you think twice. You see, she wants whoever does this to move into the house for a few weeks. I think the tight-fisted cow wants to make sure that you do some work, because I told her straight that she'd have to pay for the work upfront. We wouldn't consider taking it out of the final fee! After all, these big places often take a long time to sell – years, even – and we couldn't, in all conscience, ask anyone to do this work and then wait for that long to be paid."

"And she agreed?"

"Funnily enough, yes. I think at last she's accepted that if she wants it done at all, then she's going to have to accept something in return, albeit pretty minor. I came here thinking to say to you that maybe you could just go for the weekday nights, but now I'm thinking you might well like going and spending some time in a beautiful old house with terrific views over the Bromyard Downs?"

"Will she pay my going rate?" Cleo asked. "I can't afford to do it on the cheap for you, Angie. I've got my own pile of expenses just at the moment!"

But Angie's grin just got broader. "I told Mrs Darcy D'Eath Wytcombe that I knew someone who was the best in the business …and then added five quid an hour onto your normal rate! And I told her that you certainly wouldn't be expecting to contribute to your board and lodgings while you were there, either! You'll be living there full board for free!"

Cleo's jaw dropped. "Angie! You little devil, you!" By Hecate, it was tempting! It was more than tempting! No expenses at all for a month or two was just what she needed at the moment.

"You haven't got any jobs on at the moment, have you?" Angie suddenly thought to ask.

"Not exactly on the go," Cleo admitted. "I've a couple of folks who already knew that I was going to take a month or two to get around to them, so they won't vanish if I'm not on the case straightaway. I'm currently writing up the results of my search for a wealthy American rancher whose Irish ancestors I've been digging up, but that won't take me beyond the end of next week. Besides that I've got the usual couple of 'forlorn hopes' who I can't get anywhere with, but they can sit on the back burner for a while. Other than that I've several enquiries, but none where I've put the ink on the deal just yet."

What Cleo called the 'forlorn hopes' were those clients who just wouldn't accept that their families couldn't be traced, and Cleo had a tactic for them. She would do what work she could and make a note of the hours actually spent, but then she would pass on the initial findings, or lack of them, listen to the pleas to try again, and then put the job on one side for a month or two. She only ever added a tiny amount onto the bill (given that she only ever reread the evidence she'd found and did a couple more searches), telling her clients that she really hadn't found anything more; yet somehow that extra month or two's wait for the results seemed to finally convince them that she had done her best. And she was never annoyed with these people, because they were the ones who most often went on to recommend her to their friends. They always seemed to think that they'd got value for money out of her by the extra wait, and Cleo was astute enough to know that her fees spread over six months, instead of three or four, gave an appearance of being a better deal.

Therefore the two 'forlorn hope's she had on file at the moment would be work she could probably type up on her laptop in the evenings, after she'd finished her day's work at the house. And as if reading her mind, Angie added,

"Oh, and I told Mrs D.D.W. that you would only work office hours! Told her straight that if you came and stayed, there'd be no pushing you to work in the evenings as well! I said that you would expect professional consideration," and she gave Cleo a mischievous wink. "Wasn't going to let the old besom think that once you were there, you'd be slave driven! I said that any hint of that and you'd be leaving and she'd never find someone as good as you again."

Cleo shook her head in wry admiration of Angie's gall. "Sounds to me like you sold it to her as a done deal. What if I'd said 'no'? Or had been in the middle of a really good and lucrative job?"

But Angie was already grinning and waving Cleo's protests aside. "I told her that she might have to wait several months until you were free. ...Both for your sake and mine! I wanted her to sign the damned agreement and get the house on the market before she changed her mind. Luckily she's already had one viewing from a small company who specialise in country house hotels. They didn't want to pay the going rate, let alone Mrs D.D.W.'s idea of what it will fetch, so that didn't go anywhere – but with that being a first, at least it's made her think that we're the ones to do the job, and who'll sell it for what she wants. She'll be chuffed to bits if you can come earlier than I've told her to expect you."

Cleo sighed, but with good humour. "Looks like I'm going to be living the life of a country squire for a bit, then!" She hugged Angie. "I can't say I'm not delighted at the prospect of not having to live here for longer than necessary, and I'm well pleased that it's going to do us both a good turn in the end."

"Right! Then these are the details," Angie declared with her normal bounding enthusiasm, and proceeded to pull a huge sheaf of papers out of the briefcase she had brought in with her.

When she had gone, Cleo went and poured herself a glass of red wine from the bottle she had opened last night, and went down to the antique statue at the bottom of the stairs. Heaven knew where it had come from, but it was far older than just some modern reproduction, and in an auction would probably fetch thousands. Yet she felt a strong bond with it, and knew that she would never part with it except under the most extreme of circumstances.

"Thank you, Hecate," she said gratefully, dipping her finger into the wine and dripping a few drops onto the plinth. The flat was just the upstairs half of what looked like a normal house from the outside, but the statue was still way too heavy for her to have got it up the short flight of stairs. So instead, Cleo opened the front door and stood watching the February sun sinking over the Malvern Hills, and shining in on the old statue she had found abandoned in the garden of her previous flat.

"Maybe things are looking up after all?" she said, giving the statue an affectionate pat on the arm and putting the small posy of artificial daffodils into its arms, which was what she'd been about to do just as Angie had arrived. The hall was too gloomy for a pot of real miniature daff's to survive in, but if this job went well then perhaps, when she moved on, it would be to somewhere where she could sit the statue by a big window again.

Chapter 2

A week later

As she drove up the long and winding drive to Upper Moore House, Cleo thought that it was probably just as well that her old car had had to go. Arriving at this splendid Georgian house – a place worthy of a *Pride & Prejudice* Mr Darcy if ever she'd seen one – in the mouldy-green and rust coloured Ford would not have created the right impression. As it was, the hire car was suitably newish without creating the impression that maybe she was charging a little too much for her services, and its unexciting grey at least looked businesslike.

Not quite sure where to go, Cleo decided that parking outside the imposing front door would be frowned upon, and instead followed the tyre marks in the gravel around to the side of the house. That proved to be the right choice, because there were four older cars parked there which presumably belonged to the staff. Quite where those staff were, however, was harder to determine. As she got out of the car, Cleo was struck by the quiet which hung over the place. It almost seemed deserted.

Then around the corner of an outbuilding appeared first a wheelbarrow and then a tall, thin man in overalls pushing it.

"Hello," he said with little enthusiasm. "You come to see the place, have you?"

"Err, no, actually I've come to meet with Mrs Wytcombe. Do you know where she might be?"

"Well not out here," he declared morosely, and seemed about to carry on on his way when a voice from behind them called out,

"For God's sake, Joe! Try being a bit more polite!"

Cleo turned and saw a much more animated woman come bustling out of a door which it was now evident to see led into the kitchen.

"Hello, love, I'm Sarah Palmer – cook and general indoor dogsbody!" the woman introduced herself. "You'll be Miss Farrell?"

Cleo immediately took a liking to this woman. Of indeterminate age, but probably not far over fifty, Sarah could just as easily have been chivvying a meeting of the local W.I. to order as working in a country house, and Cleo suspected that if the house was in good order then it was probably down to Sarah's hard work.

"Yes, I'm Cleo Farrell," she said, shifting her briefcase to her other hand and holding out her right one in greeting. "I hope I'm not making unnecessary work for you by staying here?"

Sarah gave a wry grin. "You? No, I doubt you'll be any trouble at all! And anyway, Herself says you're staying so that's the end of it!" There was definitely an air of mischievous criticism in those words, and Cleo was glad that Angie had warned her about Mrs Wytcombe's aspirations to grandeur – they obviously didn't go down very well with her employees!

"I'm sorry about Joe," Sarah was continuing, "but it's been a worrying couple of months. None of us knows whether we'll have a job when the place sells and there aren't that many jobs around here, and like me, Joe's home is tied to the job."

"Oh I quite understand," Cleo sympathised. "Most of my work comes from abroad, and without that I couldn't keep going on what I'd earn from the home market. I'd have to try and find a regular part-time job at the very least, and I've enough friends who've tried to do that to know that it's easier said than done."

Her gesture of solidarity worked and made Sarah even more forthcoming. She shook her head woefully as she declared, "I'm well the wrong side of fifty to be working full-time in a supermarket somewhere, even if they'd have me. I think we all knew that Herself would sell up when Sir Archie died, but we all thought he'd be around for a lot longer. I mean, he was only just into his sixties – no age at all. We thought we'd got a good ten years left here."

"Did Sir Archie die suddenly, then?" Cleo dared to ask.

"Very!" Sarah said with the air of someone who thought something underhand had gone on. "One day he was out with the local gamekeepers and talking about this season's shoots – we have a particularly good wood and parkland for those, you see – and then the next he was ill in bed and never got up again."

"Good grief!"

Again there was that sniff from Sarah which said something fishy had gone on. "Yes. I know this sounds harsh, but I'd rather he'd died here. Then there would've had to be an inquest. Instead he was in Worcester hospital for just long enough for them to say that they'd been treating him for a perforated ulcer and internal bleeding, and so having been in there, the doctor's words were taken as gospel. But I still find it odd! My uncle had ulcers for years, and one of them perforated, but Sir Archie had had none of his symptoms. He was as fit as a flea right up until that last week or so – not a hint of trouble! And I know damned well that if I'd have served Uncle Sid with some of the dishes I cooked for Sir Archie in what turned out to be his last months, the poor soul would have been rolling round the bed in agony. So before you ask, no, I don't think that was what was wrong with Sir Archie at all."

Cleo smiled back at Sarah, but thought it odd that someone on the staff should so bluntly express their concerns to a stranger. After all, she could have been connected to friends of Mrs Wytcombe, for all Sarah knew. Deciding that she must treat this woman with some caution, Cleo followed her indoors. The last thing she needed was for Mrs W to think that she too was criticising her behind her back before she'd barely started the job. She really must make sure she kept her comments neutral to Sarah until she'd figured out what on earth was going on here.

By now they had arrived in a huge kitchen area, all kitted out with the latest mod. con's. And although there was a large dining table at the far end, it was clear to Cleo that this must be where Sarah and Joe, plus anyone else who was working in the place, came to sit and eat. The chairs and table looked well used, and not particularly fashionable. Mrs Wytcombe would have either the latest chic designs or expensive antiques, Cleo guessed, and these were neither.

"I hope I'll be joining you down here to eat," she said. "Eating up in my room all sounds a bit *Jane Eyre!*"

"God, yes!" Sarah laughed. "I'm glad you hadn't got your hopes up over eating with Herself. You wouldn't stand much chance of that, I'm afraid. Anyway, she barely eats a couple of lettuce leaves and a quail egg most days, although quite why she's so obsessed with not putting weight on at her age, I don't know."

"All the better to attract the next husband?" Cleo daringly ventured, and immediately kicked herself mentally. Damn! So much for treading carefully – that wasn't the right thing to have said at all. Her memories of her mum going on the man-hunt way too close to her dad's death still hurt, and in the current circumstances were too close to the surface. *I mustn't judge Mrs W by Mum!* she chastised herself. But she was rewarded with a chortle from Sarah.

"Oh you'll do! I was dreading having some pompous madam coming in who took Herself's word for everything. I don't think she'll pull the wool over your eyes! So just to warn you: she thinks you're going to find that there's pirates' treasure in the old ice house, or a will which proves she owns a vast former plantation in Jamaica, or the like."

"Oh crap!" Cleo sighed. "Not another one of those. Why can't people just be interested in their ancestors for their own sake?"

Sarah shrugged. "No idea! For what it's worth, I think that what Sir Archie told her about the family having some deeply buried secret is more likely to be the kind of thing she'll wish had never come to light, if you find it. Let's face it, some of these old country families did some pretty terrible things in the past – daughters walled up into rooms because they'd got pregnant by the wrong man, or some poor infant being born not right because its parents were too closely related, and getting locked away in an attic for life. Charlotte Bronte probably didn't pluck the idea for Bertha Rochester out of thin air – there were more than a few reported cases of crazy wives and lunatic sons about. If I was a betting woman, I'd be putting my money on you finding that."

Cleo smiled. "Well unless there are a lot of family papers it's unlikely that I'll find even that much detail. The work I do focuses much more on censuses; births, marriages and deaths; and the occasional land grant or deed." Then couldn't help herself adding, "But if I came across another line of the family and that the property was entailed away, so that Mrs Wytcombe had to vacate for the rightful owner, I don't imagine that would be a popular result? I'm just a touch worried that she hasn't really thought this through at all – I can't guarantee what I'll find, and once found, I can't in all conscience then bury it again. I suspect the police would regard that as defrauding someone of their inheritance."

The way Sarah's eyes brightened was enough to tell Cleo that she, at least, would love for that to happen. "You keep that in mind while you're searching," she told Cleo, "and you'll be having my best Madeira cake for Sunday tea from now on!"

However, it was now time for Cleo to go and meet the woman who was employing her, and with sinking heart she allowed Sarah to show her through to what she was told was now the TV room. To Cleo it looked as though a once pleasant if slightly dark room, had been opened out into another room to make a cavernous space but with little character. The windows, such as they were, only had a few feet before a substantial brick wall blocked the light from the first one and there appeared to be some kind of bank falling away in the others. Slightly frosted glass had been put in to partially disguise the lack of view, and most of the light came from the glass door across the hall. A quick glance up to the ceiling revealed the scars in the plaster of once substantial light-fittings, but now there was a stellar array of inset spotlights.

Rising from a chaise, Mrs Wytcombe clearly meant her first impression to be one of the suffering widow in mourning, but a daytime soap blaring from the TV rather ruined the effect. Cleo thought of herself as a fairly sympathetic kind of person, and she had no illusions about her looks either – she was at best ordinarily pretty, and most of the time felt she would pass unnoticed in a crowd. Her hair's curls usually went in the wrong directions, and her best look was the kind of tailored suit she was wearing today, when she knew that at least she looked smart. Glamorous she could never do. But in the women facing her she had found someone with no discernible good points at all, and was close to downright ugly in a harsh and calculating sort of way. Mrs Wytcombe's face was long and horsey, with protruding heavy teeth. Above them she had a patrician nose that would have looked distinguished on a man, but did nothing for a woman, and the eyes were cold and hard.

No sign of weeping there, Cleo observed, and the lavish makeup wasn't there to hide smudges under the eyes or blotchiness from crying. It had the air of being something Mrs Wytcombe automatically did on a daily basis, regardless of circumstances. No doubt they were all top of the range products, because the haircut was definitely expensive too. The stylist must have had her work cut out for her, because Cleo felt sure that the artistic layers which had been created in the short, brashly white, peroxide locks were the only ones which were even vaguely flattering. And yet it could all have been put onto a rather coarse statue for all the good it did. Nor did the brilliant and harsh lighting do much for her. But conversely, a genuine smile or sign of emotion might have done a lot to make the woman look better.

Without consciously intending to, Cleo instinctively adopted her most businesslike approach. There were very few clients she could not maintain a working relationship with, and she was groaning inside that this time, the one she might have real difficulty with was one she would have to meet regularly in person. There was a lot to be said for dealing with clients by email and transatlantic phone calls!

"I hope you are aware that I cannot promise anything in the way of results," she said firmly, as Mrs Wytcombe waved her to a seat so far away it felt as though she had to shout to be heard across the void between them. "I will do my utmost to ensure that you have all the information which can be gleaned about your family, but sometimes the records simply do not survive."

"It's not *my* family you will be investigating," Darcy Wytcombe said with great disdain, as though she would never dream of letting a mere researcher get their mucky hands on her pedigree. "It's my husband's family I'm paying you to research. I was told many times by him that there were family papers which his father had said he would become privy to, but unfortunately his father died before he could explain fully. My dear Archie was quite bereft about that."

I bet he was, Cleo thought darkly, *but more because you never stopped pestering him about it than because he was desperate to know*. Time to get tough.

"Mrs Wytcombe, can you be more specific about what it is you want me to try and find?" Cleo asked bluntly. "Only I have to tell you that official documents will only give the facts of any situation. I won't be able to prove or disprove hearsay. Do you want me to take your husband's family as far back as I can? Or do you want me to look at side branches of the family? Or both?"

"It's Mrs *D'Eath* Wytcombe," she was pointedly corrected, "and what I want you to do, is to make some sense of the pile of family papers in the library. I don't know who half the signatures belong to, or whether they've signed something important, or even if they had the right to sign anything away!"

Bloody hell, Cleo thought, *Angie was right, she's grabbing everything she can, even if it means digging the dirt on some poor old squire who's been dead for years*. But she picked up on Mrs Wytcombe continuing saying,

"The solicitors have taken what they regard as necessary in order to deal with Archie's will, but there are boxes and boxes of old paper in there, and Archie was most insistent that none of it got thrown out. He said it was all valuable. So I want you to find out what he meant by that!"

Cleo could already feel her jaw hurting from clenching her teeth and putting on the false smile. It was a good thing she was going to get paid so well for this, and it was helping her out in the other way, otherwise she would have been out of the door already.

"Right, well if I can be shown to my room, I'll unpack my computers and make a start," she said firmly.

"Computers? But there's a perfectly good one in the library!"

"Maybe, Mrs D'Eath Wytcombe, but mine have special programs on them which I will need to use, and therefore I always use two laptops."

Darcy D'Eath Wytcombe waved a dismissing hand at her as if this was all just too tiresome. "Oh, if you must. If you go back through to the kitchen, Sarah will show you to the room. When I'm here I shall require regular updates, although I expect I shall be going back up to London to my place up there soon. I have affairs which need to be attended to. You may email me weekly reports."

Cleo knew when she was being dismissed and so she got up and left, but was amused to see Sarah leaning on the door frame in the main hall which led to the kitchen, grinning. Clearly she'd been listening to every word.

"Quite a charmer, isn't she?" Sarah chuckled, as she gestured Cleo to follow her upstairs to the library.

Cleo felt all her instincts prickle again. What was it between these two women? She was going to have to ask because the potential for things to go drastically wrong was just too great if she didn't know. They climbed a stunning ancient and warped staircase with exposed timbers, which had Cleo entranced at the thought of how old they might be, but then forced herself to consider the present – time to start wondering if she could find a dendrochronologist to give her a firmer date once she'd got settled. First things first, and Sarah was top of that list.

"If you don't mind me saying, Sarah, you aren't afraid to speak your mind about your employer," Cleo began, hoping that that wasn't too blunt.

Sarah swung the door open onto a large and beautiful library which Cleo would have killed to own, but leaned on the door and snorted wryly.

"Well she's not exactly my employer. You see Archie was my cousin – well second or third cousin actually, though I never can work out how those degrees of separation work." As Cleo blinked in surprise, flummoxed over what to say to that, Sarah continued, "I'm too remote to be in the direct family line, so I don't have a cat in hell's chance of inheriting this place." She sighed regretfully. "His first wife was lovely. She and I were really good friends – and that's another thing Herself holds against me."

Sarah walked across to one of the tall windows, and Cleo realised that here at the back of the house the first floor rooms at the one end were almost at ground level because of the way the ground rose diagonally away from the building. She'd come in at the side to the kitchen, and it hadn't sunk in until now that even access to the kitchen door was cut out of a bank.

"Archie used to love it here," Sarah sighed wistfully, and Cleo noticed she'd already dropped the 'Sir'. "He loved that he could just open these French windows and walk out over the 'bridge' straight into the garden. …They were so unlucky, him and Penny. Their only son was born with cerebral palsy, and I know some people live to adulthood and beyond with it, but Simon's condition was so severe, and it wasn't his only problem, he didn't make it to his teens. He died of complications, not just the main thing, you see, and then they'd barely got over that when Penny was diagnosed with cancer. I'd come here to help them look after Simon, because my husband Jeff was in the RAF and away most of the time. Our two boys were in private school from when I was out with him in Germany for a while, so Gardener's Cottage here suited us just fine. The boys came home in the holidays and Jeff when he was on leave, but it wasn't so huge that I felt like a pea rattling round in a tin can when they weren't here."

"Oh." Cleo didn't quite know what to say. That put a whole new complexion on things. "So when did…?"

"Herself turn up? Oh, about five years ago. Penny had been gone ten years and poor Archie was feeling the pressure to have an heir for the place. There was a very distant male cousin on his father's side, you see, but then he went and wrapped himself round an oak tree in his Morgan and that was the end of the heirs. So Archie apparently started dropping hints amongst his 'county' friends of the need for a new Mrs Wytcombe, and before we knew it, there she was! Stuck in our midst like some bloody cuckoo! I told him he'd be lucky if he ever got an heir out of her, but she'd already got her hooks into him, and Archie never could stand confrontation. If I'm honest, I think he started off feeling sorry for her – you know, lady of a certain age who's been left on the shelf – although once she's got her feet under the table the pretences stopped! Before the first year was out he'd have loved to divorce her, but he recognised that to pay the bitch off he'd have to sell this place, and that he could never do."

"What does your husband think of the situation, then?"

Sarah's face fell. "Jeff's been in a coma for the last two years. A skiing accident. I was already facing the dreadful decision of whether or not to turn his life-support off before all of this. My one son is now living in Canada, and the other's in New Zealand on a five year contract at the moment, so I've been trying to put it off until he comes back in two years' time, but I don't know that the doctors will give me that long."

"Oh my God! Oh Sarah, that's awful!"

"So you'll understand that the last thing I needed was for Herself to give me orders to pack up. I do not need the stress of having to pack up my home into boxes just at the moment. It's not the money. We have enough put aside to buy somewhere else, because Archie always let us live here rent-free. He said that they'd never have been able to have Simon at home for as long as they did without my help, and that this was his way of saying thank you. It was one of the few things he stuck to his guns over when Herself arrived, actually. …That's another thing she won't forgive me for!"

"Would she not sell you the cottage?"

Sarah pulled a face. "No way! She says that the kind of owner who'd want this place wouldn't want the estate split up – that they'll probably want the cottage for a housekeeper or chauffeur. And I can't see them keeping poor Joe on either, even if they do need a gardener. He's not the easiest of men to deal with, even if he's a wizard with the plants."

That explained a lot. And Cleo couldn't help but feel sorry for Sarah. Of all the lousy timing that had to be one of the worst, and it wasn't lost on her that Sarah was potentially in a similar situation to herself. Both of them were only one step away from being homeless. However, for her part that was going to make living in this house complicated if her sympathy was dragging her away from her client's best interests.

Luckily, Sarah now waved her towards the door and said, "I'd better take you to your room. I'm afraid it's up another floor. The main bedrooms are on this floor, and you're up in what at one time was one of the reserve guest rooms on the nursery floor. I hope you're not worried about ghosts. Some people get very superstitious about these old places – although that at least has saved us from the worst of Herself's friends from staying. She took one look at the bedrooms and refused to set foot in them, saying she felt she was being watched. Strange woman."

"No, I'm fine," Cleo said brightly, thinking this wasn't the point to admit that she too was sensitive to some places.

Chapter 3

Cleo's bedroom turned out to be a lovely room facing the front, and even if it had once been part of the servants' quarters, or where the children of the house were kept out of the way, it was still more luxurious than anywhere she'd ever owned. Having discreetly confirmed that once Mrs D'Eath Wytcombe departed for London, that she would be the only one in the house overnight, Cleo felt she would be able to snoop a little on this floor at least, for she longed to see if there were more gems like the staircase. And straight away she could see why Sarah had given her this room. There were two more large bedrooms, which were each bigger than the lounge of the flat she had just left, which led off the almost-square area of landing to hers, facing front and back respectively. The front one was separated from hers by a large bathroom. Then there was a smaller bathroom behind hers, which looked onto the side roof of the rest of the first floor.

"I'd use that one if I were you," Sarah said, gesturing to the smaller one. "The heater in there actually works, and although it's only got an electric shower, not a bath, you're not missing anything there. By the time the hot water has worked its way up to this floor to the bath, it's lukewarm at best anyway, thanks to the antique boiler. The only good thing about the old wreck is that it's the reason why Herself won't linger long here – she can't heat her room to subtropical levels!"

Looking at the kink in the landing between the two other bedrooms, Cleo guessed that more rooms lay beyond there, but Sarah said nothing about them, and Cleo thought they would be better explored once she had settled in. There must be nearly the same square footage again beyond there, given her memory of the span of the frontage, and of course the elegant main stairs must come up somewhere there too. She had seen them rising from the central hall when Sarah had taken her to meet Mrs Wytcombe, and they were at the other end of the building to the lovely old stairs she'd come up.

Up here there were no exposed timbers, and she guessed by that and the rooms' proportions, that this was a Georgian frontage put onto an older building. Downstairs, apart from the glorious old timbers in the back staircase, there was no clue that the house had been built in at least two phases, aside from the main porticoed front door being on what was now the side of the house, and Cleo couldn't wait to get a chance to go exploring and start dating the older part at the back. For all that her expertise lay in disentangling the paper trails, it was always nice when you had some physical evidence to back it up. Her time at university had included modules on archaeology and art history, and both were subjects she'd continued to enjoy reading up on in the evenings, or watching documentaries on. Consequently, although she would have been the first to admit that she was not an expert, she was a very well-informed lay-person when it came to putting dates on buildings, or layers of them, and to find herself actually living in such a delightful puzzle was more than compensation for working for the ghastly Mrs W

What baffled her was Sarah's statement that Mrs Wytcombe loathed the old place. Cleo had fallen in love with it at first glance. But then on second glance she could see that if you had aspirations to knock out walls and make modern open spaces, then this wasn't a house you could do that to. Too many of the walls were structural, for a start – you didn't need to be an architect to work that out. And of course it being listed meant that there would always be constraints as to what could be done. Mrs Wytcombe must have been seething when the implications of that sunk in, Cleo thought.

However, for this first night she was glad just to get settled in, and then join Sarah downstairs for the evening meal.

"I cooked with the intention of us eating here, because I wasn't sure what you'd be like," Sarah confessed. "But once Herself has cleared off, we'll eat over at my house as long as you don't mind. It's much more cosy over there! I have to be on hand to serve Her Royal Highness, unfortunately." Then she brandished a tray on which an avocado sat in near isolation apart from some fronds of continental-style salad and a few baby plum tomatoes. "That's it! That's all she's had today since breakfast as far as I can tell."

"Blimey, I can eat more than that in a sandwich for lunch!" Cleo said, as she appreciatively sniffed at the casserole smells wafting from the oven. "I'm clearly never destined to be a fashion icon."

Once the dinner was over, and Mrs Wytcombe's tray had come back down, Cleo and Sarah retreated to a pair of old but comfortable armchairs near to the huge Aga.

"When the weather's cold, Joe brings his packed lunch in here," Sarah explained, waving Cleo to one of them as she sank into the other with a grateful sigh. "And then there's Phil who's the general handyman who comes if anything needs fixing, so I like to have somewhere comfy for us to sit and enjoy a coffee. Other folk come in as needed too, like the extra gardeners. Those were the other cars you saw when you arrived. They've gone home now, though. ...So, how does this thing work? How will you get the information?"

Cleo took a sip of the excellent coffee, but then shrugged. "If I'm honest, I don't really know. My normal work is finding peoples' ancestors. There's not usually this pressure to find out what went on around them. Mostly my clients are Americans, Canadians, New Zealanders and Australians wanting to know about the folks back home, so anything I can tell them is welcome. If there's a title involved somewhere in the dim, dark past, then that often makes their year, let alone their day, but I'm always quick to warn new customers that I may well find that they were a bunch of criminals instead, and to not get their hopes up. Doesn't always work, of course, but the warning is there in writing, so if the odd one gets nasty and threatens to sue they don't have a leg to stand on."

"Will you get Herself to sign something like that?" Sarah asked looking slightly askance. "Best of luck with that if you do!"

But Cleo shook her head. "No, I won't this time, primarily because I'm being employed by the estate agents. They're the ones I have the formal contract with, and they're asking me to do this only because it's such a lucrative deal if they get a sale out of it. What Mrs Wytcombe thinks of what I find doesn't truly come into the equation, as long as she keeps her custom with them. So if it flatters her ego to think that she's employing me then I won't argue, but at the same time I'm not going to massage what evidence I find to suit her whims."

"And what evidence is there likely to be? Where do you start?"

"Where I usually do, I suspect, and that's with the censuses. The very first one done in England is in 1841, and the last one currently accessible is 1911, so you get some very nice snapshots at ten-year intervals of who was living in a house, especially when it's a nice old place like this which would always have been here within that time frame. They also give you ages, and quite often you can pick up on name variations too. So for instance, if there's a Sarah-Jane in the 1851 census who is the mother of Harry, aged two, and Bertie aged five, then she's likely to be the same person as just 'Jane' in the 1861 census who is mum to Harry aged twelve and Bertie aged fifteen. That in turn can give you a lot of clues as to what birth, marriage and death certificates you are looking for.

"But beyond that I shall try to find a bit more about the estate in this case. With a normal house in a town there's not usually much to find, but this place looks like it's been here a very long time. Do you know how old the house is?"

Sarah puffed her cheeks. "Golly, I don't really know. Archie always said it went back to Tudor times, but I don't know enough to say which bits. It just looks Georgian to me."

"Well those timbers on the back stairs are older, I'm already pretty sure of that."

"Really? Wow! …God, Archie would have been thrilled to bits to hear you say that – how sad he's not here."

"Yes, the way it goes up in quarter turns was so that it could be supported on heavy timbers. It's from the days when the main walls would have been timber-framed with wattle and daub infill, you see – not enough support on vital sections of the stairs for a straight run, has always been my understanding. If you were to remove some of that modern plasterwork, you'd probably find that it's a glorious open stairwell. My guess is that that would have been the main stairs to an older house, and that it got covered in panels so that the servants who used it later weren't so visible."

"Well I never! So the main stairs…?"

"Tacked on with a Georgian extension, I would guess, with a half landing to link with the older, lower-ceilinged building behind it. That's not anything unusual. Fashions change, and it's always the way that when it's just grandfather's old place, it doesn't have the cachet that makes people want to preserve it as it was. Think of how many big Victorian terraces in London in recent years have had the insides ripped out of them to make 'modern' spaces. I bet in a hundred years' time our generations will be regarded as terrible building vandals as the few remaining ones in their original state get rarer."

Sarah hooted with laughter. "For goodness sake, don't say that to Herself! She has some apartment in London that's made out of the top floor of an old Georgian terrace. All the walls except the ones needed to stop the place collapsing around her pretentious ears have been stripped out, and it's all in white. Archie only ever went there in desperation. He used to come back saying he felt like he was going snow-blind after he'd been in there a few hours. Apparently the high-gloss white kitchen is open plan with the white-carpeted lounge with the white chesterfield sofas. Even the bloody modern art on the wall is fifty shades of white!"

She gave a giggle. "The last time he went, only a few weeks before he died, he said he deliberately knocked over a big glass of red wine just so that there would be a bit of colour in there!"

Cleo blinked in shock. "Wow! I bet that wasn't popular!"

"She screamed like she'd been savaged by her sodding white Persian cat! Archie said he had to slap her to stop the hysterics. She was absolutely incoherent about it, he said, talking about having to get the whole carpet ripped up the very next day. And when he said a bit of stain remover ought to do the job, she threw him out of there and sent him home. He actually thought she might ring her lawyers and ask for a divorce, she was that het up."

"I thought he dreaded that?"

"Because of selling this place? Well yes, he did. But he said that her response was so bizarre, so totally over the top, that any judge would see her as the one behaving unreasonably, and in that case, she might not get the settlement that she wanted."

Cleo felt a nasty cold lump settling in her insides. "So did she? See her lawyer, I mean?"

Sarah shrugged. "We never knew. But knowing her, I bet she did. And I bet she got told that she'd come up way shorter than her expectations if she went for a divorce." The humour drained from her as she added, "You can understand me being so damned suspicious, though, when I tell you that that all happened only six weeks before Archie died."

The lump in Cleo's stomach hardened and sat like lead. She had to ask now. "You think she murdered him, don't you?"

"To put it bluntly? Yes, I do."

Sarah got up and went and got them a top-up of the coffee from the expensive machine, which took up a whole section of one worktop. "You see, they had to go away to some house party of a mutual friend – well more of an acquaintance in her case until she got married. Archie had long since stopped meeting any of her regular friends, who are all cast from the same mould. But Philip and Tessa were the ones who introduced them, and Archie didn't want to fall out with Philip because he brings useful business our way with the shoots. So he went. But he never came back here after that. It was at their place that he took ill.

"Well once he went into hospital I went over and spoke to their cook, who's someone I know through the WI. Poor Sue was distraught that he was taken ill after eating one of her meals, but the thing is, Cleo, they had pheasant. Have you ever eaten pheasant?"

"No, I don't quite move in those circles."

"Hmm, well then you won't know that it's very strongly flavoured. I mean, you could hide a lot in pheasant! And when it's come from a local shoot, not the farmed stuff, you often bite into it and find a tiny pellet from where it's been shot. So anything gritty would go unnoticed."

"Heavens, Sarah! You've really taken this seriously, haven't you? Have you gone to the police with this?"

"And say what? That I think Herself slipped something like powdered glass into Archie's pheasant casserole? How could I prove that at this distance? You see, I think she was very cunning. I think she gave him enough to scour his insides, but not enough to actually kill him with it. ...Now Archie had a real thing about dark chocolate. He absolutely loved the bitter, dark, eighty-percent cocoa stuff. And he always had a square or two after dinner with his coffee. But that was something he bought himself, it never came through my pantry – so I had no control over it – and in the evening, when he was in the lounge with Herself, she would often take his coffee and squares of chocolate over to him, because she said he was too clumsy and kept spilling it. So how easy do you think it would have been for her to have substituted one of those laxative chocolates, eh? Archie had smoked a pipe in his youth, so his taste-buds were shot to hell when it came to fine flavours. That's why he liked pheasant and dark chocolate so much, they were things he could actually taste. But do I think he'd have known the difference between his real chocolate and a laxative? I doubt it, I very much do."

Cleo took a gulp of her own coffee. "Good God! So you think she scoured him out with powdered glass, then gave him a laxative? Christ, that's cunning! He'd have purged himself of the glass by the time he went into hospital, wouldn't he? And if there wasn't an autopsy, would anyone tell the difference between the lesions the glass made and ruptured ulcers? I mean, the hospital doctors were convinced it was ulcers, weren't they?" She was somewhat worried that Sarah was making wild accusations here, but if they weren't, then this was serious stuff.

However, Sarah was deadly serious as she said, "But that's why I think she was so cunning in her timing. The poor staff were run off their feet at that point. It was right in the middle of the Norovirus outbreak that damned near shut the hospital down, back at the start of the year."

"Good grief, I remember that! Didn't they close Accident & Emergency at Worcester Hospital for a while?"

"Yes, they did. And they were horribly short-staffed because of the doctors and nurses going down with the damned bug too. They were so run ragged, I can't blame them for not catching on to what a load of bull she was sprouting to them about Archie having had ulcers for years. But that was also what became the final straw for poor Archie. He got it too, the virus I mean, and never recovered."

She wiped away the tears that were now trickling down her cheeks. "That bloody cow had it all worked out, I'm sure she had. She knew about the outbreak from me, you see, because I'd been told it would be better if I didn't go and see Jeff, and of course once Archie was ill, the same applied. Even if I could go to see him, I wouldn't be able to go and see Jeff as well, just in case. I think she took all of that into account, because Sue told me a month or so after the funeral that Herself had specifically asked for the pheasant at short notice. Some twaddle about it being a treat for Archie when he'd been down in the dumps. It was that time of year when they had lost Simon, you see. It always got to him because it was very close to Simon's birthday as well."

"Oh my God! That's foul!" Cleo found herself gasping. "Playing on his son's death to help her kill him? What sort of woman is this?"

"A very cold and calculating one. Someone I can barely think of as human," Sarah said with a bitter sniff, as she dried her eyes and then blew her nose. "So you see, I never got to say anything to the doctors, because by the time I'd worked it out — because I'm telling you, I was infinitely more upset over Archie's death than ever she was — it was all too late. The only thing I managed to insist upon was that he was buried next to his true wife. That was what he'd always wanted, and luckily his solicitors knew that too, because the crafty baggage was all for having him cremated!"

"To destroy any remaining evidence? Oh Hell, that's too pointed for words once you have the bigger picture, isn't it?"

"Yes it is, and my God, did she ever push for that cremation! It took me being really tough and getting the solicitors to pretty much take over the funeral arrangements to get that far. ...I'm afraid I had to lie a bit and say that I thought Archie might have added something into his will to that effect. Something he'd asked me to witness his signature on. Well he did ask me to do that, but it wasn't for that reason, but I covered it with the solicitors when they later couldn't find it by saying I'd misremembered being so upset. And they saw that my grief was genuine. I think they'd already begun to see how much trouble they were going to have with Darcy-sodding-D'Eath. Poor Archie wasn't even in the ground before she was bombarding them with questions about how soon she could sell up. It didn't go down well. They're a very old and conservative firm, and they like everything done properly and with some dignity, so I was lucky that she'd ruffled a lot of feathers there. It meant that they were only too willing to side with me."

Cleo sat back and thought hard. This put a very different complexion on things. Even allowing for Sarah being naturally upset by her cousin's widow being so callous, there were still far too many coincidences for comfort here. Should she ring Angie once she was back in her room? Warn her that maybe Mrs Wytcombe wasn't necessarily the rightful heir with the attendant right to arrange the sale? But then her common sense kicked in. How on earth could she prove anything? And what if Angie spoke to her bosses and they decided that they didn't want to get involved in a sale that could backfire on them? That would harm Angie more than herself, and could she give a scrap of evidence to support these accusations? No she couldn't. But that didn't mean that she didn't want to try and find out.

Then a thought occurred to her. "Sarah, you'd say Mrs. Wytcombe is arrogant, wouldn't you?"

Sarah turned from the dishes she'd begun washing up with a snort of disgust. "They don't come much more so!"

"Okay, so does she have a clue that you suspect this of her?"

Drying her hands, Sarah came back to the chairs and flopped down in hers. "No, I'm pretty sure she doesn't. I've been very careful not to let on what I think of her. Primarily it's been because I feared if she did, then she'd turf me out there and then, and I have nowhere to go – or at least not at that kind of short notice. I need things sorted with Jeff a bit more before I dare antagonise her like that. When I can get at least one of my sons over here, we'll deal with things like inheritance, and then I can sort out the money that was in Jeff's name, stuff like his life insurance. But until then I have to tread carefully. …Why?"

Cleo gave her a wan smile. "It's just that in my experience it's the arrogant ones who never think someone they see as beneath them will see through their tricks. God knows I've seen enough of it first hand with my stepfather. Always up to some scheme or other to fleece the naive and foolish out of money, and he's always so bloody surprised when he picks on the wrong person and it all blows up in his face. Well Mrs Wytcombe told me to go through the papers in the library. She never said which ones! So I think I should make a speedy start on them, because that arrogance of hers tells me that she won't have thought that I might have the wit to look at everything I find in there. She's probably never even considered that I wouldn't know on first sight which ones are relevant to my search, and which ones aren't. I may never get the proof you'd like of her absolute guilt, but I might be able to find enough to mean that you could ask for an exhumation and a proper post-mortem."

"You'd do that?" Sarah's expression was a mixture of astonishment and delight.

"Well I'm damned if I'm going to be implicated in what amounts to outright fraud," Cleo declared vehemently. "I have my own reputation to consider, too, don't forget. She wants me to dig into the family, so dig I will! If I happen to fall over something that the police ought to know about, then it would be my civic duty to take it to them, wouldn't it? I can't think of a single instance in the past where I've felt like this," she then reassured Sarah, "and I certainly don't go through people's pasts just to muck-rake – I wouldn't last long in my field if I did. But this? This is something on a whole other scale of wrongness.

"I'm no Miss Marple, and I surely can't go trotting off to any buddies who are detectives or anything like that. But I have certain skills that I can use, things above and beyond the average person's knowhow that I've acquired in the years since I've been ploughing through things like land grants and wills. A certain understanding of legal phrases for one thing. And what I really, *really* don't like is somebody thinking that they can use *me* to help them pull off a crime, by finding them the means to fleece other relatives of something that should rightfully be theirs! I will not be a party to fraud!"

Chapter 4

Initially Cleo put down her trouble with getting to sleep that night to everything she'd been told. After all, it was hardly something she'd ever had to contend with before – sleeping under the same roof as a suspected murderess. But even having finally dropped off, she went from drowsing and slipping in and out of half-sleep, to fully awake somewhere in the early hours of the morning. Yes, the bedroom was considerably colder than the one at the flat she'd just come from, but having lived for the last two years in the ground floor flat of a huge old Victorian house with high ceilings and no central heating, Cleo wasn't a newcomer to cold bedrooms. But this was a sudden and marked drop in temperature.

She normally liked to sleep with the curtains at least a crack open, and by the light of the moon she could see most of the bedroom except for one very dark corner. Yet the window wasn't where she thought the extra cold was coming from, nor was the dark corner behind the wardrobe. It was more from over by the fireplace.

Peering up over the thick, old-fashioned quilt which had been put on as an extra layer over sheets and blankets – Mrs Wytcombe clearly not running to modern duvets and covers for a room that was hardly ever used – she squinted towards the fireplace yet could see nothing.

"Who's there?" she called softly. She hardly wanted to scream it out, not knowing where Mrs Wytcombe's bedroom was on the floor immediately beneath here, although it wasn't likely that Sarah would have done that to her, if only out of self interest in not wanting her boss to moan about her own disturbed night due to the new hired help. Yet she could be right below her for all Cleo knew, and she'd look a right fool in the morning if her supercilious boss challenged her on her nightmares on the first day.

"Anyone there?" she called again softly, and having got no answer, was just rolling over to try and get comfortable again when she was sure she heard sobbing.

She sat bolt upright in bed and switched on the bedside light. Sure enough she was totally alone in the room, as reason had told her she was. Yet even as she clutched the blankets up to her chin against the cold of the night she heard it again. Yes, it was definitely a sob.

As she listened more carefully she heard it again and thought it was definitely not a child. Not someone trying to spook her by playing a recording of a child, given that she was up on the nursery floor, then. Although who would have been playing such a prank she couldn't have said. And when it came again she was pretty sure that it was the voice of a man.

Getting out of bed and pulling on the heavy fleece which was acting as her dressing gown too for now, she shoved her feet into her slippers and moved across the room to where she thought she'd heard the sound coming from. Was it across the small landing or in the bathroom next door? She couldn't quite tell. And if so, who on earth was it?

Moving very quietly, she slipped across to the door and turned the knob. The old latch creaked a bit, but at least the door opened easily enough and Cleo stepped out onto the dark landing. Flicking the switch by her door, the old landing was instantly flooded with the stark, bright light of the modern economy bulb. Not a soul was there, but more to the point, the next sob sounded as though it was back behind her in her own room, not out here.

"What the hell is going on?" Cleo muttered, beginning now to get more than a little annoyed. If this was a prank, then it wasn't remotely funny.

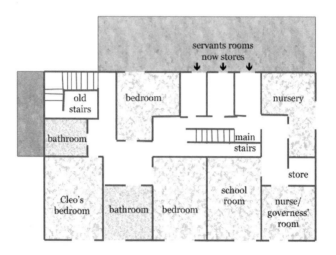

Top floor plan of Upper Moore House

She stepped back into her room, still leaving the door wide open, and wondered whether there was someone in the main bathroom which adjoined hers. Whether it was a mere decorative conceit to leave a set of fire irons beside the ornate iron grate in her room, or if they did actually light fires up here still when the house was full, such as at Christmas when it might be cold enough to warrant such a thing, Cleo didn't care, but she did take hold of the long and sturdy poker from the set. If someone was intending to play tricks on her they'd come unstuck. She hadn't been on her school's fencing team without knowing how to wield a couple of feet of hard metal to deadly effect.

And so she crept across to the other door and listened carefully. She could hear nothing, even with her ear pressed hard against the thick old wooden door. So with the poker at the ready, she leaned across and twisted the knob on the door and shoved it open hard, ready to lunge at anything which came her way.

Yet she was greeted by total silence, and when she flipped the light switch on in here the room was clearly deserted. A huge old claw-footed bath stood in splendid isolation in the middle of the room, while a hand-basin and toilet were on the far wall, with a hefty old cupboard against the landing side, but there was nothing up against her room at all – not even a cupboard someone could hide in. Perplexed, she closed the door again and opened the one at right-angles to it which led into the next bedroom. Again the modern stark light revealed a room all shut up, dust sheets over the bed and important bits of furniture, and a heavy layer of dust on the carpet which hadn't been disturbed in months by the look of it. There was no way someone had come into here and stuck a mini speaker into a wall to create the effect; or at least not unless they'd been planning this for far longer than the warning they would have had of her own arrival.

Her own bathroom was little more than a converted storeroom, but there was always the room across the landing. And so Cleo braced herself and marched over to that door, flinging it open. But when she put the light on it was even more deserted than the other bedroom. Years ago someone seemed to have used this room as a study, or small sitting room, because there was only an old-fashioned daybed under the window, its mattress showing signs of mould, an armchair which was distinctly tatty, a big old cupboard, and a nice old desk with a captain's chair.

Feeling a total idiot, Cleo shut the door and returned to her room, glad to snuggle under the heavy eiderdown quilt and get warm again. Luckily there was no repeat of the crying noise, and by the morning she was ready to put it down to Mrs Wytcombe down below. After all, she was a very manly woman with quite a deep voice, so maybe she was just not very good at showing her grief in front of someone who obviously hated the sight of her as much as Sarah did.

"You need to be more careful!" Cleo lectured her reflection in the bathroom mirror as she washed her face. "Sarah's very convincing, but you don't really know her. For all you know, she might be the nasty one, and she's trying to get you to help her to throw Mrs W out. Just because she tells a good tale, it doesn't mean that it's the truth.

"Mrs W can hardly be without any redeeming features or why would Archie have married her? Sarah wasn't around when they were courting, by the sound of it, so maybe there's a whole other side to Mrs W she hasn't seen? And just because Mrs W wasn't married before, it doesn't mean she might not have lost someone she loved deeply. It could be that what she and Archie shared was that loss of someone they loved? Come on, Cleo, get a grip! Maybe Mrs W resents Sarah because she was always sticking her nose into their marriage? Maybe she even thinks that Sarah poisoned Archie against her? For God's sake, be more careful! You can't take sides this early and without proof!"

Going down to the kitchen she found a note from Sarah telling her to help herself to whatever she wanted, and where everything was, so at least she didn't have to confront the woman she was having doubts about now. A pot of coffee was already warming on the grand machine, and Cleo revelled in the taste of what was clearly very good coffee of the sort she couldn't normally run to. Toast and local honey, with some fruit which had probably come from orchards in the grounds, made for a lovely start to the day, and so it was with considerably more enthusiasm that Cleo set off for the library and the start of her work.

In case Mrs Wytcombe came in, she booted up both laptops and opened new files ready to start inputting information. But then the question came of where to start? Now that she was having a second look at the library, she could see that while the books were all in neat order, there were piles of papers all over the place. Someone, and it had probably been Archie, had undoubtedly known which pile was which, and where he had put things, but coming into it cold, Cleo hadn't a clue as to what most of it was. There was a significant gap on one of the bookcases which looked as though several Lever-arch files had been there, and she assumed that those had been what the solicitors had taken. Presumably Archie had been organised enough to keep those official papers in order, for surely he must have had to use an accountant for the estate? But what the rest was was anyone's guess. So with a sigh, she decided the only thing for it was to start making new piles of her own.

There were three beautiful, huge old desks in the room, and she carefully lifted the precarious piles off the one nearest to the large and elegant French window which let in a lot of natural light. Where she could, Cleo liked reading in natural light, because with old-fashioned handwriting it was often easier to decipher without harsh shadows and the yellow cast many bulbs gave off. Holding a letter up to the natural light, so that it shone through the paper, had clarified what a word was for her on several occasions.

So with a clear desk in front of her, she then surveyed the different heaps on the floor. Some of them had very yellowing paper in them, and that probably meant that they were the older documents. But Cleo was disciplined in her methodology, and she liked to start from the present and work her way carefully back. It was all too easy when it came to families to spot something in the distant past and assume that there was a connection, only to find that you'd wasted a lot of time and effort on a strand of investigation which petered out thirty years before the person you thought it would connect to had even been born.

And so she went to the cleanest, brightest looking papers and began sorting through them. At this stage she was concerned with dates alone, and soon she found herself giving up on the desks altogether, and starting more heaps on the carpet. For some years there was virtually nothing, and then for others there were a lot of documents of different sorts. It certainly seemed as though for most of the time the estate ticked along at its own pace, not exactly bustling along with the twenty-first century, but equally, not mouldering in nostalgia for an Edwardian era of grandeur that would never come again.

By lunchtime she had made some progress, and went down to see if Sarah was around and what the possibilities were of getting a sandwich. Luckily Sarah was just returning with an armful of washing from the garden, and once again they had a companionable break together. However, Cleo didn't mention her broken night – that was something she'd keep to herself for a while – and Sarah seemed to be keeping her comments a little more circumspect than the previous evening. The reason why revealed itself just as Cleo was about to go back to the library. Darcy Wytcombe suddenly barged into the kitchen with a crash of the door and cut straight across Sarah's words of, "Do you like shepherd's pie?" with,

"Did I make it plain to you that I don't want you taking any food or drinks up to the library?"

Startled, Cleo blinked and said, "Err, no."

"Well don't! That's an antique carpet in there. I don't want you tramping crumbs into it or spilling coffee all over it!" and without waiting for a response, Mrs Wytcombe turned on her five-inch heels and stalked back out as fast as her skin-tight pencil-skirt would allow.

"How rude!" Cleo spluttered. "I've never been so insulted! For God's sake, what sort of researcher does she think I am? I wasn't spoken to like that even at the bloody Bodleian Library in Oxford!"

"Welcome to my world," Sarah said with bitter humour, but it settled Cleo's mind in one respect at least. Whether she sided fully with Sarah, and whether Sarah turned out to be as much of a liability as Darcy Wytcombe, she herself was not going to take that lying down. If she'd begun to tell herself not to go digging for skeletons in Mrs Wytcombe's closets this morning, she was certainly going to have a good rummage around now after being spoken to like that. Cleo wasn't a proud woman, but the one thing she could get touchy about was someone calling her professionalism into doubt.

Stomping off up to her bedroom, Cleo dug out her sports water bottle with its good seal, and filled it from the bathroom tap. It had accompanied her on many visits to archives where more valuable documents than the Wytcombes were ever likely to have had were kept, and if it was good enough for them then it was good enough for here.

"Bloody woman!" she muttered darkly to herself as she went back down to the library, and tucked the water bottle under the desk on the floor where it wouldn't be seen or in the way. This wasn't just a petty reaction, done out of spite or affront. Old paper had a way of collecting dust, and it wouldn't be the first or last time that Cleo opened a bundle of documents to get a face-full of paper dust and find herself coughing like a forty-a-day smoker for half an hour. So the water bottle wasn't there merely for thirst, but as a very practical necessity for washing the muck out of her throat, just as the large packet of tissues was there for the resulting sneezes induced by the same source.

At the end of the day she had got through the piles on two of the desks, but the third was practically groaning under old bundles of papers, and she knew that it would probably take a day all to itself just to sort into some kind of order. Going downstairs, she found Sarah taking the same miniscule salad up to Mrs Wytcombe, but then Sarah led Cleo across the old cobbled backyard to her own house. As soon as she got through the door, Cleo could see that this was a very different place. This was a home. A normal kitchen served as the dining room too, much the way the similar large room in Cleo's old flat had done, and she immediately felt much more relaxed. Brightly patterned cushions made the sturdy wooden chairs around the well-scrubbed table comfortable, and through the open door Cleo could see family photos on the hall wall beyond. Sarah's tastes clearly ran to the cheerful and comfy, with no modern minimalism to be seen.

It rather confirmed to Cleo that Sarah was what she had first seemed to be, and that her grief over the loss of her cousin was genuine. Not enough for Cleo to deliberately pry any more that evening – she was still aware of needing to find her feet – but it relaxed her enough to tell Sarah some of her own history, and how distraught she had been to have to move out of the flat she had loved. She didn't linger long after dinner, though, saying that she really needed a good night's sleep, as the previous one she'd been kept awake thinking of how she was going to attack her mammoth task.

This time, as she got up to the top floor, she went and switched the lights on in each of the rooms facing hers, satisfying herself that there was nothing and nobody up here with her.

"Not even a pigeon stuck down the chimney," she told herself firmly as she showered, glad to get the dust off her before bed, even if the temperature was dropping and made the bathroom far from hospitable. It had been a mild February this far, but English weather being what it was, that was no guarantee for the rest of the month or beyond.

Tucked up with one of her favourite novels, she welcomed the familiar characters like old friends, only putting it down when her eyes started to droop, and fell asleep straight away.

"Oh you have got to be joking!" she groaned as she rolled over and looked at the alarm clock and saw it was only three-thirty. What had woken her this time? Unwilling to even sit up in bed when the temperature had dropped several degrees since she had got into bed, she resolved to go back to sleep straight away, but then heard it again – sobbing!

"Buggering hell!" she muttered savagely, and put the bedside light on with rather more force than necessary.

With a tug of the sheet and blankets to keep herself covered, she sat up and looked around. Yet again the room was totally empty, but just as she was about to lie down again she heard the sob again, and this time she was sure she heard the distraught voice say the words, "Oh God, it hurts!"

That wasn't going to be Darcy Wytcombe, surely?
The woman was so thin her skin was tight across her big
bovine bones, but Cleo hadn't got the impression that she
was anorexic, and it didn't seem likely that she was crying
out in hunger – which was the only kind of physical pain
Cleo could imagine she might feel, although it didn't
preclude her mourning someone, even if it wasn't Archie.
And anyway, that had sounded very definitely like a man's
voice, and someone a lot more local than Mrs. Wytcombe.
For all of her airs and graces, Mrs Wytcombe still had
more than a hint of London in her voice, whereas this
voice sounded like the posher local clients Cleo had dealt
with. Someone from the Midland counties at least, albeit
filtered out through a good school, and possibly a
professional job.

"Who the hell are you?" Cleo demanded, but got no
response.

Sitting up in bed, she was glad she had left her fleece
on the spare side of the double bed, because the room was
freezing cold and she gladly pulled it on and zipped it up.
Listening intently for a few minutes, she was just about to
give up and lie down again when the voice returned.

"Why does it still hurt when it's not there?" the man
wept. "*Oooww*! My leg! My bloody leg. …Oh, Christ!"

"Who are you? …Are you there?" Cleo· called
tentatively, but got no answer.

When another series of long and pained sobs came
and she called out again with no response, she began to
think that this was very much a one-way street. Whoever it
was, she could hear him, but he wasn't hearing her. It was
an odd sort of haunting, though. He obviously wasn't
targeting her, and it made her wonder whether she was
only hearing him because she was the first person in ages
to have slept up here? Maybe he regularly called out in
pain in that previous time, and her presence here had

nothing to do with why he was audible, but was more a phenomenon of the house? If that was comforting in one way, it was also rather disconcerting in another – what was it about Upper Moore House that made this possible?

Chapter 5

"My goodness, you look tired," Sarah said, as Cleo wandered into the kitchen, yawning. "Didn't you sleep very well?"

Her response was interrupted by Darcy Wytcombe flinging the door open with a, "Where's my car?" demand. But when their employer had flounced out – or as near as someone as inelegant as her could ever flounce – with a disgruntled taxi driver shepherding her towards his car, where a ridiculously large amount of baggage was in the process of being stowed, Cleo finally managed to tell Sarah,

"I had rather a broken night, unfortunately."

"Not Herself, I hope?"

"Not unless she's reassigned herself as a man."

That stopped Sarah in her tracks, but her response wasn't what Cleo was expecting next.

"Oh Lord! Have you heard Hugh, too?"

"Hugh? You mean you know who it is? ...Errm, I mean you know what's happened? How could you?"

Looking distinctly sheepish, Sarah confessed, "Well I didn't really believe it, you see. Archie had told me that the ghost of his Great-uncle Hugh haunted what were the old bedroom suites, but you know how legends wrap around these old places. And who believes them these days?

"I'm truly sorry, Cleo. I honestly didn't even think of it when I put you up there. I was thinking more that you'd be more comfortable in one of the less cavernous rooms, and not on the same floor as Herself. She's bad enough at the best of times. I certainly didn't think you deserved to have to confront her in your nightie when nipping out to the bathroom at night – and that was before I'd even met you!"

"Thanks for the thought," said Cleo, managing a wry smile. "But who's this Hugh then? And why would he be haunting the place? He's a bit recent for the average ancient house's ghost, isn't he?"

"Oh, it's a very sad tale. Come on. Now that Herself has cleared off back to London again, we'll have a bit of peace and quiet, and I can tell you more about what's gone on here. Let's go into my kitchen. It's a good deal warmer in there than in the big house, and we won't be disturbed by the gardeners – I've left them coffee on the go and some sandwiches, so they won't go wanting."

"Gardeners?" Cleo questioned as they walked across to the cottage. "I thought Joe did all of that – oh, you said something about them when I arrived, didn't you?"

Ushering her into the cosy atmosphere of her own kitchen, Sarah shook her head. "Joe does the kitchen garden around the back of the house, and very good at it he is too. He's here all the time, because even in the winter there are winter veg's to tend to – we do well for parsnips, sprouts and some of the older varieties of veg thanks to him. It was one of the rare times when Herself didn't get her own way, you know. Archie was insistent that we could be self-sufficient, and he was most against going and buying exotic fruit and veg out of season from some supermarket. So although Herself loathes Joe – thinks he lowers the tone of the place – he got to stay. But the ornamental gardens are a different matter. One of Archie's ancestors was a keen plant hunter, and so we have some quite rare specimens here. And that's why Archie contracted an RHS qualified gardener and his assistant to come once a month in the winter, and then weekly through the summer, to keep the fancy garden in tip-top order. It's them who are here today. They were here when you arrived too. Something about some trees needing lopping before we open it up to the public again, which we do on certain days in the summer for charity."

"Oh!" That was another revelation about Archie, who Cleo was starting to have substantial sympathy for. He must have really loved this old home of his, and what a wicked trick of fate to land him with a second wife like Darcy D'Eath.

"Did the first Mrs Wytcombe like the garden?" she asked.

"Penny? Oh yes, she loved it even more than Archie. When Simon was so poorly she'd often go outside and do some weeding or pruning while I sat with him. She said it helped clear her head. I think that's another reason why he was so insistent on keeping the gardeners coming – it honoured her memory."

"I'm feeling sorrier for him at every turn."

"Good!"

"So what's this about his great-uncle?"

"Hugh?" Sarah sighed sadly as they sat down at the table. "Another poor soul who lost his life as a result of the First World War. He didn't actually die in the trenches, though. He was badly wounded and taken back to a field hospital where they had to take his one leg off above the knee. They brought him back here to convalesce."

"Not an unusual story for that time."

"No, but Archie always said what happened next really bothered him. You see Hugh was the youngest of the family. Albert – known as Bertie – was the oldest and Archie's grandfather. Then there was another brother, Charles; then Emilia, my grandmother; Verity, and then Hugh was the baby. ...Yes that's it," as Cleo began roughing out a family tree.

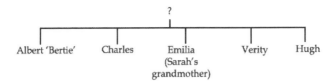

"Hugh was twelve years younger than Bertie and eight than my gran', so as children they weren't particularly close. I never knew my gran', because she emigrated to Australia and would never come back. Dad came back when he got married to Mum, and though I was born here, my older brother, Mike, was born in Oz – but he died in the same car crash as Mum in the late seventies.

"Now it wasn't the first time Hugh got wounded, the first time being at Passchendaele, but the second time it was over in Italy…"

"…Ah. The winter campaign."

Sarah looked surprised. "You've heard of it? Most people don't even know that we fought in Italy in World War One."

"Actually, my own grandfather fought there. My dad's dad, that is. Dad married quite late, so he was old to have a daughter of my generation, but it means he told me a lot about Granddad's exploits over in the Dolomites."

"What a coincidence! Well then, I don't need to tell you that the fighting over there was every bit as fierce as on the Western Front, albeit in different terrain. So when Hugh got machine gunned in the leg the second time around, he was sent to recover down in Verona."

Cleo nodded. "That was the main place they fell back to, wasn't it. I remember reading that because Verona was down out of the mountains, it was the only place of any consequence where they could accommodate large numbers of troops, and even then, they had to be strictly rotated in and out of there."

"So they did, and obviously men who needed to recuperate were given priority. To be honest, I don't think Hugh should have been sent back into the line the first time, but he was a junior officer and they were running short of them by that stage in the war. And of course he was one of the few who actually had fighting experience."

"Yes, the junior officers suffered the heaviest casualties of any rank," Cleo sympathised. "First over the top leading the men, and the first to be cut down."

"And Hugh felt a great loyalty to the men under him. He didn't want to let them down. That's the kind of man he was, and I heard that from both my dad and Archie. Hugh was the kind of officer who inspired a lot of loyalty back from his men.

"So there he was, back in Verona the second time, recuperating in one of those lovely Venetian-style houses which got requisitioned during the War. Not much to do for most of the day, and his wound was serious enough that men came in and either went home, or went back to the front, while he stayed there. Something to do with the bullet only just having missed the femoral artery, so they didn't want to subject him to the jolting of a long journey. Now Archie said that Hugh found something there in that villa, and that his own grandfather – that's Bertie I'm talking about, as Hugh's had died long before that – was very angry about it. Something to the effect that Hugh should have just destroyed it – whatever 'it' was. And it caused a real rift in the family.

"It was the reason why my granny and her husband emigrated, saying that they wanted nothing more to do with anyone. And the odd thing is, Cleo, it wasn't Hugh who they were angry with over this, it was Bertie! My dad always said he wouldn't have trusted Bertie further than he could throw him, had he still been alive, because his mum

– my granny – had dropped heavy hints that Bertie had blood on his hands."

Cleo's jaw dropped. "Good grief! That's a pretty hefty accusation to make about someone!"

"Isn't it just! Granny never said any more than that, but Archie said in later years that he wondered if his grandfather had helped put Hugh out of his misery."

"Eh? I thought Hugh came back here to convalesce? Even in World War One, I don't think they shoved soldiers out of hospital until they were out of danger. And by the sound of it, Hugh might well have been quite a decorated soldier, not some rogue from the backstreets who'd been up on endless charges. I know that their morality back then wasn't quite ours when it came to the working classes, but Hugh was far from that whatever the circumstances."

Sarah was already nodding in agreement. "Yes, Hugh had several medals, and they're carefully locked away somewhere in Archie's desk where Herself won't find them. I think Archie rather idolised Hugh the more he found out about him."

"Hang on," Cleo said, waving Sarah to pause. "I'm losing track of the generations here," and she dug into her bag for the A4 pad and pens she never went far without. "Can we start over, please? So who was Archie's father again? Was he this Bertie?"

"No. Archie's father was Bertie's second son, Horace. This is where it all went so horribly astray, you see. Horace wasn't in line to inherit. That was Bertie's oldest son, John. But John was a career officer in the army, and he died in World War Two. 1941 or '2, I think. Well by that time Bertie was an old man in his seventies, or nearly, and a lifetime of guzzling port and smoking cigars had done its worst to his system. Archie told me that when the news came that John had been killed, his grandfather had a stroke, and from then on he couldn't have told Horace much even if he could have remembered it."

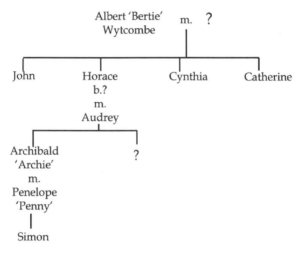

"Archie was born in 1952, and Bertie had been dead a few years by then, though I can't recall offhand when he did die – after the War, I think, but not by much. So you begin to see the problem, Cleo. Whatever it was that Bertie did that my granny so loathed, he probably confided it to John, but John never told Horace and neither did Bertie himself. Archie said his father used to go into fearful rages over the whole thing, because hints had been dropped that it was this terrible, big thing, but never enough for him to piece together. And of course Horace couldn't pass on to his own son, Archie, what he himself didn't know."

"I see. I'm beginning to appreciate the depths of the problem now. Did Archie try to find out for himself?"

Sarah gave another heavy sigh. "He did, but to be fair, he didn't even know what he was looking for. It was only when I came to live here, and told him about what Granny had said to Dad, that he thought it might have something to do with the line of inheritance. But what always puzzled him, was what on earth Hugh could have found that would have brought it into question? As far as we know, there's not an Italian connection in the family, so why would there have been something in Italy which Hugh would have found so terribly worrying? And why would he and Bertie have quarrelled so violently over it?"

"Did they? Quarrel violently, I mean? It's one thing to have a falling out. Most families have those somewhere in their history. But it sounds as though you're talking about something far more than that."

"Granny thought it was, and she was far from a fanciful woman. 'Hard-nosed old battleaxe' was the way Dad described her, even though he loved her to bits. She certainly thrived on a sheep station out in the wilds of Australia, and there're not many women who could do that back in the first half of the twentieth century."

Cleo smiled. "No, point taken. I think it would take a pretty self-sufficient kind of lady to cope with the level of isolation, and with only male company for much of the time. So if we agree that your gran' was a far cry from what we'd now call a fluff-head, I can see that we have to give some credence to her claim that Bertie acted badly towards Hugh. So where did Archie's idea that Bertie had helped Hugh to die come from? Was that from your gran' or his own research?"

Sarah frowned in concentration. "Not sure, to be honest. This is where *I'd* be glad of you sorting out the dates for us, never mind this stuff about the house. I *think* – and here I have to be honest and say that I might be hopelessly wrong about it all – that Hugh died a year or so after the war ended, but my granny and granddad had emigrated by then. I only know that because Dad told me that the first letter she had from home when they got to Australia was one saying that Hugh had died, and that it always made her cry to think that she'd not been able to go to his funeral and say goodbye to him.

"But that period was pretty stuffed with tragedies for the family. I was told that the next sister down, Verity, and her family died in the influenza epidemic of 1919, and even Dad was a bit hazy as to whether it was Verity dying that prompted granny to leave. …You know, sister and her two babies dying, when she herself had two small children, and with them both living in London with their husbands. It'd be enough to make any woman think escaping to the clean air of the wilds might be a good thing. So I'm hesitant to make too much of Hugh's death as her incentive to leave."

"Oh, I can quite see why, and it's the kind of caution I apply all of the time until I have more details. So didn't you say that there was another brother? What happened to him?"

"Charles?"

"Ah, yes, that was the name you mentioned," and Cleo scribbled it down. It would all need checking, but getting a handle on the family always helped, and knowing the generations would help her sort the documents out faster. "So there was Albert, a.k.a. Bertie, as the oldest. Then Charles, am I right?"

"Yes, and he lost his only son in World War One, too. Terribly sad. He didn't last much longer either, though what Charles died of I don't know."

"Heavens! They really went through the mill, didn't they? How many members of the family did they lose in those few years?"

Sarah began ticking them off on her fingers. "Well first there'd be Charles' son, George. Then Verity and her husband and two little ones." She paused and frowned. "Then I think probably Hugh. Then Charles. That's it for the immediate post-war years."

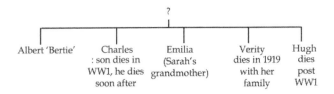

Cleo nodded as she scribbled notes. "Ah yes, I was forgetting that the other deaths came after the next war, but even so, seven deaths in the immediate family in less than as many years is pretty dramatic."

"It is, isn't it! Funny, I never totted them up until now. Never saw them clustered like that."

Cleo scanned her notes again. "And when was Horace born …Archie's dad? Do you know?"

"A bit before the First World War, I think, but he was way too young to be called up for that. I believe he served in World War Two, but he never wanted to make the army his career like his older brother did. I think he was quite old for conscription at that stage, and I don't think he ever served overseas. Why?"

"Hmm. So if we guess that Horace was born somewhere between, say, 1905 and 1914, he would still have been quite a little lad when all of the kerfuffle was going on, wouldn't he? Certainly not of an age where any of the adults were going to talk seriously to him about it, and probably young enough that they might even have consciously avoided speaking about whatever the problem was when he was around. And then his oldest uncle goes and dies before he's anything like an adult, as does his one aunt, and the other aunt leaves the country. Which really only leaves Hugh as the surviving other member of the older generation who might have known the truth of the matter, and if Horace's father coloured his point of view, Hugh may well have been seen as the problem, or even the enemy.

"So I can see how it would have come down to being a matter of Bertie choosing to tell your gran' what he wanted her to hear, and the same for his oldest son. And there wouldn't be anyone around to dispute it once Hugh was dead, would there? I presume there wasn't a huge gap between John and Horace?"

Sarah shook her head. "I don't think so. A couple of years or so, but not more than that."

"Interesting. ...So even if John was told about whatever this problem was before he died, he would have only ever heard his father's account of what went on. What applies to Horace also applies to him – he was too young to have been involved at the time. He'd never have had the chance to speak to anyone else who could corroborate or deny whether Bertie told him the truth. ...Do you know, Sarah, it might not make as much difference as you think that Horace never got to talk about it with his father, because it could have been a deeply biased account of events anyway, and a very long way from the reality."

Sarah looked at her in amazement. "Good grief! You're right! Again, I'd not made the connection about how the generations had failed to overlap properly. I supposed because I heard it from my dad, I assumed everyone else had had more of a personal connection. Well I never, quite the puzzle, isn't it?"

Sitting back and accepting a refill of coffee, Cleo confessed, "You've got me intrigued, alright. It's been worth us talking, but for the life of me, I can't imagine what this big deal could have been? I mean, it can't have been about inheritance when you come to Bertie and Hugh's generation, can it? If the estate has to pass to a male member of the family, then by the time it actually mattered, there were only Bertie's children left anyway." Then a thought occurred to her. "You told me that

Archie's heir was a male cousin. Who was that, then? Your dad?"

Sarah laughed. "Lord, no! Like I said, we're pretty distant from the inheritance, and actually it's a bit of a muddle – all to do with Bertie's sister who emigrated, so we're definitely from the female line. No, the cousin who would have been Archie's nearest heir was David, and to get to him you have to go back another generation or more. I can't recall the exact link, but he came from Bertie's younger great-uncle Edgar's line I believe, and they were thin on the ground by then."

"And could he be the problem? Was it an issue going back to an earlier generation, do you think?"

However Sarah could only shrug. "It might be, but all I can say is that it sounded a bit more dramatic than that. I know that's not much help, but it's hardly abnormal for a family to have to go back a generation to find an heir, is it? And at the time when all the trouble happened, there was no reason to look as far as …oh, golly, I suppose it would have been David's grandfather or great-grandfather?"

"No, of course not," Cleo said, mentally kicking herself for not having spotted that. Those disturbed nights were doing nothing for her clarity of thinking. "For all anyone knew, at that point even if Horace and John had died in childhood, Hugh himself was still living and would presumably have been in line. But the same still applies – no shortage of direct heirs. And I'm baffled as to what could have been so important if it wasn't about inheritance. The house had been in the family's hands for generations already by then, hadn't it?"

"Goodness, yes! The Wytcombes can trace ownership of Upper Moore to the Napoleonic era, and I think Archie once said that another branch of the same family took it back to the Civil War."

"Hmmm, seventeenth century, then. So not a case of Bertie's father or grandfather winning it at cards, for instance, and there being an ownership dispute as a result."

Sarah laughed. "No way. Solid members of the squirearchy are the Wytcombes. You can find them all planted in the local churchyard, or at least the ones who died around here."

"I think I'd better go and have a look at that churchyard, then."

"Come to church with me on Sunday, if you like?"

Cleo winced. How to put this tactfully when Sarah was being so kind? "Ah… Well I'm not exactly Christian," she said cautiously, hoping that Sarah wasn't such a pillar of the local community that she'd object on principle.

Mercifully Sarah just smiled wanly. "Oh well, never mind. There are more people who don't believe than do these days. I'm afraid it's one of the things which keeps me going, what with Jeff and all of this about Archie. If I didn't think that I'd be seeing them in the hereafter, I'd probably fall apart."

Crossing her fingers that she wasn't about to alienate Sarah completely, Cleo said carefully, "I said I wasn't a Christian. I didn't say I didn't have faith. I do believe in an afterlife, and I totally understand what you're saying. To go through what you have, faith can be the rock you need to hang on to sometimes.

"If it helps, I can't stand going into a church service, because my stepfather is the kind of Catholic who thinks he can do what he likes in the week, go to confession on Sunday, and have all his sins wiped away so that he can start being an utter shit again on Monday. That the various priests never seem to rip into him and tell him that what he's doing is downright wicked, not just unchristian, has had a lot to do with souring my relationship with what I see as the Church-corporate."

"Oh, I see," Sarah said, looking slightly startled. "Yes, well I can see that having an experience like that would tend to put you off."

"Don't worry," Cleo said with a self-deprecating grin, "I'm not about to start dancing naked around the oak trees at full moon, or sacrificing chickens in the garden at the dark of the moon. And I don't go around eating children – well not a whole one, anyway!" And the daftness of that broke the ice as Sarah giggled with her.

"I just prefer to look to a more nature-based belief set," Cleo continued, "and I'm with the Wiccans when they say that what you hand out comes back to you three-times-three. My dad's mum was Welsh and she always swore that 'it all comes back to you!' So in this case, for instance, you being welcoming to me has come back to you in me seeing Mrs Wytcombe in her true colours, and wanting to search for the truth, not just what she wants me to find. Do you see what I mean?"

Sarah nodded, smiling in a much more relaxed way now. "And if Herself is due for all the pain and misery she's handed out to come back to her threefold, I for one won't be sorry."

"Well it might just," Cleo warned her, "because there aren't that many things that the Victorians got worked up about, and if we're talking about Bertie, then he certainly falls into that moral era. They might not bat an eyelid about keeping a 'defective' relative – as they would have seen someone – locked up in conditions we would now think unbearably cruel. And men keeping mistresses was so common it was barely worth commenting upon, as long as they didn't parade them about in polite society. So if it was something which had two brothers at each other's throats, then it has to be something really grim and against their moral code, such as incest or bigamy. In which case, Mrs Wytcombe may come to rue the day she ever asked me to investigate!"

Chapter 6

Though it was well into the morning by now, when Cleo went back up to the library it was with a new sense of purpose. Whatever it was that had caused so much trouble, it had to have happened pre-World War One, she reckoned. If it hadn't, then surely it would have been contemporary enough for Hugh not to have needed to discover it – it would have been known about already, albeit maybe something that the family would not want to be made public?

So she was able to sort the modern stuff out fairly rapidly without reading it in any detail, carefully filing it in something like a sensible order, and then putting it to one side. And in fairness, Archie seemed to have been quite thorough with his paperwork during his time as owner. It was Horace's stuff which it looked as if Archie had had to struggle to get straight, but even with that, he had clearly done the best he could and there wasn't much Cleo could add to it. Even so, that still left her with a considerable pile of material to work through, and she paused to have a brief sandwich at lunchtime before getting stuck in again. By the time she finished for the evening, she had found a fair number of papers relating to Hugh, and she took them down to Sarah's house with her.

When they had eaten and the table was cleared away, she brought them out and laid them in order across the incongruously pretty cotton cloth, given the subject matter.

"He got the Military Cross *and* the first bar," Cleo told Sarah, pointing to the correspondence which related to them. "Bizarrely he was in the 12th Durham Light Infantry, which may sound a long way from here in Herefordshire, but over the years I've been doing this job, I've learned that when it comes to World War One, all bets are off as to which unit a man might serve in. The Durhams and the Northumberland Light Infantry had a training ground up on Cannock Chase, just the other side of Birmingham, would you believe, so that was probably where Hugh joined up. ...See? This is his enlistment number, and that indicates that he started his military career at the Cannock depot.

"I can probably dig deeper and find out a bit more about him, if you want, but I should warn you: an awful lot of the army's records went up in smoke in an incendiary raid during World War Two. Things like the internal transfers have all been lost to us. It's a tragedy, because there are men whom we've lost all record of, so even knowing this much about Hugh puts us ahead of so many families looking for men who served back then."

Sarah had put reading glasses on and was peering intently at the yellowing scraps of paper. "Well I never, Hugh was quite the hero, wasn't he!" she murmured in awe. "This has to be what impressed Archie so much."

Cleo nodded. "If he had the medals themselves locked away, then yes, even if he never discovered these papers, I can imagine him being very impressed with his great-uncle. Especially when you look at the date of the medal the first time. That's Passchendaele, Sarah, the battle where the war's reputation for mud like soup really came from. Every time I read accounts from men who were there, I marvel at the fact that anyone survived at all. Listen to this from this tiny letter he sent home:

Dear Bertie,

> *Please do not tell Mother about this, for it would only distress her terribly, but the mud here is beyond anything I have ever known. We have both seen the River Severn in flood, and the way that the fields turn red with the clay, but nobody ever tries to walk over that. This is like wading through a porridge of mud. None of us sleep well, for as we walk along the duckboards, where they still survive, that is, we sometimes look down and see the face of a man in the deeps, or the body of a drowned mule, its panniers still on its back. This is Hell on earth, brother, and I fear I may never close my eyes again without seeing it.*

"Did you know that it was seeing that during his own war service which Tolkien used for the Dead Marshes in *Lord of the Rings*? It left so many men with horrific memories that they couldn't lose. And Hugh was twenty-seven then, so older than many of the men he was serving with, but still a young man who probably went in hopelessly unprepared for what he was going to witness."

Sarah was reverently fingering the tiny fold-indented paper as if she could touch the past through it. "I had no idea we had actual letters from him," she breathed softly. "Passchendaele …well, well, well. …Oh my word, Cleo, am I reading this right? He stormed a machine-gun nest to save his men?"

Cleo peered over her shoulder to confirm which item she was reading. "Yes, he did, and that wasn't the only time. He got the bar to the Military Cross for doing much the same thing in Italy. That was when he got shot in the leg. ...Here you are, that's the award for that one. It's a bit sparse on detail but you get the gist of it."

They went through the other bits of Hugh's military life in increasing awe, finally packing them up again in the sleeves of special archive film that Cleo had with her, to protect them as best they could. But it was as Sarah was making a cocoa for herself and a camomile tea for Cleo, that she suddenly said,

"Doesn't all of that make you think that Hugh was the kind of man who would do the right thing, come what may?"

"Yes, it does," Cleo agreed, "and I think you're thinking the same as I did when I read them for the first time: that Hugh wasn't a mischief maker. I can't equate the man in those letters and documents with the kind of person who would deliberately stir the muck amongst the family, unless it was for an awfully good reason."

"That's it in a nutshell. Cleo, this man wouldn't have come home with only one leg, most likely suffering from what we'd now call PTSD, and then picked a fight with his older brother on a whim. He just wouldn't. Whatever it was he found, it had to have had the most profound implications. One of Jeff's old friends had PTSD, and he couldn't stand any sort of arguing and shouting around him, even to the extent of him struggling to cope with his kids' normal childish rows. He had to leave the house when they kicked off. So Hugh must have been gritting his teeth all the way over this."

Cleo yawned mightily. "Well I just hope he keeps quiet tonight, bless him. I feel like my eyes have been bathed in grit already. I don't need another disturbed night."

For a moment Sarah didn't answer, suddenly peering out through the kitchen window before saying, "I don't think you need to worry about that. I was going to ask you if you wanted to move across into my spare room tomorrow, anyway, but it's snowing out there. You can't possibly go back into the big house! You'll freeze to death up there on a night like this. The only time those top rooms get warm is when the heating is on in all of the rooms below them. Come on, leave that tea for a minute. You go and grab your overnight things while I lock the rest of the house up, then you can spend the night here."

Deeply grateful for the thought of a decent night's sleep, Cleo was even more thankful by the time she had made the dash up to her bedroom and grabbed her wash-bag, change of clothes, and her pyjamas. Her bedroom was positively arctic, and she was sure she could see the start of ice on the inside of the single panes of glass. "Bless you, Hugh, but you've got this place to yourself tonight," she said as she fled downstairs again.

Sarah's spare room turned out to be infinitely cosier, and by the time they had finished their drinks, Cleo had to admit defeat and headed for the joy of a warm duvet. Even so, as she drifted off, vaguely aware of the TV still on in the lounge below, it occurred to her to wonder which rooms of the big house had been Hugh's. Had she been in a room which he'd always used, or had he only been shoved up onto the top floor when his nightmares disturbed the other members of the household?

After a long and blissfully undisturbed sleep, Cleo woke feeling much more like her normal bright self. But drawing back the curtains, she was shocked to see how much snow had fallen in the night. Here in the open countryside it had drifted, and the lower temperature than in the towns made it different to the snow she usually encountered. Immediately she doubled up on her socks, expecting the library to be bitterly cold when she got over there, adding an extra t-shirt under her shirt as well. However, as she entered the kitchen to find Sarah making a large pot of tea, once again Sarah was emphatic about Cleo not going over to the house.

"I'd never forgive myself if you caught a chill and got sick," she said firmly. "We're not out of February yet, and if Herself can clear off to London to sit in her tropical penthouse, it's a bit rich to expect you to work in that icebox."

"How did Archie cope with a sick son over there, then?" Cleo asked, her curiosity piqued.

"Oh it was different then," Sarah declared, scooping a large portion of scrambled eggs onto thick crusty toast and handing the plate to Cleo. Helping herself to a similar portion, she came and sat beside Cleo, explaining, "The house had to be kept warm then, but Archie and Penny were more sensible about things. They kept to this near side of the house, and of course neither of them was bothered about standing on ceremony. So the end bedroom on the first floor – that's the one beneath yours – became their lounge, the room next to it was Simon's, and the room on the other side of his was their bedroom – that way they could always hear him, or either one of them calling for help. All the rest of the bedrooms were kept shut up, and downstairs we mostly all ate in the kitchen.

"But because of them keeping that clustering of rooms, not the full house, the old central heating boiler and system could cope, most of the radiators being totally shut off, you see. And of course they could light an open fire in their sitting room, and the Aga kept the kitchen warm. Simon's bedroom had once been part of another room beyond the end one they made into a lounge, so that didn't have a chimney – that's now in the corner of the middle room. So Simon's was at least bracketed by two rooms that could have fires in them, and they had extra electric heaters in there. Most of the time Archie would go and get what he wanted out of the library and bring it through to sit with Simon, so they weren't heating that room either."

"Yes, I'd wondered about the lack of chimneys," Cleo mused. "The place would hardly have been built without them."

Sarah rolled her eyes in disgust. "Oh most of the alterations were done by Horace. He was a terrible old spendthrift!"

"Did he knock through those rooms where I met Mrs, Wytcombe?"

"The 'TV room', you mean?" Sarah had put on a snobbish accent over the 'TV' bit.

"I presume so."

"*Hmph*! Well for once I can't blame Herself for that mess. They were once the billiard room and the music room, though the music room was always partly open to the main hall for the purposes of entertaining. I think Archie said that there were folding doors separating it when he was a little boy, but Horace wanted to keep up with the sixties fashion for open-plan, and so the walls got taken down."

"Ah, so have the other floors changed much since Hugh's day, as well?"

"The first floor has. What's now the master suite is a right old hash! You have to go through a bedroom to get to the master one – why on earth Horace thought that was a good idea baffled Archie as much as it does me! He once told me that the builder who did the work said as much, too, but Horace was the kind of idiot who said that if he was paying, he was choosing. But that master bedroom was once just a single room on its own, and the bedroom next to it that you now have to go through, had a bit nibbled out of the side to allow access from the landing. What is now the en-suite and a chunk of the middle bedroom was actually the original owner's big room.

Again, the wall has been shifted, because you used to get into that from what's now that middle room's doorway, but the door was right in the corner of the original room. And what became Simon's room was originally bigger, having the other chunk of the middle room as part of it."

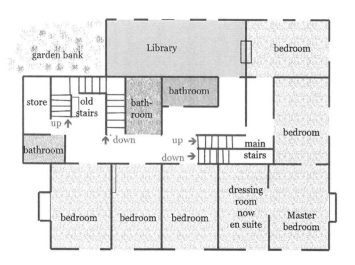

First floor plan of Upper Moore House

Cleo ruminated on that for a moment as she finished her toast, then said, "And is any of the furniture original to Hugh's time?"

"Good Lord, I don't know! Why?"

Making emphatic stabs with her fork, Cleo explained, "Well I was wondering how many people were living here at the time when Hugh was brought home? What you've just told me means that there were only four bedrooms across the front of the house, not five – I'm guessing the owner's room was the one with two windows, not one – and with a couple more on the side? So who was living

82

here then? Bertie and his wife, I presume, and then John and Horace, but the boys might have been upstairs in a nursery or away at private school most of the time? If the family did as many Edwardian folk of their class did, and regularly had people over to stay for shooting parties and the like – a bit *Downton Abbey*! – then Hugh needing a room of his own might have been more of an issue than we'd think nowadays for a house with that many bedrooms."

"Oh, I see what you mean. Yes, I think they did do a lot of entertaining, which was where Horace got his expensive tastes from. He never could quite rein it back to later-twentieth century standards. But why does it matter where Hugh was?"

Cleo laughed. "Because for one thing, I'd like to know why his ghostly calls are affecting me up on the top floor if he never went up there."

"Ah," Sarah agreed, smiling with her. "Yes, it does seem odd, put that way. Do you know, I think that they made a suite of rooms for him up there."

"So was the room I'm in the old nursery?"

"No, actually it wasn't. That's at the other end of the house. Your room and the ones by it were for the lesser guests in the house's heyday. …But why does it matter? Why are you so interested in where Hugh slept?"

Cleo picked up her mug of tea and wandered across to the window beside the kitchen door, through which she could just see the nearest corner of the big house.

"I think it matters because of this: imagine you are Hugh. You've come through hell on earth, and in a far away part of Europe you find something that's going to rock the very world of your family. Are you going to trust your word will be enough? …I don't think he would. I reckon he'd have some sort of proof, or he'd never have even brought the subject up.

"And everything I've heard about Bertie from you makes me think he was probably one of those bombastic and rather bullying kinds of men. So Hugh must have known that if it just came down to his own word against Bertie's, then his older brother would win. After all, Bertie was the one who was the pillar of the local community here, wasn't he? He was lord of the manor, so to speak, and therefore the one with all the contacts with the family solicitors, and the like."

Sarah had come to join her at the window. "Yes, of course he would – Bertie, I mean. And it's the same firm of solicitors who are handling all of the estate matters now, though none of the original families practice law anymore. So yes, they would probably have never had much of anything to do with Hugh in the past. It would be Bertie who they'd know."

"Exactly! Now follow that line of thought onwards. If you were Hugh, what would you do with that proof? You know it's going to cause an almighty row, and possibly divide the family forever. Would you really leave it lying around where your brother could find it and destroy it? Because from what you say Archie told you, Bertie actively *wanted* Hugh to destroy it! So it's not being fanciful to think that if he could have got his sticky paws on whatever it was, that he would have destroyed it without having to argue the toss with Hugh about it.

"So come on, Sarah, where would Hugh have put this thing? Not in any of the public rooms, I'll be bound! For a start off, he couldn't risk one of the servants stumbling across it. And if there haven't been many servants in the last fifty years or so, back in the twenties there would probably have still been a staff into double figures for a house of this size."

Sarah froze with her mug halfway to her lips again. "Oh my word! I see what you mean. No, he'd want it somewhere where he could keep an eye on it, wouldn't he?"

"Which means one of the bedrooms, if he was here convalescing with only one leg. He'd hardly be nipping up and down the stairs in that condition, would he? He was a long way short of modern prosthetics which can be fitted relatively soon after the limb stump has healed. He'd have been on crutches at best for months, and probably bed-bound for a fair amount of the day."

"I see what you mean! So his bedroom would be the ideal place! He'd be there through the night, so he'd know if someone came snooping. …But we don't know which room was his, Cleo."

"No, we don't. But we can eliminate a few, can't we? Unless he buried stuff under floorboards, it won't be in any of the rooms which his nephew Horace mucked about with. Even after Hugh had died, if some workmen came to Horace with a bundle of papers and said, 'Here you go, governor, we found these under the floor,' then there'd have been no reason for Horace to be so agitated every time the matter got mentioned, would there?

"Do you see what I mean? Horace could have read them, realised what they were, and destroyed them just as his father wished. After which point there'd have been no point in mentioning it to Archie; and you gave me the impression that Archie's father was wittering on about this right up into his old age."

Sarah nodded. "Yes, he did. He pretty much made Archie vow to him on his deathbed, that if the matter ever came to light, that he would destroy the evidence once and for all."

"Well there you go, then. He wouldn't have been so anxious if it had already appeared, would he? So I think we have to assume that the various knocking down of walls, and rearranging the internal spaces of the house, never brought anything to light."

"Heavens, Cleo, you're quite the Sherlock Homes!"

To which Cleo laughed. "I'm hardly the local CID. It's just that it's often helped in my line of work to be able to put myself in other people's shoes. Where would I go in such-and-such a situation? Or what would I do? It's no substitute for proof, but it can't half help cut down on the amount of time it takes in searching to find that proof.

"But seriously, Sarah, you do see what I mean, don't you? Hugh was no fool, and by the looks of it a pretty capable sort of man – not least because he survived so many years in the trenches. And that makes me think that right from the start he would have known that he would have to convince folk like the family solicitors, as well as the family themselves. So he'd never have even tried if he hadn't got something pretty convincing, and the fact that it hasn't come to light as yet means that it's still around somewhere.

"Now if Hugh had been an active man, I would say we'd have a near impossible task on our hands. After all, he might have hidden it at someone else's house or even out in the grounds somewhere, if he knew of somewhere safe from when he was a boy, for instance. But he wasn't active. He was a crippled man who certainly wasn't going to be using an old tree-house, for example. So if we work on what a man in his condition would have found accessible, I think we can only conclude that the proof is still somewhere in the house."

Chapter 7

"So where do you want to start?" Sarah asked. "I wish I could tell you which rooms Hugh used, but I can't, and I fear he may have come home to his old rooms and then been moved on into others."

Cleo smiled at her. "As I said before, I think we can discount any rooms that have had major alterations done to them. And sad to say, if there were any large pieces of furniture which went to an auction house which might have concealed stuff, then even so we might be too late. But if we go through the rooms which are still fairly intact, and also any old pieces of furniture which have been in the family for generations, then at least we can say we've ticked all the boxes that we can."

"Do you want to start today?" Sarah asked worriedly. "Because those rooms are going to be like working in a walk-in fridge in this weather."

To her clear relief Cleo shook her head. "No, I'm not that impatient. Maybe we could go and have a walk around just to see which rooms look like the best candidates? But beyond that I've got a lot of work still to do on the papers. I can bring bundles over here and carry on with them in the warm."

"Good idea. But there's something else we could do today. I need to go and do some shopping, so do you want to come with me? Then on the way back we could go and have a look at the graves in the parish churchyard. The snow's not that deep that it will stop us doing that."

Cleo jumped at the chance to get out in the fresh air. "Great! And I can get myself a new pair of wellies. My old ones had given up the ghost before this, but living in a town, I hadn't needed to replace them as yet. If I'm going to do much wandering about the place, though, I think I might need a pair."

However Sarah had to warn her that she might need to wait for that, since the local shops in Bromyard might not have what she wanted. "And that's if the independent ones are open," she added. "Most of the owners are local, and if they're down lanes, they might not bother trying to get in today, assuming that there'll not be much trade to make it worth the struggle. The local Co-op will be open for food, of course, that's why I'm going. But if we're going to go around the churchyard, I've a spare pair of rubber gardening overshoes you can use. You look like you're a size or two smaller than me, so you can slip them on over your own shoes and stay nice and dry."

They took Sarah's car, which although elderly was a four-wheeled drive, and so they had no trouble getting through to Bromyard. Cleo took the opportunity to get some thicker socks, if nothing else, and immediately put one pair on, blessing the fact that she'd brought a pair of low heeled lace-up boots with her. Fashion boots though they were, and certainly not up to hiking across the graveyard in the snow, at least she could slacken them off a bit to accommodate the heavier socks – something she couldn't have done with her smarter court shoes.

She was glad of both the socks and Sarah's loaned garden overshoes when they got to the church. Thornfield Church was set down a short but narrow lane, and in the summer Cleo could see that it would be a very pretty spot.

"The original church goes back all the way to Saxon times, we think," Sarah told her proudly. "It's something to do with a pattern in the wall."

"Herring-bone?" Cleo guessed. "That's usually the best marker."

"You do know a lot," Sarah said in surprise, but Cleo was quick to explain,

"It's more that it all came as part of the same package. I did my degree a bit later than some, though I was still only in my early twenties when I went. But it meant that I really *wanted* to do my degree, rather than going straight from school and just picking the course which sounded good. And I was already living away from home before I went, so I just carried on living in my tiny flat over an antique dealer's in Worcester. The owner was glad to have someone trustworthy on the premises at night, and I helped him out in the shop at weekends.

"So by the time I started doing archaeology modules, I'd got at least a basic grasp of stuff. I knew about dendrochronology, for instance, because I went with my landlord, Mr Wentworth, to an old house where they were having everything assessed. He went to look at some lovely old Tudor presses, but there was an expert there taking samples from the oak beams. Going into genealogy after all of that was almost a straight path, because I didn't fancy teaching, I wasn't good enough to go on and have an academic career, and yet I still wanted to be involved with history. There aren't that many jobs in the heritage sector anymore – the government funding just isn't there – so something where I was making my own choices seemed like a sound plan. And for the most part it's worked out. I'm far from rich, but I haven't starved yet, either."

They turned a corner of the squat west-end tower and suddenly Cleo spotted what she'd been looking for. "There it is! Herring-bone stonework, and a very nice example it is, too! And that's good for our quest, as well."

"It is?"

"Oh yes! You see, if the parish had expanded, you might have got a new church being built on the same site in say the 1840s. Or just as bad, the local worthies deciding that this simple church was no longer good enough, and abandoning it for a newer one down the road, at which point you might find the records don't match up. But with this having an uninterrupted run as the parish church, we can pretty much say that if there's anything to be found here, that's all there'll be. We won't need to go running around half the churches in this part of the shire on the off-chance that there are Wytcombes buried there."

As so often was the case, the church itself was securely locked up during the week when there was nobody around to keep an eye on the place. However, Sarah knew the verger, and before long she had come back from his house with the key. Letting themselves in, Sarah switched on the lights, and Cleo saw the interior for the first time.

"Well I'd say that there have been some eighteenth- and possibly nineteenth-century additions," she observed as she began walking down the nave, "especially the southern side aisle. Nice bit of Norman window there in the north wall, though… oh! And here we go! A tomb to one of the Wytcombes."

An elegant marble plaque was inset into the wall, inscribed with,

> *To the memory of Lieut. Richard Wytcombe,*
> *hero of the Battle of Lissa,*
> *born 11th Feb 1785, died 9th Dec 1838.*
> *Son of the late Henry & Martha Wytcombe,*
> *beloved husband of Francesca,*
> *father to Hector, Sophia & William.*
> *May his soul rest in eternal peace.*

And to his beloved wife Francesca,
1783-1835

"Now I wonder where he fits in?" Sarah mused. "Looks like his wife died before him and they re-did the memorial. Not much to go on for her, is there?"

"No, and that's a bit odd. Normally for the wife of the local squire you'd expect some reference to her family, even if it was something like, 'daughter of Robert and Winifred Smith'. I wonder who she was? I suppose it's possible that she wasn't from around here. He's of an age to have fought in the Napoleonic Wars, so she could be from France or Spain."

"Cleo! Look at this!" Sarah was gesturing to a rather more ornate but slightly less legible memorial higher up on the wall and a bit closer to the altar.

To the memory of Edwin Wytcombe
of Upper Moore House,
son of William & Mary Wytcombe,
departed this life 12th July 1811,
and to his wife, Anne, of this rectory,
died 16th August 1801,
and of their son, William,
laid to rest too soon,
12th Sept. 1811.

Sarah looked downcast as she read the words aloud. "Well that means that Richard can't be anything to do with Upper Moore, can he? Not when his dates overlap with these. How do you unravel stuff like this?"

However Cleo was not so dissuaded. "Don't be in such a hurry to dismiss that. There's a fair gap between this William dying in 1811, and Richard dying in 1838, and there's also nothing to hint that young William married. It would be odd to have him buried with his parents if he had. Far more likely that he would have been interred with his wife and any of their children who had died young. And I can't be sure, but I've a feeling I've seen Richard's name on some documents back at the house. I'll have to check properly, but I think it was something to do with a sale of some land, which looked like it was for death duties. If that's the case and the date is something like 1812 or '13, then he could be the heir the house passed to."

"It's all a bit far back to be connected to our problem, though."

"Not necessarily. When was Bertie born? The 1870s we guessed? Well that's only a couple of generations away from the start of that century. They could all be connected, in fact probably are, it's just working out how, and who the key players are. …Ah! Now over here we've got the more modern members of the family. Not exactly your grand memorial plaque like Edwin Wytcombe, but here's one to Bertie. …Albert Wytcombe, 1878 to 1948. So we weren't far out in our assumption."

She looked around her and spotted the wooden board at the back which listed the men lost in both world wars. Yet there was no sign of Hugh's name on it.

"Poor Hugh! Not even commemorated on the war memorial!" Sarah exclaimed in disgust as they went to look at it, but Cleo reminded her,

"He didn't die *in* the war, though, did he? And sadly, men like him who died later of their wounds don't make it onto the memorials. Although it saddens me, unfortunately that's not all that rare. He's not the first case like this that I've come across – a client absolutely sure that a relative died in the war, but who actually turned out to have died some months after the armistice, which is why he's on no memorial. Or in some cases, who died back at home from their wounds, but after having been officially demobbed from whichever force they were in, even though the war was still going on. It happened in World War Two, as well."

She looked about her again. "Is there a family tomb, do you know? I'm wondering if the family who died in the flu epidemic would be buried there?"

"It's outside," Sarah said, and led the way back out, locking the church up behind her.

The family mausoleum turned out to be an ugly pile of lichen-encrusted marble, ringed with a rusting iron railing.

"Archie hated it," Sarah said with a shudder. "He always said it looked like it belonged in a Hammer Horror film. He's not here, and neither are Penny or Simon. They're over in one of the newer graves. I think the last one to be buried here was Horace, and that was only because he'd absolutely stipulated it in his will. But Archie refused to do this thing up, and I don't think he ever came here to visit his father's grave." She waved towards another part of the graveyard. "His mum is over there, by the yew tree. I know that because I came with him a few times on the anniversary of her death to bring flowers, back in the days when Penny was sitting with Simon, and only one of them dared leave. Luckily his mum died after Horace, so she didn't get put in here – she hated it as much as Archie."

"It was a very divided family, wasn't it?" Cleo observed. "In each generation there seem to be some quite strong disagreements."

Sarah nodded. "Audrey – that was Archie's mum – married Horace at the end of the war. I think she was a radio operator in the army, and that's how they met. She told Archie later that if she'd known what she was letting herself in for, she'd have run a mile!"

"Heavens, that really sounds like it was a disastrous marriage!"

"I think for her it was. Their first two children were girls, and Horace almost took it as an affront that he had no heir. But once Archie came along, I think Audrey felt she could decline his attentions, if you know what I mean. I think he was quite rough with her, not much of the attentive lover. Clara, Archie's oldest sister, went to live in Canada to escape even before she got married, and the other sister, Emily, got measles and died. It meant that Archie and his mum were very close, but then he was very like her in personality. He said it was always a relief when Horace cleared off up to London, or to the house of one of his hunting and fishing friends.

"Audrey was the one who got Archie into books so much, and a lot of the collection in the library is hers. She was quite astute at buying and selling books, you know, and Archie once told me that there are a few first editions in there if you know what you're looking for. At the time he said it with a twinkle in his eye after Herself had had one of her hissy fits over him always having his nose in what she called his 'useless' books. He said she wouldn't think them quite so useless if she knew what they would fetch at auction."

As they squelched their way across the graveyard to take the key back, Cleo declared, "But that's another reason why the secret might have stayed buried for so long, isn't it?"

"How do you mean?"

"Well you've just said that Archie and his mum were close, and that his father made her life a misery. Under those circumstances, Archie would have been a pretty odd sort of son if he'd then wanted to help his father sort out the family mystery. It'd be more normal to think of him dragging his feet over the matter, and as a teenager just saying in very 1960s fashion, 'yeah, man, whatever,' whenever his father went off on one of his rants."

Sarah collapsed in giggles, and when she could talk for laughing, explained, "I saw some old Polaroids of Archie in his youth. Oh my God, Cleo! You so got him in one! There he was with his long hair, sandals and flares. He even had an astrakhan coat! Bless him, he laughed as hard as I did over them later on, but he admitted that half of it was pure and simple rebellion against his strait-laced father. I think his mum quite liked the idea of a bit of freedom, and she was quite happy for him to bring a succession of slightly odd friends home. He and Penny went to the Isle of Wight festival, you know, and saw Jimi Hendrix."

"Wow!"

"I know. Every so often he'd dig out his old Hendrix LPs and play them at full belt. He said he liked to shock the vicar when he was coming!"

"Mischievous old Archie!"

"Oh yes, he had a great sense of humour. That's what made his current marriage such a tragedy to my mind. He slowly stopped laughing at all."

"How terribly sad. And I don't see Darcy Wytcombe 'gettin'-it-on-down' in the Summer of Love, do you?"

Sarah hooted with laughter again. "You've a wicked mind, Cleo, but you're right!"

"Then we really should sort this out for his sake," Cleo decided. "If there's one memorial we can give him, it's to put things right the way his great-uncle Hugh wanted to do, even if that means we disinherit the new Mrs W in the process. Surely to God there must be some more deserving heir to the house than her?

"And I'll tell you something else. My friend Angie at the estate agents was saying that the house isn't worth what Darcy Wytcombe thinks it should be. At the time I just thought it hadn't been built to quite the highest standards in the first place. But now I'm realising that what's dragging the price down is all the mucking about that Horace did to it. He must have done it before it got formally listed, because he'd never have been allowed to do that rearranging of the bedroom walls afterwards.

"But you know what? That might just have saved a vital clue. Who knows what the daft old sod would have done if he'd had a free rein with the place? But once the listing went on, he'd have had to shelve any further plans he had, and that might mean that he never got the chance to rip out any more original bits."

She suddenly realised that Sarah was no longer alongside her, and turned to see Sarah a couple of paces back looking shocked.

"What is it?"

"You've gone and done it again – jogged my memory. Archie told me years ago that the final nail in the coffin of his parents' marriage was that listing. Audrey would never admit it, but Archie was sure she was the one who pushed for it with the local council. He said he thought she'd done it because she loved the old place, and couldn't stand the thought of Horace wrecking it. But also because Horace was so hopeless with money, he'd have bankrupted them with his crazy ideas of modernisation.

"Yet he also said his father apparently went completely nuts over it at the time, and nobody could understand why, other than that he was behaving like the spoilt big kid that he was. If you're right, though, and part of why he was taking the place to pieces was because he was trying to find whatever Hugh had hidden, then it explains why his reaction bemused everyone else. After all, he could hardly say to his hunting and fishing friends, 'oh, I'm taking the family home apart bit by bit to find and destroy something that proves we were a bunch of rogues,' could he?"

"No, but I'd lay good money on that being part of why he did it."

Cleo shivered as they got back in the car and Sarah turned the heating on full. "Good grief, I hope this cold is only a short snap! I want to get on with those papers now, but I won't get very far if my fingers are numb with cold!"

Chapter 8

With the winter daylight already fading by the time they got back to Upper Moore, it was hardly the time to go exploring the house, and so Cleo worked on the papers at Sarah's large kitchen table. To Cleo's relief, Sarah let her get on with the work rather than sitting chatting. Not that Cleo would have blamed her if she had – these days, life at Upper Moore would be very lonely at this time of year, she observed. It also seemed more and more as though Sarah had lost not just a relative or an employer, but foremost a good friend in Archie, and though Cleo felt she could hardly ask, it sounded as though Archie might have been repaying the support Sarah had shown him by being there for her in her own crisis. Being in the house, she couldn't help but hear the early evening phone call to the hospital, and Sarah's defeated tones. Her husband didn't seem to have long left.

She also didn't miss the worried way that Sarah confided, "I can't seem to get hold of my son, Chris, in Canada. That's the fifth time I've called him and he's not been there, and this time I got the message that the phone's not in use. God, I hope he's alright."

"He's probably just changed providers, or they've had some proper Canadian snow and a signal mast is down somewhere," Cleo consoled her, but that night she was aware of Sarah getting up in the middle of the night and going downstairs to prowl around.

Blessed Hecate, Cleo mentally groaned, *if it's not ghosts it's distraught mothers! I know she can't help being worried, and I do sympathise, but I'd like more than one decent night's sleep in a week!*

In the morning, Sarah looked tired with dark shadows under her eyes, and this time it was Cleo feeling that she shouldn't leave her which made her go and get another heap of papers from the library. Yet at just past eleven o'clock the phone rang, and Cleo heard Sarah's joyful, "Chris!" from through in the other room. When Sarah came back in it was with a beaming smile.

"He's come home! Chris has come home!"

"Where is he?"

"Heathrow, just getting the train into London. I'll be going and picking him up from the station." Then Sarah's face fell. "Oh dear."

"What's wrong."

"Erm, …you're in Chris' room."

Cleo laughed. "Good grief, Sarah, that's not the end of the world. The snow's already melting today, and if I can get some of those portable heaters you mentioned up into my room, I'll go back. You really don't need to worry about me along with everything else. I'll be fine. I've lived in cold, old houses before – I'm not like Mrs W!"

"The heaters, yes! We'll have to go and dig them out!" Sarah declared with relief. "They're a bit old now, but I think most of them are working. Can you break off now to come and look around the house?"

Blessing the fact that she always worked methodically, and would be able to pick up her thread again easily, Cleo was able to smile and say, "Of course. Come on, let's go and find them and then I can leave you to go and get your son. Would you like me to cook tonight? I'm not quite up to your standard, but I can whip up a mean lasagne. It seems the least I can do after you've helped me so much."

The relieved smile she got back was answer enough, and they donned coats and boots to go across to the big house.

"You might as well get the full tour," Sarah said, producing a large key ring with so many keys on it that Cleo was amazed that she knew what any of them were for. However Sarah didn't hesitate to pick the correct ones to use on the impressive front door. The high-tech Yale was obviously the main security, but a proper old-fashioned iron key went in to a keyhole too. Yet the door didn't budge, and Sarah looked perplexed before giving an exasperated sigh. "I must be losing it," she said with a roll of her eyes. "Totally forgot that I bolted the door from the inside! Daft woman that I am! Sorry, we're going to have to traipse back around to the kitchen."

"Don't worry," Cleo soothed her. "It's the first time I've had a chance to properly look at the whole of the outside, and that's interesting all by itself. And it's not as though you haven't been under a fair bit of stress lately. I'm just glad that Mrs W has gone and isn't throwing her toys out of the pram at every turn. You don't need that."

That made Sarah smile. "No, that is a blessing! …So what do you think of the place?"

They were walking back past what Cleo had thought was the front of the house, but now she said, "It's a curious old place. Having now seen the front door, I think the lie of the land here made more of a difference to how the Georgian extension was built than is normal."

"Really? How?"

"Well normally they would just stick a set of reception rooms across the whole front. And until you just showed me around, I thought that this big run of rooms leading out here onto the upper terrace, before the ground slopes away, was it. But having seen what must have been the old driveway with that impressive line of beech trees, I can see that the orientation of the house must have previously been very different. They clearly had to keep the main drive to the way horses could bring carriages in, not up those steep banks."

"Well I can tell you that Archie put the new drive in as a matter of urgency when he inherited. The old one comes out on a nasty blind bend, and with the build up of modern traffic on the lanes, you were taking your life in your hands every time you tried to get in or out. You were likely to end up with another car practically in with you whichever way you were turning."

"Ah! That makes sense. So for what it's worth, if we ever come across the plans for the change, we'd see that the original house was probably quite a small square affair, set back against the rising bank. Those lovely old stairs I've been going up and down were undoubtedly at the core of the house. Did you say that the room next to the kitchen is the dining room?"

"Yes, it is. I'll show it you in a moment. It's a lovely room when it's all decked out for a big, formal meal."

By now they were passing its window and Cleo looked with interest at the chimney, even taking several steps back to look at the way it rose up.

"It might be all Georgian now, Sarah, but with a chimney like that I'm certain that it's part of the old house, you know. They didn't bother fiddling around with the chimney shape, because no posh guest was going to head around the back of the house to see that it's pure Jacobean. And that could be good news for us, because it might be another room that hasn't been mucked around with much since Hugh's time!"

They went in by the kitchen door, but this time Sarah paused and opened a door on their left. "This was the old laundry. I still use it for that as you can see, but it's more of a general store room now too." She went over to a large, old fashioned cupboard and opened the bottom doors. "Ah! Here we are! These are the electric heaters Archie used last. I'm sure all four of these work. If we wheel them out and through to the main stairs, we can take them up when I've shown you the main rooms."

They went out through the other door from the kitchen, and now Cleo saw that they were in an odd sort of corridor, which she remembered from her first meeting with Mrs W, though she'd taken little notice of it that time.

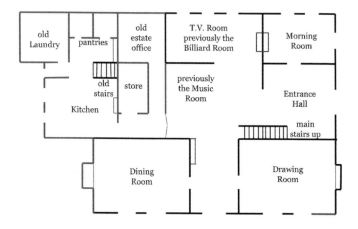

Ground floor plan of Upper Moore House

Waving her hand to the left again, Sarah told her, "There're just an old store room and the estate office down there. Archie mainly used the office when we had shoots going on. It was a good place for people to come in to with muddy boots, and it's a good secure room to have the gun cabinet in, because for some reason it doesn't have a window." She was about to wheel the heater onwards when Cleo stopped her.

"Hold on!" She began looking intently at the walls. "Oh my goodness, Sarah! This was once a lovely main hall, you know. That's why the estate office hasn't any windows – it was just the back part of a huge room which probably had lovely mullioned windows looking out down the drive." She turned around and scrutinised the wall to her right. "Yes! Got it! ...Look here, there's a line in the wallpaper where the plaster underneath isn't level. Follow that up and you can see that it's because a doorway has been blocked in here. Can you see the door's outline? Your dining room once led off *here* as the second reception room of the ground floor."

Sarah peered at the wall, making Cleo wonder when the last time she had had her eyes tested. If this son who was arriving was the approachable sort, she might suggest to him that he insist on his mum taking a bit better care of herself. Sarah's distance vision was fine, but it wasn't just the close stuff she needed specs for, Cleo thought, and that would explain why she had missed some of these clues that were so obvious to herself. It helped greatly that she knew what she was looking for, of course, whereas when Sarah had first come to Upper Moore, in contrast she would have had no reason to investigate the house itself. But to illustrate her point now, Cleo knocked firmly on the true wall, then on the infill and heard it ring hollowly.

"See? They may even have just put some wooden planking over it on this side. Why bother finishing it properly when only the servants would be seeing this side from then on?"

"Well I never!" Sarah exclaimed. "I thought it might have been Horace's snobbery that made him seal off the way to and from the kitchen – because it's quite a trek with hot serving dishes!"

"No, this happened long before Horace, I'd say," Cleo said confidently. "Look at this paper and the way it's yellowed. We reckoned Horace inherited in the late forties, didn't we, but this is much older, and just by the feel of it I'd say that there are another couple of layers of paper underneath it. Come here and knock on it yourself. ...See? It's not like you're right on the wood. It would sound even hollower if this was the only paper, but there's still definitely a cavity behind there."

They trundled the heaters a little farther on, coming out into an open area. Sarah took them straight across and parked her heater by where Cleo could now see the main staircase rose from.

"These are the easier stairs to carry awkward things up," Sarah explained. "The turns on the other one make it a struggle to lug things up that take two people. We'll carry these up between us one at a time. ...Now then, here's the front door," and she drew back two substantial bolts on it, throwing it open to reveal a perfect view down the avenue of beeches, glorious in the remains of their winter gold leaves.

"Now that's a handsome view," Cleo agreed. "That's precisely the kind of view a Georgian squire would have wanted."

However, the arctic wind whistling in swiftly made them close the door and lock it up again, but not before Cleo had turned around and seen how the house would have presented itself to the great and good who would have walked in this way. The Georgian staircase had been neatly positioned so that nobody would have a view to the passage through to the back of the house. Heaven forbid that the servants should have been seen! But when she stepped sideways to see that doorway, it also showed up something else. The double doors that they had come through from the kitchen passage were much bigger than she had realised.

"Look Sarah! That's the old front door of the house! Look at the size of it – no internal door ever needs to be that big. I was right, the estate office was part of what was once a lovely Jacobean hall. That huge chimney you've got in the kitchen that the Aga is part of? That once opened the other way and was the centrepiece of the hall. That's why the stairs up to the top floor are out of line. They probably only led up to attic rooms in the original house, and so they go up the other side of the chimney stack."

"Come and tell me what you make of this, then," and Sarah led her back through the propped open double doors and through the kitchen to what Cleo had already guessed were the pantries. "Archie and I always thought that there was a lost space here," she said, gesturing to the wall which Cleo now thought had to back onto the old hall. "Do you think there was another chimneybreast here? There isn't a fireplace in the estate office anymore, and there's no chimney on the outside."

Cleo stuck her head around the door of the nearest pantry and saw what Sarah meant. Yes, the pantry definitely dipped back farther than the wall outside. They went around to the estate office, at which point Cleo couldn't help but give a little laugh of delight. There, in what must have once been the thickness of the chimney breast, was a substantial gun cabinet, though there were no guns in there anymore.

"I'm not licensed for fire-arms, and neither is Herself," Sarah explained, "so as soon as Archie died, the local police had to come and take the shotguns away for safe keeping. I expect they'll be sold as soon as the legal stuff is sorted. There were a couple of Purdey shotguns in there, and they'll fetch a tidy amount all by themselves."

"What a fabulous old cabinet, though!" Cleo enthused. "Look at the workmanship on the decoration! And you and Archie were right. This isn't just the cabinet – the whole thing is the second fireplace to the old hall. I bet if you investigate up above the cabinet, you might even find a lovely carved stone lintel under the wallpaper. Look at the width of this, and then at the way the carpenter had to put that stout beam in to divide it in two so that you could have a double set of doors on either side of it – that's the width of the ancient fireplace. Now stand back and ignore the internal bits of the cabinet. If it helps, squint your eyes a bit. Can you see it? Those beautifully carved side pieces are actually the sides of the old fireplace!"

"So it is! Good grief, it's true what they say, familiarity really does breed contempt. I always thought what a clunky ugly old thing that cabinet was, never for a moment seeing what it might have been. But, Cleo, there's nothing left of that chimney upstairs, nothing at all."

However, Cleo wasn't dismayed by it at all. "It might be that this side of the original house got damp, what with being right close to the earth bank on this corner. And in those days, bricks got made very close to where they would be used by travelling brick-makers. So they weren't always of the best quality. It may well be that the Georgian rebuild wasn't just done to keep up with the neighbours – it might have been something of a necessity if the original bricks had started to rot. And brick can rot, you know, especially old ones made of little more than baked clay."

"You may well be right. In better weather, if you go outside onto the bank from the library French windows, you can see that in the past, a retaining wall was built to keep the bank back from the house at this point. That's the bit of wall you can see from the TV room's windows. And when we get up there you'll see that they put a bit of a roof over it, too, in between the bridges leading from the library's French windows onto the bank, to stop the rain from washing down into the gap between the two walls."

"A sensible precaution in an age where they wouldn't have had things like damp-proof courses. They probably couldn't afford to rebuild from scratch somewhere else, so they were making the best of what they had. ...So come on, then, this is getting exciting! Where to next?"

Sarah smiled, "Well you guessed right about the TV room where you met Herself. Do you want to see that again?"

"Wouldn't hurt, if only to discount it from our search."

What Cleo didn't want to say was that she had seen what might turn out to be a tiny cupboard built into the side of the huge old fireplace. It wasn't that she wanted to deceive Sarah or keep things secret from her, far from it. But she only had these precious few hours left to get a deeper insight into the house before Sarah got taken up with her own problems – and Cleo wasn't so churlish as to expect Sarah to put those on hold for even a moment. Having to make the kind of decision which was looming over her was something she wouldn't have wished onto her worst enemy, and all the worse for Sarah and Jeff seeming to have had a close marriage. No, she must get what she could out of this time, and then work on on her own.

As Cleo had expected, the TV room and the former music room had both been much too altered to have any secrets left to shed, and going on to the first of the front rooms, which Sarah said was the morning room, revealed it to be part of the Georgian revamp. It was a lovely room, filled with light being beyond the slope of the bank at the back of the house, but with it primarily facing east, it was bitterly cold at this time of year, and they didn't linger.

Across the hall from the front door was the drawing room, which was equally Georgian if warmer for facing mostly west.

"No, there's nothing here for us," Cleo was able to say with confidence. "That plasterwork is lovely, and I bet they paid an arm and a leg for it to be done back in the day, but there's not so much as an ornamental niche here where Hugh might have hidden something."

They had to go back and around the stairs, and through the music room area, before swinging left into another hall area which had its own glorious double French window leading outside. The afternoon watery winter sunshine streamed in through it, and again Cleo could imagine it full of Edwardian and Victorian ladies enjoying an evening's dancing. It was the perfect setting for that, and the elegant fireplace against the dining room wall would keep any chills at bay from having the windows open, but that was so obviously Georgian that Cleo knew it had to be part of the newer house – this was no reused relic as the kitchen chimney was. However, when Sarah flung open the door from the inner hall into the dining room, they were suddenly back into a different era. Whether the family had run out of money by this time, or someone had just loved the old wood panelling, but it had survived intact in here.

"Oh this is delightful!" Cleo enthused. "Granted they put in some longer windows to give out onto the terrace again, which is why that wall is plastered, not panelled, but the rest of this room hasn't been changed in centuries. Mind you, it probably helps that they used a paler wood than oak." Then she went to look at it closer. "Hmm. Actually, I think it's just that this wood was French polished before it became too dark, and that's what's kept this lovely warm glow. These carved linen folds are spot on for a Jacobean house."

She turned around and spotted where the old door must once have been. "Crafty devils! See, Sarah? They moved the architrave to the new door, and then they shoved this huge matching oak dresser in front of where the old door was. If you could shift this monster, I'd lay good odds on you finding bare plaster behind it." She went and peered at where it butted up to the panelling. "Hmm, actually fixed to the wall – and that may well have been a practical thing when you consider how tall it is. You wouldn't want this toppling over! Anyone standing in the way would be killed outright. But it does fit incredibly well with the room, so I think it might have been built for – and possibly even *in* – here, and that's not unknown for the period, either."

And this is another piece I shall come back to explore when I've got more time, Cleo thought, remembering some of the pieces in Mr Wentworth's showroom which had hidden cupboard spaces in them. The folk of the seventeenth century had to have places where they could keep their valuables, and in an age when they didn't have the luxury of modern safes, secret nooks and crannies might be all that stood between you and some thief robbing you of your family valuables.

Good Lord, Hugh, you weren't short of hiding places, were you? Cleo thought. *Especially if you were the lad who talked to the servants rather than being stuck up, as your brother sounds like he was.* What she said aloud, though, was, "Right! On to the next floor! Let's get these heaters upstairs and we can keep going."

Chapter 9

They took the first heaters up to the library and plugged them in.

"If we leave them on overnight, there's a chance you'll be able to work in here tomorrow," Sarah said, although she still sounded doubtful.

"I notice that the one desk is close to the fireplace," Cleo observed. "I'm used to dealing with open fires, you know. And with that big tiled grate, Mrs W's precious carpet is far enough away not to get singed. That's a substantial fireguard you've got there. It looks as though Archie was shrewd enough to be alert to the dangers of stray sparks."

"Oh, if you know what you're doing, then that's different," Sarah said with some relief.

"My old flat still had its hearths, and being the downstairs rooms, the fireplaces were a fair size. With those tall ceilings a proper fire was the only way to keep warm. The whole chimneybreast acted as one big brick radiator."

"Yes, they do, don't they. Well there's a substantial log pile out the back because I've a log burner too, so help yourself. I just wouldn't leave it burning overnight."

"God, no! Not in any library, let alone if there are first editions in here! No, Sarah, I promise I'll be extremely careful."

"Great, then let's get those other heaters up to your bedroom."

She took Cleo on the circuitous route back to the kitchen, showing her the rest of the first floor rooms, and as Cleo had feared, most were too messed about with to have any secrets left. If Hugh had hidden anything here it had long vanished in a pulp of builders' rubbish. The only room which looked as though it hadn't been disturbed was the one which backed onto the library. Like the morning room which it was over, it was a pleasant, light room, but cold as charity with its two east windows, despite the third facing south, and Cleo pitied anyone who had been put in this room on a winter's night. She just hoped that the Wytcombes had been generous with the eiderdowns and blankets.

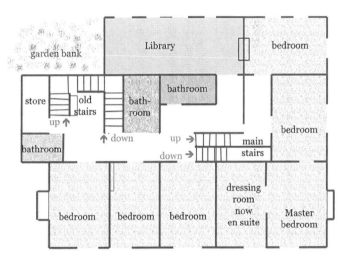

"You see what I mean about Horace's daft ideas," Sarah said, as she showed Cleo back to the stairs. "The fireplace that warms the entrance hall must have come up here to the room that goes on into the master bedroom.

That's why there's still that structural wall in the way. But there's no way of heating that room anymore."

"Another blocked doorway at that back bedroom end, too," Cleo agreed. "The two bedrooms that looked out over the portico must have had their own small landing. It's certainly a very modern doorway that leads through to the master suite now – no Georgian built to those stingy measurements!"

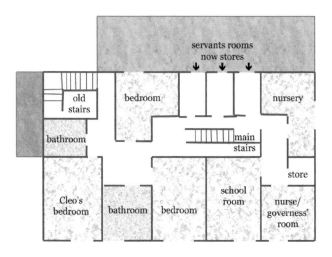

The upper floor, however, was much more fertile ground. Again Cleo pitied the poor servants, because their Georgian masters hadn't thought about how they would keep warm at night. There wasn't any sort of fireplace in any of the three little rooms that faced the back of the house, but when Cleo wriggled between the piles of boxes to look out of the middle one's window, she could see why. The chimney stack from the library almost blocked out the light from this room and the one next to it, but the servants had probably been glad of its bulk blocking the icy east winds. Indeed the roof tiles she was looking straight out onto appeared to be older than those of the main roof, making Cleo wonder whether this was another relic of the original house. Possibly the angle of the old roof had been cut into to make these rooms, though they all had a serious slant to their ceilings, and she thought a walk around the outside might show them as a run of dormer windows rather than a wholesale interruption to the roof itself. However, Hugh would have had to be pretty mobile to have found a hiding place up in any of the roof spaces here, and Cleo struck all three off her mental list of rooms to return to.

"This is the old nursery," Sarah said, opening the door to the next room along, again on the same easterly wall as the morning room. However, the children who had been in here had been more fortunate, for the slope of the roof meant that the only window faced south over the portico.

"I wonder if as boys any of the children ever sneaked out of the window?" Cleo said with a grin. "It's not such a drop down to the portico roof from here. An enterprising lad would make short work of that with a bit of rope."

Sarah laughed. "If they were anything like Chris and Aiden, they would! Heavens, I had such a job keeping them in when we lived in an old house when Jeff was stationed up in Scotland."

"Who's the older one?" Cleo asked, glad to see Sarah smiling over happier memories.

"Oh, Aiden. He's his father all over. He was forever dragging Chris off into some 'adventure', which usually ended up with Chris coming home cut and bruised. I could never get him to see that with Chris being two years younger, he couldn't reach as far, or jump as far, or whatever escapade Aiden had devised. He just expected Chris to follow, and if he didn't, he didn't look back to see if Chris was stranded."

Cleo thought Aiden sounded a selfish lad, but it wasn't something she could say to Sarah, who had to love them both equally. Instead she said, "So it's Aiden who's in New Zealand?" then was dismayed to see the way Sarah's joy drained away again.

"Yes, he is. I don't think he'll ever come home if I'm honest. Not to settle, anyway. He was a geologist working for a big energy company, and that took him all over the world. Then when he got disillusioned with that, he transferred to one of the big climate charities. He's as likely to be in a boat off the Antarctic chasing whalers. New Zealand's just his base he goes back to now and then. I can't see him ever settling down. He's now thirty-four, and yet I don't think he's ever had a girlfriend for more than a few months, though he's had plenty of them. I just wish he'd ring home a bit more often – especially with what's happening with Jeff, now."

Cleo impulsively went and hugged her, realising that this information probably meant Sarah was in her late fifties and older than she'd thought. Even if she'd married very young, if her oldest son was that age, she had been married to Jeff for over thirty-five years, so no wonder the prospect of turning off his life-support was tearing her apart. What a cruel trick of fate for her to lose him, just as they must have been contemplating what they would do in their retirement years.

"Well thank goodness you have Chris coming to support you," she said encouragingly.

"Yes. Though I can't imagine his wife is any too pleased. She never took to Jeff and me."

Bloody hell, Cleo thought. *One son's a selfish git who couldn't give a shit by the sound of it, and the one who's coming is going to be hurrying back home because of his sodding wife! Come on Cleo, get your skates on with this work, you've got to give this poor woman some good news one way or the other!*

She was introduced to the other rooms in this section, which were the former nurse or governess' room, and the schoolroom, neither of which looked particularly promising from Cleo's point of view. Both were stripped bare and had probably only ever held the most basic of furniture, nor did they have any useful nooks or crannies. And now she could see why she'd not been particularly aware of them before, because the continuation of the main stairs up to here virtually split this floor in two.

"I'm guessing that by having the servant's rooms at the back, and the schoolroom at the front, that they were guaranteeing that when there were guests up here they weren't disturbed by babies crying, or kids being mischievous?" Cleo ventured, and got a nod from Sarah.

"Definitely a case of children being seen and not heard, and not seen that often, either," she agreed. "I wouldn't have wanted my kids shut off up here when they were tiny – poor little mites could scream themselves hoarse and nobody would hear."

"Certainly not in the daytime," Cleo agreed, "And then at night it pretty much must have guaranteed that it was the servants who got up to tend to them. It was no wonder that so many people from this class turned out to be so unfeeling as adults. They must have had all the softer side knocked out of them by the time they got shoved off to some boarding school. A modern psychiatrist would have a field day with their problems with relationships."

Sarah gave a watery smile. "Archie said it was one of the things he was so grateful to his mother for. She insisted he went to the local grammar school, not be shipped off to his father's old school."

"Proof, if you needed it, of the damage this determination to remain the ruling class did to his father," mused Cleo. "I must see if there are still bills from that school, because it sounds likely it was Bertie's before it was Horace's. ...Now then, what was this room then, because it doesn't look much like a bedroom to me?" They had come to the room diagonally across from Cleo's, and the one she had looked into on her first night. "Dare I suggest it might have become a sitting room for Hugh?"

Sarah could only shrug. "It might have been, but equally it could have been changed around in Horace's time. I honestly don't know."

Cleo didn't want to push that any harder, especially as Sarah now said that she must go or she wouldn't get through the rush-hour traffic to get to the station in time. Personally, though, she thought that this room bore none of the pretensions that went with Horace's interference in the other rooms. This was the taste of someone who wanted a much simpler life, and her bet was still on Hugh.

So having made sure that the two heaters were on full in Cleo's room, positioned close to either side of the bed to give her a cocoon of warmth, they went back to the cottage, and as Sarah headed off, Cleo began making the lasagne. However, once it was all put together she had a while to go before she would put it on to cook, going on Sarah's estimations of when they would be back. That left Cleo with time on her hands, and if it wasn't enough to start on the estate office's secrets, it was for her to go back up to the top floor of the house.

Pulling on her coat, she went across and up the back stairs. This time she went into the other bedroom on her bit of the landing, which was the one she'd seen all draped with dustsheets. Walking in now, just as the light was fading rather than in pitch darkness, the single bulb was enough for her to get a better look. There was a nice half-tester bed, and if the drapery wouldn't have been quite as all-encompassing as a full four-poster's would have been, it would still have been enough to keep the draft off someone who had to sit up in bed a lot.

"So come on then, Hugh," Cleo said to the air, "was this your bedroom, or were you in mine?"

The bed she was sleeping in had a good high headboard and footboard, but not the drapery, so she thought it probably came down to whether Hugh had been able to cope with feeling that enclosed at night.

"Were you like me, getting claustrophobic in a bed like this one?" she wondered aloud again, having gone to lean in under the half-tester's drapery. No, she wouldn't spend more than five minutes in this bed without feeling suffocated, and depending on what Hugh's wartime experience had been, she thought he probably wouldn't have either.

The bathroom between this one and her room – probably originally just another smaller bedroom – yielded no further clues, though she felt sure that the claw-footed bath belonged to the Victorian era, and therefore had probably been there in Hugh's time. That at least confirmed her suspicion that Horace hadn't had time to start on this floor. The only thing worth investigating in the daylight would be the old cupboard, because to Cleo's informed eye, that had once stood in a far grander room than this. A quick look inside revealed some rather damp and musty old towels, and she thought it might be worth mentioning those to Sarah, if only to get them out before they rotted altogether. However it was now time for her to go down and get the oven on, and so she suspended her investigations for the day to concentrate on preparing the salad and garlic bread that would make the rest of the meal.

When Sarah walked in through the door with a man at her heels, Cleo had to blink and look twice. The photos of the blonde-haired little boy had done nothing to prepare her for what walked through the door. Just in time she managed to keep her mouth closed and not gawp at him like a total lunatic. *Holy Hecate!* she mentally gulped. *If Jeff looked like him at his age, it's no wonder Sarah was smitten!* Then she thought back to the photos and remembered a dark-haired man. No, Chris must take after Sarah, but Cleo hadn't thought she had once been such a stunning blonde. Either that spoke of her marriage being less joyful than Cleo had imagined for it to have taken such a toll on her; or Chris had won the genetic lottery and got the best from both parents. Startlingly blue eyes were staring back at her, but he was instantly saved from seeming like the kind of good-looking man who knew it only too well, by the natural smile that broke out.

"So you're Cleo," he said in an accent that said he must have been in Canada for quite some time, for he'd picked up some definite trans-Atlantic intonations – not that that did anything to quell the butterflies that were doing a quick flamenco in Cleo's stomach.

"Yep, that's me," she replied, then felt a fool for not thinking of something faintly more intelligent to respond with. "Lasagne is pretty much ready if you're hungry?"

"Starving!" Chris replied, the grin getting wider. "That smell has got my stomach growling already!"

They all sat down and tucked into the dinner, Cleo relieved that Sarah also came back for a second helping. If she'd passed muster with a cook of Sarah's calibre it had to be okay. And though she stayed to share a coffee with them, she soon beat a tactful retreat, knowing that they must have a lot to discuss without a stranger in their company.

It felt a bit lonely going back up to the room at the top of the house, and belatedly Cleo realised how much she'd enjoyed having some company too. After she'd more or less had to leave home in her late teens, and having been on the receiving end of the bleaker side of her mother's second marriage, she'd been very reluctant to get involved with anyone herself. But it was disconcerting to realise that just like some of the former occupants of this house, she had what most people would think of as a problem with relationships.

Friends were one thing, and she had some very good female friends, such as Angie. Men, though, tended to make her wary, and that was something which hadn't been helped by the kind of men she met. Old Mr Wentworth had been a sort of surrogate father to her, or if not quite that, then certainly a kindly but distant uncle type who she could ask for advice when needed. But Mr Wentworth had retired to the south coast, at his wife's insistence, to be closer to his real daughter. Male clients tended to fall into two camps, either overawed by her capabilities; or mildly affronted that she could do what they had failed to do in tracing their ancestors, and therefore aggressive in their attitude towards her. The later were mercifully few, but Cleo had never yet been on a date with a former client, and the dates well-meaning friends had set her up on had never come to anything beyond a few evenings of drinks out at pubs, or a meal or two.

You're a fine one to wonder about Sarah's marriage, she told herself sternly as she curled up under the quilt with her book. *Even if she's stuck it out with Jeff all these years because she couldn't get out, how has that been any worse than what you've been doing? You've hardly been making an effort, have you? If you'd really wanted to find someone you should have tried harder. All those evening classes you went to …you always seemed to end up in the ones that were female dominated. You can't get around the fact that quilt-making was hardly ever going to be filled with eligible men, was it? It might have got you a couple of new female friends for a while, but you passed thirty last year. When are you going to wake up and realise that the eligible men are all getting snapped up without you even seeing who's out there?*

And all of a sudden she couldn't bear to read another word of the romantic story which normally entranced her. Going to the window, she leaned on the sill and stared out at the moonlit garden. The remaining snow reflected the moon's glow enough that she could see more than she had in the past, and she was lost in her reverie when she became aware that the door to the cottage had opened and that someone had walked out. That someone could only be Chris, and he came walking slowly towards the terrace of the big house, hunched into his fleece jacket until he stopped and Cleo saw his hands go up to his face. She couldn't see detail or hear him, but she didn't need to be a genius to know that he was sobbing his heart out.

Oh get a grip, girl, she told herself. *He might be married and not available, but are you really going to leave the poor bloke out there? Get downstairs and invite him in for a cuppa and a chat. That's hardly propositioning him, is it? And he's about to switch his dad's life-support off, so he'd be a hard-hearted bastard if he wasn't upset. Come on, Cleo, shift yourself!*

She trotted briskly downstairs, shrugging her coat on as she went. Not bothering to put the kitchen light on, she opened the door and went out. Now she could hear the sobs, and needed no light to guide her to him.

"Chris?" she said gently. "Come on, come inside. You'll freeze out here."

With a sharp intake of breath, Chris' head came up.

"It's okay, I get that you don't want your mum to see you so upset," Cleo ventured, hoping it was the right thing to say, "but come into the big kitchen. It won't help if you catch a chill and end up in bed."

Without saying a word he followed her into the kitchen where she just put the cabinet light on under the cupboard above the kettle. Somehow she felt that he wouldn't want a stranger seeing him red-eyed and sniffling, so she only put on what she needed to find the instant decaf' and the kettle.

"Do you take milk?" she asked as the kettle came to the boil.

"Please, and one sugar, too, if mum's got it."

Cleo chuckled. "If it goes into food I think it's a fair certainty that your mum has it," and was glad to hear him give a rather choked laugh too.

"Of course she would."

She carried the two mugs across to the table, where he'd sat down in the seat next to the one she'd noticed Sarah usually sat in. Not wanting to disturb whatever associations were going on there, she sat across the table from him instead.

"Is Sarah okay?" she asked.

"Sleeping," Chris replied. "I think she's been hanging on hard for one of us to get back." He paused and then seemed to come to a decision. "Don't think me a bad son," he began. "I'd have come way sooner if I could. But the thing is, Cleo, I just couldn't. Please don't tell Mum any of this, but I want you to understand so that you don't ask the wrong question in front of her."

Startled, Cleo gasped, "It's not for me to question you, Chris!"

"No, but Mum likes you, and I think she trust you too. The last person I saw her behave like that with was Penny. That was a fair time ago, and I think she's been more than a bit short on friends since then.

"You see, while Dad was in the RAF, they moved around so much that she never got to make that many long-term friends. That was the case all the time while we were growing up. It was only when Archie needed someone here, and Dad decided to retire and take up a normal job, that she got to be anywhere long enough to get familiar with non-forces families. But while Archie offering her this post was a blessing, in another way it wasn't"

"I'm with you. She exchanged one closed community for an even smaller one."

Chris gave a gulp. "Hell, she said you were quick on the uptake! But yes, that's it. Lovely though Penny and Archie were, it was all a bit too enclosed." He paused and seemed to be wondering whether to say more. "Look …again, not a word that I've said this to you…"

"…No, of course not…"

"…but Dad didn't exactly help. I think Mum thought that when he came out, that they'd do more stuff as a couple, but he had a terrible time adjusting to civilian life. He couldn't get on with the people he worked with, and he had a succession of jobs in a short time, some of them working away from home for a lot of the time. So much so that he began to look like a bad employment prospect. But he wanted the same lifestyle as he'd had in the RAF. That was what the bloody skiing trip was all about. A piss-up of a get-together with his old mates. Mum wasn't there, wasn't even invited! He just said he was going, even though they couldn't really afford it because he was out of work at the time."

"Oh God, does that mean that your mum is misinformed when she says that she has enough saved to buy a house?"

"No, I don't think so. But that's only because of her own good sense. She'd always argued that if something happened to Dad while he was in the forces, that she might have to get out of married quarters in a hurry, and so she'd need a deposit for a house fast. So those savings have always been in her name, and I don't think that Dad ever realise how much she added to them and what they ran to – I know I never said, and I don't think Aiden ever bothered to ask her."

"And how does your brother feel about all of this?"

"Aiden?" Chris gave a bitter laugh. "If Aiden's given this more than a few minutes' thought in all of the time Dad's been in a coma, I'd be bloody amazed! He's just like Dad – single-minded and after what he wants. I tried ringing him to ask him what he wanted to do, and all he said was that he wanted his share of whatever Dad had left to him. When I told him that was going to be fuck-all because Dad had already spent it, he just put the phone down."

"Charming!"

"Well I wasn't expecting any better. I'd already rung him months before that, when I needed the money to come over and help Mum. He just said I should have been tougher with Melanie."

"Is that your wife?"

"Ex-wife, and ex for over a year now."

"Oh! The way your mum spoke I thought you were happily married?"

"I haven't dared tell her. It would break her heart. You see Melanie cleaned me out. I'm absolutely broke. I was hanging on with my job in the hope that I'd get the promotion I needed, but it turns out that the company I was with like stable, married men, and there was me newly divorced. In the end, when I couldn't bear leaving Mum alone any longer, I tapped all my friends for small loans to get the airfare together. They were all great about it, and every last one said that if I never get to pay them back, it's fine – they, at least, get it that it was so wrong to leave Mum coping with this on her own."

Cleo's head was reeling. "Surely your mum would understand?"

"Oh, she'd understand once I told her I found out that Melanie was shagging my one boss, and moved on to him as the better prospect. But what I can't tell her is that I've come home to be a burden to her. Do you see, Cleo? I can't even afford to rent a place of my own. My stuff – what's left of it – is in my buddy Tony's garage, 'cause I sure as hell can't afford to have it shipped back, so I'm here in what I'm standing up in, and what I could bring as normal baggage. That's it. That's all I've got left after seven years of Melanie. And just when I want nothing more than to take care of Mum, I'm absolutely helpless …and that just breaks my heart."

"Oh, Chris, I'm so sorry! Yes, I see that you'd feel dreadful about that. But surely to God your brother would help you in the circumstances? She's his mum too, and you'd be the one here doing the looking after. Wouldn't he be glad to give you a bit of help to know that she's being taken care of?"

Chris looked up with eyes now red-rimmed. "You've obviously only heard mum's sanitised accounts of Aiden. She can't face what he's become. But in truth Cleo, he doesn't care about anyone else in the family but himself. It might sound all very caring that he works for a charity, but the truth is, he's only doing it because it gives him the life he wants, foot-loose and fancy free. Aiden doesn't want any ties, any responsibilities, and though I wish I wasn't saying this, he's exactly like Dad in that. Dad never thought what it was like for us to be dragged from base to base. Aiden thrived on it, and because of that they both thought that Mum and I did – but we didn't, we hated it.

"So Aiden won't be home for the funeral or anything else. It wouldn't even shock me that much if we stopped hearing from him altogether now that Dad's going to be gone. It was always him and Dad doing things."

That's why you're hardly on any of the photos! Cleo suddenly realised. *It must have been Jeff getting Sarah to take those photos of him and Aiden, and you were there on the camera side with Sarah. Oh how I wish I could find some clue that would let you two inherit this place! You both so deserve a break.*

Chapter 10

Whatever the reason was, Hugh didn't disturb Cleo's sleep when she finally got to bed, having sat up with Chris for as long as he needed to talk. That was a good thing, because even so, the morning seemed to come around far too quickly for her, and it was the sound of Sarah's car pulling out of the driveway that woke her at eight o'clock. They had to be making an early start to beat the traffic up to Birmingham, Cleo thought, knowing now that as an ex-forces person, Jeff was at the big hospital up there in one of the military wards.

Shivering her way down to the kitchen, she took one look at the coffee-maker and decided that a pot of tea would be quicker and simpler. Pulling Sarah's gardening over-shoes on over her slippers, she made a quick dash for the logs, and brought a basket-full inside. Then while the tea brewed, she lugged the logs up to the library and got a fire going in the grate.

"Mrs bloody Wytcombe can sod right off if she thinks I'm going to freeze to death on her account!" she declared to the portrait of a florid-faced man above the mantelpiece. "And which one are you, then?" She peered at the frame, but there was no neat plaque announcing whose portrait it was.

They had agreed last night that Cleo would still go across to Sarah's for a shower, since the bathroom she'd been given was still arctic-cold, and so once she'd revived herself with a hot tea, she made the quick flit across the yard and let herself into the cottage. A shower and breakfast sorted, she felt more human again, and decided that the best way to help both Sarah and Chris was to keep their individual confidences, and work to find a way for them to keep the cottage.

Right! she thought determinedly, as she prepared to tackle the next pile of papers. *Where do I start today?* The library was starting to warm up to close to tolerable, and yet she couldn't settle to the job at hand. In the end, having gone downstairs for a mug of instant coffee, she realised that the estate office was calling to her. That ancient fireplace and its wooden surround were niggling away in the back of her mind, she just couldn't quite dredge the right memory to the surface to make sense of it.

Taking a replenished hot mug through to the office, she put the lights on and then stood back to scrutinise the ancient fireplace. Yes, that carved rose on the right-hand panel was definitely different from its counterpart on the left. It looked more worn, as though people had handled that particular part of the carving more for some reason. And what was going on with that leaf near it? It was crooked compared to the left side, too.

Putting her coffee down on the well-used scruffy desk, already ring-marked from many mugs in the past, she went and probed the panel with her fingers. This close to, it looked as though the leaf might be pinned in the centre and was intended to rotate, but years of polish had long since stopped that. But if it was only old polish stopping it moving, Cleo knew how to deal with that. She went back to and through the kitchen, and into the laundry storeroom, investigating cupboards until she found what she was looking for – a bottle of sugar-soap. Armed with that, a bowl of hot water and some old cloths, and an old penknife, she returned to the office. She wasn't such a vandal as to attack the leaf with the penknife, but its dull blade was ideal for wrapping a layer of cloth around to get right into the narrow places.

It took some time, and what seemed like an age's worth of grime, old polish and dust coming off, but suddenly she felt the leaf shift a little. Taking the rubber gloves off that she'd been wearing, she took a dry cloth and, gripping the leaf firmly with the cloth, gave it a twist. For a moment it did nothing, and then suddenly it came free and swivelled to right-angles to where it had been. Since she had already been working on what she thought were probably the edges of the compartment, now that she could get to the final bit that had been under the leaf, it didn't take long before a tug on the rose made the secret compartment's door open.

"Woo-hoo!" Cleo exclaimed triumphantly, as a small cupboard space revealed itself. It wasn't big, only a couple of feet either way at the opening, and not much bigger inside, though it seemed to go back an extra six inches or so. But what delighted Cleo even more was that there was a pile of letters and other things stacked in there. Surely she hadn't found Hugh's hideaway already? That would be too good for words, and when she pulled the items very carefully out of their hiding place, she rapidly revised her assessment. These looked to be from a far older time.

She checked inside the compartment with her fingers, just to be sure that there was nothing left hidden in there, but that only confirmed that someone a very long time ago had had the presence of mind to line the hidey-hole with lead, which had no doubt saved the papers from the damp and the predations of many generations of mice. Making sure that she put the precious finds well away from her cleaning stuff, she took all of that back through to the kitchen straightaway, not wanting to risk any accidents. If these things had been precious enough to hide in the first place, the last thing she wanted to do was drop them into the water bowl now!

Coming back with freshly washed and dried hands, she carefully carried the bundle up to the library, and placed it on the desk by the fire, which she'd previously cleared ready to work on.

"Now then, my beauties, what secrets are you going to reveal?" she asked softly, as she picked up the top packet from the bundle. It was an old envelope of sorts, yet there was something hard but uneven inside it. It had been carefully secured with a ribbon. Cleo undid the binding with great care and lifted the flap of the envelope, then was shocked to see what looked like gemstones inside along with another envelope.

What on earth is this? she wondered, gently tipping the outer envelope up so that its contents slid out onto the desk. It was a necklace, and for a moment Cleo wondered why anyone would have bothered hiding it, because it certainly wasn't dripping with diamonds, nor any of the more sparkling gemstones. Yet something about it made Cleo look at it harder, and with a skip of her heart, it dawned on her that she was looking at something much older than anything else in the house. Indeed the last time she'd seen anything like this, it had been on a holiday to Rome when she'd gone around the Etruscan Museum.

"Oh you beauty!" she breathed, very gently fingering it so that she eased it out to reveal its full size.

Her next move was to go and pull on one of the pairs of cotton gloves she always carried in her work briefcase. They were there for when she had to do serious archive work, for the acid from skin could do damage to ancient papers, and therefore Cleo wasn't going to risk her fingers doing the same to something this old. The purplish stones she quickly recognised as amethysts, for they were one of her favourite stones, but there were striped stones and deeper red ones in the pattern. Booting up her laptop and searching for ancient jewellery, she decided in the end that the redder stones were most likely a rather dirt-begrimed set of garnets. The striped ones, though, were a bit harder to determine, and she thought they were possibly either a banded agate, or chalcedony, which was a kind of quartz. Both had been used in Ancient Greek and Ancient Roman jewellery, but it would take a professional lapidary to know the difference.

Sitting back in the chair, Cleo regarded the necklace with awe. It had to be worth several thousand just because of its antiquity, going by her online search, and there and then she determined that she would not reveal this to Darcy Wytcombe. The woman might be paying her, but going by the rock she'd seen on her ring-finger, Mrs W was more into bling than quality, and Cleo didn't trust her not to put these dull stones into the rubbish bin as worthless. For although Cleo would have been the first to declare that she was no jewellery expert, on those times when she was up until late in the evening making transatlantic phone-calls to clients, she usually gave herself the following morning off, and she had often tuned in to various jewellery shopping channels as she sat with her morning coffee on those occasions. And so while she might not be an expert, she was a very well-informed lay person; all of which meant that she had looked at Mrs W's small boulder of a stone on her engagement ring, and had known straight away that it wasn't a true diamond. There was no fire in it, no hidden flame when the light caught it which would signify a diamond of that quality – and if Mrs W didn't even know that, then she would never grasp what this necklace was worth. Moreover Cleo reasoned that the engagement ring had to have been Mrs W's personal choice, because if Archie had been so disenchanted with her at that stage as to buy her a poor-quality, simulated diamond ring, then he could have called the wedding off before he got trapped.

"Well at least she didn't sting you for a real diamond of that size," she said to the empty room, yet feeling somehow as though Archie's ghost was at her elbow, as excited about this find as she was. "We're going to crack this puzzle, Archie, I can feel it in my bones, and it won't be your nightmare of a widow who benefits, either." Though why she felt so sure of that was also a puzzle, for Cleo knew she had to be scrupulously honest about all of this – except for the necklace, which she would get valued first to show Mrs W its worth – or her good intentions might backfire on her and ruin her reputation in the process. If it turned out that Mrs W was the rightful heir, then that was what she would have to make public, it was just that she was keeping everything crossed that that wouldn't be the case. If the necklace was claimed by a museum for its antiquity for a fraction of what it should have cost them, then that at least would be a small triumph.

Using one of her spare gloves as a polishing cloth, Cleo ever so gently began rubbing the individual gemstones, and was swiftly rewarded with a layer of dusty grime coming off. The amethysts and garnets came up the best, but that didn't deter her, for she knew that if the others were a kind of agate, then they wouldn't necessarily glow quite so much until fully cleaned – and that was a job for a professional, not her.

And so putting the necklace to the back of the desk, she turned her attention to the document that was in the envelope with it. It was firmly creased with age and she took her time very gently unfolding first the envelope, and then the paper within, aware that too much haste might have the folds crumbling away to dust, and obliterating vital words on the inside in the process. When she had opened it out, she went and brought one of her laptops over to the desk along with a magnifying glass, and with great care began transcribing the letter – for that was what it clearly was – onto an electronic document which she would be able to share with Sarah and Chris.

This letter is for my dear children, it began, and Cleo was relieved that the writer then named them as Hector, Sophia and William, but also included the writer's step-daughter Ana Kovač, of whom he said, *though I wish you had not in these later years given in to your brother's persuasions and married my illegitimate son, Tarquin*.

"Oh, so were you Ana Wytcombe by this time? Or is Kovač your married name? Tarquin Kovač doesn't sound remotely English, so where did he come from?" Cleo wondered, as she opened another e-document that she had prepared all ready to construct family trees upon. Her question was immediately answered as she turned back to the letter.

> *I have given Tarquin my name for your sake, though I cannot bring myself to make him my heir over Hector despite his protestations. He may be the oldest of my sons, but I do not think that the son I had with a parlour-maid should inherit Upper Moore. Yet I might have been persuaded otherwise had Tarquin been of a different character. Please be careful, my dear Ana! I write this knowing that my end is near and that I will not be here to watch over you. I am not yet so close to my grave as not to be able to see that Tarquin and your natural brother, Luka, are hatching some plot which I fear may involve your baby son. Be on your guard!*

As for you, Hector and William, I would also urge you to caution where those two men are concerned. Do not sign any papers without consulting my men of business, for your own innate honesty may be the undoing of you both in any dealings with those two. Luka has hated me ever since I brought him to England with your mother, and contact with him has done what I fear will prove to be irreparable damage to Tarquin, who has been far too easily led by Luka's glib lies.

It makes me wish, here at my last, that we had brought your mother's precious heirloom with us. She left it with her family in Rovigno, as you well know, believing to the very last that it had protected her from the evil her first husband brought upon the family. We never talked openly to you all as children of her beliefs in this matter, for it was already hard for a Catholic like her to allow her children to be brought up in the English Church. It was also hard for you to explain to your friends why your Mama did not come to church with us, but went to the Catholic Church in Hereford, and we felt that it was wiser to not speak of the other thing. Then as you got older, it seemed not to matter so much.

But nowadays I find myself thinking back to the things that she said in the early days of our marriage, and wishing I had listened more. I believe that old necklace she spoke of has been handed down via the women of the family for many generations, perhaps even back to Roman times. For despite your Mama's devout Christian belief

*and regular attendance of mass, she also held
onto some of the old beliefs from her
homeland. There is a book in the library on
the Romans and their gods and goddesses
which I have latterly consulted, and it seems
that some of the rituals associated with them
carried on for long after their empire fell. In
it I again came across the name of the lares,
which were the household guardians of those
ancients, some of whom would be ancestors,
and some deities. And it was here that I came
across the name of Hecate once more.*

"Hecate!" Cleo gasped. "Noooo! What are the
chances of that?" She carefully turned the letter over to
continue reading what was on the back.

*It seems that your Mama's belief that Hecate
would watch over the women of her family
was no mere fancy of her own invention, for
she appears to have embodied all aspects of
womanhood.*

"Too damned right she does! Maiden, Mother and
Crone — they're all part of her aspects. Well I never, but
why did she ever think she needed protecting?"

*There is a dark tale attached to your Mama's
family from the time they were in Rovigno,
and should you wish to know more of that,
then I would recommend you to speak to
your Uncle Ernesto, or Aunt Giulia, over in
Verona, though only Ernesto has any
memories of that time. That none of the
family came to grief over what happened,
your Mama always attributed to the
influence of the necklace, and while her
sisters lived it was always close to them in
their thoughts and prayers.*

Your marriage, Ana, had her wishing more often that she had brought it with her, though she was torn in that respect by her belief that it had kept her family safe in her absence. Moreover, Luka knows of the necklace, and has frequently taunted your mother over her lack of it. Latterly it has worried me that he should feel so threatened by it, for he once implied that there was nobody to stop him with its presence being absent, making me look at his past actions thus far in a different light. Nor did I like what I now saw, and though I would not distress you with this knowledge when your dear Mama died, I found him gloating over her body that her goddess had failed her, which was why I had the Catholic priest come and say his words over her and had the coffin sealed. There is something very wrong with Luka, and I beg you to be on your guard.

I fear that as I fade, that Luka's suspicious nature will have him searching this house once I am gone, or if not him then he will get Tarquin to do it for him. For that reason I have hidden this warning in the old hiding place which only you, Hector, know of. When you come to this I will be gone, and you will have learned of this from a copy at the reading of my will, which is also why I have spelled out for my legal men just who Tarquin, Ana and Luka are. For however much I love you, Ana, your children with Tarquin are not my heirs and never should be. May God watch over you and them, for I fear you will need His protection. Please forgive your Papa's cowardice for not having

> *the strength left to tackle Luka and Tarquin,*
> *but know that I love you all dearly and have*
> *done the best I can now to protect you.*
> *Your loving Papa,*
> *Richard Wytcombe*

"Blimey!" Cleo gasped, sitting back in amazement. What on earth had gone on here? It sounded as though this Luka, whoever he was, was a real nasty piece of work. And what was that about Rovigno? Where was that?

She connected to the internet again and swiftly discovered that Rovigno was now the lovely Croatian holiday resort of Rovinj, but that it had been part of the Venetian territories for a very long time, along with all of the rest of the Istrian peninsula at the northern end of Croatia's coast. Then another connection of her own clicked into place, and she grabbed her notepad that had been with her in the church two days ago. Yes, there it was! Richard Wytcombe and Francesca, she being the one whom Sarah and herself had remarked on, and had wondered whether she might not be English. Well she certainly hadn't been that! Not if she came from Croatia, or whatever it had been called in …she looked at the date on the top of the letter. "March 1838! Wow! So it *is* the same man who's buried in the church."

She compared the date of his burial and realised that whatever he had died of, it had given him a lingering demise – to know he was dying back in the March but not to go until the December was quite a while back in the days, when pneumonia tended to carry off those who were confined to their beds, whatever they had initially sickened of. Probably not anything like arthritis, Cleo mused, but potentially something like bronchitis which had never fully cleared, or maybe his heart was giving out? Not a stroke, or he wouldn't have been writing so coherently, nor so clearly, and Richard certainly had nice handwriting compared to some of the scrawls from that era that she'd seen.

And funnily enough, it was that distinctive handwriting triggering her memory that made Cleo realise that she had seen it elsewhere. Somewhere in those piles of papers were things that he'd written, she was sure of it, and though it went against her normal restraint to dive randomly back into the past, what got her on her feet and scouring the piles of documents was the thought of what a blessed distraction it would be for Sarah and Chris, if tonight she could tell them some of this story.

It took a while to find the right pile, but then there he was in the oldest documents, Lieutenant Richard Wytcombe, son of the younger brother of the then squire, the very same Edwin Wytcombe whom they'd also seen the plaque to in the church. *Sarah will be pleased,* Cleo thought, *to know that the Henry Wytcombe who we saw was Richard's father, was himself actually Edwin's brother. I told her not to dismiss him, and I was right!* What was made much clearer in the old will which Cleo now sat down to read, was that Edwin had been faced with the miserable knowledge that his own son wasn't likely to live long. Although the son William from the memorial had indeed inherited from his father, the will was much clearer in saying that William was known to be 'consumptive' and not likely to last. For even in those days they knew that consumption – now known as tuberculosis – was a one-way ticket, and so Edwin had tied the estate up neatly so that it wouldn't get caught up in the dreadful mess that was the Court of Chancery.

Dickens had known a thing or two about that, Cleo recalled, and anyone who had ever read *Bleak House* knew of the corruption of that court, which drained whole estates of every last penny to leave people heirs to nothing more than the bricks and mortar, if they were even that lucky. The case in *Bleak House* of Jarndyce versus Jarndyce might have been fiction in terms of names, but not in the machinations of the court. So Cleo mentally applauded Edwin for having been shrewd enough to name his seafaring nephew as the secondary heir.

But however did you get to meet and marry a woman from Croatia? Cleo wondered. *If you were in the navy before inheriting in 1811, then you were probably amongst the thousands of officers in Nelson's navy, fighting against Napoleon – which makes you a regular Hornblower type.* She began sorting at speed through the piles of contemporary documents, and to her delight found some papers which gave the names of the ships which Richard had served on.

"Fabulous names!" she found herself breathing as she picked out the ships he'd served on. "*Bellerophon, Barfleur, Phoebe, Mercury* and then *Active.* Good grief, Richard, you were quite the silent hero, weren't you! I can't wait to tell Sarah and Chris about you."

Chapter 11

As often happened when she got immersed in her work, Cleo only realised the time when she had to get up and put another light on, having only paused in between to put more logs onto the fire. Now, though, she realised that she should wrap things up for the day and go and see about getting some food on for when Sarah and Chris returned. So it was with some dismay that she came out of the back door of the big house to see the cottage lights blazing, and the kitchen window open but steamed up, speaking of Sarah already cooking.

Hurrying in, she found Sarah and Chris in the kitchen, red-eyed and silent, but with no hint of a bad atmosphere. Looking around at her Sarah gave a wan smile and said, "He's gone. They switched the machines off, and it was only minutes before he just slipped away."

"Oh Sarah, I'm so sorry," Cleo said, feeling that that was a pathetically bland thing to say, but unable to find anything better. Instead she walked over and gave Sarah a hug. "You didn't need to do this. I'd have come and cooked for us all."

"It's okay, I needed to be doing something or I think I'd have started screaming," Sarah confided. "I've already done most of the mourning I'm likely to do, and it might sound callous, but I've been crying with relief more than anything else. I'm just so glad that it's all over. However things work out, I'm not stuck in that dreadful limbo anymore. And the problem with today being a Saturday is that we couldn't do anything about arranging the funeral.

That'll have to wait until Monday when we can get the death certificate and register his death. So we came straight back, which is why we were home a few hours ago."

Cleo turned to Chris and gave him a questioning look.

"Don't ask me how I am," he replied, "because I honestly don't know. Like Mum, I've done a lot of my mourning already. It's more that it feels weird to be back here and know that he's never going to come marching in through that door ever again. I guess I'm more missing the dad I had when I was a little boy, because once I grew up we were terribly distant – and not just because of the miles between us. We could have Skyped like Mum and I do, but even when he was here, he didn't want to talk, or hear about my life in Canada. ...Shit! Sorry, Mum, that came out all wrong! I didn't mean it to sound critical today of all days."

"It's alright. I may have loved him but I wasn't blind to his faults. He was always a better dad to Aiden than you, and part of what's upsetting me more now is that Aiden isn't here. He owed Jeff that much, and I don't believe that he couldn't have got the time off if he'd have asked for it."

Sensing that this was dredging up far too much of the worst of the family's past, Cleo was very glad to be able to say,

"Well if you want a bit of a distraction, I have quite a different kind of story to tell you."

The way that they both perked up at this was evidence enough that they didn't want to be left alone with their own thoughts tonight, and so Cleo began telling them of what she'd found, though she omitted the necklace for now, thinking that a pagan goddess casting an influence might not be the image to help Sarah just at this point. Instead she focused on having found out significantly more about Richard Wytcombe, for in the bundle she had pulled out of the wall were all of his records of service – or at least if not the wholly official ones, the bits and pieces he himself had sent home to his parents.

Having covered what she'd initially found and the wall cupboard, Cleo got on to Richard himself. "He joined the navy at the tender age of twelve," she began.

"*Twelve?*" Chris exclaimed. "Really? But he was only a kid!"

Cleo smiled at him. "By our standards, yes, but it was perfectly normal in those days. Twelve was the going age for a lad to become a midshipman. With his uncle being the current owner of this place at that time, his own father hadn't got much to offer him. I haven't been able to discover what Henry Wytcombe actually did, and it may be that he was one of those hopeless sorts who lived on an inherited income which gradually got less and less. It would certainly explain why young Richard felt he had no choice but to go to sea. From one of the earlier letters, I got the impression that a maternal uncle or cousin was a ship's doctor, and it was he who pulled some strings to get Richard his first chance."

She broke into a grin. "Now this is where things start to become a bit more familiar. He joined a ship called the *Bellerophon* in 1797, and that was one of the ships at Nelson's famous victory at the Battle of the Nile a year later in August 1798. The *Bellerophon* was affectionately known as the 'Billy Ruffian' by its crew and others, who no doubt couldn't get their heads around its classical name, and when I looked it up online, it turns out to have been a very famous ship that's since been written about in its own right. So if you want to know more, it's out there. I'm guessing that it was his proud mother who kept all of these letters – particularly if the 'Billy Ruffian' appeared in the newspapers of the day – and although he addresses them all to his mother *and* father, the way he explains things in the early days makes me think that he was writing primarily for her. That's how come I can tell you that he was one of a crew of around six hundred, if you count the non-combatants like servants."

Chris looked astonished. "My God! My whole secondary school only had a hundred more than that number. That must have been a huge culture shock to a young lad from these parts."

"Oh it was, and you can tell in the early letters that he's horribly homesick. He seems to have been lucky and not got too seasick, but he was terrified of what went on down on the orlop deck, where the surgeon would work when they went into battle. And from the description of the guns firing, you can tell that at first he was downright petrified by them. Probably didn't help that some of the older men tormented him with tales of men who had got hit by huge splinters when the ship got hit by other guns. It was a bloody harsh world for a lad who'd come from the leafy lanes of Worcestershire. Martley, where his parents then lived, is about as far from the sea as you can get, so it was totally alien to him.

"Anyway, he's on *Bellerophon* from 1797 until it returned to Portsmouth in the autumn of 1800 for a refit. With the war with France in full flow, he had no trouble getting another position, this time in an even bigger ship called the *Barfleur*. The *Bellerophon* had seventy-four guns, and was classed as a Third Rate, but as Richard tells his mum, these were the workhorses of the navy. I'm no naval historian, but I think these and the frigates were the vast majority of the fighting ships at this time. *Barfleur*, on the other hand, was one of a much smaller number of prestigious, even larger ships, and had a mind-blowing ninety guns on board."

"Good Lord," Sarah gasped. "So what was that then? Forty-five on each side?"

"I'm not sure," Cleo admitted, "and I can only say from watching programs on TV on them, that I think they had some smaller guns at the bows. But how many, I couldn't guess. I'm amazed that they weren't all deaf after a battle in that monster. Richard was very proud that this ship, like his old one, had fought at the Glorious First of June the year before he joined the navy, and this time he was in the flag-ship of the man who was then Rear-Admiral Collingwood, albeit he's still a very lowly midshipman, and one of a large number of those, too. He was so proud to be serving Collingwood, who he clearly hero-worshipped.

"Sadly his good fortune didn't last, and when *Barfleur* was paid off in 1802, without a patron to push him forward, poor Richard had a hard time finding a new position. He had to write begging his parents for some funds just to buy food and what sounds like some very meagre lodgings."

"Heavens, how old was he then?" Sarah fretted, looking at Chris and clearly thinking what it would have been like for him.

"1802? He was just seventeen. So considered old enough to be out in the world and no longer a child, but not old enough to have had sufficient experience to be useful. Thankfully, his Uncle Edwin seems to have taken pity on him and stumped up the money for a new berth for him, or at least enough to sway his next captain to take him on. I couldn't help wonder whether Edwin wasn't a bit exasperated with his brother Henry, especially as his own son may already have been sickening.

"Oh and by the way, Sarah, it turns out that the William who we saw on the tombstone as Edwin's son, died of consumption – TB as we'd now call it – so he knew his son wouldn't last long after him. That's why he made Richard his heir. Personally I think he may have had a sneaking regard for the lad who had managed to get that far in the world alone, and almost in spite of his father – because you would normally have expected it to be his brother Henry who would inherit after William died."

Chris was looking a good deal brighter for the distraction and now added, "It sure adds to the impression that this Henry was a bit of a waster, doesn't it? Almost like Edwin doesn't trust him with this place."

"That's what I thought."

"So what happened to Richard next? I have to say, Cleo, this is great stuff."

"I'm glad you think so. Well Richard joined a ship called the *Phoebe* later in 1802 under a man called Captain Thomas Capel. He was still the lowliest of lieutenants, but at least he'd got beyond midshipman. In the *Phoebe* he got something of a more permanent home, and he seems to have slowly risen through the lieutenants' ranks in her. They went first to the Mediterranean, then took part in chasing French ships to the West Indies before coming back to be one of the ships at Trafalgar in 1805."

Chris' eyes were shining now. "Wow! Our own Trafalgar hero! That's great! I used to love reading C. S. Forrester, Richard O'Brian and Alexander Kent when I was a kid. You're dragging up some real old memories for me of playing battleships with Aiden, with us up some tree out in the park pretending that we were up a frigate's mast."

"Then you probably understand more about these ships than I do," Cleo admitted, grinning with Chris at the thought of the two lads fighting the imaginary French fleet out in the park. "*Phoebe* was a thirty-six gun frigate."

"That must have been much more fun for a young guy like Richard," Chris immediately said. "The flag-ship would have been prestigious, but the frigates were the young man's choice of ship. Their captains were like the rock-stars of the day, you know. Their exploits were the subject of the broadsheets back home, kinda like the newspaper writing about the Special Forces these days. Did Richard ever make captain?"

"No, sadly not. He only got as far as First Lieutenant, which I gather is the second-in-command?"

"Yeah. It should've been his stepping stone up to a command of his own, especially since the frigates tended to have the most chances of taking an enemy ship as a prize. Being put in charge of one of those prizes was usually a lieutenant's first taste of going solo."

"Then I'm glad I brought my laptop across with me, because you'll want to read the letters I've transcribed. They explain how he got stuck a bit out on the far edge of things in terms of the war. But before I pull them up, do you remember, Sarah, that we wondered whether Richard's wife might not be local? Well never in a month of Sundays would we have guessed where she actually came from, and when I first saw it I wondered what bizarre twist of fate brought those two together."

"Go on," Sarah said, leaning eagerly forward in her seat, "where did she come from?"

"Croatia!"

"What?"

"Yes, Croatia, though it wasn't called that then. It was a part of the Austro-Hungarian Empire during the Napoleonic Wars."

Sarah was stunned. "That's an incredibly long way away from here. So come on, then, how did he meet her?"

Cleo turned her laptop around on the table so that they could both see the screen, then came and leaned over to open up a document. "Here you go, I've been typing up his letters for you to read. The originals are very delicate, and to be honest, they probably belong somewhere like the Maritime Museum at Greenwich, because it's rare to have someone's whole career tracked like this. You can read the others later on if you want, but this first letter I'm showing you sets the scene for the later end of his career."

She scrolled down a little and the letter sprang into view.

November 1808

Dearest Father and Mother,

I bring you good news – I am to be made acting First Lieutenant on the Mercury! When I wrote to you last so unsure of my future, I know you will have been concerned, for the change of a captain can make a huge difference to a humble lieutenant like myself. Indeed, I will be sorry to leave the Phoebe and the friends I have made there, but I shall not miss the freezing waters of the North, nor the tedium of blockade duties, even if we did secure a prize on our last outing.

My change of fortune came about as we were ordered to sail to the Mediterranean, and it was as we entered that sea that I was told to report aboard the Mercury. It seems that their First Lieutenant had an accident and had to be put ashore at Lisbon, which was when the Admiral looked for who could be sent to replace him. I confess to being greatly excited at this opportunity, not least because the Mercury's captain is Capt. the Hon. Henry Duncan, son of Admiral Duncan, and a captain of whom I have heard many good reports. I am hopeful that the much needed prize money I would require to help further my career might be forthcoming in his service, for though I am deeply grateful to Uncle for using his influence to help find me a new commission, I also appreciate that the estate at Upper Moore House is not possessed of endless reserves which I should ever presume upon. Please write to Uncle on my behalf and tell him of my progress, for though I will endeavour to do so myself, I do not know when I shall next have chance to send letters home, and I only had time to write to you.

Your loving son,
Lieut. Richard Wytcombe

"Oh bless him," Sarah gasped. "He really appreciated what Edwin did for him, didn't he?"

However Chris had picked up on a different detail. "Blockade duty. That was in the Channel and the Bay of Biscay, I think. Bloody freezing in the winter, and though I'm going back a ways now, I seem to remember the heroes in my books cussing that bit of the war, because the dreadful weather caused all sorts of damage to the ships. They had problems with masts breaking and sails tearing in the gales that Biscay's famous for."

"He does sound glad to be heading for warmer waters, doesn't he," Cleo agreed. "So the next one he sent home is this. As you'll read in a minute, the big difference with them heading for the eastern Med' was that there weren't many ships heading back to England to carry post back and forwards, so his letters are a bit spaced out from now onwards."

February 1809

Dearest Father and Mother,

I hope that this letter finds you well. I am pleased to tell you that I have made a favourable impression on Capt. Duncan and that I am settling in well with my new fellow officers. It is harder having to keep a seemly distance from the others now that I am First Lieutenant, for every time one takes a step up the ladder, the greater the gap between oneself and those below you. However, I do not want for company, and blessedly we seem to be free of trouble-makers amongst us.

We are now entering the Adriatic, and are sailing northwards towards where Bonaparte's ships are active. Even in these cold, dark days, the coastline here is beautiful, with little coves filled with white houses, and fishing boats anchored at the quays, all of which remind me of the villages I saw from the sea when I last saw the coast of Cornwall, though the houses there are grey stone, not white. In that sense it is sometimes hard to remember that we are at war, for when the French are not around it is a most lovely place to be.

I have just picked up my pen to you again to tell you that I have now seen some of the wonderful houses which Grandfather described seeing as a young man on his Grand Tour. It seems that the eastern coast of this sea was also once part of the great Venetian Empire, and as such, the great houses are very much as Grandfather described seeing in places like Venice. I wish I had my sister's talents with a pen and *brush so that I could sketch them for you, but my poor efforts would not convey their grandeur and would leave you with a wholly erroneous impression. I must finish now, for the post is about to be sent across on its journey to England, but I will write again soon,*

Your loving son,
Lieut. Richard Wytcombe.

"This is great!" Chris enthused. "Next one, please!" and Cleo scrolled to the next letter.

April 1809

Dearest Father and Mother,
Our audacious captain sent in our ship's boats on a raid a week ago, with one of them under my command. We went in under fire to seize the French gunboat Léda, which was anchored in the harbour of a beautiful little town called Rovigno, and after some fierce fighting, we succeeded in taking her. Capt. Duncan was most anxious to ensure that we had not left any of the French behind in the town, and so I led my men ashore. Never have I been so glad that Grandfather taught me what he knew of the Italian language, for the native language is like none I have encountered before, but most of the better people of the town speak Italian because of dealings with their Venetian overlords for centuries.

The town is a maze of cobbled streets, and for a while we were deeply suspicious of the quiet, fearing an ambush. But when we came to the top of the steep streets, we discovered an open space around the magnificent church of St Euphemia, as I now know it is called, and here we discovered the townsfolk praying for their lives. It took much convincing before they believed that we were not about to massacre them where they prayed, but as best I could understand, they have been caught up in this war with no desire to take anyone's side, desiring only to be left in peace. There seem to be few young men in the town, and the ones who are left are those incapable of fighting. An older man, whom I could understand better than most, told me that the Venetians called up their local militia some ten years ago, and that few of those men have returned home.

I felt great pity for him and his family, and in particular for his oldest daughter who reminded me so much of your cousin Georgiana, Mama, for she is likewise widowed with two small children, and with little prospect of finding another husband when so many other young women are available and the men so few. This family kindly offered us a billet for the night in their house beyond the ancient city walls, and when we got there it was a magnificent affair. It was bigger even than Upper Moore! A grand portico was flanked by three large windows on either side, and I recalled how entranced my sister and your nieces were, Mama, with their visit to Bath with its Royal Crescent, and thought how they would be enthralled to have stayed in such a grand place.

Yet the tragedy is that this lovely house is becoming dilapidated, for the family can no longer afford any servants, and the aging cook and her son the stable boy seem to be staying out of loyalty rather than for any pay. Truly war is cruel when such gentle folk are left so destitute, and I felt obliged to pay for what we had eaten, even though my captain afterwards expressed the opinion that they should have been grateful to have been rescued. As a result I paid for it out of my own purse, and was glad to add a little extra for the kindness we were shown. I cannot imagine what this family has endured, but they appeared to be in a constant state of anxiety as to what might happen next.

Once again I have chance to pick up my pen before I send this letter.

We did not linger at Rovigno, and swiftly moved on in convoy with Spartan and Amphion, commanded by the leader of our little squadron, Capt. Hoste. He led us across to the south of Ravenna, and now a little over three weeks since we were in Rovigno, we are bombarding Pesaro, a small coastal town which has the misfortune to have been appropriated by the French. I have no qualms about fighting ship to ship, but sometimes I feel great pity for the people of this coastline who are caught in this war through no fault of their own. I confess that this is in no small measure to my chance to renew my acquaintance with Mdm. Francesca, the young widow I wrote of. I was sent ashore to oversee resupplying, for which

I chose to enlist her father's help, since he could negotiate with the locals better than I. Their quiet dignity has much impressed me, and particularly hers. I wish there was more I could do for them.

Your loving son,
Lieut. Richard Wytcombe

"Madam Francesca," Sarah giggled. "Ooh, Richard, you romantic sailor, you! Golly, Cleo, this is quite the regency romance, isn't it!"

"Where *is* Rovigno?" Chris wanted to know, and when Cleo told him it was Rovinj, gasped, "No! I went there on holiday. Jeez! Fancy me walking in our Richard's footsteps all these centuries later on! In that case I know the church he's talking about, too. It's up on the steepest bit of the headland, kinda towering over the town. There's a fabulous view out over the little islands from up there, and it's kinda like a tiny version of Venice, but without the canals."

Cleo reverently brought out two tiny items and laid them on the protective film she had carried them in.

"Then you'll recognise the style, Chris, because these are two pen and watercolour paintings Francesca brought with her of her home in Croatia. She must have painted these to go in the oval and round frames that were such the fashion back then, but they say on the back in a very spidery hand, 'my home in Rovigno'."

However, it was Sarah who first commented, saying, "Oh my goodness, the house is in that red colour you see in Venice. I have to admit, I really don't like it – it's sort of bloody!"

"Oh Mum!" Chris laughed. "It's not that red – more of a sort of dark salmon colour – but you're right, that

colour seems to crop up everywhere that Venice had influence. But I don't think it's any worse than the dark red of our bricks here, and nobody calls them blood-red. I think it only looks different because those houses were rendered and then painted.

"But look at the size of the place, Mum. I bet Richard wasn't half glad that he'd inherited Upper Moore by the time he brought Francesca home, because I can't imagine that his own folks lived in anything quite that grand – certainly not after what Cleo's just told us about him having to struggle to get into the navy."

Cleo had been thinking the same. "She must have found this big house at least partly familiar when you look at the dimensions of the windows, and that porticoed doorway, in her old home. A Tudor half-timbered place would have seemed far more alien."

"Are there more letters?" Sarah asked, looking eagerly to the screen.

Cleo moved the document so that the next letter came into view. "And here's where you start to hear him worrying about money again, Chris. Poor chap, he seems to have been permanently skint and living in hope of prize money that never came."

Sept June 1809

Dearest Father and Mother,

Since my last letter we have been patrolling the Adriatic in Capt. Hoste's squadron, harrying the French. The outcome of the bombardment I wrote of was that our squadron captured no less than thirteen coastal vessels, but our leader is far from happy. For want of men we have no way of taking these prizes to be returned to the Admiralty, and therefore we shall not receive any prize money. This is a matter which Capt. Hoste feels most keenly, as do the rest of us. We rarely see any other ships from England, which I must explain is why you have not received more frequent letters.

We then had excitement of a very different sort when shortly afterwards we attacked the fishing port of Cesenatico, for we ran aground in the shallow waters there. We brought our guns to bear on the battery defending the town with great effect, but were much relieved when we were able to float our Mercury once more. I was then involved in the sally ashore to spike the two guns of the battery and render them useless, and in the process we once again took many of the coastal vessels which carry supplies up and down this coast. It may sound harsh to deprive these local men of their trade, but we cannot have them used by the French to keep them supplied to our detriment.

This month we have continued to move farther south, and have attacked the town of Manfredonia in the region known as Apulia. Again we have deprived the French of the chance to use the coastal vessels to resupply their ships and troops.

Sept: Once more the lack of ships home means that I must add more to this letter before sending it.

This month we are back off the coast of Apulia, but I am pleased to say that our main action was to cut out the French schooner-of-war Pugliese from the waters near Barletta. I confess the attacks on the towns are *increasingly less to my taste, not least because I have been unable to forget Mdm. Francesca and her two children. The thought of them haunts me every time we bombard one of these small coastal towns, and I imagine other families huddled in fear as our canons pound away at their walls, for they did not choose to side with Bonaparte, yet are suffering for being amongst his conquests.*

Rather more worrying is the news that Mercury may be heading to England to be paid off. Much as I would like nothing more than to see you all, with no patron to further my prospects elsewhere, I must continue my career for as long as possible and seek another ship with all speed if this should come to pass.

Your loving son,
Lieut. Richard Wytcombe.

Cleo now showed them a map on screen, saying, "These places I've marked are where he was talking about, so you can see that essentially they were patrolling up and down the Adriatic, making attacks on what we'd now call the Italian east coast. In Richard's day, though, Italy wasn't united, and the southern towns he writes of them bombarding were in the Kingdom of Naples, which only fifty years before then would have been part of the Kingdom of the Two Sicilies. Then when he gets to talking about the towns near Ravenna, they would have been part of the Papal States before Napoleon invaded. It's no wonder the whole of Italy fell to him so easily – there was nobody uniting its defence."

"So where was Richard based?" Chris wondered. "If they weren't coming home to England, they must have been resupplying somewhere. Was that why he kept running into Francesca?"

"Partly, but the British Navy also had a base on the island of what's now called Vis – so in the middle of Croatia near to Split, not in the north – but back then was known as Lissa."

Sarah looked up at her. "Wasn't that a name on his memorial?"

"Yes it was. Here, you'd better read the rest of the letters."

Chapter 12

Dearest Father and Mother,

I was greatly pleased to receive your letter telling me of my sister's wedding. Do tell Lydia that I shall be delighted to meet my new brother-in-law when I eventually return home. However, I must tell you that that may not be for some time. As I feared, Mercury has returned to England, but to be paid off and, in fear of not getting another ship, I was grateful to take the chance to transfer to the Active, which is remaining here in the Adriatic. Unfortunately I will no longer be First Lieutenant, for that position was only ever acting in Mercury and was not made substantive. Therefore I am back to my old rank of Second Lieutenant, but grateful to have a berth at all when there are lieutenants with more glorious records out there still waiting for promotion.

My former captain, Henry Duncan, left Mercury with me and has taken over Imperieuse, previously and most famously commanded by Lord Cochrane, and has gone westwards towards Sicily and thence I know not where, which may have you wondering why I did not beg to go with him. Unfortunately there was no opening for an officer of my rank, but also I confess to you now, there is another reason why I wished to stay in the Adriatic. I have become much attached to Mdm. Francesca Kovač, and if we have not met much in person, it has been easier to correspond with her than it has with yourselves, on account of it being possible to send letters when we make landfall for supplies. It is harder for her to write to me, for she does not know where I shall be next, and I can only hope that she receives my attentions with the same depth of feelings as my own. The Latin I learned from the Reverend as a boy has proven useful in a way he could never have expected, for it helps me put my words into what is no doubt terrible Italian, but since Francesca cannot read English, I can only hope she understands me.

My new captain, James Duncan, has been sympathetic to my situation, saying that he has known many a man who has courted his wife with no more time to meet in person, for such is the fate of seafaring men like ourselves. However, unlike me, most of the rest of the crew have come fresh from England, for Active had to be refitted after being badly damaged by a bombardment, so my knowledge of the local area has been greatly appreciated. I will write again soon, but the problem of few ships returning to England still remains. Please do not let this prevent you from writing back – I long for news of home after such a prolonged absence.

Your loving son,
Lieut. Richard Wytcombe.

"So he was planning to marry her pretty quickly," Sarah observed. "I'm amazed their marriage lasted. So many of those 'love at first sight' romances end in disaster once people get to really know one another."

"And it does seem to have worked," Cleo agreed. "You get the impression that he genuinely grieved for her when she died, and they'd been together ...oh, twenty years, so it wasn't a short marriage."

They turned to the screen again.

June 1810

Dearest Father and Mother,

I do not know whether I told you in my last letter, but the commander of our small squadron remains Capt. Hoste, and as ever we have pursued the French and their allies with vigour. At the beginning of the year we were once more at the northern end of the Adriatic along with Cerberus and Hoste's Amphion, engaging the enemy at Grado, and though we were harrying the coastal vessels, once more the poor folk of that town found their homes being reduced to so much burning rubble.

This more than anything has made me beg Francesca and her family to find refuge elsewhere, for their home on the coast at Rovigno is too vulnerable, and I do not know what I should do if such a fate befell them. I know now that the man whom I thought to be her father is in fact her mother's brother, and mercifully he has trading links to the area around Venice. He himself has lost his family, and is doing his best to care for his widowed sister and the rest of the family. There are so many vulnerable women in this family it breaks my heart. Would that I could bring them aboard and transport them across to Venice if not closer to home – for even life there would be safer – but at least I have been able to tell them of the safest places to cross. I tell you now that it is my intention to propose to Mdm. Francesca at our next meeting and bring her back to England with me, for I believe she is kindly disposed to me asking.

Late June: once more in company with Cerberus, and with Swallow, we captured three gun-boats. God willing, this time we shall see some much-needed prize money, for it seems churlish of the Admiralty to deny us our rewards when they give us no means to claim what we have earned. Capt. Hoste has become much disillusioned over this, for like the rest of us, he has great need of more income, in his case to support his father. I too would dearly love to be able to keep my intended family in a proper manner. It would be a grim fate if I were to rescue them from the war, only for them to have to go a begging in England should something happen to me, for I know that I could not presume on yourselves for such a degree of support for what is already a complete family.

Your loving son,
Lieut. Richard Wytcombe.

"Hell!" Chris breathed. "He really didn't have much faith in his parents, did he? I can see what you mean now, Cleo, about Henry possibly being feckless. Surely even in those days, the widow of the oldest son in a family would have been looked after? Maybe not in luxury, but that reference to 'go a begging' really sends shivers down your spine."

"That's exactly it," Cleo agreed. "I was pretty horrified by that, so I went and had a rummage through the estate accounts. It seems that by this time, Henry and Martha were living on Edwin's charity in a cottage on the estate. For a moment I wondered whether they were here in this one, but then it turned out that Edwin put them as far from the big house as he could, almost as though he was ashamed of his brother."

"And yet given Edwin's generosity to Richard," Sarah added thoughtfully, "you can't imagine that he was just indifferent to their poverty. I wonder if Henry was the sort to try and wheedle money out of Edwin's guests? You know, plead poverty and make out that Edwin somehow deliberately kept him short?"

Cleo nodded. "I think you're right on that score, because I found an admiralty paper in amongst the letters which shows that Richard was having some of his pay sent to his parents. It wasn't a lot, but then if he wasn't getting much in the way of prize money, he'd have needed his pay to live on. But that and living rent-free on Edwin's estate should have let them live well above what the average farm labourer was on, for instance. So I think Richard knew that his parents wouldn't lift a finger to help his wife, even if it had been an English girl from closer to home."

Sarah snorted in disgust. "Sounds like Bertie wasn't such a one-off waste of space after all! Dear Archie was the family cuckoo in that respect!"

Cleo brought the next letter up. "This is where you hear about Lissa."

March 1811

Dearest Father and Mother,

In February we attacked and captured four local cargo vessels from Ancona in a raid on Pescara, as a result of which the cargo of one of them was transferred to our ship, and we find ourselves fully supplied for once. Only five days later we raided Ortona, another coastal town not far from Pescara, and to our great credit we captured ten Venetian vessels which we sent to the island of Lissa on the eastern side of the Adriatic, which is serving as our base. They were carrying supplies to the French at Corfu, and were laden with all manner of things such as wheat, rice and oil; but also planks and cordage, which will now be used to repair our own vessels. In addition we were able to burn two warehouses containing things such as sailors' uniforms, cables, blocks and hawsers, the loss of which will deal our enemy a bitter blow.

Then this month we were involved in a battle at Lissa itself, where our four ships encountered a combined French and Neapolitan force of five frigates, a corvette, a brig, two schooners, a gun-boat and a local trading vessel. I am proud to tell you that though we were out-manned three to one, and with only half the fire-power of our enemy, we carried the day with great honour, capturing two of the frigates, and causing another to run aground where she blew up.

As the only British ship still capable of giving chase, we in Active pursued the Venetian frigate Corona, Capt. Gordon manoeuvring our ship until we had the best position, at which point it only took us three-quarters of an hour to force her surrender, by which time she was on fire. Our comrades in Cerberus had earlier inflicted much damage on Corona, but having been badly damaged themselves, had not been able to join in the chase, and so our gallant company took the day!

This middle section of the Adriatic seems to be forever under fire, and I am glad that my dear Francesca's home is far to the north of here, for she and her family have not managed to leave as yet. This is the second time that the French have attempted to wrest Lissa from us, the last time being in October of last year, when they temporarily managed to land a force on the island and burn some of our own supply vessels. Therefore I am proud to tell you that it was our ship which this time raised the alarm of the approaching enemy, and upon receiving our signal, Capt. Hoste responded by signalling to the squadron, "Remember Nelson," which was greeted with much cheering from all of us.

This time I do hope we will be receiving prize money, for I still intend to ask Francesca for her hand when we next meet, there being no father of hers for me to ask of, and her mother is so distraught by her widowhood that it is Francesca who cares for her, not the other way around. I am beginning to realise that Francesca's own *husband was something of a brute, and that neither she nor the children miss him, but we have yet to have the time for me to hear the full story.*

> *Your loving son,*
> *Lieut. Richard Wytcombe.*

"A bit of a brute?" Sarah was startled. "That has to be saying something, given that those were hardly enlightened times for women."

"Yes, it comes out in the final letter Richard ever wrote to his children that I've been able to find," Cleo admitted. "It seems I may not have solved any of Hugh's mystery, and instead added another one to the list. Something went on back in Croatia and it was very dark indeed. But let's get through Richard's own story first."

Aug. May 1811

Dearest Father and Mother,

The summer months have kept us busy in this seemingly endless war of raid and counter-raid. If I sound weary, it is because I am.

Following the action at Lissa which I wrote to you about, we discovered that despite having surrendered to Capt. Hoste, the captain of the French ship Flore most connivingly pretended to have submitted to each of our ships that he passed as he left the battle, and then once through our line, fled the scene for the protection of French-held Lesina*. Even worse, the French have repeatedly refused to surrender this ship to us, despite it having been formally taken.

Capt. Hoste is furious about the matter, for such an abuse of custom (since Flore had surrendered to prevent further loss of life on their part) is beyond dishonourable and goes against what is recognised behaviour by both sides. But worse, the remaining captain in command of the French squadron is rebuffing all of Capt. Hoste's requests to hand over Flore. I fear what this may mean for further engagements should one of our ships fall into French hands.

All of our squadron is now in desperate need of repair, and I did not wish to worry you, but I was one of the wounded at Lissa. Mercifully, the large splinter of wood from a mast which was driven into my arm was able to be removed without the ship's surgeon taking my arm off, and it has continued to heal without festering, so that I am almost back to my old self again.

Aug: I can now add that we saw action again in July, and that I was amongst the landing part which went ashore at Rogoznica, which is near to the old Roman city of Ragusa*. We captured the fort up on the hill which overlooked the port, thus allowing our other boats to enter. Here we captured three gun-boats and twenty-eight transports, ten of which we burned, but managed to bring the rest out, this time with no notable casualties, which has done much to raise morale. Please God this war ends soon, for we all long to return home now.

Your loving son,

Lieut. Richard Wytcombe.

"You put an asterisk by Lesina and Ragusa," Sarah noticed. "Where are they?"

"Lesina is now called Hvar, so it's right by Lissa – a.k.a. Vis – in the centre of Croatia," Cleo told them. "So that was another fight right on the doorstep of their base. Ragusa in the south is now Dubrovnik, so again that locates it all for you."

"And he was wounded," Chris said with a frown. "A splinter would've been pretty serious in those days because of the risk of septicaemia, surely?"

"Yes, he had a lucky escape there," Cleo agreed. "As I was reading these letters I could tell that by now his heart wasn't in the fight anymore. So this last letter really shows his relief at being able to come home."

Dec. 1811

Dearest Father and Mother,

We have been in action again, but this time with a less happy outcome. We intercepted a French convoy on their way from Corfu to Trieste, and our three ships met their three in an even fight. Sad to say, this time we got badly mauled, and Capt. Duncan had his leg shot off below the knee. He now has a wooden peg, but refuses to let that hold him back. More of a problem in our already depleted crew has been the loss of eight souls, and twenty-six more wounded beside the captain. We have been told that we will share the prize money from the frigate and store-ships that we captured with the other five ships that were involved in the action – meagre reward when split five ways.

I am deeply saddened to learn of the death of Uncle, but at least he had reached an advanced age. My poor cousin William, on the other hand, seems never to have been strong, yet I never thought he would be carried off within weeks of his father, leaving me as heir to Upper Moore. My sorrow for them is coupled with a great relief for myself, for Active is set to return to England early next year, and I will be able to surrender my berth and return to you. However, if it proves possible and I am able to leave the ship early, I shall first return to Rovigno and claim my dearest Francesca and her children, and bring them home with me, though I do not know what kind of circuitous route I shall have to bring them by.

I look forward to seeing you with all my heart,

your affectionate son,
Lieut. Richard Wytcombe

"So did he do it?" Sarah immediately wanted to know. "Did he bring her back with him?"

"No, he didn't. And he was certainly the faithful sort, because it took until the first fall of Napoleon before he could travel to Italy to collect her. It seems the family had made it to Venice by then – there are some very scratchy letters which I suspect were written by the uncle just telling Richard where they were. He was quick off the mark, too, because the moment the British and Prussians captured Paris early in 1814, he was travelling to get her.

Luckily they got back to Upper Moore before Napoleon escaped from Elba. But they didn't marry here. They got married in Venice!"

Sarah clapped her hands together in delight. "Oh how lovely! Oh I'm so glad that they got together. Do we know which church?"

"San Moisé, it seems from their marriage documents. It's all in Italian, which I can speak but I'll have to ask my friend who translates for me if she can double-check the details, but it looks very much as though the family fled Croatia as soon as they could, though I don't really get why."

"Oh?" Chris was curious.

"Well everyone thought Napoleon was gone at that point, right? So in that part of the world they'd have presumed they were going back to being under the governance of the Austro-Hungarian Empire. That was nothing new to them. And if it was hardly great, it doesn't explain why the family would take such a huge chance and leave their home. The house in Rovinj might have been getting a bit dilapidated, but at least they had a home there. What was there in Venice for them? Despite what Richard thought, that had been as badly affected by the war as their home town. So I think they had to have been running away for another reason." She turned the laptop back to herself and read them the edited highlights of the letter she'd found with the necklace. "Now doesn't that sound to you like a reason why a whole family might have left in a hurry?"

They mulled it over for a while, with Sarah serving up the evening meal, but couldn't unravel the puzzle. Sarah and Chris insisted that Cleo stay in the warm for a while, and so they all decamped to the living room, but within minutes of the TV going on, Sarah was nodding off. It had clearly been an exhausting day for her, but Chris now gestured Cleo back to the kitchen.

"Okay, what weren't you telling us?" he asked her, once they'd softly closed the door on Sarah.

Cleo felt an uncomfortable twinge. "I know this is probably an odd question to start with, but how religious are you, Chris?"

He pulled a face. "Not very, if you mean church-going like Mum. To be honest I'm rather dreading tomorrow, because I know she'll want me to go with her to the morning service, but it doesn't sit very comfortably with me these days. While Archie was alive and twenty-pound notes were going in the collection plate on a weekly basis, they were all over him and Mum, but they've been sod-all support for her since he's been gone, so let's just say I'm not a fan."

Cleo felt a degree of relief. "Okay, then let me show you the full letter that Richard wrote to his children when he knew he was dying."

She turned the laptop back on and this time let him go through the whole of her transcription.

"Bloody hell! Hecate?" he breathed softly as he came to that part. "That's a bit odd for a devout Catholic, surely?"

"Yes and no. Over here, yes it would've been, but you're talking there about the Balkans, albeit the westernmost edge. Even the Inquisition had a hard time weeding out the local folklore over there, you know. In my degree, I came across some academic works which had looked at how the ordinary people would turn up to mass every time, yet still held on to old ceremonies and beliefs which had to date back to long before Christianity. My Romanian friend, Oana, who speaks several languages and does the translations, knows an old lady who swears that some of the roadside shrines to 'the lady' in rural Italy are more than a bit ambiguous! She can bear an odd likeness to Diana or Minerva or Vesta – whichever you want to call her – or to Hera. It all starts to get a bit fluid, you see.

"Hera, for instance, could be worshipped as the maiden, or as the mother, or as the 'crone', but don't let that word fool you, there was nothing of the Shakespearian witch about it. A better name would be 'wise woman', someone who had lived enough and had enough experience to be looked up to and consulted on all sorts of matters. Your mum would have filled the role in that kind of society, if you think of her as having travelled a lot and yet managed to raise a family. Life experience was highly valued. Do you see what I'm getting at? It's only our later western society which degrades and looks down on mature female wisdom.

"And Hecate was another of the goddesses associated with the wise-woman trope, though less with the maiden or mother image. I happen to be rather fond of Hecate myself, which is why I know this. There's some real rubbish been written about Hecate, as though she was some sort of voodoo-like 'dark' goddess, but that's a twisted understanding of her role as the 'crone'. It's a bit easier to think of the whole triple goddess thing as equated with the phases of the moon. The waxing of the moon is growth, the full moon as reaching a peak, and then the waning moon as the passage back into the quiet of the new moon; but you can't have the full moon without the dark of the new moon, it's all about regeneration, basically." She didn't want to press the matter and have Chris think she was some closet nutcase, muttering spells over pentagrams and crystals, with candles and wreathed in incense smoke while dressed in a hippy's kaftan, and so hurriedly moved on with,

"So there's nothing weird in Francesca looking to Hecate to protect the women of the family beyond a looking back to ancient times and traditions. I just didn't say anything to your mum because she's already suggested I go to church with her and I had to explain that I'm not exactly Christian, which she wasn't altogether comfortable with. I felt dragging Hecate into the conversation when she's already had the worst of days wasn't being kind."

Chris gave her one of his devastating smiles, making Cleo wish that he didn't have quite such twinkling blue eyes, because they were doing terrible things to her equilibrium. "Thanks for that," he said, genuinely meaning it. "Too often folks see Mum as the strong, capable one, and don't take her issues into account."

"Well I could see that the Church had been her prop through all of this. I've had my own run-ins with the kind of attitudes you describe, so I'm not surprised by them, but even before you told me, I felt that it wasn't fair to seem to knock the thing that's kept your mum going."

Chris leaned forward and scanned the letter again. "Do you think, though, that this might be connected to what Hugh was trying to get his family to see? Mum filled me in during the various long waits at the hospital, and on the journeys – God knows we needed something other than Dad to talk about. And I have to say I'm dead impressed with you finding that secret compartment in the chimney. I'd never have guessed that Uncle Archie's gun-cabinet had had a previous life!"

Cleo laughed. "You make it sound as though it had a life of its own, but I get what you mean."

"So do you think there are more? More hidden places?" He got up and went to put the kettle on, gesturing to the mugs in question as to whether Cleo wanted a mug too.

"Decaf for me at this time of night, please," she replied, then as he made the coffees continued, "and yes, I think there have to be. It's the only thing that makes sense of Horace tearing down walls and getting into such a froth all the time. Even if his dad Bertie didn't tell him the half of it, I think Horace had to be at least vaguely aware that something potentially dangerous was lurking in the house. Something which could end up with him going out on his ear. And I don't think he was the imaginative sort who would have shied at hints and whispers. I think he had to have honestly believed it was something more concrete than that, in which case it had to be something which would stand up to legal scrutiny. So what else could it be other than some kind of documents?"

"Well you can count me in on the search!" Chris said, bringing the mugs over. "I could certainly do with the distraction."

Chapter 13

Knowing that Chris was dreading the church visit on Sunday morning prompted Cleo to offer to go with them. She knew it would please Sarah, and the look of gratitude he gave her when she told them over breakfast confirmed that she was doing the right thing.

"How approachable is your vicar?" she asked Sarah, as this time they used her car to drive out to Thornfield Church.

"Oh, she's lovely," Sarah said without hesitation. "She's only been here a couple of months, though. I don't think she'll be able to shed any light on our mysteries."

"I was thinking more of whether she'd let us see the parish records," Cleo admitted. "Some counties have been great about getting all their parish archives into one place and online – Dorset, for instance. But it could be that Thornfield's are still at the church, and if so, it would incredibly useful if we could see them. She isn't in Mrs W's pocket, or anything, is she?"

"Lord, no!" Sarah snorted. "Herself thought Thornfield a terribly rural backwater of a place, and her coming the high and mighty with the new vicar over Archie's funeral didn't go down well at all. You could see that she really got to Emma – that's the vicar – with the way she spoke to her, though Emma was very good at keeping it civil."

Cleo couldn't help but smile. Mrs W certainly had a knack of turning people against her, and it might make all the difference between this vicar being reluctant or willing to help. On the other hand, that made it all the more puzzling as to why Archie had ever married Darcy D'Eath in the first place. Surely he had known what she was like? Or had he? Some people were very good at keeping their dark sides hidden, as Cleo knew from watching her step-father operating on his next mark. Or was it even that Mrs W had expected a very different kind of marriage to the one she had got? If she was the city girl Sarah made her out to be, then it could be that coming to the countryside – where everyone knew everybody else's business – had come as an unpleasant shock, and if Archie had refuse point blank to spend more time up in London with her, then that might account for a lot.

Don't dismiss a simple marriage gone wrong as the motivation in all of this, Cleo reminded herself firmly. *Much as it sounds as though Mrs W may have committed murder, you've got no actual proof of that yet. The circumstantial evidence might be piling up, but her determination to get every penny's worth out of the estate might come from her feeling let down, and therefore what she's owed; particularly if she waited most of her adult life to get married and then found she was competing with the ghost of Penny all the time. A much loved dead wife could turn out to be a dreadful rival to someone like Mrs W, who's better at ruffling feathers than making friends. I really do have to ask Sarah more about how they met.*

The church service went very much as Cleo had expected, the worst being afterwards when Sarah was subjected to a barrage of platitudes from the rest of the congregation, most of whom were over fifty and of a certain class – the evangelical side of the Church of England hadn't reached this bastion of the middle classes as yet! Sarah seemed to be genuinely glad of their attentions, but Chris' expression became more and more fixed, until Cleo linked her arm through his and led him away to look at the tombs before he spoke his mind. When everyone else had finally piled back into their Range

Rovers and other high-price-end vehicles, the vicar seemed to realise that they were lingering to speak to her.

"Is it about Jeff's funeral?" she asked Sarah, who was quick to say,

"Not today. I'll come and see you once I've had chance to see the undertakers. No, this is Cleo, and she's researching the family of Upper Moore House for Mrs Wytcombe. But things aren't quite going the way we expected."

The vicar's scarcely concealed delight as she said, "Oh really?" meant that Cleo had no reservations in coming forward.

"Hello, nice to meet you," she began, handing Emma one of her official business cards to illustrate that she was a serious researcher. "I was wondering whether you still have the parish records here? You see we need to get to grips with the nineteenth-century family, because something just isn't adding up with them. Sarah and I visited the church the other day and found the memorial to Richard Wytcombe, but I was wondering if we could see the registers of baptisms, marriages and burials, please? I have some names of the people I think were his children, but it would be great to get some dates attached to them. There are online resources I could use, but they're not always that complete for rural communities like this one, so it would be good to go back to the primary source."

Clearly relieved that they weren't asking for something beyond her remit, Emma replied, "Oh those, yes, they're kept in the vestry. I'm afraid I've got to dash – a starving husband and two children wanting Sunday lunch! But since I know Sarah, I don't have any problem with you going to have a look. Just drop the key back to me when you've done – I don't need to emphasise that you need to lock the church up, do I?"

"Not at all," Cleo assured her. "I'm fully aware of the problems of vandalism."

Emma led them through to the vestry where, to Cleo's dismay, the old records were quite literally in a parish chest. As Emma disappeared off to tend to her roast beef, Cleo turned a horrified gaze back to the ancient oak chest.

"This is vandalism of another sort!" she exclaimed. "A bloody chest, for…!" she just about managed to stop herself from blaspheming in front of Sarah. "I thought all churches had got their heads around the need to store this stuff properly?"

"To be fair, Emma has had her hands full with working her way into this parish," Sarah confessed. "The old vicar, Mr Gibbons, had been here decades and was very set in his ways. He looked on this as *his* church, and nobody was going to tell him how to do things!"

"Then it's probably a good thing that he's gone," Cleo said emphatically, "because I'd have been having strong words with him over this. I might even volunteer to come back and sort this lot out for Emma once I'm done up at the house, because if nothing else, some proper folders and archive quality wrapping would go a fair way to protecting these."

With great care she began lifting the books out. The modern one they swiftly discarded, for it had only been started in the sixties, and had nothing more than Archie and his family in it. Putting the next one on the vicar's desk for Sarah and Chris to start looking through, Cleo went to the chest and reverently brought out the much older book. The leather binding was cracked and crumbling, and the pages inside yellow with age, but it had been good paper to start off with, and in some ways it was faring better than the one Chris and Sarah were leafing through. However Cleo wanted something to lay it onto so that she wouldn't crack the spine.

"I know this is probably very bad of me," she said to the other two, "but I'm going to sneak this one back to the house. I've got some foam wedges with me that will support this properly while I'm going through it, and I'll be able to treat it much better up there than here. How are you getting on?"

Chris pointed to the notepad he'd been jotting names down on. "We found Archie's sister pretty fast. She died in 1959, so Mum's granny was right about her dying young. But at the moment we're looking at Horace's generation. The first one we found was Cynthia, who was a daughter of Albert and his wife Clarissa, who was born in 1914 and who died of polio in 1938. It was obviously noteworthy because they don't seem to be putting cause of death in for other people, but there were four youngsters in the parish who died of that around the same time."

"Oh, polio was a killer back in those days," Cleo confirmed, "and I'd have thought even more so out here. In the cities there'd have been a chance of sufferers being put into what they called an iron lung to help them breathe, but by the time they got them up there from here, it would no doubt have been too late. Have you got the christenings for the others of Bertie and Clarissa's children?"

Sarah looked up from where she had been tracing her finger down the long list of names. "Well if nothing else, we can confirm that John, the oldest, was born in 1909, then Horace in 1911. So that makes Cynthia the third child, after which there was Catherine born in 1919. I've just found Catherine marrying a Howard Grosvenor in 1944, but then nothing else for them, so I guess they moved away. Looks like Howard might have been in the army because he's referred to as a captain but not RN – so not navy."

"Have you found Clarissa's death?" Cleo wondered. "It would have to be after 1919 when Catherine was born, but if she died before John the oldest son, then she'd be another person gone before Horace could find out what the family secret was."

They leafed through the book again and found that Clarissa had died in 1929, but also the burial at the same time of an unnamed infant, which Cleo added to the family tree she was sketching out.

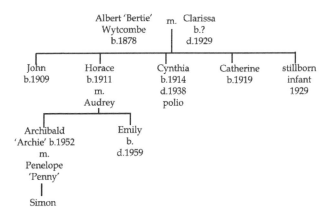

"*Hmph*, another victim of a late pregnancy," Cleo observed. "Even as late as then, it was dangerous to run into complications during pregnancy or a birth, and the upper classes weren't exempt. Anyone else from the family?"

Chris tapped his notebook. "Only Horace marrying Audrey in June 1945." He gave a wicked grin. "Clara seems to have been born a mere five months later, so it looks as though Horace and Audrey might have been doing a bit of 'celebrating' while he was home on leave! Naughty old Horace!'"

Sarah rolled her eyes at her son but agreed, "She wasn't an end-of-war-celebration baby. …Oh, and we have Emily's death in 1959 – that's Archie's sister who died of measles, but we pretty much knew about her."

But yet again, it was Cleo who could put some perspective on this. "It makes Audrey's attitude to Horace rather more understandable, though, doesn't it? Back in those days, if you got pregnant you got married. You had no option. So if she met Horace during a wartime fling, she might barely have known the man she married, especially if she discovered she was pregnant and had no choice but to go through with the wedding. Poor woman – one tipsy night with Horace might have been all it was, but then she finds she's stuck with him for life. That would sour anyone."

"Gosh!" Sarah gulped. "No wonder she might have deliberately spited him by getting the listing on the house. There mightn't have been any love to lose if it was like that."

On her own, Cleo would have carried on, but she recognised that Sarah and Chris wouldn't have her stamina for ferreting through old records, and Chris' stomach was starting to growl audibly – clearly he needed feeding.

"I'll come back when I've had a trawl through the censuses," she told them. "Those records will back up anything we find in this book anyway. It's when you get back before the first one in 1841 that the church records become vital. Come on, let's go home. If I smuggle this book out, can you take the key back, Chris?"

He immediately caught on that she didn't want Sarah to do it. If trapped in conversation with Vicar Emma, Sarah was too likely to say something out of her innate honesty. As they were driving back, though, he asked her,

"Do you always get involved with sneaking documents out of places?"

"Bloody hell, no!" Cleo exclaimed, horrified. "I can honestly say that I have *never* done this before. But then in fairness, I've never come across valuable old records treated with such blatant disregard before, either. And if I had, I would normally head for the local county archives in a hurry and tell them that the stuff was in danger. They're the ones who would have the authority to do something about it, and that's precisely what I will do as soon as I can. But I can't explain to you the weird feeling I have that I *have* to get to the bottom of this mystery, and fast. Honestly, Chris, I've never felt this compelled to dig so deep. It's the strangest feeling. …And by the way, I will return this book, albeit wrapped in as much protection as I can manage. It's just that I want to look at it now, not wait for months until it makes its way into Hereford or Worcester's county archives."

Back at the cottage, while Sarah got started on the rest of the Sunday lunch – the roast having gone on to slow cook while they were away – Chris accompanied Cleo up to the library, where with great care she opened the register up. Once he saw how gently she was treating it, and propping it up on either side with the foam wedges, he began to understand why she'd been so appalled to find it just dumped in the bottom of an old oak chest. When she opened the first page and said reverently,

"Oh my word! This starts at the Restoration!" he realised how old this must be.

"You mean the restoration of Charles II?"

"Yes, see here? 1660! Heaven knows what happened to the previous one. Possibly burned by some Roundhead troops who passed this way, who knows? But this is going to be the book that gives us the low-down on Richard and his family, I think."

She continued to carefully turn pages, adjusting the book's position every now and then, until she came to the end of the eighteenth century.

"Here we go!" she said, using a soft stylus to carefully point to a line. "Richard's christening in 1785, and then three years later the sister Lydia he referred to in his letters." She turned more pages before finding Lydia's wedding in 1809. "Robert Ralph, farmer. Well at least she must have known him before she wed. I doubt there were many surprises for her in the early years of her marriage. …Oh, and only a few years on from that in November 1814, here's the birth of a son, Hector, to Richard and Francesca Wytcombe."

It didn't take long for them to discover that Richard and Francesca had then had Sophia in 1816 and William in 1819.

"I'm not surprised that they didn't have any more children after that," Cleo told Chris. "From the marriage document," and she took him across to show him it, "she was born in 1783, so by the time William was born she was thirty-six. You wouldn't really have expected her to carry on having kids much beyond that, and if she had, it might well have killed her in the way we saw it did Clarissa a hundred years later."

She carefully closed the book up. "I'll have a go at tracing those three on through the records tomorrow, but I'll show you the census online tonight, if you like?"

"Great!" Chris enthused, and they hurried down to where Sarah had dinner almost ready.

That evening Cleo connected up her various bits of equipment, making Chris observe, "It's way more high-tech than I expected."

Cleo smiled at him as she logged into her accounts. "I have to use my phone as the link because I can never guarantee that there'll be free wi-fi where I'm working. At home it's different. I don't have to fiddle around like this because my home hub connects everything, but here we go, these are the censuses I was telling you about. Now let's search for Bertie and Clarissa."

Methodically working back, Cleo gradually revealed that Bertie had been the oldest son of Sydney Wytcombe and Millicent Powderham, and that he'd had a brother, Charles, who had been born in 1880; then a sister Emilia born in 1882, who had emigrated to Australia in 1920 and who was Sarah's grandmother. Then the sister Verity whose family had died in the flu epidemic was born in 1885, and Hugh who all the mystery surrounded came last in 1890.

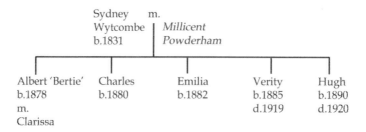

"I see what you mean about being able to verify everyone," Sarah said, impressed. "You can see the family from its earliest days in the 1881 census, through the 1891 one and on to the 1901 and 1911 ones. And I'm amazed that you found Emilia's emigration papers to Australia! That's definitely her husband with her, isn't it, and my two older aunts are girls of fourteen and sixteen, though I hadn't realised that there was such a big gap between them and my dad, because he was born in 1934."

"You said life was tough for Emilia," Cleo reminded her. "That might be why the gaps were bigger, and of

course she was getting older. The young woman of
…hang on a moment, Sarah, this isn't adding up! If your
dad was born in 1934, Emilia would have been fifty-two!
That's insanely old to become a mother in those days,
especially for someone living quite a rugged life. I hate to
drop this on you, but I think your dad was more likely the
illegitimate son of one of his supposed sisters. If Lilly was
sixteen when they went out in 1920, then she'd have been
thirty when your dad was born, and Lois, twenty-eight.
Did your dad ever talk about them?"

While Chris snorted with mirth at yet another
skeleton coming out of the closet, Sarah looked stunned,
and not in a good way.

"Sarah, are you okay?"

"Errm, …Dad told me that Lois died around the time
he was born. He only ever remembered Lilly as a sour old
woman – something to do with her husband running off
with not just another woman, but an Aborigine one, which
she thought was the ultimate slur on her. But he called her
a wicked old besom for going on about how her sister had
brought 'it' on herself by marrying a cousin. Don't ask me
what 'it' was, or which cousin, because I don't know, but
do you really think that Dad was actually Lois' son?"

Feeling awful for having unwittingly caused Sarah this
distress, nonetheless Cleo felt that there was nothing to be
gained by offering platitudes now, and said truthfully, "I
think it's highly probable. There was nothing exceptional
in a daughter's child being brought up by its grandmother.
If anything, your family's story is odd in that it seems likely
your dad was legitimate, more because quite often it's the
grandmother who takes on the child to preserve her
daughter's good name when she's not yet married. It
almost certainly means that your dad's father felt he
couldn't look after him on his own, and again that's not

odd for the time. Men just didn't stay at home to be house-dads in those days. I've got some links to international records, I'll see what I can find out for you – Mrs W can wait for a day or two if necessary."

However she wasn't expecting to be the bearer of the lesser bad news to Sarah for the day. That evening Chris got a text message which made him frown in puzzlement.

"Excuse me," he said, getting up from the sofa beside Sarah. "This is just weird. I'm going to have to call Marty back," and he got up and went out of the room. Hoping that it wasn't more bad news concerning his divorce, Cleo stayed with Sarah, watching the latest period drama on TV which tended to be a staple of Sunday night viewing. When she heard him come back into the kitchen, she made the excuse of offering to make Sarah a coffee and went out to him.

"Is everything okay?" she asked softly. "Not your ex-wife, I hope?"

Yet Chris shook his head, but looking very worried. "No. Marty said someone tried to ring me at my old job. It was the British embassy in Thailand, in Bangkok. Something to do with Aiden." He looked worried sick. "Bloody hell, Cleo, he's not supposed to be in Thailand! What could have gone so wrong that the embassy needs to contact me? Would you look up the time over there for me on your computer? Oh, and compared to Canada? Montreal to be precise."

"Sure. ...Here we go, Thailand is seven hours ahead of us, so it's early morning there – no, I'm going the wrong way, make it the middle of the night! And Canada is five hours behind us, so that puts Thailand twelve hours ahead of Montreal."

"Shit! Marty said that they called the switchboard at work a couple of times – but of course it would have still been at night over there – and in the end security put them on to him as the person who could best contact me, but they must have been trying to get me since the early morning their time. Oh crap, Cleo, I don't like this at all! Why was Aiden chasing me when he knows where Mum is?"

"Have you got a number for them?"

"Yes, Marty wrote it down and he's just passed it on to me."

"Okay, then use my computer to make the call. An internet connection will be far cheaper than you ringing on your mobile. Let me take this coffee in to your mum, and then I'll come back in – that's if you want me to?"

"God, yes! I feel like I might need someone to hold my hand over this, because I've got this horrible queasy feeling in my gut that something's gone terribly wrong. Please God he's not dead too!"

As she carried the coffee through to Sarah, Cleo offered up a prayer of her own. *Hecate, if you can hear me, don't let this be something that will finish Sarah off*, she mentally pleaded. *If you looked after the women of Francesca's family, then please look after Sarah.*

Making the excuse that costume dramas weren't Chris' thing, and that she was just going to chat with him, Cleo hurried back through to the kitchen to where Chris was hunched over her computer.

"Oh my God!" she heard him say, horror-stricken. "Whatever possessed him to do that?"

"I have no idea," the disembodied voice on the other end said, "But I'm very sorry to have to tell you that there's nothing more that we can do in this matter. He was caught red-handed, and there's no doubt at all that he was the one trying to persuade the two women to carry the drugs for him."

"Drugs!" Cleo mouthed silently to Chris, feeling her stomach take a lurch.

He nodded, tears already running down his face as he asked, "Just how much are we talking about here? Could it in any way be justified for personal use?"

"No, Mr Palmer, I'm afraid not. Not that much cocaine. He was handing a rucksack full to each of the two women, and there was a holdall with three other rucksacks in it between his feet. He's the trafficker, not a mule."

"Oh Christ!" Chris gulped, and Cleo could only come and wrap her arms around his shaking shoulders. "Is there any chance of him getting off with a fine?"

"No, not remotely, and he only made matters worse for himself by offering to bribe one of the court officials when he came to trial. There's no getting around it, Mr Palmer, your brother is going to do thirty years in a Thai jail, and that won't be anything like an English one. If his health seriously suffers, we might eventually reach a point where we could negotiate for him to finish his sentence in a British prison, but not at the moment. The Thai authorities are convinced that they have caught the ring-leaders of a significant drug-trafficking gang, and just because one of them is British, they're not going to go easy on him."

"Oh God, what am I going to tell our mother?" Chris sobbed, making Cleo feel she had to join in the conversation.

"Hello, Mr…?"

"Mr Crossland. I'm sorry, who are you?"

"My name is Cleo Farrell and I'm a family friend staying with them for the moment. Mr Crossland, I don't know if Mr Palmer has had a chance to explain this to you, but he and their mother had to turn the life support off on his father yesterday. This couldn't have come at a worse time. They haven't even had chance to plan the funeral yet, and I know that Mrs Palmer was dearly hoping that her other son would be coming home for that. From what you've just said, though, I can't imagine that the Thai authorities are likely to allow that to happen?"

"Oh good Lord, I'm so sorry," Crossland said, sounding genuinely taken aback that he'd had to break this news at such a bad time. "No, Miss Farrell, I'm afraid not, no question at all. The other Mr Palmer won't be seeing the outside world for a very long time."

She was just about to say goodbye to Crossland when a thought occurred to Cleo. "Mr Crossland, I know this might sound a daft question, but what was Aiden doing in Thailand? The last the family heard he was working for a charity in New Zealand."

She heard Crossland's disgusted huff even down the long-distance connection. "Then Aiden Palmer has been pulling the wool over your eyes, too. When I contacted the charity, since he had used them as his legitimisation for being in the country, they told me that Palmer had only ever had a six month contract when he went out to them, and though they would normally have renewed it, in his case they were glad to see the back of him. Something of a trouble-maker, it seems. He'd already sailed a little close to the wind in terms of encouraging violent protests, and they didn't want him dragging their name into disrepute. I'm so sorry for the rest of the family. Had his father been ill for long?"

"In a coma long-term," Cleo told him with a sigh of her own. "It seems the prognosis had never been good, and Aiden knew that. I wish he'd given his poor mother's feelings a bit more thought before he got himself into all of this."

"That a sentiment I hear all too often, I'm afraid. Goodbye, Miss Farrell."

"Goodbye, Mr Crossland, and thank you for your trouble."

Then the voice neither of them wanted to hear spoke just as Cleo severed the connection. "What trouble? What's happened? Chris, why are you crying?"

Chapter 14

Monday morning came in wreathed in fog, as if the weather was trying to hide the painful revelation of the previous night, and Cleo knew she was going to have to put her research on hold. Chris wasn't used to driving on the left anymore, and Sarah was in no fit state to be tackling the traffic up to Birmingham. So Cleo got them both into her car and wrote the day off as far as any further work was concerned.

As they got onto the M5 and headed north, she was very glad that she'd ignored Sarah's protests that they'd be alright. The fog was thicker here, if anything, and the thought of a distracted Sarah driving in these conditions was enough to give Cleo palpitations. So they did the various necessary legal bits up in Birmingham, then came back and went across to Ledbury, to the nearest branch of the undertakers to arrange Jeff's funeral, all of which meant that the day was almost over by the time they finished, and this time Cleo insisted that they eat out. The large hotel in Ledbury was suitably anonymous, and doing food on a quiet Monday night out of the tourist season, and though nobody was terribly hungry, they all made an effort to eat.

Once back at the cottage, an exhausted Sarah went straight to bed after ringing the vicar with the funeral details, and this time Chris wasn't far behind her. The previous night both of them had insisted that Cleo used what had been Aiden's room, since there was no likelihood of him needing it for the funeral now, and Cleo hadn't argued, wanting to be on hand in case any other dreadful news arrived. She and Chris hadn't said a word on the subject, but every time the words 'Thai jail' came up he'd looked to her with desperation written all over his face, and Cleo knew what he was thinking – Aiden would be very lucky to survive this.

But that left Cleo sitting alone at the kitchen table at eight o'clock in the evening, tired but not yet ready for bed. She couldn't stand the inane chatter of the TV, and anyway, she didn't want the noise to wake Chris, knowing from her own time in there that his room was over the lounge. She hadn't the enthusiasm for tackling the deeper history, but then thought she might at least have a look at the Australian records she had access to. If she could shed some light on Sarah's family it might be welcome, though if she found anything worrisome she'd keep it to herself for now.

There was a certain soothing aspect to getting back to the things she was familiar with, and soon Cleo felt herself relaxing as she dived into births, marriages, deaths, and other records. It was also good to switch off from her thoughts about Chris, because she couldn't avoid facing up to the fact that she was becoming ever more attracted to him. *Don't even think about it, girl,* she told herself severely. *He's going through a very rough patch at the moment. Just because he wants you around now, doesn't mean he will in the future. Be the friend he needs, and leave the rest well alone.*

It didn't take her too long to track down Sarah's marriage to Jeffrey Palmer and to see that her maiden name was Denby. Sarah had already told her that her father's name was Thomas, and so Cleo started digging into Thomas Denby. With both him and her mother being deceased, she had no trouble with access to their information with regards to privacy laws, and the first clue came with his marriage to Jane Osmond, Sarah's mother.

His surname might have been Denby, but his father's name in the relevant spot on the marriage certificate was George Carrington.

Now that's interesting, Cleo thought, having come across similar situations before. Having now got his date of birth, she decided to try a different tack and look for Thomas' birth certificate, for that would surely give her his mother's name and confirm whether he was indeed Emilia's son, or her daughter's. It helped enormously that Cleo knew that Emilia had left England with her husband Frank Denby, and of course at that point Lilly and Lois had both been Denbys too. So the key items she was looking for were the birth certificate and a marriage for Lois, or even Lilly, to this George Carrington. Being able to bracket her search to between 1920 when the family had left England, and 1934 when Thomas had been born, also cut down the potential list. So it didn't take her long to find the marriage in Alice Springs in 1932 of Lois Denby to George Carrington, whose father's name was Ernest Carrington, wine-merchant of…

"What?" Cleo yelped aloud. "Verona?" Then clasped her hand over her mouth and hoped that neither Chris nor Sarah had heard her outburst. But Verona? What on earth was a man with the terribly English name of Ernest Carrington doing in Verona? Another look at George confirmed that he too had been born in Verona, though at the time of his marriage to Lois his occupation was vineyard owner and travelling wine-merchant. And how odd that Verona would be the very place Hugh had done his recovering in; but surely there wouldn't be any connection between the two, would there, beyond Sarah's now *great*-grandmother being Hugh's sister? That link didn't go back far enough to be part of the older mystery.

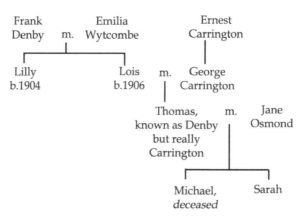

"Where the heck did you spring from, George?" she murmured softly. Well at least she would be able to tell Sarah in the morning that her dad was definitely the product of a legal union. But why had the sister, Lilly, been so disapproving of George? Cleo knew only too well that family legends often got very blurred down the years, so that someone who was convinced that they came from a noble family, with one of them swearing that a posh carriage had come for a grandmother, might turn out to be nothing more than another member of the family owning and running a Hansom cab and coming to visit. Or in the case of some of her American clients, being convinced that they had native Indian blood in the family going back five or six generations. But this was a bit closer in time than most of the cases she dealt with. This was about someone who had turned out to be Sarah's grandmother. And with the person making the accusations being her sister, Cleo was inclined to give more credence to the rumour.

"Why did you think he was a cousin, Lilly?" she muttered as she combed the archive for further evidence. "He was a Carrington, not a Wytcombe. Who on earth in the family had that surname?"

In the end she gave up and went to bed, recognising when she was tired enough that all she was doing was going in circles. Even so, she was up well before Sarah and Chris, and having made a pot of coffee for them in Sarah's much more user-friendly coffee machine, she left a note on the table to say that she was going across to the library and left them to sleep in peace. It was a good thing she had, for she'd barely got into the big house before she heard the phone ringing.

"Hello?" she said tentatively, picking it up, and was rewarded with Darcy D'Eath's haughty demand of,

"Who's that?"

Resisting the impulse to swear volubly, Cleo replied, "It's Miss Farrell, the researcher."

"Oh. Well where's Sarah? I've been ringing for the past hour!"

"Her husband died on Saturday," Cleo said frostily, wanting to deliver a severe verbal slap to this cold-hearted bitch, but knowing that she mustn't. "She had quite a rough day yesterday organising the funeral, so she's only just coming over," she lied smoothly. To hell with Mrs W thinking that Sarah was lazing in bed!

"Oh. …Well it was you I wanted to speak to, anyway. Have you made any progress?"

"Mrs D'Eath-Wytcombe," Cleo responded in her crispest business tone, "it's very early days yet to be talking about progress when there are so many documents to process. Yes, I have sorted them out, and I can confirm that there is nothing of interest in those which relate to your late husband, and as far as I have got with them, neither with your late father-in-law."

"I knew that!" snapped Darcy D'Eath.

To which Cleo fired back, "You may have *assumed* that, but that's not what you demanded the estate agents find out! You said you wanted something which would stand up as *proof*, so one of the first tasks is to make sure just how far back we are talking about. Can I presume that it was you who went through your late husband's papers before me?"

"Of course I did? Why would I pay you if I could have found it for myself?"

"Well you'd be paying a good deal less if you hadn't left them in such a mess," Cleo said coldly, "because you muddled up papers from different eras and it's taken me several days just to sort them back into some kind of logical order where I can process them."

There was a stunned silence on the other end for a moment before Darcy D'Eath came back at her with, "I don't think I like your tone of voice, Miss Farrell."

"You don't have to like me, since I'm being employed by your estate agent," Cleo reminded her. "You wanted them to find someone competent to sort out this god-awful tangle, and that person is me. I'm not here to throw you false hopes, I'm here to conduct a forensic investigation into the Wytcombe family estate to establish its bona fides for your sale of it and increase its value, if I can. And that is exactly what I am doing. I do not do slap-dash work, nor do I just skim through documents for speed, and vaguely hope that I have understood what they are saying. When I have something worth reporting to you, you can be assured that I will tell you, but in the meantime I am *not* going to invent false results just to make it seem as though I have got farther than I have. Now since I cannot tell you what I haven't found as yet, is there anything more I can do for you?"

"No, that will be all for now," Darcy D'Eath said haughtily and put the phone down on Cleo.

"And fuck you too!" Cleo said to the dead phone in disgust.

The next moment the door banged open and Joe stomped in, stopping in his tracks as he saw Cleo. "What? No coffee *again*?" were his first words.

Gritting her teeth, Cleo responded sharply, "No, Sarah's husband died on Saturday. She spent yesterday with people like the undertaker."

Joe blinked and looked owlishly back at her in surprise, clearly not expecting to get snapped at like that. "Bloody hell!"

"Sorry," Cleo apologised, "that was the arch-bitch herself on the phone from London, who couldn't even be bothered to pass on any condolences to Sarah. Rather got me off on the wrong foot this morning."

"Aye, well it would do," Joe conceded.

"Look, I haven't a clue how to work this monster of a machine, Joe, but if you're okay with instant, I'll put the kettle on."

Her concession clearly hit the spot with Joe, and he kicked off his muddy boots to come into the kitchen.

"You started early," Cleo observed.

"Aye, I normally has some breakfast with Sarah after I've done the first rounds of the garden," he hinted heavily, making Cleo inwardly sigh as she realised she'd have to fill in on the cooking front, too.

"Will bacon butties do for today?" she asked, as she investigated the depths of the huge fridge.

"Be fine, m'dear."

Not having eaten anything beyond a couple of slices of plain toast as yet, Cleo decided that she might as well join him, and so she soon had a pan full of bacon sizzling away. Luckily Joe wasn't a great one for conversation, and so Cleo didn't have any awkward questions to answer, but she did warn Joe not to ask about Aiden, giving him just the simplest explanation that he'd got into some trouble abroad and wouldn't be able to get back for the funeral.

"When be the funeral?" Joe asked. "Only I'd like to go for Sarah's sake."

"A week on Wednesday was what we arranged with the vicar, although it'll be at Hereford crematorium, not the church. Ten o'clock in the morning."

"Righty-oh, I'll be there," Joe said solemnly, and went out to hoe the vegetable beds.

So it was with considerable relief that Cleo finally got up to the library and got the fire lit once more. The weather had warmed up, but it was still far too cold to sit in the cavernous room with only the two heaters to fend off the chill. Pulling the desk chair right up to the fireplace, and cradling her mug of hot coffee in her hands, Cleo tried to organise her thoughts as to what to do next, thinking as she sipped the warming drink before she went back to the documents. She'd been distracted by the discovery from Richard's era, and there was a part of her that wanted to keep going with that. That parish register ought to be got back to the church as fast as possible, for a start off, and that more than anything else made her decide that she would continue with that for today.

Once she could bear to move more than a couple of feet from the fire's warmth, she donned her cotton archive gloves and opened the old register to the place she had marked back when she and Chris had been looking at it.

"Right, Richard, let's see if we can get anywhere with your family," she said decisively. "So we've got your son Hector born in 1814, but you talk about a step-daughter Ana in that letter of yours, so she has to be older than him. And what about this illegitimate son of yours, Tarquin? You imply that Ana marries him, so let's see if we can get anywhere with all of these names."

Carefully working her way through the register, Cleo was glad that Thornfield seemed to have always been a small parish, and there weren't that many events to each year's entries. As she would have expected, family surnames from the district cropped up regularly, but most of them were to do with the local farmers and the families who worked the land hereabouts – including the family Richard's sister had married into, though she and her husband had clearly moved elsewhere, going by their absence. However, after the birth of Richard and Francesca's youngest son, William, in 1819, the family up at Upper Moore were absent from the register until 1828 when suddenly Cleo spotted Ana. She wouldn't have made the connection, because there were a profusion of Mary-Anns and Annies, but this Ana only had one 'n' in it, and of course, she reminded herself, this young woman would have been literate enough to point out the difference to the vicar of the day.

There it was in the ponderous legal form of the day: 'Marriage solemnised at *the parish church* in the *parish* of *St Mary and All Saints, Thornfield* in the County of *Herefordshire*' the officiating clerk having filled in the appropriate points, and then the individual details: '*May 16ᵗʰ 1828   Tarquin Vyvyan, 26, Batchelor*' and '*Ana Kovač, 23, Spinster*'. Tarquin Vyvyan's occupation was given as 'gentleman', but Cleo guessed that this might have been Richard doing his best to give his errant and illegitimate son at least the semblance of respectability – either that or Tarquin was the kind of regular scoundrel who had no compunction about lying to the Church! Cleo looked at the 'Residence at time of marriage' and saw that Ana had been living at Upper Moore House. Tarquin, however, had given an address in Worcester, which Cleo knew hadn't been in a particularly salubrious part of the old city at that time. Ana really had married beneath her station, and Tarquin's pretension to being a gentleman was so much hot air.

Why did you let them marry, Richard? Cleo wondered. *You surely could have put a stop to it if you thought it was such a disaster?* Then it occurred to her that this might have happened when Richard was away from home. What if he and Francesca had been on the continent visiting her family? That kind of gap would give plenty of time for something like this to happen.

She looked further along the document and saw that Ana's father was named as Filip Kovač, deceased, and although Tarquin had put Richard down as his own father, Cleo now noticed that Richard was not amongst the witnesses to the marriage. Instead, there was a Luka Kovač as one of the witnesses, and that name rang bells with Cleo from Richard's last letter. Pulling her transcription of that up on the laptop, she saw that she was right, Luka was Ana's full brother.

So that must mean that Francesca's first husband was this Filip Kovač, she mused. *Kovač – that's more of a native Croatian name than Italian. I wonder if this Filip was marrying up into one of the Italian families who had settled across the Adriatic from Venice? What a shame that Richard's own marriage documents don't give Francesca's maiden name, only her widowed surname.*

A sudden shiver ran down her spine, and it was as though a ghostly voice said inside her head, '*Watch out for Filip! He was a bad man.*' She shivered again. Wherever had that thought come from? Certainly Richard had implied that Luka was less than reputable, but why did she feel like someone had walked over her grave whenever she read the name 'Filip'?

Well you're not going to find the answer to a Croatian mystery standing staring at a British parish register, she told herself sternly, and made herself focus and turn the page over. But there, only a year later, she saw an entry which made her shiver again. There was Ana, now Ana Wytcombe, with her husband, Tarquin Wytcombe, at the christening of their baby daughter, Sabina.

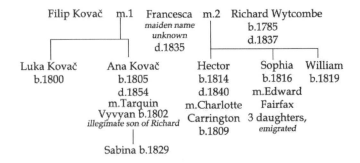

Oh my God, I'd have taken ages to find this online, she thought with a shiver, *because I needed that marriage with the two surnames. This must be after Richard gave Tarquin the Wytcombe name.* And indeed there were Francesca and Richard as one pair of little Sabina's godparents, presumably to make sure that their granddaughter was properly looked after.

Two years later in 1831, there was the baptism of the next of Ana's children, a boy called Sydney, and for a moment Cleo didn't realise what she was seeing. It was only when she had turned another page and got to the baptism of their third child, a boy called Edgar, in 1834, that the alarms bells in her head really started ringing. What was it that Sarah had said to her right back at the beginning about a cousin of Archie's from his father's great-uncle? Was this where she should be looking?

Frantically going back to her rough notes, she skimmed through them, but realised that Sarah had never been able to give her all the names of the older generations. Was this the right Edgar, or was there another? These generation ages were approximately right to be talking about Bertie's parents and their siblings, but she had nothing more than that on them at the moment. So why did she have that feeling once again of a ghost walking across her grave whenever she looked at Sydney? Why would she have the shivers over him?

Giving herself a mental shake, she carried on through the register and was rewarded with finding in 1835 the marriage of Richard and Francesca's son Hector to a young lady named Charlotte… No! Surely not? Charlotte *Carrington*? Wasn't that the name she had been looking at with Sarah's family? But Charlotte became quite legitimately Mrs Wytcombe, so any children of hers would have been Wytcombes too. Had Lilly got all of a muddle, and thought that the child of one of Charlotte's siblings, or even a more distant relation, counted as a blood relative? It was possible, Cleo had to admit, but if Emilia was the kind of no-nonsense kind of woman Sarah had described her as, she couldn't really see her daughter being that befuddled, either.

Despite wanting to go and boot up her other laptop and get into online searches, Cleo forced herself to continue with the aged book. That valuable clue about Tarquin's original surname was proof enough that she might find other snippets in here that wouldn't be in the wider records, and she needed to get through it. 1835 also saw the burial of Francesca, and Cleo now knew that she was getting to the end of Richard's lifetime. Yet two years on again, in 1837, there were a slew of family records. First came the baptism of yet another child to Ana and Tarquin, a daughter Olivia, but also the baptism of Hector and Charlotte's first child, also a daughter, called Julia. Then later in the year, Richard's beloved daughter Sophia married Edward Fairfax, and this time Richard was there as one of the witnesses – proof, had she needed it, that he hadn't been present at Ana's wedding. But only a year later, there was Richard's own funeral, and it was tempting to stop there.

However, forcing herself to patience, Cleo continued on, with the next couple of years turning up nothing until she got to 1840. A fifth child for Ana was baptised – another son, this time called Bertram – but the shocking entry which made her go cold was the death of Hector, and the tiny additional note in the old book of 'murdered'.

Chapter 15

She was still staring open-mouthed at the entry when Chris came in.

"I thought I might find you here... Jeez, Cleo, what's wrong?"

Pulling herself back to the present, Cleo gestured to the book. "I've just found the death of Richard's son, Hector. Someone made a note in the parish record to say that he was murdered."

"Hell! That's a bit extreme for these parts, isn't it? You don't think of sleepy Herefordshire as a hotbed of violent crime, not even in those days."

"And it wasn't. Oh my G...! I've just seen another entry. His poor wife must have been pregnant, because there's a baptism of Hector and Charlotte's son early in 1841. Poor souls. Baby Clifford couldn't have ever known his father, and Charlotte would have been all alone bringing up their two children." She checked her notes. "Their daughter Julia was only three when he died. What a tragedy." Then she stopped and looked up at him. "How's your mum?"

"Cleaning the cottage like a dervish. I've left her to it, because this is her way of dealing with things. There's no point in me saying, 'Mum, it can wait', because she then gets waspish for having no outlet for all of her frustrations. So it was come up to you, or risk getting stuck up in the vacuum cleaner!"

He said it with wry humour, and Cleo laughed with him, but she also realised that they'd have to keep an eye on Sarah over the next couple of days. With Jeff now gone, it might well be that some of the less pleasant memories of her marriage might float to the surface, and of course there was the ongoing problem of Aiden. How Sarah was going to deal with that was a total unknown – who in their wildest dreams expected their child to end up in a foreign jail?

"Well I've got some interesting news for her," Cleo told Chris. "Her dad was definitely legitimate and the son of Lois and her husband, George Carrington. So no skeleton's in that cupboard beyond the fairly normal slippage of a child taking their grandparents' surname having lived with them for all of their life. That's more common than you might think, and if her dad had gone through everything such as school with that surname, then because it was what he was known as for all of his life, it wouldn't be illegal to marry with that name. It might even have been that if Emilia and Lilly were so disapproving of Lois' marriage, that they might have given Thomas the impression that it was more respectable to have their family name."

Chris gave a sigh of relief. "That's all to the good. So do we know anything at all about this George guy?"

Cleo explained about the connection with Verona, but then added on what she'd found about Hector marrying a Carrington. "I was about to carry on trawling through this book when I got stopped by what happened to Hector," she concluded. "Fancy lending an extra pair of eyes on the search? We'll just be scanning for names, I'm afraid, but I'd really like to know what happened to those children of Ana's, and also to Hector's kids. They were the direct heirs after all, and that ought to lead us to Bertie."

Glad to have something to do, Chris came and pored over the old register alongside Cleo, but to their confusion it was as though Hector's Julia and Clifford simply vanished off the face of the earth. If Clifford was the obvious heir to Upper Moore House, Cleo would have expected him to have been brought up here. But beyond a final entry late in 1840 for a daughter born to Sophia and Edward Fairfax, it was as though the whole of that strand of the family vanished. And their search wasn't helped by the fact that this register ended in 1851, making it impossible, for now, to look for the marriages of the children when they reached adulthood, though Cleo was surprised not to see the widowed Charlotte remarrying – as would have been quite normal in those days – or alternatively dying. Had she moved right away from the family?

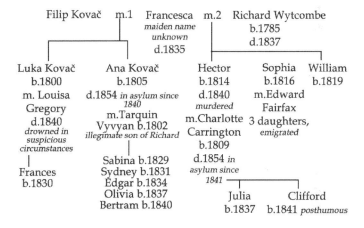

Taking a break, Cleo then got Chris to help her swaddle the old book in protective coverings, and sent him on the mission to get it back into the church under the pretence of wanting to double-check an entry for Cleo. It would be more reasonable for him to want to look at the family entries in the later books, should Vicar Emma ask, and he was positively eager to have something active to do. Sarah had emerged from the cottage, and so while she prepared some lunch for Joe and themselves, Cleo brought her up to date on her own family, relieved to see Sarah brightening with the distraction. She also told her of fielding Mrs W's call, and got profuse thanks for that.

"I don't think I could face speaking to that bloody woman, not even on the phone," Sarah said with feeling. "She's hardly going to understand how I feel."

So with that in mind, and seeing that Sarah was burning with nervous energy like a nuclear reactor at the moment, Cleo came up with an ingenious idea. "Why don't we give *this* house a spring clean?" she suggested, and with Chris having returned by now, she saw him giving her a delighted thumbs-up behind Sarah's back. "The rooms Mrs W has been using won't need it, but then it's the other rooms which might have secrets to give up. How do you fancy giving that huge dresser in the dining room a lick of polish?"

Later she would kick herself for not going back to her computers that day, for she might have found vital links sooner, but it was her sympathy for Sarah which won the day. In this instance, there was far less of the usual stuff to be done at the death of someone, for Sarah had needed to have power of attorney for the years while Jeff had been comatose, so for most of the things such as bank accounts it was more of a formality, this ending having long been foreseen and measures put into place. So whereas she might normally have been running around passing on death certificates in a hurry, so that she would have access to money for the funeral and the like, today Sarah had none of that to do, and it was doing her no good to sit and dwell on things.

So, armed with various cleaning products, rags and a couple of buckets of warm water, the three of them trekked into the dining room. They spread a plastic sheet out at the foot of the dresser to protect the old carpet, and then with Chris up a large pair of steps tackling the topmost layer, they began to clean the old polish off.

"I've never dared do this before," Sarah admitted. "I knew that some of the stronger cleaners would be disastrous, and I vaguely thought that I might destroy the patina and reduce its value."

"Well you do have to be careful," Cleo admitted, having taken the bottom of the dresser to save Sarah kneeling on the floor. "But that's why we're using very natural stuff. Archie's determination to be 'green' means that this soft liquid soap, for instance, will just get the grime off without stripping everything else away."

Certainly the buckets of water were soon turning murky and had to be replaced, but they were rewarded by a warmth of colour coming out in the dresser that hadn't been visible before. Spurred on by their success, and giving the outside time to dry thoroughly before re-polishing, they decided to have a go at the inside too. It was something of a mammoth task, because the dresser contained the Wytcombe family china, and there was a complete Spode dining service for twelve stored in there, complete with huge serving dishes, platters and coffee pots.

"Sarah, this is worth a fortune!" Cleo said in awe. "It's complete! Do you know how rare that is?"

"I don't think it was used for a very long time," Sarah confessed. "Both Horace and Archie thought the design hideous. That black decoration with the gold overlays was almost funereal in Archie's eyes. And Bertie bought an Art Deco set which is in another cupboard – he was another one who liked to have the height of fashion!"

"Art Deco?" Cleo felt her insides give a little skip. "Can you show me? I don't mean get it all out, just let me have a quick peek at it." If this family hadn't realised the value of the Spode, which unless Cleo had completely misremembered what she'd seen back in Mr Wentworth's antique shop, was probably from the very early nineteenth century going by the design and markings on the underneath, then they might have another treasure hidden away too.

She was totally floored, though, when Sarah opened a large cupboard in the hall, and Cleo saw what was inside.

"Holy crap, Sarah! This is Clarice Cliff! You have an absolute fortune hidden away here! It's not all one set, I can tell you that, but a compilation of various designs, but then I don't think she ever did whole dinner services. That doesn't reduce the value of what you've got here, though. That jug alone would fetch over five hundred pounds at auction …and those coffee sets …oh…my…God! …Please tell me Archie had this insured?"

"I don't think Archie had a clue what it was," Sarah confessed. "He didn't bother much about china, plants were more his things. He cared a lot about the arboretum."

"Well if he'd sold even just a few of these pieces, he'd have been able to afford an entire army of landscape gardeners to come in and restore it," Cleo said, barely able to keep breathing as her eyes picked up piece after piece that would have been the centrepiece of any museum display. "For God's sake, lock this up and don't tell a soul! You need a specialist company to come in and assess this, and either take it into safe keeping or seriously upgrade the alarm system here."

"Not my choice to make," Sarah reminded her wanly.

The very thought of Mrs W getting her hands on this was enough to make Cleo weep. Pearls before swine wasn't even close! But what nearly made her jump out of her skin was the voice coming inside her head again, saying, *This is Sarah's inheritance, you mustn't let the 'other one' have it!*

Mercifully she covered her squeak of surprise with a cough, and Sarah didn't notice, being too taken aback at the sudden wealth Cleo had revealed. Where was that voice coming from? Because she was one-hundred-percent certain that these weren't her own subconscious thoughts! And then it happened again, but with the image of the necklace flashing into her mind with the words, *And she must* not *get this*!

Shaken, Cleo was relieved to close the cupboard doors on the Clarice Cliff and head back into the dining room, glad that Sarah was telling Chris of their discovery the moment they got through the door, which covered her own appearance of shock.

"Should we go ahead and get these sets valued for insurance, do you think?" Chris wondered. "If we do it now, then Herself can't accuse us of wrong doing, because we'd be actually protecting her assets. …Well okay, she *could*, knowing her! But you know what I mean, if she threatened us with her solicitors, she'd look a bit of a fool, wouldn't she, once they realised that we were acting lawfully."

"Oh please, no," Sarah pleaded. "I'm sorry, but no. …I know we ought to. But I just can't face the thought of any confrontations with her at the moment. Yes I know they're worth a fortune, Cleo, but they weren't what Archie loved, and it wouldn't matter to him if they did get sold."

Feeling that Sarah had rather missed the point that they might not be Mrs W's to sell, and therefore should be kept for the rightful owner, Cleo nonetheless let the subject drop and they went back to cleaning the inside of the dresser. The work seemed to soothe Sarah, and they chatted about random things as they worked, relining the cupboard shelves with fresh paper before they restocked it. While they had the steps in place, both Chris and Cleo climbed up and shone torches down into the slim gaps behind the decorative panelling, which at least confirmed Cleo's deduction that the remains of the original doorway was there, but apart from a forlorn, forgotten toy soldier that had been lost behind there, the dresser revealed no other secrets. That rather disappointed Cleo, who had been hoping for a secret compartment, but if the dresser had ever had one of those it had long since vanished, and she couldn't even see where one might have been. So much for Hugh hiding something there.

Cleo thought she'd hidden her disappointment behind a succession of non-committal replies, but when they went back to the cottage at the end of the afternoon, while Sarah bustled about sorting out the meal, Chris sidled up to her and asked,

"Are you okay, Cleo? You went very quiet this afternoon."

Slightly taken aback that he would notice when his own feelings must be in turmoil, Cleo then felt more than a little guilty that she'd not covered her own better. "I'm absolutely fine," she reassured him. "It's just that I've got this weird feeling that time is of the essence with this search, and that phone-call this morning from Mrs-bloody-Wytcombe only made it stronger. I don't think the damned woman is going to be patient over this, going by the way she was trying to push me, and that makes me think that your mum's suspicions about her might sadly be true."

Chris looked at her slightly askance, and so Cleo drew him into the lounge and explained Sarah's reservations about Archie's death. "May Hecate intervene in this," she finished, "but I fear that Mrs W is nothing short of desperate to get her hands on every penny she can before someone starts asking awkward questions. And I'm sorry, Chris, but I also fear that she knows the one person who might do that is your mum – and that's another reason she wants the estate sold and your mum out of the way!"

"Holy shit!" he growled. "I hadn't realised that! You mean that Her-fucking-self is trying to kick Mum out of here?"

"Oh shit, you didn't know about that?"

"No, I didn't!"

Cleo grimaced. "Oh flaming hell, then I'm afraid it might have been Aiden who she mentioned it to in the hope that he'd come home and help her sort it out."

Now it was Chris who visibly winced. "If he gets out of that jail in one piece, I'm going to have one hell of a row with him for leaving Mum hanging like that. Why ever didn't she come to me?"

"I suspect because she knew your ex wasn't fond of her or your dad, and she didn't want you to be tugged two ways. After all, Aiden is the single one of you two."

That was such an obvious reason that Chris could only wish aloud that he'd told his mum about his divorce long ago. "If I'd have known it would make this much difference it would have made that decision so much easier," he groaned.

"Hindsight is a wonderful thing," Cleo said sympathetically, giving him a hug, "but you can't turn the clock back, sadly."

With that in mind, when they got up on Wednesday, Chris insisted that Cleo get back to her research, confiding to her that while donning rubber gloves and cleaning the house was far from anything he'd normally want to do, if it made Sarah's life easier, then he would gladly do it. But he was also in tune with Cleo now in hoping like mad that some other relative would come to light who ought to inherit Upper Moore. Almost anyone looked preferable to Darcy D'Eath right now! And so once again Cleo climbed the stairs to the library, although Chris gallantly hauled another basket of logs up for the fire for her.

Come on, Cleo, she thought, once she was alone again, *stop this flitting around and get methodical again. You're wasting time chasing all these nineteenth century leads until you can get the rest of the family back beyond 1900.* And with that in mind, she turned again to the bundles of papers which had been abandoned for the last few days. Some serious application soon filtered out those documents which solely concerned the workings of the estate, and though Cleo filed them in proper order, relabelling some boxes as she went so that the solicitors could access them if needed, she felt she could now disregard them. Whether this field had been sold off, or that woodland coppiced with the timber sold off, was not going to get her any further in her quest. But that meant that she had a much smaller pile to start going through now, and she set to with a vengeance.

Almost immediately she came across something which sent more shivers down her spine. It was a letter to Bertie from Emilia in Australia, and the letter would almost certainly not have survived had it not slipped into an envelope of totally unrelated things from the estate, falling from the larger envelope when Cleo had pulled a land grant out of it. Certainly Cleo felt that Bertie wouldn't have wanted it to be reread, because its contents shocked her to the core.

14th May 1920
Alice Springs

Dear Bertie,

Your news of the family breaks my heart. For this to happen so soon after us losing our dear Verity and her family is just too much. What a cruel thing to befall them all.

And here the page was smudged with tears that Cleo felt sure had to be Emilia's, for she couldn't imagine Bertie being the tearful sort. Yet she nearly dropped the letter when she read the start of the next paragraph.

> *Whatever possessed George to take his own life? Poor Charles, he must be beyond distraught at losing his only child, and only five years after Janette died, and then Verity last year, too. I will write to him, but if my letter is delayed, please tell him that it just is not possible for us to come back now for the funeral, nor would I wish to ever set foot in England again.*
>
> *Please tell me that you have not been up to your old tricks with them? You cannot fool me, brother, and I wish Hugh had come with us to Australia, for you worry me with your rages over what he says he found, and he is not strong anymore. If anything befalls him, know that I shall not forgive you, nor will I forget! And Charles knows my reasons for leaving, so do not think to blacken my name with him, nor paint me as the hysteric – I know you and how far you will go to get your own way, and I left because I did not want you near to my girls. It would be just like you to attempt to force one of them into marriage with Cousin Edward's grandson David to keep things within the family, and I was always too good with the horses not to know how dangerous close breeding can be. I repeat, you cannot fool me, brother.*
>
> *So I ask again, do you know why George took his own life? He did not go through the war as Hugh did, being too young to go overseas despite having been called up. So he*

> *cannot have had Hugh's nightmares. I will be*
> *writing to dear Charles, and should I find*
> *him fearing that you dropped poisonous*
> *words into George's ear, I will not hesitate to*
> *inform the proper authorities.*
>
> *Give my love to Clarissa and the*
> *children,*
>
> *your sister Emilia.*

"Bloody hell!" Cleo gulped. So it hadn't been Hugh's death which reached them as they got to Australia. It had been the second brother Charles' son who had died. And suicide? Not in the war itself, as Sarah had thought? As Emilia had hinted, if George had been through the trenches like Hugh then it might not have been so inexplicable, for although Cleo didn't know the exact numbers for post-war suicides of veterans, there must have been a fair number of poor souls so traumatised by what they'd experienced that they couldn't cope. But by the sound of it, George had never left England, so what had tipped him so over the edge?

Then another thought occurred to her. Where was George Wytcombe buried? Because as a suicide, he might not have been put into the family crypt if the parish priest of the time had been a bit hard-line – it wasn't just the Catholic church which could look down on such things, Cleo knew, and with the option of cremation having been available for several decades by then, George might have been sent that way. Certainly Sarah and Chris hadn't spotted his death when they were looking in the parish register, so he probably wasn't buried at Thornfield.

This time she did go to her laptop and start an online search. What she wasn't expecting to find was both his death and then his father's only two years later at the start of 1922. Normally she would only have started requesting copies of the death certificates after presenting her findings to her clients, and asking them how many of the family documents they wanted their own copies of, for they weren't cheap once you started multiplying the charge. But this time she wanted answers herself, and so she logged in to the government records with her password and sent off her requests, having found the individual record number for each one. And one of the joys of modern technology was that she could specify them just sending her a PDF of the document, so she wouldn't even have to wait for them to be posted. *Please let them come quickly*, she prayed, because she was getting a nasty feeling about what Emilia had said about Bertie's 'old tricks' and 'poisonous words'.

She would have loved to know what the next letter said, but that seemed to have got lost in the mists of time. What she wasn't expecting to find was that George had died only six weeks before Hugh. George died at the end of January 1920, with Hugh dying in mid March, and that had her logging on again and requesting Hugh's death certificate, too.

Feeling very disconcerted, Cleo forced herself to work onwards, for it was still only approaching lunchtime and she had no desire to waste the rest of the day. *Find George's birth*, she told herself, and began going back through the records for 1900 when he had been born. When she picked him up it was to see that his parents were Charles and Janette, just as in Emilia's letter, and being rigorous, she double-checked to confirm that George had been the only child. What was heartbreaking was to see via the 1911 census that Janette had had still-birth after still-birth after George, because that was the first census which recorded the number of children born and how many were still living, something which had no doubt hastened Janette's own death in 1915. *Blessed Hecate, this really wasn't a lucky family*, Cleo thought sadly. *If you are watching over this family, what was it about Janette that exempted her from your care?*

Daft though others might have thought her, Cleo felt deep in her soul that there had to be some reason why a goddess who cared for women would turn her back on one and yet look out for others – and though she'd never have said a word to anyone else, she was increasingly sure that it was Hecate who was whispering in her ear. Every time she came into the library now, with the necklace carefully hidden in her laptop case, it was as if there were spiders creeping over her skin. There was a definite presence in here, but it wasn't malevolent – or at least not towards her, and she didn't think it was to Sarah or Chris either, but it really didn't like Mrs W at all.

Chapter 16

After lunch, in which she said nothing to Chris or Sarah, instead letting them talk about their morning, she went back to her work, but this time deciding to see what she could trace of Janette. The spelling was a touch off, for Cleo would have expected it to be Jeanette, and that made her wonder whether there was any foreign connection there. What bothered her even more was the age Janette must have been when she married, because it dawned on Cleo that when Janette died in 1915 she had only been thirty-three, and contrary to popular belief, it was unusual for people to marry very young back then.

When she found their marriage in 1899, Cleo couldn't help but feel sad. Just seventeen, that was all that Janette had been, and a quick totting up of the months between that and the birth of George hinted that either he was premature – not impossible when you took into account Janette's subsequent disastrous pregnancies – or she had already been a couple of months pregnant. Not that Charles was exactly ancient at his wedding, either, being a mere nineteen, and though the minimum legal age to marry was sixteen, with him being under twenty-one, he would have needed parental consent, as would Janette.

What were your parents thinking? Cleo thought in dismay, bringing up the electronic image of the marriage document, noting that it had taken place in Hereford, not at Thornfield. Janette turned out to be Janette Franks, daughter of Mortimer Franks, farmer, of Little Pencombe, but the real shock was to see that Charles was the son of Sydney Wytcombe and Millicent Powderham.

"What?" she exclaimed, because suddenly the penny dropped, and she remembered where she had seen that name before. It had been when she had been looking at Ana!

Pouncing on her notes from the old parish register to make sure she wasn't mistaken, she had to sit down in shock when she realised that, yes, Charles had descended from Ana Kovač and Tarquin Vyvyan – neither of whom had a legitimate claim to Upper Moore House! And if Charles had, then so had Bertie! How far back did this go? Was it a scam? Or had Sydney been decided upon as the heir because nobody else was left? It was stretching the imagination a bit to think that things had got so desperate that the inheritance had to go to the child whose father had had to be legitimised, and whose mother had been only adopted into the family by marriage.

"Oh God, Hugh! Was this what you found out? Did you discover that your father had come from a tainted line and wasn't a legitimate heir? Was that what Bertie got so frantic about? Because, of course, Ana's Sydney was his father," she muttered as she sketched the family tree out.

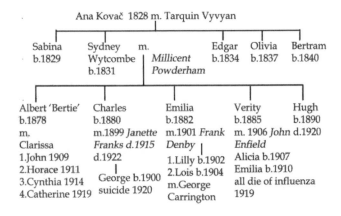

She sat there feeling faintly queasy as Chris hurried in.

"Cleo? Are you okay? We heard you call out. God, you've gone awful pale. What is it?"

Carefully taking him through the documents, Cleo explained how she had tied Bertie and Hugh's brother back to Ana.

"Holy crap!" was all Chris could say for a moment, but then he began shaking his head.

"What is it? What have I missed?" asked Cleo, fearing that she had let her emotions cloud her judgement and that she'd missed something obvious.

Chris frowned as he pointed out, "But this can't be what Hugh found, can it? Whatever that was, we know that he brought 'it' back from that house in Verona with him. Well this lot seem to have barely made it out of the county, much less all the way to Italy!"

"Are we absolutely certain of that Italian connection?" Cleo wondered.

Shrugging, Chris said, "Absolutely? Well I suppose not. But look at it from another way. You're only talking about three generations unless your family tree sketch, here, is way out. Ana was Bertie's grandmother, unless I've misunderstood you, so why would that be news to him? When did Ana die? Do you see what I mean? If Bertie ever met her, and that's not beyond possible, then none of this would be the kind of thing that Hugh could have held over him."

"I must be losing my touch," Cleo groaned. "How did I miss that? You've hit the nail on the head. In fact, wouldn't you think it more likely that this family secret is what Emilia is referring to when she talks of Bertie being up to his old tricks? If he was masquerading as the squire of Upper Moore as though he came from an unbroken line, then knowing of her grandmother, Emilia might well have thought her brother habitually rewrote the family history to suit himself."

"That sounds far more like it," Chris agreed. "Damn it, why couldn't Hugh have left us a bit more of a clue?"

"I don't suppose you found anything stuffed into a random cupboard?" Cleo asked hopefully, but Chris shook his head.

"Not a thing. A few old receipts for stuff, and behind the one bureau, a family of dead mice that must have been poisoned, but nothing else. Mind you, Mum told me about you saying that the ground floor rooms weren't ever likely to have stayed that undisturbed, and we've been doing the morning room and drawing room."

At that moment Sarah poked her head around the door. "Sorry to disturb you both, but Chris would you come with me? The bank has just rung and they want me to come over and sign the last of the papers. It's just stuff they couldn't complete until Jeff was actually gone, and I'd rather get it out of the way. It's only formalities, but better to get it finished with."

"Of course!" Chris agreed with alacrity. He turned back to Cleo with a knowing wink. "You keep digging here. I'll tell Mum what you've found on the way."

Yet left to her own devices, once again Cleo couldn't settle. It frustrated her because this wasn't the way she normally worked by any means, but getting annoyed with herself wasn't doing much for her focus. *Who of this disjointed family have I got a fair chance of tracing?* she thought, pushing herself onwards. If Hector of Richard's direct heirs had been murdered, she ought to try tracing the others, because that would possibly make more sense of the other line inheriting if there was nobody else.

Hector's widow, Charlotte Wytcombe seemed to have vanished, and she'd not got any further with Ana, so what of Sophia? Broadening her search, she found that Sophia and Edward had had three daughters in all, but not here in Herefordshire. They seemed to have gone to London, and then in 1843, when the youngest was still less than a year old, they emigrated to America, taking a ship from Southampton to New York where they both eventually died. Yet Edward's name came up twice more earlier in the records of ships leaving England, leaving for France and then returning, and that was in late 1841.

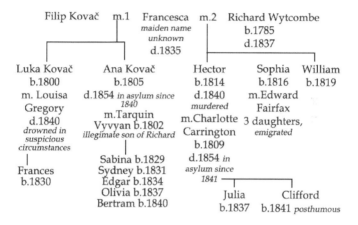

"What were you doing in France?" Cleo wondered, because he was gone for several months, and in those months Sophia had given birth to their second daughter. "Did you go to find Francesca's family?"

She checked back to Richard's last letter to confirm that Francesca had had a brother Ernesto and a sister Giulia, and from the way he wrote, it seemed reasonable to conclude that the two families had stayed in close contact, and that someone would have still been alive for Edward to go to. Then her eye went down a line on the embarkation document on her screen.

"What? …Julia Wytcombe and Clifford Wytcombe?" She sat back, aghast, for little Clifford was just a few months old, possibly only just weaned. Where was Charlotte, then? Why wasn't their mother travelling with them? She scoured the documents, even searching vessels leaving later in the year, in case Charlotte had been unwell at the time and unable to travel but had followed on; and she even checked the 1841 census in case Charlotte had been resident with Sophia in London, though why she would have let her children go abroad alone was a mystery. Nor had Edward brought them back. He had definitely returned alone.

A wider search in case Charlotte had died, showed no death for her in England between Clifford's birth in 1841 and 1900, at which point Cleo realised she'd need another clue to find her. Then just on the off-chance, she searched for Charlotte under her maiden name. No more records came up for her beyond her birth and her parents' names, but being thorough, Cleo noted in the family tree that Charlotte was the daughter of a Clifford Carrington senior and Elizabeth Gregory. Another box ticked, was how she thought of it, and then for no logical reason, she found herself typing in a search for Charlotte Gregory, with the time-frame still kept. The website refreshed with the new search and there, right at the top of the list was a census entry for 1841.

Feeling her heart skip, Cleo clicked on the link for the whole document and then nearly cried. Charlotte Gregory was one of inmates in the Hereford Lunatic Asylum in the grounds of Hereford Hospital, though run as a separate institution. Hurriedly searching for the 1851 census, Cleo could feel herself choking up as she found Charlotte still there. Doing another search on a different site revealed that the lunatic asylum had closed in 1853, with all inmates being sent to Abergavenny Asylum until a new one could be built.

"Oh Charlotte, you poor soul!" Cleo sniffed, having to get her tissues out. Her incarceration coming so soon after her husband's death and the birth of her child, might well mean that she had been suffering from serious post-natal depression, but in those days people got locked up, not treated. The records for the asylum were at the county record office, Cleo noticed, and immediately decided that she'd head that way tomorrow, and so she rang them to make sure she could get access to the records she wanted. Having been there many times before, the staff knew her, and she was able to book one of the computers for first thing the following morning, for many of the locals looking up their families didn't get there the moment the doors opened, and Cleo was confident that she wouldn't need too long to find what she wanted.

With a trail to follow now, she then looked more closely at Abergavenny, and there, in 1854, was Charlotte's death. She would have to make absolutely sure that it was the same Charlotte, but Cleo had a horrible feeling that it was, for if nothing else it explained why her children had gone abroad with Edward Fairfax without her. Had they gone to their family in Croatia – or were they in Italy permanently by now – and if so, why? Had there been nobody on Charlotte's side of the family who could have looked after them?

More searching revealed that Charlotte had indeed had two married sisters and a married brother, and even if one of those families couldn't have managed both children together, it was odd that with three potential homes, that none of them could have taken in one extra child – especially since Charlotte's siblings hadn't had huge families themselves. That had Cleo really puzzled, especially because of baby Clifford and Julia's ages and the length of the journey they'd been taken on. Why hadn't the Carrington families held onto them until they were at least a bit older to tackle such a voyage?

Trying to tie all the loose ends up as best she could, Cleo decided to look at the Abergavenny Asylum in the 1851 census, if only to make sure that there wasn't a Charlotte Gregory already in there, who might therefore have been the one whose death was recorded and with no connection to her search. Bringing up the census and starting at the beginning, Cleo began to carefully scroll down the list of names. Charlotte definitely wasn't there, making it far more likely that she had been transferred there from Hereford, but another surname caught her eye. Vyvyan!

"No! No way is that coinci…! Oh no! No, no, no!"

There in the record was Ana Vyvyan!

"Ana, what in God's name were you doing there?"

Her heart racing, Cleo went back over her data, realising that she hadn't found a death for Ana Wytcombe, and with trembling fingers now did a search for Ana Vyvyan. To her horror, she found that Ana had died at the same time as Charlotte, and when she came to find the reference number for their death registrations in order to get their certificates, was even more distraught to realise that they were sequential. Ana and Charlotte really had died together!

Another log-in on the government portal had her ordering the death certificates for them both; though going back that far she knew she'd have to be lucky to get them both, because official registration had only started in 1837, and in the more far-flung areas they might have been slower to implement the changes. Many was the time she had gone chasing agricultural labourers, and found no record because they had been too poor to pay the registration fee, but then this was an institution, not a family, who would have done the registering.

Then another thought occurred to her, for this was the era of small, local newspapers, most of which had long since vanished, but the deaths of two women in the same institution on the same day ought to have been newsworthy. It took a good deal longer to find what she was looking for, and following link after link to get the right archive, but finally she found *The Monmouthshire Beacon* – a newspaper founded as far back as 1837 and still going. If anything was going to have the dirt on Ana and Charlotte's deaths, this ought to be it, making Cleo grab her phone and hope that the offices didn't close early. She was in luck and they answered her call. So with an appointment to visit their archives after Hereford the next day, Cleo began to feel as though she had done the best she could for these tragic ladies for now.

However, Richard's warnings about Luka Kovač and Tarquin Vyvyan or Wytcombe, whichever he was calling himself, now plagued her. She'd already failed to find Tarquin's birth, not even as a Vyvyan, but given how lowly that had been, it wasn't terribly surprising. And Cleo had also come to the conclusion that Richard had probably been being more than charitable in calling his mother a 'housemaid', for given Tarquin's age at his marriage, when had Richard had the chance to move in such circles at the time of his conception? 1802 fitted for Richard being in England, alright, but his letters home had had him frantically chasing for posts, not enjoying wining and dining here at Upper Moore. Therefore Cleo thought that 'Portsmouth whore' might have been a better description of Tarquin's mother! In which case, Richard had been more than charitable to acknowledge him at all. Indeed if what she suspected of his mother's 'profession' was true, then there was a high probability that he wasn't Richard's at all. Tarquin had been another malevolent and toxic cuckoo to invade the Wytcombes' nest!

But when had Tarquin died? Cleo now realised that by getting distracted she hadn't answered this question, and she also felt a burning need to find out where Luka Kovač had got to in his life, for the two of them could be partners in crime. Luka couldn't have come to England before 1814 when Richard had brought Francesca home, but Cleo could find nothing of him until he appeared at Ana's wedding in 1828, and she wished – not for the first time – that the censuses went back farther than 1841. That way she might at least have found out whether he was resident at Upper Moore before then. Undeterred, she continued to search for Luka, finally coming across his own marriage to Louisa Meredith in 1829, not in England but in Wales. They had married in Abergavenny, and knowing of Ana's fate, that all by itself gave Cleo the shivers again. In the 1841 census, they were missing and Cleo could find no hint of them.

The 1851 census had Luka with a twenty-one-year-old daughter, Frances – who presumably had to be Louisa's as well – living here at Upper Moore, but still with no Louisa, and with a heavy heart Cleo went back to search for her death. When that came up in Abergavenny in December of 1839, Cleo couldn't avoid the conclusion that Louisa might have come to a bad end. After all, less than two years separated that from Hector's murder. Unfortunately, in this case there was only an index reference surviving, so she could get no more details on that – there wasn't a digital copy of the death certificate, and it probably wasn't worthwhile trying to get a copy from the government records. Had Luka been worried that Louisa might blow the whistle on him for whatever he had planned for Hector? It was a chilling possibility. Either that or Louisa had found out that Luka had some unsavoury plan for Frances, and that made Cleo determine that Frances would be one of those at the top of her list when she got chance to get back to the searches, which would probably be on Friday, if she was going to be spending Thursday dashing between Hereford and Abergavenny.

Reluctant to stop, but feeling by now as though her eyes had been bathed in grit from so much staring at her screen in the poor light of the library, Cleo closed everything down. Going across to the cottage, she found that Sarah had left a pie ready to go into the oven with instructions for her, and so having put the oven on to warm up, and then preparing some vegetables to go with it, Cleo was at a bit of a loose end until the others got back. Still fidgety and unable to just sit and watch the evening news on TV, Cleo got up and went back over to the big house, although having added an extra layer for warmth.

Up in what was nominally her bedroom, she sat on the bed and looked around her. If this had been Hugh's bedroom, where could he have hidden anything? Because now that Chris had pointed it out to her, she couldn't forget that whatever part he'd played in this mystery, the probability was that it didn't concern events in England, if only because he'd been away for so long in the army.

Running on instinct now, Cleo pulled out the tea-lights that she'd picked up from her suitcase, and also the little charcoal holder which she used to burn incense on. For now she was only thinking of setting the right atmosphere up here, but with luck she might get up here to meditate on one of the days when Sarah was well occupied elsewhere. Meditation was a great way to clear her thoughts, and sometimes she had moments of clarity when it was as if some ethereal being decided to drop her a heavy hint, so maybe Hecate would do that now?

Also, she had a friend whom she wanted to consult. Jen was her go-to person for anything spiritual, and some of Cleo's most revealing insights had come after a meditation at Jen's retreat. So now Cleo wanted a chance to talk to her friend openly, and without needing to moderate what she said in case Sarah was listening. This feeling of Hecate almost looking over her shoulder was starting to disconcert her, and she wanted to know what sort of meditation to do – the last thing she wanted was to open herself up to something which could potentially take her over, even though it didn't feel like that at the moment. So she set up her scented tea-lights where she was sure they would be able to burn safely, and then lit a charcoal disk with some frankincense and myrrh resins down in the grate, where she knew there was nothing which could catch fire. Even as they began to warm up, she could smell the familiar ancient scents starting to percolate the room and found that soothing.

But now she heard Sarah's car coming up the drive, and so she hurried down to meet them at the cottage, feeling sure that Sarah wouldn't be too happy about her druidic inclinations. It was a good thing she had kept that quiet, because Sarah was in a foul mood, and for the first time Cleo got a glimpse of a woman who could be an awful mother-in-law. Nothing was quite right, no matter what Chris and Cleo did, and by the time the knives and forks had been rearranged twice on the table, and the oven heat had been tweaked up and down, causing the shepherd's pie to burn on the top, it was all Cleo could do not to bite back when Sarah as good as accused her of not putting the oven on to the right temperature in the first place. Chris was looking more and more embarrassed, and yet didn't stand up for himself, and so as soon as the meal was over, Cleo told them that she was having an early night because of going to Hereford in the morning.

What she wasn't expecting was to have Sarah cross-examine her as to the reasons why.

"I thought you did everything on those computers of yours?" Sarah snapped, making it sound like an accusation more than a query.

"I *do* do a lot of it online," Cleo responded through gritted teeth, "but it's not unusual for me to have to go to an actual archive to find information."

"*Hmph*! So what have you got to find this time?"

"Mum!" Chris protested weakly, but by now Cleo had had enough.

"Look," she said tersely, "I'm trying to save you from some very distressing information I found out about Richard's family this afternoon. So please don't press me anymore. I've only got half, or at best two-thirds, of the story so far and you've had a tough few days yourself, so let me just get to the bottom of this, and then I'll fill you in."

"I'm not some bloody china doll!" Sarah snapped. "Honestly! Some people! First the bloody bank manager and then the solicitor, and now you! Jeff's been dying for years, don't you get it? I'm not about to fall apart now. I could have done with the sympathy and help back when he went into a coma, not now, when everything's close to being sorted."

"Well I wasn't here then," Cleo said coldly, "so don't take your frustrations out on me when I was only trying to be considerate." And turning on her heels she marched out of the room. Not to her bedroom in the cottage, though, but up to the one in the big house. If Sarah was going to start picking on Chris now, it would be better if she couldn't hear her, because Cleo thought that just at this moment Sarah was being pretty thoughtless towards him. And going by the way he'd come in looking haggard and stressed, she must have been wittering to him all the way home.

You're not even his girlfriend, she told herself sternly as she tramped up the turns of the old staircase. *You can't get involved, and the last thing you want is Sarah cross-examining you, wanting to know what your intentions towards her son are, because how could you answer her? Or at least, how could you do it without having to tell Chris at the same time that you fancy the pants off him?*

Thanking her lucky stars that she'd left her second small suitcase in this room, so that at least she had clean clothes for tomorrow and a clean pair of pyjamas she could use, Cleo went and grabbed some of the logs from the library and lit a fire in the small grate, her incense having now gone out. As the logs flickered into light, and the electric heaters going full-belt got some warmth into the room, Cleo heaved a sigh of relief for the silence. She was so used to living alone that it hadn't occurred to her how much of a strain it had been being around other people twenty-four-seven – and especially because these particular people had needed so much propping up. Worse, she was becoming disconcerted by these yo-yoing feelings of being glad of the company and then wanting to escape.

She drew the heavy curtains tightly, and then lit more tea-lights so that she could switch the main light off and just have the two bedside lamps on. The last thing she felt like doing tonight was reading, and she belatedly realised that another thing which had been fraying her nerves was the way the TV was always on in the evening at Sarah's, even if nobody was actually watching it. At home, although she did have a TV, she was more likely to watch something on-demand just for an hour or so at the end of an evening, and it would be something she purposely wanted to watch, not just random banal screen-time to fill the silence.

It also made a big difference to how she felt about being alone up here that she'd been at Upper Moore for over a week now, and it was starting to feel familiar. Far from the sensation of being abandoned up here, as she'd had on her first night, this felt more like an old house that she could live in permanently.

"Hecate, if you can hear me, please help me to find a lovely old place of my own," she prayed, starting to feel a bit tearful. It had been an emotionally draining few days for her, too, and somewhat belatedly, it occurred to her that what had got to her about Sarah speaking to her in those tones, was that it was far too close to the way her own mother spoke to her. Never a word of praise for what she had done, only picking fault and moaning about what she hadn't. Oh dear, she really ought to apologise to Sarah tomorrow when she got back, but not tonight. Tonight it could end in disaster if Sarah said the wrong thing and hit one of her own raw spots, and Cleo knew that she had all too many of those where mothers were concerned. And so undressing and creeping under the heavy, old-fashioned eiderdown quilt, she let her tears flow, finding a blessed relief in letting go of everything she'd been holding onto over the last couple of weeks.

Chapter 17

In her exhausted dream, Cleo was an onlooker in the bedroom she was now in, but it was a different time and place, and rather than herself in the bed, a pale young man lay there, his face creased in pain.

"Oh God it hurts!" he wept. "My leg, oh God, it hurts. How can it hurt when it's gone?"

The door was flung open and the florid-faced man Cleo recognised from the library marched in.

"Bloody hell, Hugh! Shut up! You're scaring the children! We've moved you as far·away from everyone as we can. Do we have to put you out in the gardener's cottage?"

"Sorry, Bertie, but it hurts so…"

"We know it bloody hurts! You never stop telling us it hurts! God in Heaven, how did you manage to be an officer for so long being such a bloody coward?"

Even in her dream state, Cleo was incensed. Had Bertie not seen Hugh's medals? How dare he call him a coward? Yet there was enough steel left in Hugh's soul for him to answer Bertie back.

"Coward, am I? Well I'm not the one too scared to do the decent thing and put right the old wrong."

"You'd have me impoverish my own children for a fault that isn't theirs? Damn you, Hugh!"

"Impoverish? God in Heaven, Bertie, you have a strange notion of what that truly means if you think that what we'd be left with would have driven us that low. You might have to live without your finest cigars and the special port you have imported, but none of us are likely to starve. And John and Horace were never going to somewhere like Eton anyway, so how are they going to suffer?"

"If you were a father you'd think differently. But then what woman is going to want a cripple like you?"

Cleo saw Hugh wince and knew that Bertie had hit a sore spot, but he wasn't down and out yet.

"You just can't help yourself, can you, Bertie? Always the one with the cruel joke or the barbed comment. And what have you found out now? Because when poor young George came to see me this afternoon, he looked like the world had fallen away from under his feet – and he'd been speaking to you down in the library before he came to me. I know he had, because I could hear you bawling at him from up here. So what did you say to the lad, hmm?"

"If you must know, I told him that it was a good thing I have two boys of my own, because I shall make damned sure that he never inherits."

"Christ, Bertie! He's not likely to anyway, so why torment him?"

"Because he's a perversion, that's why."

Cleo's dream self saw Hugh looking shocked as he demanded, "What in Heaven's name makes you say that? Honestly, Bertie, sometimes I wish you'd had to go through some of what I've had to – though I wouldn't put Passchendaele onto my worst enemy – because it might have woken you up to the things that really matter in life."

"Oh this matters, by God, it does! The lad is unnatural! An abomination! Says so in the Bible, and would you argue with that?"

"What are you blathering on about?"

"His mother! His bloody mother is our second-cousin! Our dear grandmother's great-niece …or was it great-great-niece? Oh, never mind! He's too close, d'you understand, man? We can't let him breed. Be likely to spawn brats with one eye in the middle of their foreheads. Can't have squinty-eyed idiots in the family, by God, we can't! Told him! Told him straight – you can't breed. I won't have it! I won't stand for it! Never mind what that fool of a father of his says, I'm the head of the family, and what I say goes."

Hugh leaned back on his pillows, closing his eyes with a grimace. "Emilia was right. You drink too much and it's pickled your brain. Haven't you grasped yet that George isn't that way inclined?"

"What d'you mean?"

"A touch of the Oscar Wilde. Do you understand what I mean?"

Bertie's face went such a deep red that Cleo wondered that he didn't have a stroke on the spot.

"Filthy pervert!" he screamed. "He shall never darken my door again!" and slammed his way out of the bedroom, leaving Hugh wan and pained, saying,

"Oh God forgive me, what have I done? I should never have breathed a word."

What happened next Cleo never found out, because she was woken by that same door being flung open in her own time, this time by Chris rushing in demanding,

"Cleo! What on earth are you doing up here? Why are you here?" and thoroughly waking her up in the process.

Feeling completely dislocated as she tried to reconnect with where she was and why, Cleo took a moment to be able to answer, by which time Chris had come to sit on the bed beside her looking anxious.

"You've been crying! Oh no, Mum didn't upset you that much, did she? I know she can be a bit much when she gets like that, but I thought you understood that it's only when she's upset herself."

Struggling upright, Cleo managed to straighten her thoughts out enough to tell Chris about her own mother. As she went through the successive dramas, where her mother had always somehow turned things around so that she could blame Cleo – even when there was no sane way that a child of that age could have engineered situations, much less be responsible – Chris' expression became more and more appalled.

"Oh Cleo!" he sighed, as she finished telling him about why she'd been so glad to come to Upper Moore. "I'm so sorry. Does Mum know any of this?"

"A fair bit. Certainly why I was glad to be able to stop here."

Chris' expression turned to one of anger. "Then she's going to apologise to you tomorrow!"

"No, Chris, it's alright. I'll say sorry to her and then let it lie."

"No, I'm sorry, Cleo, it's not alright. Mum can't have it both ways. She was getting ruder and ruder with the people we saw yesterday, who were only trying to be kind, and I had it all the way back home about how she doesn't need treating with kid gloves. Well if that's the case, then she ought to have been able to remember that you've not had it easy, either. If she doesn't want folk to pussyfoot around her, then she's got to stop lashing out at everyone."

"And that includes you," Cleo added with a watery smile. "It's not fair that you've become her emotional punch-bag just because your brother has been a prat. And I do think that most of this fury we've been seeing is to do with Aiden, not your dad. That's why she doesn't recognise what she's doing. Given that none of the people she saw yesterday know about Aiden, they see her upset and naturally think it's grief for your dad. But it isn't, is it? She's being completely truthful when she says she's already done her grieving for him. But Aiden? I don't think she's even come close to processing that she may never see him again, much less accept it."

To her amazement, Chris tugged her into his arms and kissed her warmly. As she blinked and gasped for breath as he leaned back, he said,

"You really are an amazing person! I don't know of anyone who could have been dealing with so much of their own crap, and yet who could be so insightful and compassionate towards someone who's just lashed out at you the way Mum did. But you've spotted what I hadn't, and you're right. This isn't about Dad at all, and that's why she's so all over the place."

He came and moved around so that he could sit alongside her on the bed and put his arm around her shoulders, giving her a hug.

"Bless you, Cleo. I was an inch away from having a go at Mum after you left, and it was only her storming off into the lounge and turning the TV up loud that stopped me – and that was only because I hadn't got the energy left to start shouting over the top of the damned thing. I'm so glad I came and found you …though I confess that – after I'd stopped feeling sorry for myself and had a stiff whisky – it was more because I just wanted someone to chat to who wouldn't keep snapping my head off. I can't claim any virtue for coming to find you because I'd spotted that you were upset."

"I don't suppose there's any of that whisky left? I feel like I could use one of those myself."

Chris stopped looking slightly embarrassed and grinned. "Come and pick one yourself. Mum's only tipple is a sherry with Sunday lunch, as you've no doubt spotted, but Archie had a selection of good single malts, and it seems a shame for them to go to waste. Apparently Herself prefers those technicolour cocktails that look like some kid upended a paint pot in a glass, so she's hardly going to drink them."

Shrugging on a sweater over her pyjamas and her thick fleece against the cold of the house, Cleo went with Chris down one floor to the bedroom which was beside the library.

"I think Archie sometimes used this as his hideaway," Chris confided. "With the chimney being shared with the library, once the fire's going in there it does take the chill off this room. And look here…!"

He went across to what appeared to be the kind of gentleman's wardrobe Cleo was familiar with from the antique shop, and which she'd not really looked twice at, dismissing it as probably early twentieth century, and therefore not likely to have hidden compartments. However what were hidden in here were not documents. Instead, the shelves on the right side of the wardrobe, which had once held smaller garments, now had some rather nice cut-crystal glasses and individual water jugs. The hanging space, which had always been short because of the presumption that only jackets, and trousers folded over hangers, would go in, was now divided in two by an extra shelf which stood on its own four legs on the wardrobe's floor, which was itself above the two rows of drawers at the wardrobe's base. And these two shelves were filled with bottles of malt whisky.

"Good old Archie!" Cleo giggled. "I'm so glad he had his own anaesthetic against Mrs W. She'd be enough to drive any man to drink, but Archie had the sense to make sure that was the best."

"And even divided by region," Chris said with a waved hand at the different groups of bottles, as he picked up a glass for her and another for himself. Then fooling around, asked in his best imitation of an unctuous butler, "And what would milady like tonight? A Highland or a Speyside? Or perhaps an Islay?" As Cleo got another fit of the giggles over his faux accent, he reached in and picked out a bottle. "I have a soft spot for the Bruichladdich Rocks, myself. A proper Islay malt, but not peated, not even as much as Caol Isla, let alone a peat-monster like Laphroig or Lagavulin."

"I've not tried that," admitted Cleo, "go on, I'll have one of those, please."

He poured her a considerably more hefty measure than she would have done for herself, at which point Cleo realised that she'd probably be driving to Hereford with a thick head the next morning, but just at the moment she didn't care. Archie had even had little bottles of spring water to go with his malts, and when Chris dripped a little into her glass, 'to bring out the bouquet', she realised that Chris was something of a connoisseur of malts. So for a while they chatted about the array of bottles in Archie's secret stash, Chris revealing that he'd belonged to a whisky society over in Canada, and that that had been his sanctuary when everything had been going wrong in his marriage. The close friends he'd vaguely referred to before turned out to have been part of this, and his times spent with them hadn't just been about getting drunk. In fact Cleo was glad to realise that he'd probably never got truly drunk beyond the once, because he spoke of the night when his divorce became final as the one night when he'd gone out and got spectacularly hammered, and never having had a hangover like that before or since.

They refilled their glasses, this time with a Cragganmore, and went up to Cleo's room as being warmer than the still-chilly first-floor room, and with the whisky having relaxed her, Cleo confided to Chris what she had been dreaming when he'd woken her.

"The thing is," she said, "is that portrait in the library really Bertie? Or did I insert him into my dream as the one family member I have a face for? And did I just make Hugh's face up?"

"Hold that thought!" Chris instructed her, putting his drink down and vanishing back downstairs. When he returned it was holding some large albums which turned out to be full of family photographs. "I'm not going to tell you who's who," he said. "You just pick out anyone who looks familiar. This lot are all from the Victorian era through to the 1920s, and from back when I was a kid and used to come and sit with Archie to look through these, I'm pretty sure I can still spot all the key people."

They leafed through the albums, starting with one which was almost all Edwardian parties at the house. Black and white photos showed ladies in snowy dresses parading on the upper patio outside the French windows, or ones where gentlemen with huge moustaches stood posing over large numbers of dead pheasants, ducks, or fish. Only occasionally did the children feature in these photos, but as soon as she saw him, Cleo picked out Hugh. Thinner faced than the other boys, he was also fairer haired.

"I'm sure that's the same person," Cleo said, peering closer at the group photo.

"Well done, Sherlock," Chris praised her. "Bang on the money. That's Hugh. Now can you spot Bertie?" It wasn't such an odd question, because the group had to include some of their cousins from their mother's side, or maybe the sons of friends of the family, and so there were nine boys of varying ages in the group posing beside some rowing boats, as if they'd been competing against one another.

"Him," Cleo said, pointing to a more round-faced boy, who although not the oldest, seemed to have an air about him that said he would be getting his own way. It wasn't just that about him which made Cleo certain, though. It was the line of his brow and the jutting bulldog jaw which were quite distinctive, and some high cheekbones that could well have come from Ana's side of the family. "I can see something in him of the man in the library painting, too."

"Well spotted," a surprised Chris said. "You've one heck of an eye for detail. ...So that's Bertie, and this lad over here is Charles."

"Ah, I can see it now. Yes, he's like a mixture of Bertie and Hugh, isn't he? The family gene permutation threw up a different combination with him. He looks a bit of a dreamer."

"I think he was. …Okay, what are you thinking? I'm getting to know that look."

Cleo huffed and wriggled herself into a more comfortable position. "It's that marriage of his to Janette. They were both only kids, Chris. So I'd thought maybe Charles was the kind of sexually mature lad who chased the girls from a young age, and got Janette pregnant so that they had to marry. But seeing him now, I just don't imagine him being like that. Look at the way he's staring off at the birds on the water. There must have been some of the female cousins and guests around, and they'd have been back behind the camera, higher on the bank. So a lad who fancied his chances would have been eyeing them up, and therefore staring toward the camera, not being completely indifferent to them even being there."

She turned the page to two more photos of what must have been the same family regatta. This time it was the older men who were posing, but they were harder to identify, primarily because of the wreaths of whiskers which hid facial features. "So who's who here?"

Chris pointed to the bottom of the page where, in some very faded white ink on the dark paper, there were names laid out to show who was at the back and who at the front. It now turned out that this had been taken in 1902, and the huge man seated in the centre of the group, positively overflowing from the sides of his chair, was Sydney Wytcombe.

"I think that's only a year or two before he died," Cleo told Chris, "so I'm not surprised he looks ill there. He was only in his fifties, if I remember right, but look at the paunch on him – he was hardly healthy."

"Another one who liked the fine living too much," Chris agreed. "You know looking at this now, I'm seeing it in a different light. As a kid I just used to laugh along with Archie at the ridiculous moustaches and the tweed plus-fours in the hunting photos; but reading the names now, while you can dismiss some if not most of them as just visitors, there are others I'm curious about. This guy," and he pointed to a younger man at the side of the group. "He seems to be nobody in particular, but he's on lots of the family photos." Chris had to angle the album to read the faded name. "Mortimer Franks. Who the heck was he?"

Franks had a grim, forbidding look about him, and that certain something about him that made you think, 'he's a nasty piece of work', even if you knew nothing of him.

"Look. He's here," and Chris flipped back two pages, "…and here…and here. It is the same guy, isn't it?"

It certainly was, and all the clearer for him never seeming to have followed the fashion for a bushy moustache, so that his high cheekbones and brooding brow stood out clearly.

"Oh poor Janette," Cleo gasped. "This is Charles' future father-in-law! He looks a cruel man. I couldn't understand why he would let his seventeen-year-old daughter marry, but seeing him here, it's as though you can see him trying to wheedle his way into the big house. Damn it! I don't think either Janette or Charles can have had much say in their getting wed."

She had the feeling that there was something else about him, too, but the whisky was making her feel fuzzy by now, and her eyes were beginning to droop.

When her alarm woke her in the morning, she was completely thrown by finding Chris on the bed beside her. Her pounding head reminded her of the whisky last night, and she had vague memories of getting back under the bedclothes for warmth as they'd looked through the albums. Those were still on the bed where they'd been dropped, and at some point in the night, Chris had obviously crept under the eiderdown quilt – still fully dressed – for the extra warmth, too. Currently he was dead to the world, snoring gently and with one arm thrown back behind his head, oblivious to the alarm's efforts.

"Oh crap!" Cleo winced, as she forced herself out of bed. She'd not had that much that she wouldn't be safe to drive first thing, but she was sufficiently unused to drinking for the two large whiskies to have hit her hard. For once prepared to face the icy bathroom next door, she went and put the heater on, then when she felt that she could just about face stripping off in there, went and poured herself under the shower, putting it on full blast. It must have been a relatively recent installation, because it had a fierce set of jets, and they did a lot to return Cleo to the land of the living.

With Chris still not having surfaced, she went downstairs and was relieved to unearth an Italian-style Moka espresso pot in the big kitchen. Dumping fresh, ground coffee into its top part and filling the bottom with water, she put it onto the hob to boil. Some toast went into the toaster, which looked as though it had hardly ever been used in Sarah's world of fried bread with fried eggs and bacon on it, but today the last thing Cleo could face was one of Sarah's cooked breakfasts. Barely skimming the toast with the spreadable-butter, she had to get the first coffee down her before she could face eating it.

As she was cradling the second large mug of coffee, and feeling the effects of the two aspirin she'd taken and the caffeine kicking in, Chris wandered blearily in through the door.

"Morning. Is that coffee I smell?"

"Sure is."

"Thank God!"

Cleo couldn't help but laugh. "Well if you will pour half a tumbler of malt at a time you can't be surprised at having a thick head the morning after."

"Did *I* do that? Surely not. Must be some other guy you're thinking of," but he smiled good-temperedly, and that, Cleo thought, said a lot about the kind of man he was. Other men she had briefly known were unbearable with even a fraction of the hangover he must have. *God, you'd be nice to wake up to on a regular basis*, she thought, then was glad she had her back turned to him to cover her blush as she replenished the Moka.

He came and wrapped his arms around her as she put it on the hob, doing all sorts of things to her fragile equilibrium.

"Mmm, you smell nice in the morning."

"You wouldn't have said that if you'd caught me before my shower. Crabby old crone might have been closer to it."

"You? No, never," he laughed with her, then became serious. "I haven't forgotten our talk last night, you know. I will be having a word with Mum about yesterday, and about taking it out on us over Aiden."

"Then I'm glad I'm going to be out of the way. I'm sorry, Chris, but I really do have to get going or I'll miss my time-slot at Hereford."

Whether he'd have repeated the kiss of last night she never found out, and was only glad that he'd gone to put his mug of coffee on the table as Sarah came in like a whirlwind.

"There you both are!" she exclaimed. "Why are you making coffee in here when I've done it in the cottage?"

"Gotta go!" Cleo squeaked, and grabbing her laptop case and shoulder bag, she fled from the kitchen before things could get any more awkward.

Chapter 18

Hereford on a Thursday morning rush-hour was every bit as frustrating as Cleo remembered it being, especially as it was always a challenge to be able to park even halfway close to the archive. Having had to leave her car several streets away, it was refreshing to make the walk in the bitter cold air, and it drove the last of her headache away for the time being at least. She had more aspirin with her, though, just in case it crept back after the current tablets wore off.

At the archive she went through booking herself in, and then settled down at one of the desks to start going through the asylum records. It was grim reading. So many of the inmates had what would now be treatable problems, and Cleo offered up a prayer of thanks that she'd been born in modern times. The twenty-first century might have its issues, but at least she wasn't likely to be locked up for being nothing more than a menopausal woman, and she had a strong suspicion that some of these poor souls had been nothing worse than that. Rather worse, though, were the younger women whose diagnoses were so vague that you had to wonder whether some avaricious relative was just getting them out of the way, and when she finally tracked down Charlotte, she felt that there was more than a little of that about her being shoved into the asylum.

Charlotte's diagnosis was no diagnosis at all. She was just admitted as 'mad' on the thirtieth of March 1841, but what chilled Cleo to the bone was that the man who had taken her there was recorded as 'Luka Kovač, brother-in-law'. Even worse, she had been put in there barely a month after little Clifford had been born in early February. What that separation must have done to Charlotte didn't bear thinking about, so no wonder Luka had been able to portray her as deranged – the poor woman must have been beside herself with worry and the incredibly strong maternal drive to be with her baby. The entry rattled her that badly that she had to go out to the coffee machine and grab a cup of the anonymous liquid it disgorged, before going outside so that she could fume without disturbing other researchers.

"Bloody 'brother-in-law'!" she muttered darkly, wishing she'd brought a flask of the proper coffee from Upper Moore. In the past she'd been able to drink vending machine coffee, but nearly two weeks of the good stuff had completely spoilt her taste-buds, and she ended up pouring the last half of the small cup down the nearest drain. "He wasn't her brother-in-law! Hell's teeth, how much did he give to someone as a back-hander to get her put in there? Because I don't believe for one second that the people in charge of the asylum didn't pick up on their totally different surnames. And why didn't they at least ask why someone who was far from English was doing this, because he must have still had a foreign accent?"

Going back in, she found that the person who'd booked the next session at her terminal wasn't coming in after all, and so with a bit more time to spare, she thought to look for the death of Luka's own unfortunate wife, Louisa. However, although she found Frances' birth in 1830 at a farmhouse near the Welsh border, and baptism at a small church just on the Herefordshire side – for clearly Richard was not letting Luka into the big house while he was still alive – there wasn't a scrap of evidence that Louisa had ever crossed the border from Wales beyond that one time, which made Cleo add her to her list of persons to trace in Abergavenny.

And so feeling more than a little gloomy, Cleo left and went into the city centre, but with a bit more of an appetite now, topped up her energy with a large cappuccino and a lemon muffin. Feeling more human again after that, she got back on the road and headed for Abergavenny, which was an easy run from Hereford. At *The Monmouthshire Beacon's* office, she explained why she was there and what she wanted to look at. Her credentials were impressive enough that they got her access to the archive, and soon she was sorting through the back copies from the start of the paper in 1837. She'd been intending to go straight for 1854 and the double death of Ana and Charlotte, but with her head now buzzing with caffeine, she was determined to discover Louisa's fate, if she could, with Frances still lurking in the wings, too.

Being of a mind to be extra careful, she began searching through the notifications of deaths, but also for any pieces which looked as though they might be about a suspicious death. Hector had been murdered in early August of 1840, and Louisa had died at the end of the previous year, so Cleo reasoned that she might well have 'conveniently' been shuffled out of the way before Hector, if Luka was worried that she might give his plans away. Add to that the incarceration of Charlotte only months later in the following March of 1841, and you couldn't avoid the conclusion that someone was doing a very good job of tying up loose ends.

She didn't have far to look. There in one of the news columns, was a small item recording that a woman had thrown herself into the River Usk in the December of 1839. '*Her husband, Mr Kovač of Blorenge Villa by Llanfoist, told the coroner that she had been distraught for months following her second miscarriage in as many years,*' the newspaper reported, but Cleo had her doubts about that. Luka and Louisa might only have had the one daughter, but Cleo thought that might have had more to do with Louisa rejecting Luka's unpleasant advances; because otherwise it was a shocking coincidence that the one person who might have discovered Luka plotting was the first one to die. And when the paper said that they had come to the house at the foot of the Blorenge Mountain in an attempt to get Louisa away from the place of her losses, it seemed more to Cleo that Luka had been keeping the family moving so that nobody got to know them well enough to get suspicious.

"You poor girl," Cleo sighed, as she took a photograph of the article with her i-phone. "You didn't stand a chance, did you? Nice lass from the Valleys coming up against a villain like that."

She worked her way through to 1854, and didn't know whether to be glad that she found what she was looking for, or even more distressed at finding the two other victims of Luka's machinations. This time the article was more headline news, for somehow, Charlotte and Ana had managed to elude whatever security there might have been at the asylum, and had climbed out onto the roof together. An unnamed member of the asylum staff said that 'Mrs Vyvyan' had been greatly troubled when she had been brought in, in December 1840, and that she had been greatly agitated for her first few years, frequently trying to harm herself. Mr Vyvyan had brought his wife in following the death of their infant son, the source continued, and had greatly regretted having to place his wife in the asylum, but with him fearing now for the safety of their older children, he felt that he had no choice. Every effort had been made to find Mr Vyvyan in subsequent years as his wife had seemed to improve, but to no avail. However, Mrs Vyvyan's condition had undergone a rapid decline upon the arrival of Mrs Gregory from the Hereford Asylum.

"I bet it bloody did!" Cleo breathed softly. Then thinking, *She discovered that her half-sister-in-law had just met the same fate as her! Both of them severed from their baby sons before they were barely weaned, and both of them shoved into asylums at Luka's instigation – because I'd bet good money that Luka was the one chivvying Tarquin along. And Luka couldn't bring Ana in, could he? Not even as her brother. Not when he must have been seen in front of the local court for his own wife's death only months before. This might have been a relatively quiet backwater back then, but that would make a foreigner like Kovač really stand out from the crowd.*

The newspaper went on to report that Ana and Charlotte had somehow climbed out onto the roof, and begun screaming their demands that their children be brought to them. When it became clear that this would not happen, nor would either of their husbands come to account for their actions, the two of them had clasped hands and thrown themselves from the highest point. Neither had survived the impact with the cobblestones below.

At this point Cleo had to lean back from the old papers for fear of dripping tears onto them. "How bloody desperate must you have been to jump?" she sniffed into her tissues. "God almighty! You must have felt there was nothing left to live for." Then a thought occurred to her. "Did you tell Ana something, Charlotte? You had a whole extra year on the outside before you got put inside. What had you discovered in that time?"

That made her think that she really must put some more dates onto Ana and Tarquin's children, realising that until she'd come up against this conspiracy, she had only really looked at Francesca's children and grandchildren with Richard.

"Did your baby boy really die, Ana?" she wondered as she left the newspaper office and got back into her car. "Damn it! I dropped the ball with you, didn't I! I got distracted by Hector getting murdered, if I remember right, but I should have carried on filling in the blanks for your children too. And when did bloody Tarquin die? Did he live the high life as Luka's side-kick, or did he meet a sticky end once his usefulness had passed?"

For all that the month had turned into March in the time she'd been at Upper Moore, the days were still short, and Cleo soon found herself driving back in the dark, but itching to get into another set of searches. So it was with dismay that she got up the drive to the cottage to see everywhere in darkness. Hurrying to the cottage door, where she could see that a piece of paper had been taped to it, she read, 'Mum had chest pains. Taken her to A&E. Chris'.

"Oh bloody hell, that's all we need!" Cleo groaned, feeling bad that she hadn't been here to help Chris. On the other hand, she was currently well and truly locked out of both the cottage and the big house, because Chris had had the presence of mind to lock up before he went. Worse, she didn't have a mobile number for him, and she knew he wouldn't have hers and neither did Sarah – there'd never been a need to exchange them until now.

Aware that she was also getting very hungry, and that she had no idea which A&E Chris might have gone to – having a choice of either Hereford or Worcester hospitals – she decided that the only thing she could do was go and find somewhere to eat. And so despite being tired from driving around all day, she forced herself back behind the car wheel and headed into Bromyard. Yet before she found a pub doing food, she noticed that the local Co-op supermarket was still open, and decided that it might not hurt to get herself something to take back with her.

As she perused the shelves, she realised that she'd been longing for more fruit for days, and promptly picked up several of the pots of prepared fresh fruits. Sarah was a wonderful cook, but although she cooked plenty of vegetables with every meal, it dawned on Cleo that they'd had meat every night, and quite large portions of it, too. At home she would have eaten vegetarian or fish as much as meat, and suddenly she was longing for something less weighty than beef, pork, or lamb. A salmon sandwich went into her basket, too, and it was all she could do not to start tearing into it before she'd even paid for it, so that by the time she got to the checkout, she had a regular hoard of more healthy food to take back. After all, with the bedroom in the big house being so cold, if she put stuff on the window sill it would probably be colder than in the fridge, and that way, Sarah need never find out that Cleo was supplementing her diet.

In one of the pubs on the high street she found what she was looking for – free wi-fi and a good selection of food – and with relief she tucked herself away in a corner and booted up her laptop once she'd ordered. *Now then*, she thought, *let's start double checking on you, Ana.*

Looking back at the notes that she'd made, she confirmed that she had stopped at the baptism of Ana's son, Bertram in 1840, after which she'd discovered that Hector had been murdered and had focused on what she'd presumed to be the main strand of the family. So, now she turned to the 1841 census, and was dismayed to find the entire family absent from it. That of itself wasn't so strange, because that first census hadn't been quite as all-encompassing as the government might have hoped, and Cleo had come across other instance of families being missed in that one. On the other hand it was odd in a family as prestigious as the Wytcombes, but she wasn't going to zoom in on that detail to the exclusion of everything else just yet.

However, with the 1851 census it was a different matter, but what was alarming was finding not only Luka and Frances in residence at Upper Moore House, but Tarquin there, too. With him were his twenty-year-old son Sydney; then seventeen-year-old Edgar; fourteen-year-old Olivia; and bizarrely, a ten-year-old boy called Clifford.

Where did the rest of Richard's family get to? And where the heck did Ana's Bertram go? Cleo puzzled. Had Ana's eleven-year-old son really died? Then she peered harder at the entry again. This Clifford was definitely listed as Tarquin's son, and there was no sign of a new Mrs Wytcombe to hint at a second family. Anyway, Cleo knew that Tarquin wouldn't have been able to remarry, because you couldn't divorce someone if they were insane in those days, and back when this Clifford had supposedly been born in 1841, Ana had still been very much alive. Had Tarquin messed up by claiming this new 'Clifford' as his own because this was really Bertram under a new name? Had Luka been planning on passing this fake Clifford off as the real one, who'd just been adopted by his half-uncle, thereby ensuring that one of Luka's blood inherited instead of Richard's true heir?

Did you bugger up Luka's plan's, Tarquin? Cleo thought as she devoured an excellent poached salmon, salad, and rice. *What a tangle! Charlotte's Clifford vanishes abroad and a new one appears in his place... Is that what you did?* Cleo wondered. *Did you substitute Ana's Bertram for Charlotte's Clifford? But if so, why? This new Clifford wasn't the one who ended up inheriting Upper Moore, the oldest son Sydney did. So why the subterfuge?*

Sitting back and looking through the files again, Cleo was cross with herself for having allowed herself to get sidetracked so often. If she'd been working from home this would not have happened, and had 'home' been her old flat, she might have decided to go back there for the night now. The thought of the brown-painted temporary flat, however, was far from as appealing, especially as it would be freezing cold after having been empty for so long, and she decided instead that she would stay here – buying as many cups of decaf' and soft drinks as she needed to to justify her holding onto the table – until she could be sure that someone would have got back to Upper Moore to let her in.

The other thing she could do, however, was make that call to Jen, and as the pub got noisier, and with less chance of someone listening in on her conversation, she rang her friend.

"You will not believe what I've been dragged into!" she began, and then told Jen all of what had happened. As she'd hoped, Jen was very interested in the Hecate link.

"Have you thought that the old necklace might have come from some shrine to Hecate?" she asked Cleo.

"No …no I hadn't!"

"But it's the right age for it, surely?"

"Yes, it is."

"And I wouldn't discount that She might feel that you were particularly receptive to her. It's too coincidental that all of this is coming to light just when you turn up. You did say that the family had been looking for decades, didn't you?"

"Err, yes I did."

"And Cleo…? As your friend, I have to say to you, don't dismiss the idea that She might be looking out for you too."

"Me?" Cleo was rather taken aback.

"Yes, you! When was the last time you had any man take any interest in you? You hide yourself away behind your books and charts, but you're an attractive young woman, and I don't think it's coincidence that the one point when Chris really hinted at how he feels about you, was when you two were alone in the house where the necklace is. If someone 'up there' was loosening his inhibitions…"

"Oh heavens, Jen! He's only just split from his wife."

"Cleo! Stop making excuses! He told you he got divorced nearly a year ago. Well that doesn't happen overnight, not even in Canada! And that means that he probably broke up with her well before that. So he's hardly on the rebound anymore, is he? …*Is he*?" Jen insisted into Cleo's silence.

"No, I suppose he isn't."

"There's no 'suppose' about it, my girl! So don't you go putting him off just because you don't think you deserve him, or any rubbish like that."

"No, Jen."

"No, and you remember that. Repeat after me: I am worth it, I *am* enough!"

"I am worth it, I *am* enough."

"Good, now go and solve this mystery! And come and tell me all about it when you've done …and bring Chris with you!"

Ending the call, Cleo hoped she hadn't gone as scarlet as she felt. Jen had been telling her for ages that there was a special man heading her way, but she'd never dared to believe it. But Jen was right about something else, too: Cleo had to sort out this mystery, and with new resolution she decided that tomorrow, providing she could get into the big house, she would go and do a proper search of the places where she had felt Hugh's presence the most. For one of the things Jen had agreed with her about was that Hugh wanted this story of his to be found and told, and that whatever it was, it was even more than what Cleo had found so far.

Chapter 19

When she got back to Upper Moore, Cleo was much relieved to see Sarah's car there. Had that not been the case, then she might well have had to drive back to what she couldn't help but think of as the 'brown flat', or spend the night in her car – neither of which was good. The cottage was unlocked, however, and on the kitchen table was a note from Chris.

Mum's okay, he wrote, *had me worried but it's nothing serious. Will tell you all tomorrow. Too beat to sit up for you – sorry! See you in the morning, Chris xxx*

It was an instant relief to know that there was nothing drastically wrong with Sarah, and for a moment Cleo debated stopping in the cottage for the night. What made her pause was not knowing whether Chris had had any chance to clear the air on her behalf before disaster had struck, and the last thing she wanted was to get up to some confrontation over breakfast. But on top of that, she was feeling a strong pull to get back up to the top floor of the big house. The cottage was cold, anyway, with the heating having been off all day, and so it wouldn't make a lot of difference to her going up to the cold room in the other building.

Leaving Chris a reply of: *Glad Sarah is fine. Didn't want to wake you so went back to other room. Whoever gets up first makes the coffee ☺!* she grabbed the keys for the main house and made her way over there.

She took a hot drink up with her, and then settled into the bed once more, glad of being able to take her business suit off, and wrap herself in her fleece and comfy pyjamas. Nor did it take long for her to drift off to sleep, snuggled under the warm eiderdown.

Once more her dream self was looking in on the room as it had been a hundred years ago. Yet this time Hugh was moving fretfully about the room on his crutches, a worried frown on his face. He seemed to be looking for something, for he went first to the big old wardrobe and then the chest of drawers, but each time stopping in front of them to stare and then shaking his head.

A young woman came into the room, saying to him, "Oh Hugh, can you not settle?"

"No. …Oh Verity, I know this is a terrible thing to say about our brother, but I don't trust him."

"Is this about what you found in Verona?"

"Yes it is. We are not the rightful heirs to Upper Moore, Ve, we truly aren't, and I do not believe what Bertie says, that if there had been members of the proper heirs left that they would have come forward. I think after what I read that they were in fear of their lives if they came back."

"You're being very mysterious, Hugh. Why won't you let Emilia and me read these letters? We could lend our support to you if we understood."

Hugh's expression of pain got deeper, but Cleo didn't think that it had anything to do with his wound, and his next words proved it.

"Bless you both, Ve, but I won't put you in danger by telling you."

"Oh come now, Hugh, you can't think that Bertie would do anything to us …do you? …Oh Hugh, no! No! Bertie is many things, and some not good at all, but he would never do anything to Emilia or me."

"Really?" Hugh was looking at her with sad eyes. "Ve, I've started asking Mrs Murray to start bringing me up just light meals away from the main family dining times. I did it because I was

starting to get the most fearful cramps in my belly, and I thought I was just not used to rich food anymore. I never thought anything of it when I asked her, but that night Bertie came up to me with a plateful from the main table, and it suddenly occurred to me to wonder why he would put himself out like that? He's normally the first to demand that the servants do the running around. And then he went into a fearful rage when I told him I'd already eaten, calling me an ingrate and several other terrible things which I won't repeat to you.

"Yet the strangest thing was that within a day my pains had stopped and so had the blood in my …err-hmph! Well you get the idea, I'm sure! I had begun to truly fear that I must have got some shrapnel in my belly which hadn't been noticed, what with the way I was covered in blood when they took me into the hospital. And I could only think that it must have suddenly started moving all these months later. But it wouldn't just suddenly stop again, would it? And then for the next couple of days Bertie kept coming up bringing me all sorts of strange things, like chocolates.

"Again, I didn't eat them because I just couldn't face them, not to spite him, you understand, I genuinely couldn't. But then by the third day he started looking at me oddly whenever he came up, and kept asking if I was feeling alright, though not in a nice way. So I thought I'd better get rid of the blasted things — which I'd been hiding under the bed — in case he came a hunting while I was in the bath, or something, so he wouldn't fly into another of his rages when he found his discarded 'gifts'. But the thing was, *Ve*, when I chucked them onto the fire, they burned with a very strange flame. …I…I think he put arsenic or something like it in them!"

"No! No, Hugh, you must be mistaken!" *Verity* declared, backing away from him in horror. "Oh my poor brother, what that terrible war has done to your mind that you could think such a thing!" and she fled from the room.

"And that's why I'm not telling you the rest," Hugh said, easing himself into the chair by the window. "If he'd do that to me, what would he do to you?"

In her dream, Cleo saw him brush away tears as he picked up a large, well-hugged old teddy bear of the vintage kind, and said to it, "I read Great-aunt Sophia's letters to Claudio and Cinzia. I know what she thought had happened to Great-aunt Charlotte and Great-aunt Ana, and why she left England. There's too much of Filip Kovač's blood running through Bertie's veins, and I just pray it never comes out in mine. If they could be locked up as insane, then Bertie might try to paint you two as the same, with madness being in the women of the family. God preserve me, I couldn't live with myself if I thought I'd brought that taint down on you and your children."

The dream faded, and if Cleo dreamed of anything else that night she certainly didn't remember it in the morning, but the dream of Hugh was as clear as if she'd been standing in the room with him. And if he'd been that certain that Bertie was trying to murder him, then what he'd been doing was looking for somewhere to hide things so that Emilia and Verity wouldn't stumble across them, as well as keeping the evidence safe. Nor could Cleo dismiss what she had witnessed as a product of her own imagination. However crazy anyone else would think her, she was sure she'd been given a glimpse of the past by Hecate, though how she was going to explain that to Chris rather worried her.

Deciding that she was being rather foolish hiding away up in the attic, so to speak, she hurriedly dressed and went downstairs, walking in through the kitchen door of the cottage just as Chris came in by the other door from the hall. The coffee machine was gurgling away to itself, making him say,

"I found your note. Coffee is on its way!"

"Wonderful! You've really been spoiling me with this, you know. I nearly spat out my cupful from the machine, yesterday – heavens, it was dreadful!" and they both laughed. "So come on, what's happened to your mum?"

Chris grimaced. "Oh, man! You'd only just gone when I caught her rubbing her arms. I asked her what was wrong, and then she said she had pains all up her upper arms and in her chest. God, Cleo, it was a wonder *I* didn't have a heart-attack! I got her into that car so fast her feet barely touched the ground, and I sure hope I didn't pass any of those speed cameras, because I'm going to be picking up traffic fines like confetti the speed I went.

"Well we got to the A&E department at Worcester – 'cause I didn't realise that there was one at Hereford too, having at least seen the signs to the Worcester one the other day when we went on the motorway. I got Mum inside and told the doctors what I feared, and to be fair, they were amazing. They ran all sorts of tests, but decided that it definitely *wasn't* a heart-attack.

"So then the head nurse starts asking me if Mum's been under any stress lately, and I'm like, 'where the hell do you want me to start?' I managed to get her away from Mum, and then told her about Dad, but also about Aiden and what you thought was going on. So top marks to you, Cleo, because the doctors agreed with you. And then I remembered that the day before, while you were sleuthing and Mum and I were cleaning, I kept turning around and finding her shifting heavy furniture on her own. I kept saying to her, 'Mum, ask me to move that,' but you know what she's like."

"Oh I'm getting there," Cleo agreed, coming to give him a hug. "So was it a combination of stress and pulled muscles?"

"You got it." Now, though, he went and made sure that the door through to the hall and staircase was shut before continuing much more softly. "They wanted to give her anti-depressants and some gentle tranquillisers. I told them, 'For God's sake don't tell her what they are! If you do, she won't take them and they'll go in the garbage as soon as she gets home.' …Oh man," he groaned, "you know she told me she did that when the GP prescribed her some when Dad first had his accident, which worried me sick back then when I was thousands of miles away. I used to plead with her on the phone to take them. 'Cause they were just to help her, but she wouldn't have it – too much of 'what will I say to the folks at Church?' to which I said to hell with them, which didn't help, either. So I told the doctors this time what she'd done."

Cleo could see his exasperation over this. Sometimes Sarah was her own worst enemy when it came to people trying to help her. "So what did they do?"

"They were great! They told Mum that the one lot of pills are just to help her muscles relax – which apparently isn't a total lie, because it is one of the additional effects of the anti-depressants. They said it would help stop the cramping, but that she must take it easy for a day or two. Then the other pills they said were to ease the other side effects, and the one nurse was great at being not very specific, but they're really to help her sleep." He heaved a sigh of relief. "This is the first night she hasn't woke me up prowling around, so I know they've kicked in. And as I said to the nurses, Mum can barely work the laptop enough to Skype me after I set it all up for her, so there's no chance she'll do an internet search for what the pills are – anyway, I've got them, so she can't check on the name!"

"What a day," Cleo sympathised.

"Sure was. How was yours? …Sorry, by the way, that it never occurred to me that we'd locked you out until we got back."

"Heavens! Don't be silly, you had more important things to worry about than me." Then the odd look that Chris gave her made her think that maybe Jen's intuition hadn't been so wrong after all. Did he think her important?

Covering her confusion by bringing Chris up to date while they had breakfast, it was only when she got to her 'dream' that she became more reticent. "Look, Chris, please don't think me some weirdo, but I don't just think that I made this up. It was so vivid. I could smell the coal from the fire — you know, that really distinctive smell proper coal has when it first starts to burn. And I could *feel* that it was warm! I mean, summertime warm, not just because the fire was on. The big window was open at the top to let some fresh air in for him, and I think they only had the fire lit because he was so frail by then and those cavernous rooms so bloody cold. I could smell mothballs as well. I haven't smelt mothballs up in that room the whole time I've been here, so it wasn't that triggering my subconscious."

"I believe you."

"Wha...? Really?"

Chris laughed. "Don't look so shocked. I believe you. My one buddy in Canada has a grandma who is full Anishinaabe Indian, and the tales he's told me didn't even come close to preparing me for meeting her. She couldn't have known some of the stuff that she told me details of. For instance she described this cottage, and Tony had never even seen a photo of it to be able to tell her, and I know that because I had to take one of it for him after that when I came back home for a visit, to prove to him what it was like. So, yes, I believe you. Whether it's this Hecate, or you're picking up on some vibe left in the house, I don't know, but I think you definitely tuned into something up there."

Cleo relief was clear, and so he now asked, "So what's first today? Do we search or do you do those family trees?"

"I'll go and bring my stuff down here so that we can keep an eye on your mum," Cleo decided. "I know anti-depressants can have some really unpleasant side-effects because I just can't take them."

"You?"

Cleo gave him a wan smile. "I was fourteen when we lost Dad. And my mother started hunting for a replacement long before I'd finished grieving for him. It meant I kept a lot of stuff bottled up, and it all came out a few years later. But the anti-depressants were all wrong for me. I became almost non-functional and so physically sick I couldn't keep any food in me. So I weaned myself off them and went down the alternative route. It probably took me longer to get right, but it was the better, healthier path for me. On the other hand, a friend of mine had her own issues, and they were an absolute miracle drug for her, so it just depends on your mum. Hopefully they'll work for her."

Setting up on the kitchen table once more, Cleo pulled up the blank document for family trees to show him. "I can expand this out as far as is needed, but for now I want to try and get to grips with the major strands of the family, so I'll do you smaller ones by hand for now." She quickly filled in a basic tree. "So here is Richard and Francesca's tree."

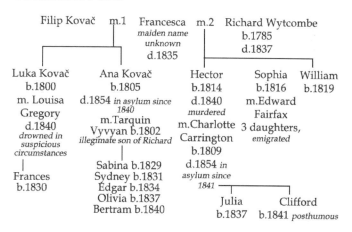

Chris scrutinised the tree. "What happened to William, their youngest one?"

"I have no idea. He vanished."

"And you said that Julia and Clifford got taken abroad by Edward Fairfax?"

"Yes, and that's the last I can find of them. But I don't know where Bertram went to, either; or whether Tarquin was trying to pass Bertram off as Clifford, though I can't for the life of me work out why."

Chris nodded thoughtfully. "You'd have to have assumed that William was well out of the way to go to all that trouble, wouldn't you? Because when Hector died, nobody could have known for sure that Charlotte would have a son, so William would have been the automatic heir. It makes you think that there was some serious plotting going on. Have you looked to see if William died just before 1840?"

"Oh yes, and that's what I meant about him vanishing from the records – nothing. And you're right, I think that maybe they miscalculated somewhere along the line. I don't think that they could have done much until Richard died, so things couldn't be planned before late 1838, even if the dreadful Luka had secretly schemed on his own. To me, the death of poor Louisa – you remember, the poor girl Luka married – conveniently just before Hector, speaks of that plan starting to be put into play."

"Agreed, that's suspicious to me, too."

"But also, there wouldn't have been any point in even going that far if Luka and Tarquin thought that William was still on the scene by then, wouldn't you agree? Let's face it, with the fashions of the day, they may not have been aware that Charlotte was even pregnant. Because if you do the maths, Clifford was born on the eighth of February, which means that he was conceived somewhere around the May of 1840, and Charlotte probably didn't start to show until well into the autumn. She might not have said anything to anyone until Hector was killed, and she knew she'd be on her own with the child.

"So to take the events in order, Richard dies on the ninth of December 1838. That means that nothing much was going to happen before the January of 1839 at the earliest, and you have to allow for the legal system of the day grinding exceedingly slowly for checking that there were no other heirs, or whatever they might have looked for – they hardly had internet searches in those days! Also, the official handing over of the estate to Hector probably wouldn't have happened much before the Easter of 1839, but that would have been the point when Luka and Tarquin start feeling they've been short-changed in the inheritance stakes."

Chris agreed with a thoughtful, "I think that's pretty much a given, then."

"Then wouldn't you know it, Louisa throws herself into the River Usk in December of 1839. That shifts her out of the way. I have the awful feeling that she stumbled across something she shouldn't have, you know, at which point she became a liability to Luka. But I don't think at that point Luka and Tarquin realised that they'd have to get rid of Charlotte too, or at least not permanently. So I think she may have managed to keep her pregnancy quiet from them at least that far. They probably planned to marry her off to some crony of theirs, because that was acceptable in those days, and she wouldn't have expected to run the estate herself. Possibly Luka was even going to marry her himself to legitimise his position here, because he could have as a widower by then."

"So when did you say that Hector died?"

"Sixth of August 1840."

"Holy crap! Poor old Hector! His last fling with Charlotte might well have been when he fathered Clifford!

But what a facer for the terrible twosome, too! They just think they've got shot of the remaining legitimate heir, and then as if from the grave, Hector goes and scuppers their plans by fathering a son. ...So you said Charlotte was put in the asylum only a month or so after Clifford was born?"

"That's right."

"And they're missing from the 1841 census?"

"Yes, and that's odd if we're talking about the family of a big house like this. I mean you lose families who were in the industrial slums of Birmingham, for instance, but the more I think about it, the odder it is that they aren't recorded here."

She went back to her computer and found the 1841 census for the area. "How odd, all the servants are listed, but none of the family. I wonder if they told the census takers that the family was away somewhere?"

"Well they couldn't actually have been at some friend's house," Chris pointed out, "because they'd have been listed as guests there, wouldn't they?"

Cleo nodded. "Oh yes, and again, especially in that sort of prestigious house. ...Do you know, I'm beginning to think that they just scarpered for the day? Threatened the servants with God knows what – because they must have known what Luka was like by then, and probably been scared stiff of him – and then returned when the coast was clear."

"That sounds feasible. After all, this is fairly rolling countryside around here. There must have been dips and hollows where they could pull in a carriage out of sight if you knew the area well." Chris stared out of the window as if seeing across the parkland to some hideaway. "And when does Ana vanish, did you say?"

"Harder to say precisely, but Bertram, her youngest child was born in April 1840, and christened here, so she must have still been here then. I could only get a date of

December 1840 for her being incarcerated at Abergavenny Asylum, but I reckon that soon after Bertram's christening she might have learned that Charlotte was pregnant. I mean, they would have talked, wouldn't they? Two young mothers in the same house, who'd both had daughters in 1837 – they would have had a lot in common. So if Ana got wind of her brother and her husband plotting to do some harm to Charlotte, she might just have tried to warn her sister-in-law."

Chris whistled softly, "And never knowing that those bastards were planning on substituting her son for Charlotte's to make sure that a child with Kovač's blood inherited Upper Moore." He looked at the family tree again. "When does Luka Kovač die?"

With a groan at another point missed, Cleo again tapped into the archives and shortly came up with some worrying information.

"I can't quite believe this," she told Chris. "Bloody Kovač! Talk about the Devil looking after his own! He's in the 1861, the 1871, and the 1881 censuses, living like some malevolent spider right here at Upper Moore. He only dies in late 1881 at the ripe old age of eight-one years old. Sodding hell, Chris! He lived long enough that even *Bertie* would have known him while a toddler!"

Chapter 20

"Bertie?" Chris exclaimed. "Are you sure? I mean he was way after Luka!"

"Positive," Cleo replied. "Don't forget that Bertie was born in 1878, so he'd have been three years old when Luka died in October 1881. That's certainly old enough for him to have some kind of memory of Luka."

Chris shivered. "That's just made me go all goose-bumpy. Okay, then, what happened to his partner in crime, Tarquin?"

"Already ahead of you," Cleo said, typing furiously into the searches. "...God! Tarquin died in September 1851. That's right after he must have mucked up the census return!"

"Hell! Luka was bloody ruthless in getting rid of anyone who stood in his way, wasn't he?"

"Very!"

"Do we know how Tarquin died?"

Cleo shook her head even as she continued typing. "No, but I'm going to request his death certificate and see if it's on there. Luka was being very cunning, so I think it might have been in such a way which could have been covered as an accident. It's only when you start putting the whole picture together that it starts looking so bloody suspicious. ...And of course at the time, none of the family could have anticipated what was going to come next and so soon."

"Would Luka be on any of those family photographs I was showing you?"

"He might be. Family portraits really got going in the 1860s, and for a wealthy family like this it wouldn't have been beyond them to afford. Even quite humble families start having formal photos taken for major events within his lifetime."

"I'll go and fetch them," Chris volunteered and got up. "Oh, by the way, what happened to Luka's daughter?"

"Frances? She's another one I'm about to chase up, because up until yesterday I didn't think she'd be significant. I'm almost dreading now what I'm going to find."

As Chris disappeared off to the library to reclaim the albums, Cleo began searching for Frances, and it wasn't long before she came to her. In 1855 Frances married a man called Algernon Franks, and for a short while Cleo dared to hope that she had escaped the clutches of her father, for in the 1861 census she found Frances and Algernon with a little boy called Godfrey, who was three, and another little boy, Mortimer, aged six months. But it was Chris coming back in and looking over her shoulder who made the chilling connection.

"Mortimer Franks? He's the guy in the photo albums!"

Cleo buried her head in her hands. "Oh no, not another kid who Luka got his filthy paws on!"

"Luka?"

"Mortimer was Frances' son."

"Jeez! I didn't see that one coming."

"No, neither did I."

"So what happened to them?" Chris asked, dumping the albums on the table and shifting his chair around so that he could watch as Cleo typed.

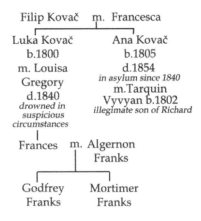

Filip Kovač m. Francesca

Luka Kovač
b.1800
m. Louisa
Gregory
d.1840
drowned in
suspicious
circumstances

Ana Kovač
b.1805
d.1854
in asylum since 1840
m.Tarquin
Vyvyan b.1802
illegimate son of Richard

Frances m. Algernon
Franks

Godfrey
Franks

Mortimer
Franks

She began checking for the different names and found that Frances and Algernon, along with Godfrey, all died in 1864, which looked very much as though something like influenza or pneumonia had gone though the family, as they died within weeks of one another. At least they had taken themselves well away from Upper Moore, for they'd been living in Ledbury at the time, and so it seemed unlikely that this set of deaths could be pinned on Luka.

"What rotten luck for the poor kid to have had to come back here, though," Chris sympathised. "I mean, you can see that it would make sense, because if nothing else there were servants here to look after him, given that he would only have been four or five years old."

Cleo was hurriedly scanning through her notes, adding, "And I think you might be right about that – the servant bit, I mean. There are no children of a similar age here …no, hang on, that can't be right."

"What can't?"

She brought up the census for 1861. "Look here. There's a Sydney Wytcombe, aged seven in the house, but I'm sure I found Sydney as the father of Bertie."

"So?"

"Well if Bertie – or Albert as he appears in the official records – was born in 1878, then how can *this* Sydney be his father?" She began hurriedly sketching out a new tree for Chris.

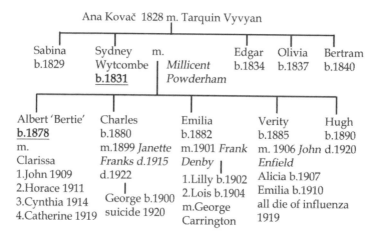

Ana Kovač 1828 m. Tarquin Vyvyan

| Sabina b.1829 | Sydney Wytcombe **b.1831** m. *Millicent Powderham* | Edgar b.1834 | Olivia b.1837 | Bertram b.1840 |

| Albert 'Bertie' **b.1878** m. Clarissa 1.John 1909 2.Horace 1911 3.Cynthia 1914 4.Catherine 1919 | Charles b.1880 m.1899 *Janette Franks d.1915* d.1922 George b.1900 suicide 1920 | Emilia b.1882 m.1901 *Frank Denby* 1.Lilly b.1902 2.Lois b.1904 m.George Carrington | Verity b.1885 m. 1906 *John Enfield* Alicia b.1907 Emilia b.1910 all die of influenza 1919 | Hugh b.1890 d.1920 |

"Do you see? Ana's Sydney was born in 1831, which would have made him forty-seven at the time of Albert/Bertie's birth. Now that's not impossible for him fathering a child by any means. But do you honestly think that as the male heir – as Luka would have perceived him – that Ana's Sydney would have been allowed to wait until his forties to start knocking out heirs to the place?"

"Oh, I see what you mean. No, Luka would have been dragging him down the aisle with some lass as soon as he could, wouldn't he?"

"So that means that I've either missed an earlier marriage for Ana's Sydney, whose family didn't survive – which is always possible given the way infectious diseases could rip through a family – or there's a new member of the family who I haven't linked in yet." She sat back and thought hard while Chris topped up the coffees. "You know it's downright common for sons to be named after their fathers. I wonder if this is the case here?"

However, Chris had a different idea, flipping open the albums. "We might find a clue in here, you know. I was only showing you the later one to find Hugh. But this is an earlier family album. Let's see who is in here."

This time they began from the back of the album, finding more photos of the Sydney who had appeared in the group photograph in 1902, and rapidly tracking him back to being a boy in the 1860s.

"I don't like the way that that older man has him pulled towards him, do you?" Chris said, wrinkling his nose in distaste. "Do you think that could be Luka?"

The very much older man was in stark contrast to the already podgy boy, saturnine in appearance and staring back out of the page at them with a sharp-eyed glare. There was no smile for the camera here, and although Cleo knew that back in that time few people did smile for the camera because of the time it took to get an image, nonetheless he still looked particularly stern. But where was the boy's father or mother? In none of the photos did anyone appear who looked vaguely as though they might be his parents.

Taking a grateful swig of the coffee and accepting a chocolate biscuit from Chris, who had raided the cupboards and brought a tin over, Cleo decided,

"We've got to marry up these two lines of the Wytcombes. We've got Richard's line coming forwards, and Hugh and Bertie's line going back, but somewhere in the middle of the nineteenth century we've got a big hole. I'm going to be a stickler over this, Chris. I'm going to trace backwards, because I'm damned sure that in all of this I've missed something."

"Who are you going to start with?"

Cleo returned to her own records. "I'm going to the Sydney Wytcombe who married Millicent Powderham, because we know for definite that he's the father of Bertie and Hugh." She brought up the record image that she'd saved on her laptop. "Here we go, this is where I got to. …Ah, and here's where I think I jumped the gun a bit. I assumed that the Sydney Wytcombe who I found registered as Charles' father at his marriage, must have been Ana's son. …Oh heck! That's what's been bugging me for days. Charles – that's Hugh and Bertie's brother I'm talking about – married a Janette Franks, and *her* father was *Mortimer* Franks!"

Chris stared at her open-mouthed, too stunned to speak for a second. "You mean the Mortimer Franks we found as the surviving son of Frances and what's-his-name?"

"Algernon Franks? Yes! That little boy who had to come back to live here, is the father of Janette who married back into the family."

"Draw me a tree!"

Cleo rapidly sketched out the connection.

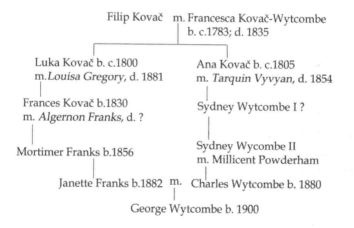

"Shit!" Chris breathed. "Your dream was right, Cleo, it was an unnatural connection. If Mortimer was Luka's grandson, then that makes Janette his great-grand-daughter, and Charles was Ana's what…?"

"…Great-grand-son, if you accept that there's another generation in there. Otherwise he's her grandson."

"Jeez! And Luka and Ana were full siblings, weren't they!"

"Yes. …Yuk! It's not exactly incest, but it's pretty bloody close, and in this instance I can begin to see why Bertie was so outraged. Charles and Janette's son might always have been a bit genetically entangled, if you get what I mean, a bit fragile or what we'd class these days as mentally disabled, though I don't think he could have had any physical disabilities because of going into the army. If he could hold it together enough to pass being called up, even merely being in the army could have been too brutal for him to cope with – he wouldn't have had to survive the trenches like his Uncle Hugh did, for him to have been horrifically stressed. And if Bertie then callously told him that he was what, even politely, would have been called inbred…"

"…Then you can see why the poor sod topped himself," Chris concluded. "Bloody hell, Bertie really was being damned cruel, wasn't he? Because even if he hadn't known earlier of how he and Charles connected to Janette, he must have known what sort of boy Charles was."

Cleo gave another shiver. This was nothing like anything she'd ever researched before. The way these family lines kept coming back to one another was both creepy and rather nauseating. But she gave herself a mental shake and refocused.

"Okay, revolting though this all is, let's see if we can find a bit more about the Sydney who was Bertie, Charles and Hugh's father. …Here we go, this looks promising.

Sydney Wytcombe and Millicent married in 1874, which might mean that Millicent lost a child before Bertie, because four years without a kid when she then has a run of them is a bit odd. But that's by-the-by, because that child never appears anywhere. So let's look at the fathers at the wedding… Oh, and here we go, Sydney's father is another Sydney. *Woo-hoo*! Got him!"

"But look at the witnesses," Chris said in dismay. "Can you believe it? Bloody Luka again! You were right when you called him a spider, Cleo. He's like bloody Shelob with his webs!"

"And our new Sydney is already deceased at the time of his son's wedding. That gives me something to work with. The Sydney who is getting married must have been born in 1854 if he's twenty at the time of the wedding, so let's search for him then. …Uh-oh! This is why we didn't see him in the parish register here. Sydney was baptised at St Helen's in Worcester, not here, and his parents are Sydney and…" she had to peer at the digital image and zoom in on it, "…Fiametta? Blimey! She doesn't sound local, does she? Let's see if we can find a marriage."

It was a harder search, and had it not been for the bride's rare name they might not have found them, but in London early in 1855 they found Lieut. Sydney Wytcombe, Royal Welch Fusiliers marrying Fiametta Marinelli. Yet to Cleo's surprise, when she came back to the list of results, not only did she realise that this marriage must have been only a formalisation of a marriage which had already taken place in Italy – because baby Sydney was listed as the son of a married couple – but Fiametta then married again in 1856 to Edgar Wytcombe!

"She married his brother?" Chris exclaimed. "Isn't that illegal?"

"Not if his brother was dead. And… Yes, here you are, the Royal Welch Fusiliers served in the Crimean War.

Well that would explain why I didn't find any death for that Sydney. He's probably in an unmarked grave in Russia, or what is now the Ukraine." She did more searches for Edgar. "And now Edgar disappears along with Fiametta. He's not in the 1861 census at all, and neither is she. I wonder if they went back to her family, wherever they were? It would make sense. And could he be the Edgar whose descendent would have inherited this place when Archie died – if he'd lived?

"But to come back to the family tree, I don't think I'm stretching it too far to think that the reason why Sydney senior and Fiametta had a second wedding in England was so that they could leave the country with their little boy, Sydney. Or am I?"

"Could Luka have been blocking that? Would he have legal grounds?"

"I don't know about legal grounds, but I reckon he could have been making it very difficult for them. Let's face it, little Sydney ends up staying here despite his mother leaving, and you can't imagine she left him willingly. You'd expect her and Edgar to be moving heaven and earth to get the child away with them. So it says everything for Luka's grip on things that they failed. God, it's chilling isn't it, that Sydney II was totally under Luka's thrall – and he lived on into the twentieth century. So did he try to mould Bertie in Luka's form as well? He was around for long enough."

Then she had to swallow hard as she realised, "Oh, hell! Look at the date, Chris! Sydney II arrives just after Tarquin dies! If Sydney I and Edgar and their sisters had the slightest inkling that Luka had killed Tarquin, then no wonder the family was scattering to the four winds!"

Chris looked at the family trees again. "What about Sabina and Olivia? Where do they get to?"

Sabina was soon found to have died in 1847, so given her age of eighteen, it seemed likely that she had died in childbirth rather than of a childhood illness – tragic, but not something they could lay at Luka's door. And that also explained why she hadn't shown up on the 1851 census. Yet it took Cleo expanding the search to the whole of the UK, not just England, before she found Olivia, for she and her husband, Henry Thompson, had run away to Gretna to get married when she was just eighteen.

Cleo puffed at that. "Wow, you can't help thinking that that was a girl on the run. Her oldest sister was dead – so no refuge there – and you have to think that Sydney I was already in the army by then. This was in 1855, so did she hear of Ana and Charlotte's deaths? Did someone send her a newspaper cutting? And since Edgar wasn't at Upper Moore back at the 1851 census, he possibly wasn't around either. Elopement was the one way she could have avoided having to get parental permission since she was under twenty-one, and she must have known beyond a doubt that Luka would have made sure that never happened unless it was to someone who would benefit him. She must have been determined to get out of this house before she met a sticky end."

"Where did they live?" Chris wondered.

"Hang on… Looks like Pershore. Yes, Henry's family were farmers there. It's close enough that she might have met him through mutual friends, but it took her far enough away that she wouldn't have seen her family more than a couple of times a year, in all probability."

"Lucky girl, she made it out alive." Chris was once again looking at the family trees Cleo had roughed out. "Okay, so if we've sorted Bertie and Hugh's grandparents' generation out, what about the one in between them? Who else was there besides the Sydney who married Millicent? He's a generation on beyond where we thought he'd be now, and we've got an almost empty line in the tree beside him. What about his siblings or cousins?"

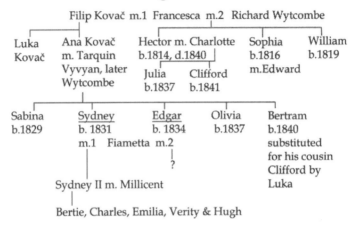

Cleo could only shrug. "Unless we get incredibly lucky, I doubt we'll find anything on the children Edgar and Fiametta had. The trouble with tracing people in Italy is that you keep running up against the brick wall of the Vatican – and they don't play nicely with anyone, unfortunately, when it comes to accessing their records. I shall do my best with Olivia, but I haven't looked yet."

"What about the fake Clifford? What does he do?"

"Not a lot, as far as I can tell. He seems to be living at Upper Moore, but in the censuses he's always down as single, and as a profession he's calling himself a scholar. It might be that he was an academic at one of the universities, but he always makes sure that he's back at Upper Moore when the census comes around. That might be Luka stamping his foot again, of course, especially if he was originally counting on sliding 'Clifford' in as his heir. And even if Luka was getting on a bit to go chasing around the country in the later years, he probably had

Mortimer Franks and then Sydney II well trained up as his foot soldiers by then."

"And how long does 'Clifford' live for?"

"As best I can tell – in other words, providing I've got the right Clifford Wytcombe, though I've not found another one – he lasts right up until 1903, dying at the age of sixty-three here at Upper Moore, but he must have been cremated for us to not find him amongst the burial records. Nary a sign of him marrying, or ever having children, and that includes the six census returns he appears in. He's always down the bottom of the list, defined by his relationship to the main householder at the time – even though in 1891 and 1901 that's his nephew Sydney – never as a head in his own right. Poor bloke, it sounds as though he took refuge in his books and never came out."

Chris sat back, stroking his chin thoughtfully. "Okay, so we've got the English family as far as they go. ...Do you know what's bugging me? That Italian connection via Fiametta. Am I presuming too much to think that maybe she was connected to Francesca's family in some way? And why do the family over here run east whenever trouble strikes? It takes until the twentieth century before folks start heading for the States or Australia."

"Not exactly. Don't forget Sophia and Edward, they leave for the States earlier. But I see what you mean. This family looks back into Europe for security; few of them are obviously making new lives in the New World."

"I think we've got to start doing a detailed search of the house for whatever Hugh found," Chris decided. "I'll go and make sure Mum's woken up and get her some brunch, then as long as she's okay, you and I will go and start shredding the big house."

Sarah turned out to have woken up and was watching her portable TV in her bedroom. She was feeling groggy, but had luckily avoided the dreadful side-effects that Cleo had had. Chris thought she was slightly woozy mainly because she had finally stopped running on adrenalin and her body had been forced to relax. And so once they'd got her downstairs and tucked up in front of the TV with a large plate of bacon sandwiches and a pot of tea by her side, Cleo and Chris were free to go exploring.

Cleo was all for them heading up to the top floor, for she was convinced by now that Hugh had regarded anywhere else as compromised. However Chris hadn't forgotten Hugh's medals.

"They have to be somewhere in the library," he said firmly. "We're talking about something Archie would have hidden from Herself, not anything before then. Have you searched inside the desks?"

Admitting that she hadn't, beyond making sure that no major stashes of documents were in the drawers, Cleo agreed to start there. All three of the desks were old and beautifully made pieces of furniture, and not for the first time Cleo wished she could have even one of them.

"My IKEA flat-pack desk isn't a patch on these," she told Chris wistfully, as they went to the first one by the French windows. "Burl walnut, no less – such a pretty wood. Just look at the natural patterns in the grain," and she ran her hand lovingly over the top. When she looked up, Chris was giving her another of those odd looks, as though he was halfway to offering her it or something of a similar nature.

"Chris? Are you okay?"

He heaved a sigh. "It just seems so bloody unfair that you and I, who would love and cherish this old place and everything in it, aren't the ones who are going to have the looking after of it." The way he said 'you and I' made it sound very much as though he was thinking of them as a couple already, and Cleo had to turn to the desk again to cover her confusion.

She therefore began to run her fingers across the underside of the desk top, and then pulling the top drawers out to be able to feel those parts of the top too.

"Do you want me to lift the other drawers out?" Chris offered.

"It might help," Cleo agreed. "Certainly the top two on either side, please, even if the big bottom ones are too heavy to lift." Archie seemed to have had a morbid fear of running out of stationery, for the bottom drawers had packets of printer paper, printer cartridges, and packs of envelopes and pens, most of which had never even been opened.

Once Chris had lifted the top two of three out on the left side, Cleo knelt down and began examining the inner depths of the desk, while he moved the two drawers on the right. Apart from some pieces of paper, which had obviously fallen out of the upper drawers but which were of no significance, there was nothing there. But on the right-hand side the top drawer was shorter, so that it didn't go as far back as the others.

"Hello! What have we got here?" Cleo murmured, sitting down on the carpet so that she could angle herself to see better. Chris passed her a torch and she shone it into the gloomy depths, exclaiming, "There's a little hidden drawer back here!"

Carefully pulling it out, it turned out to be where Archie had hidden not only Hugh's medals, but a couple of very old keys, too.

"Now what on earth do these fit?" Chris wondered, turning them over in his hands.

"I'd say a cupboard or drawer. They're not big enough to be a normal door key." Cleo looked around her at the library. "How intriguing. Looking at the state of these, and the box that the medals are in, Archie must have looked at them relatively recently. That plastic box the medals are in is positively modern. So what was he hiding and why?"

They put both the keys and the medals on the desk and went to explore the other desks, but neither of them had any secrets to give up, and Chris was starting to say that they'd just had beginner's luck in finding the medals. But Cleo had no doubts.

"Archie was hiding something and it was recently, so who is the obvious person he would be doing that from, eh? It certainly wasn't your mum or his first wife. It can only be something he didn't want the gorgon he was latterly married to to find. Come on Chris, we've got to do this for his sake! You start at that side of the door, and I'll start at the other. Look along all of the bookcases for something that might just be a keyhole. Oh, and I don't mean a nice neat little metal plate, either. Just a hole in the wood where one of those keys might fit in."

"Heavens, woman, you're like a bloodhound on the trail!" he teased, but went to do as he was told.

It was a good job that there were library steps at both ends of the room, so that they weren't having to keep swopping a ladder to reach the upper shelves, and Cleo was working faster than Chris because of knowing more what she was looking for. So it was after she had already gone along the long stretch of wall which she knew backed onto the two bathrooms, and was at the turn which backed onto the older staircase, that she found something promising. The only trouble was that she couldn't see how anything would open. It was right in the angle of the wall.

With great care, she began taking books off the shelves on either side, only clearing the top three shelves of the cases, for the potential opening was one shelf down from the topmost one, and she had the suspicion that this wouldn't be the whole case opening up.

"What *are* you doing?" Chris' voice came from behind her, as she put the last of the books at her feet on the wooden steps, and began tapping at the wood of the shelves themselves.

"This hole," Cleo said, pointing to something which could have been mistaken for the kind of hole left when a knot fell out of the wood. "It's right in the corner, so I haven't dared to try and put one of the keys in to turn it, in case I jammed the mechanism by forcing it to try and move the books as well."

Chris dashed back to the table and brought the two keys to her. "Here you go, try them. See what happens."

Shining her torch into the hole to see where the metal was, Cleo very gently inserted the first of the keys, but that clearly wasn't a fit. Undeterred, she tried the second one, and was rewarded with it sliding in perfectly and turning easily with a soft click. As it did so, one of the uprights on the corner of the bookcase popped half an inch to the side, and when Cleo gently pulled it, it swung open to reveal itself as a proper little door masquerading as part of the corner side of the bookcase. Without having the books off the shelf it had been impossible to tell what it was, but now Cleo could see that within the angle of the two built in ceiling-to-floor cases, there was a cupboard space.

Chris whistled. "Well I'm damned! Is there anything in there?"

Cleo reached inside and pulled out a whole pile of things, but most unexpected was a very modern looking document, which when opened turned out to be a new will made by Archie.

"Holy crap!" Chris gulped. "He's disinherited Herself of everything in favour of Mum!"

"And it'll stand up, too," Cleo declared with an excited high-five with him. "Look at the witnesses! None of them involved with this estate at all. I wonder why he went to a solicitor in Worcester rather than his own chaps in Bromyard? Could it be that he knew that Mrs W would contest this, and he wanted a big firm who would be able to stand up to any London lawyers she brought in?"

"What do I do?" Chris asked, visibly shaken.

"Get in your mum's car and go into Worcester with a copy of Archie's death certificate, *now!*" she told him. "I daren't be the one to do it. Not when I'm supposed to be working in the gorgon's favour. And anyway, you might need my testimony later to say that you found it after discovering the keys. You had a perfect right to go looking if you tell them that Archie had promised you Hugh's medals. They have no monetary value to speak of, and it's the sort of thing a man like Archie would do – promise a war memento to a favourite child of a friend and relative. And from all you've said, you and Archie were close when you were at home during the holidays."

"Yes we were. Dad and Aiden would be off somewhere jumping off cliffs, or whatever, but I used to come up here and chat with Archie – or Uncle Archie as he was to me then."

"Then that's exactly what you tell any solicitor who asks," Cleo said firmly. "Forget that we were hunting for clues as to the family mystery. You just wanted your little pieces to remind you of him, which is as normal as it gets. Go, Chris! Now! Get that will into the hands of the solicitors before anything more can happen! I'll keep an eye on Sarah. You go and make sure that she gets to keep her home!"

Chapter 21

They both went to check up on Sarah, and covered Chris going out on the pretext of needing more milk and bread. Since Sarah was still dozing on and off, she was hardly curious, and so with the promise of popping back in an hour to check on her, Cleo headed back to the house as Chris sped off down the drive.

"Now what have we got here?" she mused, as she spread the other documents from the hidden cupboard out on the nearest desk. "And if one key fitted this cupboard, what does the other one fit?"

Forcing herself not to get engrossed in the papers, but nonetheless noticing that one bundle seemed to include letters, she scanned the rest of the library. Could there be another cupboard like this one? Somehow she didn't think it would be in here, not least because once one hiding place had been found, then the other one would give up its secrets too easily. However, she made herself finish a full check of the library first, if only to confirm that there really wasn't another cupboard behind any of the other cases.

There wasn't, and so she went back and looked at the remaining key. If anything it was slightly bigger than the other one, but every bit as old. Not of the age of the estate office's hidey-hole, but still much older than the twentieth century. *Who would have built you?* she wondered. *Who would have had reservations about Luka?* Probably not Richard himself, because by the time he'd woken up to the looming danger, he was a bit too old and ill to have been overseeing new building work. But what about Hector? He'd had that brief spell between Richard's death in the December of 1838 and his own death in the August of 1840 – eighteen months, not long enough to build anything major, but plenty of time to have brought in a carpenter to do some small projects. And the more she thought about it, the more Cleo believed it had to be him, if only because after that Luka had been on hand too much, and would have wanted to know what was being hidden from him. But what if Hector was trying to hide things for his missing brother William – who might not have been so missing at that point?

Spurred on by that thought, Cleo wandered out of the library and onto the first floor landing. Which rooms could Hector have convincingly got a carpenter in to work on without exciting too much curiosity? Obviously the library, which would probably have been considered his preserve as the new head of the household, and which he'd maybe shared in the past with his father and brother – that if nothing else accounted for the three equally good desks in there, if they'd each had their own.

Then with a sudden squeak of excitement, Cleo realised that she hadn't looked hard at the exterior of those desks. Not the fronts, but the backs! All three desks were quite deep, so of course the drawers hadn't extended all of the way to the back, but hadn't one of them seemed to have less of a gap back there than the others? Hurrying back into the library, she now took into account that while the desk with the secret drawer they'd found sat at right-angles to the French window, with its back exposed, and the one she'd been working at was similarly placed at right-angles beside the fire, the third desk was almost up against the far window. If she'd thought anything of that at all before, Cleo had assumed that the gap between it and the wall was to allow the heavy drapes to be drawn across in the winter, not to be able to get to it. But now she also realised that this was the one desk where you couldn't see its back.

Scrutinising the right-hand side of it, which was well lit by the French windows as well as the window it was by, she could see that there was nothing there at all. *But then why would there be?* she chided herself. This was something that had been made to remain unseen. And so she got down on her hands and knees, realising that there was plenty of room to get down on the other side of the desk without getting stuck up against the bookshelves, and that it was in relative darkness. Shining the pocket torch along the rear side edge of the desk, she suddenly found another of the fake knot-holes.

"Oh you beauty!" she breathed and fished the key out of her pocket. This time there was nothing to get out of the way, and once again the key fitted perfectly. Yet when the click of the mechanism moving came, a panel at the back of the desk seemed to pop out, but not at an angle as if it was hinged.

Getting up and going around to the other side, by the window's light she could see that it looked as though that far panel of the three on the back of the desk might slide. And so very carefully she gave it a gentle tug towards her. It moved enough to show her that this was indeed the way it was supposed to move, but this time the muck of ages in the tiny channel it had to move along was blocking its way.

"Sorry, Hector, or whoever it was who had these lovely desks made," Cleo apologised, "but I don't have the time to be so careful right now." And going up to her bedroom, she found her small penknife which had useful things like a mini screwdriver and a bottle opener on it.

She'd hardly ever used the knife part, and it was stiff to open, but being a small blade, it was ideal to carefully work along the channel. Most of what came out seemed to be the residue of generations of enthusiastic housekeepers polishing everything, and the wood was hard enough that Cleo's little knife made no impression on it. Compared to modern furniture, which she would have been gouging out chunks of by now, the solid hardwood desk stood up to her ministrations remarkably well, and before half an hour was out, she had managed to slide the hidden door along very nearly to the end of the groove. The maker had been most cunning, for the other end panel didn't sit quite flush with the middle one, making it look as though the end ones ought both to be slightly more prominent.

"Clever you, whoever you were," Cleo complimented them, then again sat on the floor and wriggled behind the desk so that she could see inside.

This time, however, it was clear that nobody had touched this in ages. But then, Cleo thought, Archie would have had trouble getting down to this one as he got older, and there was always the possibility that he had kept the key to this one safe only because he knew the other one opened the bookcase hideaway, not because he knew where this space was. Nothing like as deep as the square space behind the bookcases, this was only a few inches deep and had a shelf across its width halfway up. That had undoubtedly been there partly to give some support to the thin wood of the panels which formed its front and back, so that it didn't buckle compared to its slightly more substantial neighbours, but also, without the shelf the hiding place would only have been useful for large but flat documents. Instead, it held small packets of letters, all of them old and yellowing.

Reverently, Cleo lifted them out into the light. This time there were post-marks which showed that they had come from Italy, and not just anywhere in Italy, but Verona! *This is the link to Hugh!* Cleo thought excitedly, but then looked harder at the letters and knew that these were from long before the First World War. So this had to be an earlier link, and that made it even more intriguing.

Feeling almost breathless, Cleo took them over to the desk to join Hugh's letters, then had a horrible thought. Mrs W had no idea of the bomb that was about to drop into her lap, but what was the betting that when it did, she'd be back here from London on the next train, screaming blue murder and wanting vengeance? So none of this should be where she could get her hands on them, because everything Cleo had seen and learned of Darcy D'Eath Wytcombe said that she was the kind of woman who would throw stuff on the fire, regardless of what it was, if she thought it would spite someone else.

And so emptying one of the cases that she carried her laptops in, and shoving the spare cables and memory cards into the other case, she carefully put the letters into the different compartments, and hurried across to the cottage. Sarah was fast asleep again in front of the TV, but seemed to be breathing normally, and so rather than wake her, Cleo crept up to the room she was using and slid the laptop bag with the letters under the bed, while leaving the other one on show for the curious. Other than her own car, that was about as safe a place as any for now, and in this cold weather, Cleo didn't want the precious old papers getting anything like damp in the car.

She made herself a coffee and prepared something for the evening meal while she thought. This had been a remarkable day so far, but nevertheless, she still hadn't found anything which looked as though Hugh had sent it home from Verona. His letters thus far had all been very much the standard kind of small notes that she had seen so many times in her dealings with other families, and somehow she had the unshakable belief that what she was looking for was something more bulky, or at least different.

Use your other talents, the voice came inside her head, and in that moment Cleo realised that she could try dowsing for this.

Rather glad that Chris wasn't here to see her doing this, Cleo went back up to her suitcase and found the small yellow jade pendulum she always had with her, but on an impulse, also put the ancient necklace in her pocket too, in case that might aid her search. Some friends, such as Angie, had laughed at her dowsing to find lost objects, but find them she always did, and Jen had said that she had a particularly strong talent for dowsing. So pocketing the yellow stone on its silver chain, Cleo checked on Sarah again, and leaving a note for her and Chris that a casserole was on in the oven, slow cooking – careful not to say that it was vegetarian, with the Quorn slices in that she'd bought, not meat – she went back to the big house.

This time she went up to the top floor, convinced that the first floor had given up all that it had. Pulling the jade out, she gently warmed it in her hands, then held the chain loosely in her right hand so that the gem could swing whichever way it wanted. The way it had always worked for her was a back and forth swing for 'no', and a circular rotation for 'yes', and so when she asked out loud,

"Can you help me find what Hugh hid?" she was pleased to see the jade start to gently rotate on the chain.

"Is Hecate helping me with this?" got another rotation, but more vigorous.

"Okay, then." She went and stood in the room she'd been using. "Was this Hugh's bedroom?" The answer came back 'yes'. "But did he hide what he brought back in here?" This time the pendulum did a vigorous swing back and forth. So she'd been right to think that Hugh had thought this was too obvious a room to leave anything in.

Moving out onto the landing, she thought she would at least check that neither of the bathrooms were contenders, but the pendulum – or Hecate, or whoever was guiding her at the moment – was in agreement that the bathrooms held no secrets. Nor did the other bedroom at the front of the house, or any of the nursery suite, as Cleo thought of those rooms. She hadn't expected any of them to yield a positive response, but by checking them first, she was at least convinced that it wasn't just her own desperation to find something that was making the pendulum swing to an answer.

"Right," she said, as she came back along the landing, having worked her way methodically along the front of the house, then to the rear to the nursery. "A quick check of the store rooms and then it's on to that back bedroom."

She stepped into the first of the former servants' rooms, and edged her way into the centre past the packing cases full of stuff from who knew how long back. Fully expecting the pendulum to swing in the negative when she asked, "Is there anything I should look at in here?" she was aghast to see it start to rotate and then pick up speed. "Oh crap!" she muttered despairingly, looking at the removers' kind of hefty tea-chests, which were piled three high around the room. "I don't suppose you can tell me which one?" then started, as she realised that she was still holding the pendulum in the correct position for it to be rotating again. "Oh! You can?" It rotated a bit faster.

Feeling a little relieved, Cleo rummaged in her fleece pocket and found a marker pen, and so going steadily along the rows of cases one at a time, she marked a small cross on the ones she could discount and, having got through them all, was glad to discover that there were only two which she needed to investigate. With all of her intuition now running at full speed, Cleo addressed her invisible helper.

"Thank you so much for all the help so far. I promise you I will come back to these crates, I will. But I'm really worried now about that bloody Wytcombe woman, and what kind of tantrum she's going to throw when she gets a phone-call to say that her husband specifically disinherited her. I can't move these cases on my own, so I've got to wait until Chris gets back and can help me," for irritatingly, both the ones she needed were on the bottom of their stacks. "But I don't want to waste time either. So I'm going to move on and check the other rooms, if that's okay?"

The pendulum circled in agreement, and Cleo moved on to the next of the servants' rooms, and then the next, with not so much as a twitch from the pendulum except slight swings in the negative. For herself, though, the longer this went on, the more she felt the hairs on the back of her neck standing up, not helped by the warm tingling sensation that was creeping through from where the necklace sat in her pocket. She'd had one or two strange experiences in old houses before, and twice in her life she had seen what some people might call ghosts, but which she had felt were not so much haunting a place or person, but were more stuck in that place because of some terrible thing which had happened to them there in the past. And right now she was getting that feeling again as if she wasn't alone – and it was more than one person, too!

For no reason other than instinct, she turned the landing light off and stood there in the late-winter afternoon's darkness for a moment. Yes, over there there was definitely a shimmering of something, and she thought it felt male and might well be Hugh's essence or spirit, whatever you wanted to call it. But as she turned around she felt herself starting to shiver as she saw what looked like several others, and this time she could swear that they were all female. And with them came the sensation of unbearable sadness.

"Ana?" she found herself calling softly, her voice choked with emotion. One of the blurs seemed to glow a bit brighter. "Oh sweet goddess! Are you all of the women Luka wronged?" she gulped, and suddenly the landing wasn't so dark anymore, but there was also the sensation of something much older and more powerful coming in with them, and it was willing her forwards. It held no danger to her herself, of that Cleo was sure. If it had any feeling towards her it was of great approval of what she was doing, and that was so unaccustomed for Cleo that she was almost reduced to tears.

But there was that sense of terrible urgency building again, and so, with it taking all of her spiritual strength to keep herself focused and moving, she turned the handle on the door to the back bedroom. Immediately the strange swirls of ethereal lights were surging past her into the room, and Cleo resisted the urge to put the light on. The 'ghosts' went, not to the old desk, nor to the armchair and the stubby chest of drawers beside it which had probably served as a side table, but to the big old cupboard in the corner of the room.

Opening its doors, she found a conglomeration of bits and pieces in baskets, most of them seeming to relate to the generations of children who had been in the house. There was a doll's house on the bottom shelf which these days would be considered an antique and again worth a mint, and half a dozen large dolls which Cleo guessed had probably been Emilia and Verity's, going by the clothes, but to her eyes all of them were hideous, and would probably give a modern child nightmares with their harsh china faces. But there on the top shelf, all alone and looking very forlorn was a large bear. Instantly Cleo recognised it as the bear she had seen Hugh hugging in her dream, and as she lifted him down she almost heard the sigh of relief from behind her. This was what she was meant to find.

As she clasped the bear to her, his long legs hanging down to beyond her hips, for he was a classic old teddy bear of the long-limbed variety, Cleo could smell the distinctive scent of his sawdust filling. Back when she had been a little girl, and her dad had taken her to his parents, there had been another old bear whom she had loved dearly, and who had once been her dad's. She had never found out where Bruno had gone to, because by the time she had found out that her grandparents had had to go into a nursing home, her aunt had gone through their cottage like a whirlwind and thrown everything out. Had her dad still been alive at the time, they would have gone up to the cottage and helped with the clearing, and she might have rescued Bruno, but her aunt and her mum had hated the very sight of one another, and by the time the news had filtered through her mum's indifference, it was way too late for Cleo to go looking. But it meant that she pulled this teddy in tight to her and hugged him hard.

He crackled. Or rather, he rustled! Something papery was inside the bear!

"Oh Hugh, you genius!" Cleo gulped, hurrying to the light switch. When the feeble light came on, she couldn't see any signs of tampering with the teddy's seams, but she knew from having seen other families' heirlooms, that men of the First World War era could produce some lovely needlework. Hand-stitched regimental badges sent home to loved ones were often beautifully worked, and so she wasn't surprised that she wasn't seeing any crude stitches up the teddy's back.

It almost made her wish that she wasn't going to have to unpick him, because her own work wouldn't be that good when she came to repairing him, but unpick him she must. Not here, though. That was a job to be done in the sanctity of the cottage. And so hugging him with one arm, she made one last attempt at dowsing, but whether she had run out of energy or there was nothing to find, she got a very feeble 'no' when she asked if there was anything more to find up here.

Chapter 22

Hurrying back to the cottage with Bruno II, as she'd decided to call him, she took him straight up to her bedroom, not wanting to have Sarah think that she'd totally lost the plot in getting attached to a teddy bear. It was also rather worrying that Chris wasn't back yet. Coming this way, by this time he shouldn't have had any of the usual bottle-necks of rush-hour traffic to get through, and Cleo began to fret that he might have had some kind of accident if he was upset and driving on unfamiliar roads.

At six o'clock she served up the casserole for Sarah and herself, just about managing to fend off Sarah's drowsy queries about where Chris was. But when he walked in through the door at just gone seven o'clock, she was past any restraint and threw her arms around him in relief.

"Oh, blessed Hecate! Am I glad to see you!" she gasped. "The later it got, the more worried sick I was!"

Chris was hugging her back, but said thickly, "Could you let me breathe, please?"

"Oh!" Cleo gulped, mortified, but realising just how hard she'd been holding him around his neck.

He only waited until she'd backed off enough for him to see her face to face before kissing her, though, and it was only after several minutes that he said, "I hope that's some dinner I can smell, because I'm starving!"

Ushering him into the lounge to Sarah, Cleo brought him through a large pasta-bowl of casserole on a tray, and on his instructions while he ate, she went and found one of the bottles of prosecco he said was in the under-stair cupboard.

"Chris? What's all this about?" Sarah asked, having at last seeming to have surfaced from her exhaustion and looking much better. "What have we got to celebrate?"

Between them, Cleo and Chris told her about finding the new will, and of Chris' mad dash to get to the Worcester solicitors before they closed for the day, though not yet of her being the one to inherit. In the briefest of conversations they had agreed that if Archie might turn out to not be the rightful owner, and therefore have no right to hand it on, it would be cruel to get Sarah's hopes up that she could stay here.

"They've said in terms of procedure it's a bit irregular," Chris told them, "but there's no question about it, this new will is legal and it will stand up in court if necessary."

"What about Diglis and Marchand, though?" Sarah asked, referring to Archie's normal solicitors.

In answer, Chris turned and smiled at Cleo. "Well it's a good thing you had the presence of mind to grab that envelope of theirs off Archie's desk along with all the other stuff." He turned to Sarah. "Cleo said we might need to put them in contact with one another in order to speed things up, and though Archie did mention them by name in the new will, it made things go a whole lot faster that the new guys could just pick up the phone without having to track them down – particularly as I reached them towards the end of their working day.

"When the Worcester guys phoned them, it seems that in amongst Archie's papers that Diglis and Marchand came and took away, there was a letter to them apologising for having to act without them. Unfortunately, they had no clue as to what for, and certainly not that it was about a will. The thing was, this all happened so close to when Archie died, I don't think he'd had chance to finish doing all of the preparations he'd intended to make. The new solicitors said that although the new will was all drawn up, Archie had told them he'd be coming back to see them when he got back from his visit to the friends where he died.

"Well not knowing where he'd gone to, the new guys thought he might even have gone as far afield as Australia to watch the cricket – especially after having seen Archie in his Worcester County Cricket Club blazer. So while they were expecting him to come back and finalise some of the details at some point, they weren't concerned as yet that he hadn't turned up, especially as he'd seemed in good health. And to be frank, as a large multi-branch company, they handle so many cases they were hardly going to worry over one will that was taking a while to do the last bit of box-ticking. But to give them their due, once I'd told them everything, they were onto the other guys straightaway. And I'm afraid your friend isn't going to love you for this, Cleo, because the sale of the house has to stop right now."

"Oh no! Angie!" Cleo gasped, suddenly realising the full implications. "Oh damn! She was counting on the commission to be able to buy her and the kids a place of their own. What a lousy friend I am."

"No, you're not," Chris said firmly. "And for all we know, in the end the house may well go on the market, in which case we can ask Angie to handle the sale." He gave Cleo a meaningful look over that, for he'd very carefully skirted around the inheritance issue regarding Archie, simply saying that he'd not had chance to read the new will. Instead, he said they had realised that it must supersede the old one and had taken it straight to the solicitors, because he and Cleo had feared Mrs W turning up unannounced and discovering it. That was satisfying

Sarah for now, and she didn't need the prospect of fighting Darcy D'Eath looming over her. If she'd not been able to face phoning her over insuring the china, this would involve ten times the confrontations. Better also, that Sarah give an honest reaction of shocked disbelief if confronted over inheriting, even if Mrs W might not believe her despite that.

"God, I'm beat," Chris declared leaning back with relief in the armchair. "I'm so not used to driving these twisting country roads."

"Then I'm sorry to have to ask you this," Cleo apologised, "but in a minute, would you come back over to the house with me? I just need you to help me shift a few boxes. I won't ask you to do any more than that, but I can't lift them on my own."

"Surely it can wait until the morning?" Sarah said, puzzled.

"I'd rather not," said Cleo with a wince. "I can't explain why, but I think there'll be explosions when Mrs W gets the news tomorrow, and what will happen if she comes up here and locks us out of the house? She can't legally do anything to you here, Sarah, but I think there are some old things we need to get out of there just in case. I'll be bringing the rest of my stuff over here, too, if you don't mind and for the same reason. I don't think I'm going to be her favourite person in all of this."

However, Sarah didn't grasp Cleo's feeling of urgency, saying it would be fine in the morning, because how fast could Herself get here from London? Being more used to that trip than Sarah, Cleo couldn't bring herself to say that even on a Saturday the trains would start in the early hours, and that a train at just gone nine o'clock would have Mrs W here not far off midday, and if she got the train any earlier, then it might even be before eleven o'clock.

"Don't worry," Chris told her as they went to go to bed. "The solicitors told me that we'd have the weekend in peace, because they won't ring Herself before Monday morning. You see, I told them about us losing Dad and then what's happened with Aiden, and they were really sympathetic. The main job as far as they're concerned is telling the estate agents to hold fast on the sale, and they've done that by an email."

"Which Angie's company will get first thing," Cleo pointed out. "If it's Angie's turn to work the Saturday, then she'll do me the courtesy of ringing me first. But if it's one of the other partners, they might be straight onto the phone to Mrs W."

Chris looked horrified. "They'd do that?"

"Why wouldn't they? As far as they're concerned, Mrs W has led them a right merry dance, and if they're feeling really snitty, they might see it as them being landed with my bill for work which they'll have to pay up for, but with no recompense to them in the way of a sale."

"Holy shit!" The thought had stopped Chris in his tracks at the bottom of the stairs, Sarah having preceded them in going to bed, so at least they didn't have to explain it to her. He gave Cleo a worried look. "You've been right at every turn so far, and that makes me think you will be on this. But are you so sure we need this stuff?"

Cleo took his hands in hers and looked beseechingly up at him. "I get that you're exhausted, and I wouldn't dream of asking if I didn't believe with every fibre of my body that this needs to happen tonight." She drew him back into the kitchen. "I haven't had the chance to tell you all of my news, but let me just say that I have made some serious discoveries of papers. There hasn't been time to read any of them yet, and they're safe up in my room for now, but they're old letters, okay?"

"Letters?" Chris' eyes widened at that. "Uh-oh, that's significant."

"Very. Now you know my whole Hecate thing? Well, while I was upstairs hunting, I was… 'directed' is the best word, I suppose, to the old servants' rooms. Now two of them were just junk rooms like we thought, but the thing is, Chris, I can dowse, and my dowsing took me to two specific packing crates in the third room. Just the two. But they have other things piled on top of them. That's what I need you to help me move. Just four crates. Then you can come back and go to bed. I'll carry on on my own after that."

"Alright. On one condition."

"What's that?"

"That while you sort through that case, I get to liberate Archie's malt whiskies!"

Cleo laughed. "I think we might even take a stiff one each upstairs to help with the moving."

"Damn it, you're a hard woman to refuse when you talk dirty like that!"

When they went in through the kitchen of the big house, Cleo remembered seeing some bottle-bags in the utility, and so they took those up for Chris' quest. But up at the top of the house, he was suddenly more serious when he saw how she'd marked every one of the cases.

"You dowsed over every one of them?"

"Yes, I did."

"Wow, that was pretty thorough. Okay, I'm convinced that *you're* convinced, even though I always thought dowsing was one of the more way-out things." And he went to the top box of the first pile. It took the two of them to lift it down and move it out of the way, for whoever had packed these things up had got the maximum into each tea-chest. However, when the two marked crates were exposed, Chris insisted on being the one to use the steel floorboard-lifter they'd brought upstairs as well to prise the lids off.

As the first one came free, and Cleo picked it up to put on one side, Chris whistled. In neat handwriting on an envelope on the very top layer it said, 'Verity's things'.

"This is the Verity whose whole family died?" Chris asked Cleo in amazement. "Why would her stuff be here?"

Cleo shrugged. "I suspect that they had to clear the house she and her husband had in London, and the personal stuff had to go somewhere. Even Bertie must have had feelings for his kid sister, especially if she was always the peace-maker, and we know next to nothing about his wife, Clarissa, do we? It might have been a marriage very like Archie's parents, where she couldn't stand the sight of him after a few years. So maybe she and Verity wrote to one another? Because I can't imagine that her dresses and hats are that important."

The top layer of things were neatly folded dresses, obviously of very good quality and the height of fashion in around 1919, and possibly worth handing on to a museum of fashion, but Cleo knew that lovely though they were, they weren't what her spectral guides had been pushing her to find. And so she began gently lifting the clothes out while Chris went to rescue the whisky. It was only when she was almost at the bottom that she found them. Neatly tied up in a blue ribbon were a handful of letters.

Cleo put them on one side and, having checked that there was nothing left in the rest of the case, put the dresses back in and placed the lid back on the case. It wouldn't pass close inspection, but she didn't expect Darcy D'Eath to come in here. It was simply the worry of not having any access to the house which was plaguing her to get these tonight.

What she wasn't expecting was to find that the other case contained more women's things, but of a woman of a clearly bigger build than Verity. In a much less practiced and rougher hand, the envelope being used as a tag in this case said, 'Lady Clarissa's things', and had clearly been written by a servant. Whoever that servant was must have loved her mistress dearly, because some of the ink was tear-smudged.

"I'm glad someone cared that much for you, Clarissa," Cleo said, wondering if she had been another of those wavering lights that had been here before. So many women in this house seemed to have over-written by the malevolent men around them, or killed off before their time. Where had Hecate been then? *What took you so long?* she wondered. *If you can be so alert to me, where were you when these women needed you?*

However, she was once again digging down through layers of silk and lace, all carefully interleaved with lavender bags and cedar balls to keep the moths at bay. Then once again down at the bottom she found a bulging envelope. *Mistress bid me put these here for you to find when you come home, Miss Emilia*, it said, *or for Miss Cynthia or Miss Catherine when they am older.*

Cleo sat back on her heels. This had to be Clarissa, but when had she died? Later than Verity and the others she recalled, though not the exact date, so this had to be referring to Bertie's daughters. Interesting that Horace's wife, Audrey, who was of the same generation, wasn't mentioned. Had Clarissa thought she was too brow-beaten by him, or just too plain afraid of him, to be trusted? Or maybe it was even the sympathy of one bullied wife for another, who knew how hard it could be lie to them? That all by itself said a lot about the man, even if Cleo now knew that Audrey had had inner steel in her soul that had made her defy Horace in her own quiet way. Yet for now, all she could do was to put Clarissa's clothes back as best she could, and the lid back on the box.

As she hurried downstairs, it was to see Chris filling the last of the bottle-bags, and she helped him carry them across to the cottage, locking the big house up securely behind them.

"Are we being overly dramatic, do you think?" Chris asked as he picked up two of the bags and Cleo the third.

"I wish I could say yes," Cleo said with a backwards glance at the house, "But all of my instincts are saying not."

Saturday morning began with the phone ringing. Mercifully Sarah's house phone showed the identity of the caller, and so they knew it was Darcy D'Eath and let it ring out.

"Come on, Mum," Chris said cheerfully, "let's lock the cottage up securely and then go and do some shopping. We're running out of everything anyway, and we don't need to be here when that bitch gets here. She can swear herself hoarse at the empty cottage while we enjoy a pub lunch." He didn't add that the final thing that he and Cleo had done last night was scour the big house for any keys to the cottage. The last thing they wanted was for the dreadful black widow to let herself in and trash the place in their absence. By now Chris was thinking the same as Cleo, which was that Darcy D'Eath's spite might know no bounds at being so thwarted.

What they weren't expecting was to be halfway around the Tesco in Ledbury when they got a call from Joe on Sarah's mobile.

"I called the police," he said, his voice full of righteous indignation. "Her done call me a fuckin' yokel! Her was bangin' and kickin' your front door. I told her there weren't no need for that, 'cause you'd be back soon enough, but then her picked up one of the rocks on the edge o' the drive an' threw it at I!" As Cleo and Chris stifled their mirth at the thought of Mrs W's nemesis being the unlikely person of Joe, Sarah stood aghast in the middle of the frozen isle, a bag of oven-chips hanging limply from her hand, as she took in Mrs W's violence towards Joe.

He continued, "I ain't standin' for that! Mr Archie were a proper gent, but she aint' nothin' but some cockney whore – an' I told the police that, too! So they'm comin' out to 'ave words with 'er." The more indignant he got, the thicker his local dialect became.

"Joe?" Cleo said, since the phone was on speaker and she was the only one who could respond at that moment. "We'll come straight back, okay? We won't be long. Just make sure that you stay well out of her way. We don't want you getting hurt."

"Don't you worry, I ain't goin' anywhere near *her*!" Joe said with conviction. "I'm a' waitin' at the bottom o' the drive for the coppers. I ain't goin' anywhere near the big house without an *escort*," and he made it sound as though he was expecting an armed response unit to turn up, which reduced Chris – already struggling to keep his laughter inaudible – to have to smother his mirth all over again.

When Joe had rung off, he managed to gasp, "What's he expecting? A SWAT team to turn up? For one upper-crust widow who's throwing a hissy fit?"

Cleo could laugh with him more than Sarah could, but sobered him with, "Don't forget what we fear she might have done to Archie. If Joe's called the police because of her doing criminal damage to the cottage, we've got an unrivalled chance to get our version of events over to the police. Don't you see? We have what might be a one-off chance to play the innocent victims to the police, and in the process say that we feel there's a real danger from Mrs W because of what we fear she might have done to Archie."

Her memory of similar dealings with her own family made her point out, "*We* didn't call them in. *We* aren't making wild accusations about a woman who appears all calm and reasonable. We can simply be answering questions about what's going on with a woman who's already threatened a member of staff at her house with physical violence."

With Sarah and Chris suddenly getting what Cleo was driving them to see, they finished the shopping at speed and drove straight back to the cottage, all thoughts of lunch now on hold. When they got there it was to find a police car in the middle of the drive, and Darcy D'Eath swearing and screaming abuse at a bemused constable and his accompanying Police Community Support Officer. As they got out of the car they could hear the constable saying,

"Madam, if you don't stop this right now I'm going to be arresting you for…" he never got the chance to finish because Mrs W spun on her heels, stormed in through the kitchen door, and slammed it behind her. Even as they walked across the drive to the policemen, they could hear the bolts being shot on the other side of the kitchen door. Mrs W had gone into siege mode!

When the basic introductions had been made and it transpired that Joe had gone home, vowing not to set foot in the place while 'she' was here, Sarah invited the policemen into the cottage.

"Do come on in and have a cup of tea," she said, just being herself, but providing a stark contrast to Mrs W's screaming harridan, especially when she just tutted and shook her head sadly at the huge gouges in the cottage's door, which had probably been made by Mrs W hammering on it with one of the driveway rocks.

That morning Sarah had felt enough like herself to have made a Madeira cake before going out, which had been cooling on the kitchen table while they shopped, and so now the police found themselves being plied with particularly scrumptious cake to boot, all of which was creating the right impression, Cleo thought. It took a very quiet word in the PC's ear, but she managed to engineer it so that the PCSO took Sarah through to the lounge to get a statement about the state of affairs at the house. That left Chris and herself free to speak more openly to the constable, and to explain what a rough time Sarah had been having, and how Mrs W had been threatening to evict her despite having no grounds to do so. It also gave Cleo the chance to explain her presence in the household, and just why she had been rummaging around through the family papers in the first place.

"I warned her right at the start that she might not like what I found," Cleo told PC Willis. She shook her head wearily. "It's always the ones who have such high expectations of them being related to the royal family, or worth a fortune, who are most disappointed and who get ratty about it. The people who come to me with much lower expectations are the ones who tend to go away delighted that I've found more than they ever anticipated."

"And you say that it's the estate agents who employed you on Mrs Wytcombe's behalf?" PC Willis double-checked.

"Oh yes. To be frank, the first time I met her I thought that if this had been a direct commission, I would have walked away there and then. It was only because I was helping a friend out by doing this that I stayed on. You see, I wouldn't have trusted Mrs W to pay me if I didn't find what she wanted, but because it was through the agents, I'd get paid out of the proceeds of the sale.

Mind you, I wasn't expecting the sale to get stopped in its tracks."

"And it's the stopping of the sale that's caused the disturbance this morning?" Willis asked, rapidly writing notes.

This time it was Chris who replied, "Yes it has. Well the sale couldn't go through once Cleo and I had found that new will. We didn't read anything beyond the fact that Sir Archie had cut his wife out of his will. Cleo found me the address of his current solicitors, and I jumped in the car and drove to Worcester, hoping I'd catch the new solicitors before they shut up for the weekend." He handed over one of the company's business cards which they'd given him. "I only just made it, but to give them credit, someone stayed on and rang Sir Archie's family solicitors. From now on it's between them. We have no say in any of it, but I don't think Herself quite sees it like that."

"Can I add something?" Cleo asked tentatively.

Willis looked up. "Yes. What sort of thing?"

Taking a deep breath, Cleo relayed what Sarah had said to her when she'd first arrived, but making it sound as though now Sarah herself might be in danger from Darcy D'Eath. She made sure that if anything she underplayed the suspicion of murder, concluding with, "I don't think anyone would have thought much more of it if Mrs Wytcombe hadn't been so passionate about demanding Sir Archie be cremated, which was so against what he'd wanted. Sarah had quite the fight on her hands with the woman, and she only stuck up for Archie as hard as she did because she'd long known that he wanted to be buried with his first wife and his son. She didn't think anything suspect at the time, you see. It was just about respecting the memory of a relative and good friend. But the more time has gone on, and Mrs Wytcombe has pushed and pushed for a high-value, speedy sale, the more suspicious she's become.

"And if I'm honest, the longer I've been here, the more I've thought that there was something very wrong in all of this. I've never had a client who wanted results so fast, and was so focused on how much *money* she could make from it. I've had clients who wanted impossible connections before, but never one who expected to so specifically have a financial gain out of a genealogical search."

She gave a rueful smile. "I'm not a closet Agatha Christie fan or anything, but even I've wondered if she wanted the money so that she could skip the country before she got found out. Daft, I know, but you know what it's like once an idea takes root – you can't always shake it off."

Willis very tactfully said nothing, but Cleo was secretly delighted to have noticed that he'd made a lot more notes, especially about the idea that poor Archie had been fed powdered glass and then laxatives. If they were really lucky, he'd be disinterred and a proper post-mortem carried out, but even if that didn't happen, she was sure that by now the police were seeing Mrs W as a very dodgy person indeed.

Chapter 23

When the police finally went, having tried to get Mrs W to answer the door but without success, Cleo insisted that they all still go out for the pub lunch.

"If bloody Shelob is sitting in her nest waiting for a chance to come and start bawling at us again, let's not give her the opportunity. By the time we get back, hopefully she'll have hit the wine cellar and be too drunk to do anything. And there're things I want to tell you, Sarah, without her screaming through the window at us, or listening at the door."

At the lovely old pub out on the Bromyard downs, they were just in time to order a late lunch, and then while they were waiting for the food, Cleo began telling the other two about the letters she'd found.

"Good grief!" Sarah gasped at the end. "Fancy Hugh being cunning enough to stuff them into the bear!"

"I don't know quite what's inside him," Cleo admitted, "but I think Hugh knew that his beloved antique bear was one thing he could leave in the cupboard which the servants wouldn't throw away. Going on that tear-stained writing a servant left with Clarissa's things, there were people in the house who genuinely cared for the nicer members of the family, and I reckon of that generation Clarissa, Verity and Hugh came into that group, as probably did the two daughters in the next, Catherine and Cynthia. I don't think Hugh would have actually said, 'don't throw the bear away,' because that would have been something Bertie could bully out of a servant. But I think he was sharp enough to realise that Bertie wouldn't go ferreting in the storerooms – because post-war, the house would have been running on a fraction of the staff, and therefore not needing those rooms as mini dormitories – and the servants would leave well alone out of respect."

"We need to get back and start reading," Chris said firmly.

"Yes, we do," Cleo agreed. "But what I didn't want to happen was for the police to leave, and for us to start spreading the letters out on the table, only for Mrs W to come nosing in through the window. I can't explain why, but I really don't want her to know that we have those letters. I think it might be because I fear she may try and convince a solicitor that they are her property, and force us to hand them over. Even if she's being denied the sale of the house, she might think she can get her grubby hands on the fortune she thought Archie's family had hidden, and at least make off with that before she's caught."

Sarah and Chris took her warning to heart, and so when they got back to the cottage, the first thing they did was check around outside. However, wherever Mrs W was, it wasn't in any of the rooms they could see into on the ground floor of the big house. And although Chris went up onto the bank at the back of the house to be able to look into the library, he reported back that nothing seemed to have been disturbed. That sounded very unlike Darcy D'Eath Wytcombe, but with both the outer doors still securely locked, they could only presume that she was drinking herself into a stupor up in her bedroom.

Nevertheless, when they came to get the bundles of letters out, Sarah suggested that they spread them out on the lounge floor. The lounge window gave a glorious view out over the landscaped garden by virtue of being right at the top of the next bank in the series of terraces – the same one that the first terrace of the big house was on the edge of too. Short of bringing a ladder with her, Mrs W had no chance of being able to peer in at that window, which Chris and Cleo agreed was perfect.

The first thing to do was to find what Bruno II had hidden in his innards. And so with Sarah and Cleo carefully unpicking his back seam, kneeling like two surgeons beside the bear laid out on the large footstool, they all found themselves almost holding their breaths in anticipation.

"Jeez, it's like waiting to become a father!" Chris laughed nervously, and got a withering look from his mother from over the top of her reading glasses.

"I hope when the time comes you're considerably more excited over *that*," she remonstrated, but only got a cheeky grin back.

They had to unpick almost all of Bruno's back, but then they could see how Hugh had carefully cut into the stuffing to slide a bundle of letters inside. Cleo immediately carried Bruno back upstairs, for they would need to replace his stuffing before sewing him back up, and she told the others that he was enough of an antique for it to be worthwhile taking him to a proper restorer, rather than trying to do it themselves. But once she was back in the lounge, they looked at the letters and decided that these were almost amongst the oldest of the bundles, except for a few modern ones which were clearly from Hugh.

"I think we have to start with Hugh's last letters home," Cleo decided. "If they shed light on what he found and where, then we might start to make sense of all this."

And so very carefully they opened out all of the newer letters and spread them out on the floor. There were only four of them, and they were swiftly sorted into order.

"Hugh must have retrieved these from the other pile of his letters I found in the library, once he realised how hostile Bertie was," Cleo deduced. "They're on the same sort of paper, and I won't go back and check at the moment, even though the others are upstairs now, but I think these must be the last ones he wrote from abroad."

Chris agreed. "He may even have heard from Verity that she and/or Clarissa had kept his letters, and become worried what Bertie would do if he found them. He may not have had to go looking for them. He could as easily have asked her to show them to him, and when she wasn't watching, just pulled out the ones he was most worried about. That gets around him not being mobile enough to go hunting – or at least not in the early days when he came home."

"I think that's probably as close to the true version of events as we'll ever get," agreed Sarah. She pointed to a letter. "So is that the first one?"

With Cleo being the one most used to reading all sorts of handwriting, she was the one who picked up the letter with its tiny script and began to read aloud,

> *Via al Cristo*
> *Verona*
> *5th November 1918*
>
> *Dear all,*
>
> *I do not wish you to fret, but I have been wounded, and quite badly too. On 27th October, we advanced across the River Piave. I have not seen such carnage since Passchendaele. So many of my men are dead or wounded and I wonder why I am still here? I have lost my right leg, so will be here*

quite a while recovering. Just now I am too
done in to write more. I will write more when
I feel up to it.

Hugh

"Poor man," Sarah empathised. "He obviously had survivor's guilt."

"And not without reason," Cleo said sadly. "The crossing of the River Piave was an absolute massacre that hardly gets talked about these days. Everyone remembers the Western Front and Gallipoli, but the River Piave in north-east Italy almost wiped out Hugh's regiment. Later on I'll find you the numbers if you want, but the 12th Durham Light Infantry were never the same again."

"At least he made it to Verona, though," Chris observed, and Cleo felt the chill down her spine once more. There it was again, that feeling that it was just too much of a coincidence that Sarah, and therefore Chris, had their own link to that city. But forcing herself to focus on what they had in front of them, she read the next letters out.

Via al Cristo
Verona
18th November 1918

Dear all,

I am mouldering here with the rest of the wounded as what are left of our units get sent back to the Western Front, and thence to home. We are all finding it hard to rejoice that the war is over. Too many friends lie in shallow graves across this land for that. I dream of them at night, but have also started having very strange other dreams – I am not sure which I fear the most. Maybe it is remembering those few Christmases that we spent at Great-aunt Olivia's, when she used to tell us tales of going to visit her cousins in Italy? It was Verona where they lived, was it not? All my dreams are very vivid, and I asked the nurses if it was anything to do with the pain medication I am on, for I believe it to be morphine. If so, I cannot wait to come off it and have a quiet night's sleep.

I have no idea as yet when I will be returning home. They say they have to get me more stable before I can travel. Something about some shrapnel still being near a nerve in my back.

  Your loving brother,
       Hugh

       Via al Cristo
        Verona
     26ᵗʰ December 1918

Dear all,

  I had so hoped to be home with you for Christmas, and was very low once I knew that I would not even be on my way. Only a few of us are left here now, and in the care of the Italian doctors and nurses for the most part. Just one doctor of our own remains, for he will travel back to England with us.

  Yet the strangest thing has happened. I have discovered that this is the very house that Great-aunt Olivia used to talk about. I am living in the house which was once our cousins'! This is where Claudio and Cinzia Marinelli lived, whom Great-aunt Olivia talked of, and her cousin Julia with them until she married Pietro, though I do not yet know where their descendants are. And even odder, one of my dreams would not leave me alone. It kept showing me some papers hidden in a hollow book in the library here. I say library, but it is not as grand as the one at Upper Moore, but more of a gentleman's study lined with book cases.

It plagued me so much that I asked the nurses if I could go and find a book to read from there. As we have all read what few books that were left behind with us several times over by now, they agreed. I cannot tell you what a strange sensation came over me when they wheeled me into that room. It was as though I had known it all my life. And once they left me to roll my chair along the bookcases, I knew beyond a doubt which book I was looking for. Is that not the strangest thing?

Yet even odder was that when I found it, to my shock it was indeed hollow and there were letters inside. I felt most faint when I looked at them and saw an English stamp upon them and that they had come from <u>home</u>. I only found them a couple of days ago, and the nurses have been so good to us arranging jolly things for Christmas, so I have not had chance to read them yet, but I am bringing them home with me, along with an old necklace that was hidden with them, and seems to have belonged to the family.

Your loving brother,
Hugh

"So *Hugh* found the necklace!" Cleo gasped. "He *must* have known about the hiding place in the estate office, then!"

"Or somebody he trusted did," Chris pointed out. "It would have been a tall order for him to get downstairs and into there in his state. And now I think about it, would he have been able to get to the library, either? I wonder if he was friends with one of the gamekeepers or somebody like that? A servant of some sort? A person he felt he could trust with his secrets?"

Cleo frowned in concentration. "Do you know, I think in some of those estate papers I went through, it said something about one of the estate manager's sons being killed in the war. I wonder if the lad went off with Hugh and never came back? If so, it would be understandable if his father or his brother, who also served, had come to speak to Hugh when he returned.

"And if Hugh knew that the letters were dynamite, he might not have wanted to fully hand them over to whoever it was, for fear of what might fall on the father, particularly if he was still employed by Bertie and in a tied house on the estate. But he could have said, 'hide this for me until I can hand it on to my sisters.' After all, neither Verity nor Emilia was living at Upper Moore at the time, were they? They only came back to visit. So it would be a much more reasonable sounding request if Hugh couched it in terms of wanting the necklace to go to one of the family, rather than an in-law, regardless of whether he liked Clarissa or not. And I think the same goes in this situation as we've said before, Chris. He may have feared that Clarissa was too much under Bertie's thumb. After all, Hugh had been away for five years and wouldn't have had the time to see what the state of his brother's marriage had degenerated into. Or on the other hand, coming back after so long away might have meant that he observed their relationship with fresh eyes, and didn't like what he was seeing."

"But how would that other person have known about the secret hiding place in the gun cupboard?" Chris wondered. "That has to have been somewhere that Bertie didn't know about. But then how would Hugh have known it existed?"

Cleo frowned. "Point taken. Maybe the gamekeeper always knew about it when members of the family had forgotten? He would have been in that office more than anyone, especially given the huge tallies of dead birds and fish that I came across from Bertie's hunting and fishing parties. That man was probably the person who made sure that no river got fished out, and that enough pheasants got reared each year for the shoots. And if Bertie was as unpleasant a character as we now believe, and Sydney and Mortimer even fouler, you can imagine a long-suffering family in service to them taking secret delight in knowing something about the old house that they didn't."

"Families stayed on these estates for generations," Sarah agreed, "and much of the time they would have struggled to move on because they were in cottages tied to their jobs. So they couldn't just sell up and move on, and there was no such thing as social housing in those days for the likes of them."

"Precisely," Cleo said. "And let's not forget poor Clifford, or Bertram as he was originally. The quiet scholar, the bookworm. Hugh would have been…" she did a quick check on the laptop which was beside her, "…thirteen when Bertram-Clifford died. Like you did with Archie, Chris, he may have been the one to go and spend time with an uncle who everyone else thought a bit dotty. But Clifford might have been daft on the right side, as my old granddad used to say. A case of hear all, see all, and say nothing where his father and then oldest nephew were concerned, but who might have told his more bearable youngest nephew of some old hiding places.

"That would mean that Hugh could have told someone else where to hide things, even if he couldn't get there himself. And if it was the other son of the gamekeeper, a man whose courage had been proven in the war, and someone who wasn't even going to be living on the estate anymore, then he would have been safe to do that, wouldn't he? If that chap was soon going to be long gone, Bertie couldn't bully the information out of him. I know this is grasping at straws, but doesn't that sound at least likely?"

"I think you've come up with the most reasonable scenario," Sarah agreed. "So what's in the next letter, Cleo?"

> *Via al Cristo*
> *Verona*
> *8th January 1919*

Dear all,

> *I scarcely know how to begin to tell you this, but we are not the rightful heirs to Upper Moore. A terrible crime was committed by our ancestors, and it is one that in all conscience I cannot keep silent about. I am bringing the evidence home with me, so you must not think me imagining this, Bertie, for I know you will be angry at what I have found.*

> *I believe the main instigator of all this is Great-great-uncle Luka, or whatever relation he was to us. I never met him, which now I am most thankful for, for he sounds a truly evil man and he has blood on his hands – the blood of some of his own family. We always*

*knew that going back to Richard Wytcombe
we had connections with this part of the
world, but I had no idea until now that they
had only fled here from farther afield. And
that that flight was triggered by Luka's
natural father, another evil man.*

*Like you, I already knew that Great-
aunt Olivia wrote to her cousin Julia, but not
that Julia had come to live here in this very
house where I have been, until now. Because
Julia was not Italian! She was Richard
Wytcombe's son <u>Hector's</u> daughter, and
Olivia writes to her including her brother –
another Clifford – so they did not die as we
thought. They fled England after Hector's
murder.*

*Worse, we were always told by Father
(and you, Bertie, by Luka and Mortimer, as
well) that Hector's brother William was
killed at sea. Well he was not! He lived and
married over here in Italy! And he did not
come home to England to claim what was
rightfully his because the Italian family knew
that Luka had murdered Hector, and feared
for William's life. Yet even worse, Clifford
lived on, taking his mother's maiden name
for safety, and unless I am much mistaken, he
had a son called Ernest Carrington. I do not
yet know what has happened to William's
heirs, if any, but the Carringtons through
Clifford and Hector are the rightful heirs to
Upper Moore, and if they have been cut
down in this dreadful war, then we must do
the right thing and try to find who is the true
heir.*

Therefore it was a terrible lie told to us by Great-great-uncle Luka and others that Richard Wytcombe's other children did not survive to inherit. I profoundly apologise for the distress I know this news will bring you, but I felt it only right to forewarn you of the news I was bringing home. Believe me when I say that I have found out something else, which is about myself, and which is equally disturbing, but which requires much greater investigation once I am well enough.

Your brother,

Hugh.

"Well! Isn't that an eye-opener!" Sarah gasped. "You were right, Cleo, Luka was a right nasty piece of work. When you told me that Hector had been murdered, I thought he'd just fallen prey to some footpads out on the road, or thieves breaking in and hitting him over the head or something."

Yet Cleo was sitting cross-legged on the floor, glad that she couldn't fall any farther. Ernest Carrington? That name had cropped up in Sarah's family tree, surely? *Blessed Hecate!* she thought with a shiver. *Does this mean that Sarah and Chris are the rightful heirs to Upper Moore even without Archie's will? If so, this could get really ugly when Mrs W finds that out. I have to make absolutely sure of this before I dare tell anyone. I must protect them in case she really loses it and tries to kill them, because if she could murder Archie in cold blood, what's she capable of in a rage?*

Chapter 24

With Hugh's part in the puzzle as sorted as it could be for now, the next question was, who were the other letters from, and to whom? Having carefully laid them out across the carpet like some enormous tarot card spread, they could at last see that they fell into distinct groups. The oldest ones were between Francesca and her family, and these were written in Italian, which meant that Cleo would have to translate them for Sarah and Chris. There then seemed to be a brief gap before there were letters in English from Francesca and Richard's daughter Sophia in New York, to Francesca's sister Giulia of the Italian family, though the letters sent in response to Sophia's were not amongst any of the others, and probably didn't survive. The next batch seemed to be between the two cousins who had been born in 1837, Ana's Olivia writing from England – which had been in amongst those Hugh had brought back from Italy along with Sophia's – and Hector and Charlotte's Julia's replies written from Verona, which had been found in the back of the library desk. The final bundles had come out of the packing cases, and were all in English and between Clarissa and Verity, with everyone now having a terrible sense of foreboding over what they would say.

However, Cleo thought it best to start with the oldest letters, if only because they would give the best background to the whole tangle of lies and deceit.

"Okay, here we go, then," Cleo declared. "I'm probably going to be a bit slow at this, because it's been a couple of years since I've been able to afford to go over to Italy and get my language up to speed, thanks to my damned step-sister, but I'm giving it my best shot. I'll get my friend to double-check my translations later, but for now this will give us an idea, at least," and she began to read the letters out loud.

Upper Moore House,
Bromyard
21 October 1814

Dearest Ernesto,

I have put pen to paper as soon as I could, knowing that you felt that I was making a dreadful mistake in marrying Richard, and so wanted to set your mind at rest. The journey to England was incredibly long, and for a while I feared you had been right, and that I should have taken my chances remaining with you all. I miss you all terribly, and all the more so for I know that we may never meet again in this life, the distance between us is now so great.

However, Richard has proven to be the kindest and most considerate of husbands. He never made us travel for longer than we could cope with, and though my Luka was quite shockingly behaved towards him, and far from the behaviour I would have wished from a boy approaching manhood, Richard never lost his temper with him in the way that Luka's own father did. Indeed, it is only now that I see the dreadful effect my late husband had up on his son, and I pray nightly that Richard's calmer influence over him may prevail. As for my little Ana, Richard absolutely dotes upon her, treating

*her as if she were his own, and not the eight-
year-old he has inherited along with me. I can
say in all honesty that we have found the
sanctuary we desperately needed, so please
tell Mama and our sisters this, though I
know Mama will scarcely understand.*

*Upper Moore House is not quite as
grand as the home we once had when dearest
Papa was still alive, but is still a very
substantial house. It has three floors, the
upper one of which will be the nursery for the
newest member of our family who will arrive
soon. Yes, I am to be a mother again, and I
am delighted this time in a way I never could
be before.*

*And now I must entreat you to look to
yourself. You and our beloved uncle have
done so much to try and protect our family
after Papa was forced to marry me to Filip
Kovač, and please believe me when I say that
I hold no grievance against Papa. He was put
in a hideous position, being forced to choose
between sacrificing me, or watching everyone
else in the family being turned out of our
home penniless, and with Nonno and Nonna
dal Zotto…*

"that's granny and granddad dal Zotto, so one or the other
set of grandparents," Cleo interrupted herself to explain,

*…being in their seventies, it would have
killed them if none of the rest of us. It made
me glad at the time that Mama's parents
were not alive to suffer that anguish, and
having seen her distress since then, I fear it
would have been the end of her too, if she had
had to watch her own mama being so sworn
at as Nonna was by Filip. That Filip would*

even consider doing such things was bad
enough, but his continued persecution of
Papa even after I bore him Luka, makes him
barely human in my eyes. I certainly have no
remorse for turning his own dagger upon
him.

You and I share this secret which none
of the rest of the family are burdened with,
may the Lady be blessed, but it means only
we can comfort one another and plan for the
future. They still believe that Papa was able
to strike back at Filip even as he shot poor
Papa, not that I was the one who stabbed him
in the back. However, I must warn you and
beg you to caution now, because members of
Filip's family are less trusting. His cousin
Georgi, for one, is such a man of violence that
I do not think he ever believed that it was
Papa who made the fatal blow. But while
Napoleon was at large, and his army
wreaking havoc across the whole of Europe,
Georgi could not reach us. Now, though, the
barriers are gone, and I feel the greatest of
distress that one day soon he might come
from Laybach seeking revenge.

Please, I beg you, persuade Mama and
our sisters to pack up our home and move to
the other side of the Adriatic, at the very
least, for I shall not rest easy until I know
you are beyond that monster and his other
cousins' grasp. I am writing to you in Italian
as I know that neither Maria nor Guilia
learned it well enough to write, and the
servants will not be able to read this letter
either.

Your loving sister,

Francesca.

"Where the heck is Laybach?" Chris wanted to know.

Cleo had to pause and do a quick internet search, but was then able to tell them,

"It's now Ljubljana, the Croatian capital city. But back then it would probably have been a provincial capital, nothing more. It's more significant that it would have been deeper into Austrian held territory, and so Francesca was right in one respect – it would have been harder for these men she speaks of to get to visit them once they were over the water in the Veneto region of Italy. In Rovinj they really were far too vulnerable."

"It's good to hear that Richard was being the proper gentleman," Sarah said with a wistful sigh, making Cleo think that she was maybe a little sad that she didn't have quite such glowing memories of Jeff. "But oh my God, that poor girl! To have witnessed her husband killing her father! And what's that about her stabbing him?"

Cleo had scanned the letter again to make sure she'd got the right sense of it. "It sounds bloody awful, doesn't it? The bit about her father having no choice but to marry her to this Filip bloke, or the whole family would have been turned out …that's just horrible. Your heart just bleeds for the poor man. So it sounds as if this Filip might have been a blackmailer, or something even worse, because there's no sense that the family had ever done anything to bring him down on them like a horrible curse.

"And the way Richard talked in his letter about the women in the family being so alone, as well. That has to be after that awful time, and you get the feeling that this hidden crime of theirs was hanging over them like a black cloud. It might have been self-defence, but they were clearly worried to death that it would come back to haunt them."

Chris agreed with her, adding, "And you get the distinct sense that they didn't want to drag the younger sisters into it, just in case the authorities got involved. So what's the next one say?"

"It's a reply from Ernesto, her brother…"

> *Rovigno*
> *26th January 1815*
>
> *My dear sister Francesca,*
>
> *Plans are afoot! Uncle Arduino has been working as tirelessly on our behalf now as in wartime, and I am delighted to tell you that the whole family is about to move westwards to Verona. Uncle Arduino is going into partnership with an old friend of his, and I am joining them. It seems this friend has trading contacts who are eager to explore the opportunities offered in Istria now that the war has ended, and one of them has made an offer for our family home. Of course it is far below what it was once worth, but it is better than receiving nothing at all, which is what would happen if we simply upped and left. If nothing else, it will allow me to rent a decent home for us all in Verona until such time as I can afford to buy something more fitting.*
>
> *Please do not reply to this letter, my dear, for I do not know how swiftly our move may come. I will write to you as soon as I can, sending you our new address. In the meantime, know that I am greatly reassured by your description of your life with Lieut.*

Wytcombe. I am much relieved that he has turned out to be a true gentleman, and therefore a far cry from that evil man you had to endure before.

> *Your loving brother,*
> *Ernesto*

P.S. I have taken your lead in not writing in our own language. I feel you are right to remain cautious of our secrets being revealed – as far as I can tell, the servants we have now have no allegiance to the Kovačs, but I would not dismiss the possibility of those evil men threatening one of our folk, and cowing them into doing their wicked work for them. But please, do not forget that it was I who dealt the final and fatal blow. When we come before Our Lady at the end, and beg for her intercession, you were not guilty of taking his life. That is my sin to bear, but I believe most devoutly that She will understand our fears that he would have murdered us all had I not done so, and sooner rather than later, too.

> *E.*

"Holy shit!" Chris gasped. "So Ernesto had to finish this Filip guy off because he thought he was going to kill the whole family? That's pretty extreme stuff."

"It is," Cleo conceded, "but if you think of them being on the fringe of the Austrian territories at a time when the Austrian Emperor had barely managed to hang onto his lands around there, there probably wasn't much in the way of law enforcement going on at the time. Think of the atrocities that were committed in the Balkans between the Serbs and the Croats only a decade or two ago. There was nobody to stop them then, either, so Filip sounds like someone who saw his chance to steal everything that was this family's, and then pass it off as his own after the war was over. He was committing little short of a war crime, so we shouldn't think too badly of Francesca or Ernesto."

Sarah meanwhile was thinking of Francesca. "Is that what her brother calls him? 'That evil man you had to endure'? Goodness me, that's pretty strong stuff when talking about one Georgian era man's perception of another, isn't it?"

"Very!" Cleo agreed. "It might well be that she had to suffer Filip raping her many times over, and that just make me feel sick. ...Oh, here we go, the next one is from Ernesto too..."

Via al Cristo
Verona
4th April 1815

My dearest sister,

> *Despite the return of Napoleon from his captivity, we have made the journey to Verona. Our new home is near to the Ponte Nuovo, one of the main bridges in Verona, and our house faces onto a pleasant little square. We do not have the separation from our neighbours that we once had, but I take consolation in the fact that the violence we endured in our old home would be audible here, and would arouse the concern of these neighbours. A man like Filip would find it infinitely harder to carry on his*

wicked ways in this house, for we are not so separated.

The journey itself went with remarkable ease, and our sisters Maria and Giulia are blossoming in this new home. They have lost the worried frowns which were close to being permanent, and to my great delight, are beginning to behave more like the twenty-one- and eighteen-year-old young women that they are, instead of old women before their time. Poor Mama, though, is much unsettled by the move, and regularly cries out for Papa to come and rescue her. I fear that the prolonged stress of sharing a home with your evil late husband, and then losing first Lucieta and then Papa in the midst of such danger, has permanently affected her mind. Whether she will ever be the same again is in some doubt. I briefly considered whether to ask you if Richard would allow you to have her with you in England, but then Maria pointed out that in her present state of mind, poor Mama would never cope with being surrounded by strangers who also spoke another language. Within our house, she at least has us and our few loyal servants to talk to. So she will stay here with us in Verona.

For my own part, I also have good news to send you. PierAntonio has a baby sister, who we are calling Lucieta in memory of our dear sister whom we lost so tragically. My beloved Anzola was due to give birth within the month even as we made arrangements to leave Rovigno, and we were all most apprehensive as to the advisability of her *travelling so far. However, she was most insistent that we go, saying that she wanted her child to be born without the threat of the Kovač family's revenge looming over us, and so no sooner had we landed on the Venetian shore than Lucieta arrived. Maria and Guilia are both besotted with their baby niece.*

And there is more good news, for Maria has married Gennaro Pierucci, who is the captain of the boat which brought us here. His family are from Puglia, and so although he knows Uncle Arduino and his partner from their business, he is mercifully unaware that Filip Kovač even existed, much less has any connection to him. You are the only one to whom I can express such relief, and I know that you will join me in rejoicing that at least one of our sisters now has another family who will care for and watch over her, and also the children she and Gennaro will undoubtedly have. It was a courtship even faster than your own, but he adores her and I know you will understand the reasons why neither Uncle nor I opposed the marriage.

Your loving brother,
Ernesto

"Oh bless them!" Sarah gulped, deeply moved by the letter. "Oh it does sound as though they were living in a permanent state of terror in Rovinj, doesn't it?"

"If it was having such an effect on the younger two sisters, then yes," Cleo sighed, feeling terribly sorry for this family whom she would never meet, but who seemed destined to be a part of her life. "In 1815, Francesca would have been coming up thirty-two, so there was quite a big gap between her and the other two girls. I did wonder if there were children in between, of which I presume one was Ernesto, though I don't like the sound of Lucieta's death. It makes me wonder whether Filip was more than a little responsible for her dying too. I'll have another go at looking for more siblings when I get the chance, especially now that I have a surname to work with. Mind you, it's not unknown for women to have a break in their fertility if they're under huge stress, and if this wasn't the first time Francesca's mother endured that, it might account for it. …Okay, now we're back to Francesca…"

Upper Moore House,
Bromyard
23 May 1815

Dearest Ernesto,

You send me all good news. I am so delighted that you have escaped unscathed. My heart bleeds for poor Mama, and her confusion over having to leave her home of so many years. Once upon a time we shared so much love and laughter in that old house, and in latter years, I often wondered whether in Mama's empty gaze she was looking back to those happier times because she could not bear the pain of the present. I am so glad that you and Anzola have another child. I can but hope that the sound of children playing happily once more will rouse Mama, and that it will prove to be the tonic she needs.

On November 5th I gave birth to a lovely baby boy, named Hector after Richard's grandfather. Ana is a doting big sister to

him, but the one blight on our happiness is
Luka. He has shown terrible jealously
towards the baby, and after months of trying
to reason with him, Richard has finally sent
him away to become a midshipman. He
assures me that in the mixed company of the
navy, Luka's less than perfect English will
not be too much of a barrier, and he believes
that having to find his own way in the world
will do Luka much good.

I have not yet found the courage, nor, I
confess, the words in English to be able to tell
Richard all of what befell us. Therefore he
does not fully comprehend the malign
influence of Filip upon my son, and I have
only been able to explain in the poorest of
manners how Luka believed he would inherit
all of his father's wealth. That that wealth
had vanished in Filip's gambling, drinking,
and hopeless grand schemes long before we
left, is something that Luka refuses to hear.

I am glad that Richard could not
understand the foul names that my son
sometimes called me, for I know that Richard
would have been angry beyond words. Yet he
is no fool, and he told me that it was not just
for baby Hector's sake that he was sending
Luka away, but for Ana's and mine too. I do
not understand all that he tells me yet, but I
fear that the one night he was trying to tell
me that he had found Luka in Ana's room.
What went on Ana will not say, but since
Luka has been gone she has treated Richard
like her saviour, and only you can guess what
I fear that signals, for she is now the age
Lucieta was when Filip began preying upon

her. Please Our Lady, Luka has not inherited his father's perverse tastes.

However, for now our household has settled into something which resembles the happy home life that you and I once knew, and I am daring to hope that my remaining children will never need to worry about that dark cloud which once hung over us. Give my love to all of the family, and tell Maria that I am glad now that I left the family necklace with her and Giulia, for Mama always swore that that was our protection, and I now have my guardian in Richard.

> *Your loving sister,*
> *Francesca*

Chris was wrinkling his nose in distaste. "Luka in his sister's room? Oh yuk, that really is gross! He was one nasty pervert, wasn't he?"

Cleo nodded. "A real chip off the old block by the sound of it. God, that part about Filip preying on Lucieta sounds like he was a paedophile to add to his sins, doesn't it? You could argue forever about nature versus nurture, but in Luka's case, if his father set him off on the wrong path, then he certainly doesn't seem to have been receptive to Richard trying to put him back on the right one. He appears to have been determined to be his father's son."

Sarah was silent, but glancing at her, Cleo saw her looking at Chris and giving a watery smile – he was the son who hadn't followed his father's lead, and had proved to be the better man for it, even if Sarah would never say so out loud. Damn, that part had hit a bit too close to home.

"Interesting about the necklace, too," Chris was carrying on, oblivious to his mother's looks. "That's one heck of a strong belief they had in it. You get the feeling that they were deeply torn as to whether to give it to Francesca for protection – 'cause let's face it, they hardly knew Richard from Adam, did they? – or to hang onto it for their own safety. But believe in it they did."

Cleo picked up the next two letters and noticed the black edging on the second one. "Oh dear, this doesn't look like good news. Here we go…"

> *Via al Cristo*
> *Verona*
> *29 August 1815*

My dearest sister,

> *In amongst the wider rejoicing at the downfall of Napoleon, we have joyous news of our own. Maria is expecting a baby in December! Giulia is blossoming in this new place, and is becoming quite fluent in Italian, but as yet she has not mastered the written language, so yours and my 'conversations' are still private.*

> *Sadly, Mama is declining, and I fear that by the time you read this she will no longer be with us. Do not mourn too hard for her, though, for life has become an intolerable burden to her in these last years. She now thinks that Maria is you, and that Guilia is Maria, believing that our baby Lucieta is her own infant Lucieta, and no matter how many times I tell her otherwise, she believes me to be Papa, and asks where her son Ernesto is. Guilia is the best one at comforting her, for I*

fear I cannot find the right words most of the time. How can I tell her that Papa is not here without digging up the memories of Filip and all that he did? And she does not deserve to have those brought to light if she has forgotten them.

Uncle Arduino and his partner, Matteo, are doing very well here, as a result of which they have taken on more men and put me in charge of them. I am very grateful of the increase in income with the new mouths to feed, so please thank Richard for me for the money he sent, but assure him that we should be able to support ourselves from now on.

As for your news of Luka, that disturbs me greatly, and I cannot but applaud Richard's decision to remove him from your home. I had begun to fear that Filip's bad blood had been passed on to him undiluted even before you left. After his evil father had died, I sometimes found him looking through family papers which he had no right to be doing. When I would ask him why, he would look at me with those hard eyes which no child of his age should have, and demanded to know why we were keeping him short of the luxuries of his father's time. Nothing I could say to him would convince him that Filip had squandered every coin, sold every jewel, and even sold off most of our land which was not his to sell.

It is a terrible thing for any mother to have to do, but I would counsel you not to press Richard to allow him back any time soon. If Luka does reform, then when your children are old enough to stand up to him it

*may be different, but for now do not blame
yourself for what Luka has become. Between
the Kovač bad blood and the example their
father set, instead give thanks to the Lady
that your dearest Ana has turned out to be
such a sweet soul.*

*I will write to you as soon as anything
happens with Mama,*

Your affectionate brother,

Ernesto

*Via al Cristo
Verona
30 October 1815*

Dearest Francesca,

*Our beloved Mama is
gone. She slipped peacefully away in her
sleep a week ago, and has been laid to rest. I
only wish that we could have buried her
alongside Papa where she would have wanted
to be, but you are the one member of the
family, aside from Uncle Arduino, who
understands fully why that was never going
to be possible. We have consoled Maria and
Guilia with the excuse of the distance, but I
confess I had to be most insistent with
Maria's Gennaro to stop offering to transport
Mama's coffin home. He loves Maria very
much, and only means to please her and ease
her grief, but in the end Uncle and I had to
have a more frank conversation than we
would have liked with him, and if we did not
tell him all, we did at least convince him that
there were men back in Rovigno who would
be seeking us to do us harm. May the saints*

be blessed that he is not a curious man, and
so asked no more than what we told him, for
how could we tell him that his sister-in-law
stabbed her husband, and that I made the
killing blow when he turned on you, despite
the many blows you had already delivered?
How could a man who has only ever known a
loving family comprehend a man like Filip,
who would shoot his father-in-law in front of
his own wife for no other reason than his own
malignancy?

Your grieving brother,
Ernesto

"Oh how terribly sad," Sarah said with a sniffle into her tissue. "That poor mother."

"Steady on, Mum," Chris consoled her, coming to give his own mother a hug. "It sounds more than a bit like Alzheimer's to me. And it might have been a blessing, as Ernesto said, that in her last years she didn't really know what was going on."

"But she missed her late husband so much," Sarah wept. "They must have been so close."

Chris said nothing but gave Cleo a despairing look; and knowing now that Jeff had swanned off on that last skiing trip regardless of Sarah and what she had wanted, Cleo could only sympathise with the turmoil of feelings Sarah must be going through. So she hurried on with the next letter.

Upper Moore House,
Bromyard
24 December 1815

Dear Ernesto,

I write to you on this Christmas Eve with many mixed emotions. For all that you have told me of Mama's decline, I have still wept many tears over her passing, remembering the wonderful loving mother that we had. She and Papa were so happy together when we were all children, and she did not deserve the monster which war brought into our midst. May God forgive me, but I still pray that Filip rots in the lowest levels of Hell for what he brought down on us all. I cannot tell you how many times I have knelt before the image of Our Lady and asked Her why his regiment had to come to our town? What terrible trick of Fate sent him to us? Why were they not with the rest of the emperor's army, like our late and beloved Uncle Ernesto was? How could he have died and yet Filip live? It seems so unfair. I am glad that all of us have escaped from the lands controlled by the Austrian Emperor, for the ease with which Filip's family would have been able to get to us still haunts my dreams.

Yet I have happier news of my own for you. In the spring I shall be a mother again! Hector will have a baby brother or sister, and my dearest Richard is thrilled, as is Ana. Of Luka we have had no direct word, though an old friend of Richard's has informed us that the ship he is on is in the West Indies. That is a relief for me, for it means that he will not be home in a while, and I need not fear him turning up unannounced while this new baby is tiny. That feels such a terrible thing

*to say, for I can still remember him as the
first child I cradled in my arms, but the
person he has become is now a total stranger
to me.*

*I have prayed that Maria has been safely
delivered of her first child, and that you will
all be celebrating Christmas, remembering
with joy how Mama and Papa so loved
having us altogether at this time of year.*

    Your loving sister,
        Francesca

"And poor Francesca, too," Chris breathed. "Wow, what an awful thing to have to say about your own child. Luka must have been one hell of a monster for even his own mother to think that."

"And of course by then he wasn't a little boy anymore," Cleo pointed out. "In 1815 he would have already turned fifteen, and well capable of inflicting some terrible damage on a fragile newborn, or even Hector as a toddler. You can understand why they were glad he wasn't around. Look at some of the cases that come up in the papers these days, where teenagers of that age commit murder – it wasn't just a Georgian era problem, some kids just can't seem to help being drawn to the dark side of life."

"And in his case with no excuse for having been brought up in poverty," Chris added pointedly. "That house in Rovinj might have been getting dilapidated, but it was a very far cry from some poor farmer's hut. And he came here to Upper Moore to be waited on hand and foot." He looked at the diminishing pile beside Cleo. "So do these letters start to run out?"

Cleo had been scanning the rest as they spoke. "I don't think so much run out as this remainder being just them keeping the few significant ones from now on. I wonder whether young Giulia suddenly proved to be better at Italian than Ernesto thought, and he and Francesca had to start being more circumspect?"

She waved one letter gently. "This one from Ernesto in 1818, for instance, seems to have been kept primarily because it included the invitation to Giulia's wedding. …Hmm, Guilia dal Zotto to Alvaro Marinelli – that's nice, two more surnames I can work with!"

She had a quick look at Richard's family tree, then telling the other two, "Francesca didn't have our missing William until the next year, so it's possible that she and Richard and the family went over for the wedding. What a pity it's too early for there to have been any photos. I'd love to put faces to names."

Chris nodded. "Ernesto sounds like such a cool brother to have had. He really did his best for them, didn't he? And maybe if the Wytcombes went over to Verona, then they would have all been able to talk about what had gone on, meaning there'd be no need for secretive letters."

"So why keep them, then?" Sarah wondered.

"Insurance?" Cleo guessed. "Richard and Ernesto sound very much feet-firmly-on-the-ground sort of men. Maybe they agreed that the letters should stay with Richard, just in case anything should happen to the family in Verona? That way he would be able to set the local authorities moving – don't forget that in that era to be an English gentleman was to have no small standing, even in Europe. If Richard kicked up a fuss, he'd be likely to be believed." She turned the envelopes over to look at the stamp marks, then pointed out, "We found all of these in the one place, so I reckon Ernesto handed over Francesca's letters back to Richard, and he was keeping them safe in that hidden partition in his desk. He couldn't have had them openly in the house in case Luka came home, but I bet his sons later knew about them, even if they couldn't read any Italian."

Chris rubbed his hands together. "Wow! This is getting exciting. So we know that Francesca was forced to marry Luka and Ana's father, and she then murdered that evil first husband with the help of her brother, Ernesto. Come on, Cleo, let's have the next instalment!"

Chapter 25

Cleo carefully put the letters she had read into some protective film and set them to one side. "Okay, we're now into something of a one-sided conversation. Unlike the ones we've just read, which were hidden here in the desk, these are amongst the papers Hugh brought back from Verona with him, because these are amongst what came out of our furry friend upstairs. I think I'm right to say that they're between Richard and Francesca's daughter Sophia, and Francesca's youngest sister Guilia, but we'll be able to tell better when we get into them." She took up the first one causing Chris to groan,

"Oh no, not another black-edged one! That can't have been good news."

"I don't think it is…"

> *Upper Moore House,*
> *Bromyard*
> *14th August 1840*
>
> *Dear Aunt Guilia,*
> *I scarcely know where to begin with our awful news, and now I have such sympathy for you having to write to us four years ago to tell us of the tragic loss of Aunt Maria and all of her family, plus your own two dear ones…*

"Good Lord!" Sarah exclaimed. "That's terrible! What on earth happened to them?"

But Cleo held up a finger for quiet and continued to read,

...Yet heartbreaking though your news was, the way Cholera swept through poor Gennaro's family in Puglia, and with them having the simple misfortune to be there visiting at the time, at least made it an act of God, however incomprehensible. Oh that my own news was so blameless!

My beloved brother Hector is with us no more, and I can scarce write this for weeping, for my dear, sweet brother was murdered. You know how devoted he was to his beloved Charlotte, and to baby Julia, and you will therefore understand why we do not believe what we have been told. He was found on the morning of 6th August in an alley of ill-repute, running up into Worcester from South Quay beside the River Severn. I cannot bear to write its name, but it is where the women of loose morals ply their trade.

Forgive me for this tear-stained page. This is the fifth time I have tried to write this letter, and each time I get to this point and cannot hold back from weeping. Dear Edward offered to write this for me, but he has been left with the burden of arranging the funeral and so much more, and I felt that you should hear this news from one of us close to you. My dear brother, who would not harm a fly, and who so loved singing in Church on a Sunday, had his throat most vilely cut.

"Fucking hell!" Chris swore, and Sarah was too shocked herself to protest. "There's no getting around that as murder, is there? Nobody cuts their own throat. I mean, even with the sharpest of knives you couldn't get enough pressure to do it. Sorry, Mum, I'm not being ghoulish. It's just that I saw a program about a murder investigation, and they made the point that it's all just hokum to think that people can do that with one quick swipe of a knife. Apparently we have a lot of cartilage and muscles in our throat that make us able to do things like swallowing. So it takes a lot of strength and knowhow even to do it to someone else, and is damned near impossible as a means of suicide, despite some gory films claiming otherwise, or at least not unless you want a long and drawn out death. Poor old Hector, what a horrible way to go!"

Cleo was nodding, "And even a gentlewoman in those days would have known about things like slaughtering the meat that came to the table. Back then they didn't pick up neat packages from the supermarket – they would have heard the pig being slaughtered out in the yard – so no wonder Sophia's so upset, she knows exactly what's happened to him. And Hector sounds as though he was a thoroughly nice bloke like his dad. She goes on…"

> *What is almost worse, the men of the city watch and the magistrates have blindly assumed that Hector was visiting a woman in that wicked lane, and fell afoul of one of the ruffians who watch over those women, or maybe a cutpurse. When my Edward protested that Hector would never have visited such a place, he was distraught to have the magistrate tell him to not be so naive; that men of standing still had their appetites. Yet we all know that he would not have, not because he was so very saintly as to never notice another woman or have manly urges, but because Papa warned him most vigorously to avoid such places, since that was how Tarquin has come to be amongst us,*

and none of us want a repeat of that situation!

Edward was greatly distressed when he came home after having been told all of this, not least because he then had to tell Charlotte and myself that while the watch will do what they can, they believe that it is highly unlikely that the miscreant will be found. Yet there is worse to tell. Though Edward did his best, they would not take seriously his demands that they look at Luka and where he was that night.

I know from when we came to see you that you share my distrust of Luka, so you will understand when I say that he protested his absence from the area a little too much. He claims he was in Abergavenny at the time of the murder, yet he was here too fast for the news to have reached him there and then to have set out. If he was any farther afield than Bromyard or Ledbury I would be much surprised. Sadly Edward tells me that we must be careful in this matter, for if we are believed to be slandering Luka's good name, then it will be we who fall afoul of the law, not Luka. May God forgive me for saying so, but like his thrice-be-damned father, Luka has the luck of the Devil.

After the funeral, Edward and I must return to London, for his business will not cope with his absence for longer, yet it distresses me greatly that we cannot persuade Charlotte to come with us. Ana's baby, Bertram, is still too small to travel far, and little Olivia has shared the nursery with Charlotte's Julia so much that they are more like twin sisters, all of which has Charlotte declaring they she will stay with Ana. So far Tarquin has been remarkably silent about Ana separating herself and the children from him, which Edward and I also believe does not bode well, and had we the room here, we would have Ana with us too. Charlotte believes that they will manage until such time as young William can return from the navy to claim his inheritance, but it is unfortunate that he is at present in the Indies, and not likely to return for several months yet.

Please respond to me at our normal address, for we had to leave my baby Arianna with her nurse while we came here, and I long to be with her again. I will write again as soon as I have any further news,

Your loving niece,

Sophia.

Cleo finished and leaned back to look at Sarah and Chris. "Well that's a bundle of news, and no mistake! So Ana was trying to separate from Tarquin, was she? Hardly surprising."

"Could she do that?" Chris asked. "I thought a divorce was next to impossible in those days?"

"If you were poor, yes it was," Cleo told him, "because the lawyers didn't come cheap then any more than now. And before 1857 it actually required an Act of Parliament and was only available to men – so it was definitely the preserve of the rich back then. So for a woman like Ana in the 1840s it would have been most definitely a case of separation, because she would never have got a divorce. At least it sounds as though Hector was being a star about the whole thing and letting her live at Upper Moore. She wasn't having to pass herself off as a widow in some scummy lodging house far from where anyone knew her in order to get free of him, and yet still try and maintain some vestige of respectability. We'll probably never know the full details, but if Tarquin was truly brutal with Ana at the point when Bertram was conceived, that had to have been no later than the summer of 1839; so little Olivia would only have been two at the most, and therefore that's why Upper Moore was feeling like home to her. So the chances are that Ana had been living at Upper Moore for the best part of a year when Hector died, maybe more if they were already there and it was Hector who chucked Tarquin out."

"Which is why she clearly thought she was safe," Chris sighed. "Doesn't this make you wish you could scream back through time at them and tell them, 'Go to London with Sophia!' Even a rogue like Luka would have found it harder to do his worst there."

However Cleo shook her head. "Actually, it would probably have been the reverse. There were some very dark parts of London in the mid nineteenth century, and a truly evil man like Luka would soon have sniffed out others like himself. For all we know, he might have arranged a house break-in, and Sophia and her family might have been killed too. ...But I'm jumping the gun with that. Let me read you the next letter..."

North St.,
London.
28 November 1840

Dear Aunt Giulia,
May God watch over us, for
I have even more disturbing news. Ana has
vanished! Since our return home, I have had

weekly letters from both Charlotte and Ana, and for the first week or so all seemed to be well. But then disaster struck! Luka and Tarquin turned up together, supposedly to bring about some form of reconciliation between Ana and Tarquin. However, right from the start, Charlotte told me that she feared there was more to it than that, for she now believes that little Sabina has been spying on Ana and writing to her father. At eleven years old we must only pray that she knew not what she was doing, for it would be a wicked thing if she turned out to be another such as Luka, and evilly knowing at that age. But now Charlotte is the one who cannot travel far, for she is with child and will, God willing, give birth early in the new year. Oh how I wish Hector was still here to hear that happy news.

We were due to travel to Upper Moore as soon as Edward's business allowed, for both Ana and Charlotte wrote that Luka was claiming that there ought to be a man's presence on the estate to oversee things until William returns. Given that neither even attended dear Hector's funeral – which was commented upon by our neighbours, I will have you know – it is ridiculous for them to claim this for themselves when it was Edward who sorted the estate out. So we were due to travel next week anyway, but then two days ago an urgent letter arrived from Charlotte.

She got up one morning and felt dizzy and heavy-headed, and was then shocked to find that it was close to midday. When her maid came in to her, the girl looked half frightened out of her wits, seeming too scared to even speak to her. Yet when Charlotte went in search of Ana, both she and her children were gone, and Tarquin with them. She managed to get the letter to me out of the house via Mrs Gormley, our stout-hearted cook, who has never liked Luka, but Charlotte writes that Luka has her virtually imprisoned in the house, and she believes that she was drugged the night they took Ana so that she would know nothing. That alone makes my blood run cold, for who would do that to a pregnant woman unless they wanted her to miscarry, too?

Edward now fears it will not be wise for me to travel there with him, and will go instead along with the man he employs to guard him when carrying large amounts of money. And in truth, I am once again prostrate with morning sickness, which has laid me low since I last wrote to you, and so I would have struggled to travel anyway. However, Edward will now go and endeavour to bring Charlotte and Julia back here with him, even if it has to be a slow journey.

I will write as soon as I know more,
Your deeply worried niece,

Sophia

"Oh, this isn't going well," Sarah sighed. "It's bad enough for us to have just had the bare facts you found, Cleo, but to hear Sophia worrying herself sick over Charlotte and Ana makes it even more heartbreaking."

Cleo read on…

North St.,
London.
20th December 1840

Dear Aunt Giulia,

I am now beside myself with worry. Edward has returned from Upper Moore with a broken arm, having run into a gang of ruffians whom Luka has prowling about Upper Moore estate. My brave husband did his best to try and get past them to the house, but after they had pulled his manservant from his horse and beat him near senseless, claiming that Edward and he were trespassing, Edward felt it politic to retreat. He told me he feared had he pressed on he would have left me a widow.

Yet as they were having their wounds patched at the inn in Bromyard, Mrs Gormley came to find him. She has been dismissed from Upper Moore, but since Lady Attingham has always coveted her services, it was not long before she was re-employed. For that I am glad, for she was a good and faithful servant to us all, and did nothing to deserve her dismissal. However she told Edward some most unsettling news. It seems that somehow, Luka has become fixated on the idea that Uncle Ernesto murdered his father with Mama's connivance. It is all nonsense, of course, but he seems determined to blacken all of our names with this allegation, and I fear I must warn you that he has even gone so far as to say that once he has his share of the estate, as a rightful heir alongside William, then he will be using his

money to press for Uncle Ernesto to be
brought to justice.

Where he has got this ridiculous idea
from that he is a joint heir with William, I
cannot imagine. Upper Moore was our
papa's house, and Luka is no blood relation of
his at all. However Edward has said that he
will be watching very carefully for such
claims through the courts, for being at Grey's
Inn, he has the means to do so. In the
meantime, please warn Uncle Ernesto. It
may all come to nothing, but I would be
distraught if Luka now brought misery on
your family the way his father once did.

Your loving niece,
Sophia.

As Cleo finished, all three of them sat back and stared
aghast at one another.

"How the hell did Luka find that out?" Chris
wondered in disbelief.

"Well it can't have been from any of the letters we
found," Cleo declared. "He'd have taken them and used
them to blackmail the Italian family, wouldn't he? Possibly
very successfully, since they were clear evidence of his
suspicions. After all, what he really wanted was money and
power, and the letters could potentially have provided him
with both. And clearly Sophia herself didn't know the
truth at that stage – so she or her siblings couldn't have
told him."

Chris gazed off into the distance as he thought, then
proposed, "Do you think that he came across one of those
cousins of Filip's that Francesca talked about?"

"But where?" Sarah protested. "They'd be a long way away from here."

However Chris pointed out, "Yes, but Luka was in the navy, wasn't he? What if his ship took him back to the Adriatic? And let's face it, we don't know how long he lasted in the Royal Navy, do we? He could have jumped ship and joined up with a merchant ship. Trade would have still been going on, even if a cessation of hostilities with the French meant that there were less naval ships in the eastern Med'."

"That's a good point," Cleo agreed. "I can't imagine Luka enjoying navy discipline for long, but he'd have fitted right in with a bunch of piratical mercenaries, looting their way around the Med'. We've got a big gap in his history until he marries Louisa. I'd assumed that it was Richard who gave him the funds to rent, if not buy, that villa by Abergavenny which I found the record of. But if it was more that Richard wouldn't have anything to do with him, then Luka might well have bought the place himself, however unlikely that might sound – and he wouldn't have done that doing unskilled work in rural Wales! Going into the navy as young as he did, there was no chance for him to become articled to any professional man, where he might eventually have earned such money honestly. And outside of wartime, he'd have had to live on his wages from the navy, not save them up, and certainly not enough to get a house with, which rather points to him having some ill-gotten gains."

"So are we coming up to that point when Edward takes the children abroad?" Sarah asked, and Cleo picked up the next letter.

North St.,
London.
24th January 1841

Dear Aunt Giulia,

We still have no news of Ana, which worries us all desperately, especially as Tarquin appears to have returned to Upper Moore without her. He, along with his five children, now seems to be living there with Luka and his daughter, Frances. Charlotte is kept in her rooms along with little Julia, and we fear for their safety.

We have this news because Edward now has three men in his pay to watch the house and grounds as best they can. Luckily, Luka's main gang of ruffians soon went, though to who knows where, but there are still two men of very bad character kept about the place as if guarding it. It is wearing beyond belief, for we live in a constant state of alert, just waiting for the message to come that Luka and Tarquin have left the house for a few days, which might give us our chance to free those we love. Edward has even gone as far as to tell his men to seize Charlotte, Julia and Olivia if they get the chance, and to get them away by any means, for he knows it may take too long for him to get there himself from here before those two demons return.

I am beside myself with worry,

Sophia

"My God, Edward really must have been worried if he did that," Chris said. "It's little short of kidnapping if someone misread the situation, and since it sounds as though he was a lawyer, he would have known the consequences."

"And to risk taking Olivia, too," Cleo agreed. "I suspect they thought she was in danger because of her closeness to Julia."

North St.,
London.
24th February 1841

Dear Aunt Giulia,

> *I do not know whether to be glad or appalled at your news, but I do know that I am relieved that Uncle Ernesto and Aunt Anzola have decided to go to America with their children. Maybe that will be far enough for them to be beyond Luka's evil? Yet it does not seem right that they have been driven out from the house that Uncle Ernesto worked so hard to make into a home for you all. Part of me wishes I had not said anything to you about Luka's accusations against Uncle, but then I turn to the increasingly bad news I keep sending you, and know that I would never have forgiven myself if I had not warned you, and he had followed through with those threats.*

> *As for that news, oh Aunt, Charlotte has had a little boy whom she has called Clifford after her mama's brother. Again we have the loyal Mrs Gormley to thank for letting us know, for she heard Luka speaking with the vicar arranging his baptism. Yet I wish desperately that she had had a girl. A little girl would not be in line to inherit anything in the way of the estate, and in time, Charlotte and her babies might have been allowed to leave. But Luka will not let any potential heir out of his clutches!*

And there is worse. Luka has been to see lawyers in Hereford with a letter which claims that my brother William is dead, and therefore that <u>he</u> is now the heir to Upper Moore! Neither Edward nor I believe this, or at least not this version of events, because had William died in service, then <u>we</u> would have been informed by the navy as his next of kin. Edward has managed to find out through his contacts that Luka's letter supposedly claims that William died while on a shore party in India, but when Edward enquired of the Admiralty, he was informed that at that point William had already left the service with the intention of returning home. Truly, I do not know what to believe. Part of me longs to see my brother again, yet another part hopes he never sets foot near Upper Moore again, for with Luka there I do not think he would live through the first night. How that man manages to get away with his plots and schemes I do not know, but it shows him to have a mind of unrivalled deviousness.

We still live in hope of rescuing Charlotte, but my own pregnancy advances and with it my nightmares that I may never see her again.

Your loving niece,

Sophia.

Cleo gasped as she read the last sentence. "God, that was prescient of her, wasn't it? She really didn't ever see Charlotte again. It'd be another thirteen years before Ana and Charlotte jumped to their deaths, but the way they died make it clear that none of the rest of the family ever found either of them."

Sarah nodded. "Poor Sophia. Your emotions are all over the place when you're pregnant anyway, and with all this stress, I'm amazed that she didn't miscarry – especially when you consider the lack of medical care she would have got."

"And it sounds as though she thinks that Ernesto left just because of that threat," Chris observed. "I think the Italian family still hadn't told her that her mum and Ernesto actually *did* kill Filip, albeit in self-defence. They were all being very cagey about the past, weren't they?"

"And I suspect with good cause," Cleo agreed, picking up the next letter to read,

> *North St.,*
> *London.*
> *5th April 1841*

Dear Aunt Giulia,

> *You have no notion of how relieved I am to hear that William is safe with you. He may have thought that his journey went dreadfully awry when he found himself stranded on the coast of the Red Sea, but to my mind he was saved by that, and all the more so for having found his way to you. God be praised that he remembered where you lived! I am also forever grateful to you for having persuaded him to stay with Cousin Claudio and his wife Cinzia. My little brother will be infinitely safer with your son and his family than ever he would be here, especially as Luka has no idea where he is now. It may even be that Luka was behind William getting stranded, but if so, then his*

undoubted intention of leaving William to die on some foreign coast has vastly failed.

You will understand my mixture of relief and despair even more when I tell you that we have now also lost Charlotte. I do not mean that she has died. In some ways that would be a blessing, for then we would know that she is beyond any suffering. No, she too has vanished from Upper Moore, and we do not know to where. My heart breaks with this news, and I sometimes wonder how much more we must bear.

Edward's men have continued to watch the house, and it is to them that we must give thanks for the one happy outcome. I for one will feel forever in their debt, for they watched and waited, and one night, Luka and Tarquin left in a carriage. Edward and I now fear that it was that night that they took poor Charlotte away, because when the house went quiet, two of our intrepid men dared to break in through the library window. Creeping up to the bedrooms, they found Tarquin's children locked all together into one room on the first floor, though they dared not turn the key to check on that. Sadly, Sabina, Ana's oldest, seems enthralled with her Uncle Luka, and the men reported that having watched the way she spies on the younger children, they feared they would not get Olivia away before Sabina raised the alarm.

However, Julia and baby Clifford were locked in the nursery on the top floor, and they managed to pick them up and carry them out before they woke. I had told the men *that the back stairs were better to remain unseen upon, and also that they would get access easiest through the library French windows. Yet they got in so fast, they said they wondered whether one of the servants had spotted they were there and had deliberately made their task easier. If so, I do hope that that brave soul does not forfeit their life for their courage. But the best news is that we now have Julia and Clifford here in London with us in safety. If we can ever find where their mother is, we may yet reunite them. That is looking like an increasingly faint hope, though. Edward has even enquired at the local hospitals and asylums, but no Mrs Wytcombe has been admitted, and I now fear that Charlotte may have gone to join Hector.*

Please write and let me know that everyone is still safe with you,

Your loving niece,

Sophia.

Cleo huffed in dismay. "They really weren't any match for Luka, were they? They didn't think to look for Charlotte under another name. Isn't it weird that the one branch of the family doesn't have an ounce of guile in them, and yet the others are almost evil beyond belief?"

"And well done those men for getting the little ones out," declared Sarah.

Chris wore a pensive frown as he added, "And I reckon the men were right to think someone let them in. Have you looked at those old French windows? I don't know what the doors are made of, but it's good hard wood. It's barely warped or rotted in all the years it's been in, and the locks might look a bit old fashioned now, but back then they would have been state of the art, wouldn't you say, Cleo?"

"Oh definitely! And if you think that if Julia and Clifford were in the nursery, then they would've had to be carried almost the full length of the upper landing to get to the back stairs. Do we think for one moment that not one of the servants heard a thing? Not one creak of the floorboards? Especially as they were sleeping virtually above the library. So I think those men of Edward's must have been chatting up the housemaids, or buying the grooms a pint in the local inn, and getting them on their side. And if those servants were mostly the ones who'd been with the original family, hearing Charlotte and Ana being mistreated might have had them already wondering if there was a way they could get them out. It might not have taken much persuasion at all."

She suddenly had a thought and tugged her laptop to her across the carpet. "Hang on, let me look at the censuses again. We said it was odd that the family were all missing when the 1841 one took place, but that the servants were there. Let me check them against the ones who were there in 1851. ...Yes! Almost a total change of staff – not even any of the same surnames, which could have been just a change of family member serving there. And that again is not normal. As you said, Sarah, on those old estates, families would be there for generations. But if they realised that there was nothing left that they could do – or, heaven help them, they got threatened for helping the true family – it's not so odd to see them leaving the place once Luka and Tarquin were in permanent residence. They might have had to work at that move over a few years, but during that ten year period, if they were really determined, I reckon they could have got out – especially if Luka was developing a foul reputation in the neighbourhood. That might have made other landowners more sympathetic to workers wanting to leave, if they'd had their own brushes with Luka and Tarquin's bad tempers."

She picked up the next letter,

North St.,
London.
17th June 1841

Dear Aunt Giulia,

Edward and I are in total agreement with your plan. With Cinzia having been so ill with measles, I can fully understand her and Claudio's fear that now they may not have children of their own. It is a bad illness to have as a child, but have had it as a young woman, as Cinzia has done, can leave weaknesses which she may not recover from. So I know that Julia and Clifford will be loved and cared for as if they were their own, and will grow up in safety, never having to worry about Luka threatening their lives. He was never around when the friendship between the two sides of the family was rekindled, and so that was his undoing in his plotting against Uncle Ernesto. Since he has such a low opinion of women, he undoubtedly never even bothered to find out your married name, and so your son being called Claudio Marinelli is as good as being a total stranger to him.

Even though it will mean Edward cannot be here when I give birth, he feels the urgency of getting our two little guests away as soon as possible, and so he has already booked a berth on the next available ship for

*France. God forbid, but Luka may think to
come here and watch our house for them. We
have also talked about leaving England
ourselves. Much as it grieves me to leave
behind all that I love, I find I am unable to
face the prospect of living the rest of our lives
looking over our shoulders for Luka. If he can
murder Hector, and make Ana and Charlotte
vanish, we truly are not safe anymore.
Therefore Edward had asked me to ask you to
put him in touch with Uncle Ernesto. There
must be opportunities for a man with
Edward's legal experience in New York, and
if we can be with at least some others of our
family, then it will not seem so very far
away.*

*Please write and let me know that
Edward has arrived safely,*

Your loving niece,

Sophia.

"And how soon after that did you say they leave?"
Sarah asked.

"Only a couple of years later," Cleo said, checking the
date in her records. "They probably only waited that long
because Sophia got pregnant again so quickly. It was far
from an easy voyage in those days."

"So what does the last letter say?" Chris asked.

North St.,
London.
6th October 1841

Dear Aunt Giulia,
*My dear Edward is back
safe with me, and has been introduced to his*

new daughter, Francesca. I am so pleased that Julia and Clifford have settled well with Claudio and Cinzia, and I think it a good thing that for now they will have the Marinelli name as far as your neighbours are concerned, but that on official documents they use their mother's name. They cannot avoid the fact that they were born here in England, and should they want to return when they are adults, it would be better if they did not have the name of Wytcombe.

I also think you are very wise to consider moving house, too. Claudio and Cinzia are safe since Luka never met them, but he might yet recognise you, and of course he would definitely know William by sight. The expansion of your husband's trade across to Genoa gives you the perfect reason to leave for there, and yet leave Claudio to run the Verona vineyard. So none of your neighbours are likely to be over curious, but it lessens the danger should Luka head your way seeking his perverse revenge.

We too are now determined to leave England as soon as we can. Alvaro's kindness to Edward in providing him with a contact name in Boston has made him convinced that we can thrive over there, and we both feel that if we can provide another safe haven – though please God we will not need it – then that would be a very good thing. Edward is still trying to locate Ana and Charlotte, but is finding that men of law out on the edges of Wales are not kindly disposed to what they see as London men meddling in their affairs. Under other circumstances, we would find their pomposity a minor irritation, but it drives me to distraction whenever I think that my step-sister and my sister-in-law's lives might depend on their cooperation.

Please write to me as soon as you have a new address in Genoa, for once we have that, we shall hasten our own plans to leave. I will not have little Arianna and Francesca suffering at the hands of Luka the way their namesakes' great-grandmamma and grandmamma did at his father's.

With deepest affection,

Sophia

"So that's what happened to them!" Sarah said, relaxing a little. "But how tragic that the local solicitors, or whatever they were in those days, didn't take Edward more seriously. Can't say I'm surprised, though. It can get awfully parochial out in the shires, and back then this would have been a very quiet little place."

However Chris had picked up on something else. "That's why there are no more letters! If Guilia and her husband – it was Alvaro she married, wasn't it? – went to Genoa taking William with them, then any further letters will be hidden somewhere over there."

Cleo agreed. "And if the memory of the necklace and its significance to the family was starting to fade, then while Giulia probably deliberately left it at the Verona house to watch over her son and his wife, you can easily see that for Claudio and Cinzia, it might have become something of nothing, if they remembered it at all."

Chapter 26

"Another good thing," Cleo added, "is that we now have a name for Francesca's mother – Arianna. I must admit this is all very useful in terms of the search possibilities, but I'll wait until tomorrow to do any of that. I know it's getting late, but I don't think any of us want to stop just yet, do we?"

Chris shook his head. "Not likely! This is way too exciting! They knew that William was *alive,* but that he wasn't going to claim his inheritance because they feared Luka would murder him, too? Jeez! You can see why Hugh thought this was dynamite, can't you?"

"So who did you say the next batch of letters is between, and when?" Sarah asked.

Cleo looked at the dates and envelopes. "Definitely between Olivia, who was Ana and Tarquin's youngest daughter, and who was living near Pershore, and Julia – she was Hector and Charlotte's daughter who got taken into hiding in Italy. So these are the two half-cousins who spent their early childhood together before being forcibly separated. Julia's over in ...*oooh!* Genoa, at that point! That's interesting; I wonder what made her leave Verona? ...Hmm, we start in 1865, so let's see what was going on with them then.

Lower Hopyard Farm
Pershore
26th August 1865

Dear Julia,

> *I am so sorry to hear of Aunt Giulia's death. Poor Uncle Alvaro, he must be devastated, as must Claudio and Cinzia, and I know that you, Clifford and William all loved her dearly as a grandmother, too. It is at times like this that I wish I knew what had happened to my own dear mother. I know that Aunt Sophia has long believed that she died when those two demons took her away, and having become a mother myself, I now know just how much she would have fought to get back to us if she could.*

"My God, how prophetic was that!" Chris exclaimed. "Isn't this around the time that Ana and Charlotte died?"

"No, they'd been dead a bit over ten years at this point," Cleo confirmed. "How sad is that? She never knew her mum had died trying to get to her," and she heard a sniff from Sarah and looked across to see her wiping her eyes. "I know, it chokes me up too. I hope the rest of the letter isn't like this or we'll need another box of tissues…"

> *I am glad beyond words that with me now well established as the wife of my dear Henry and his family here in Pershore, it is now safe for us to exchange letters, and that Claudio felt it no longer dangerous for me to know where you are. When you vanished all those years ago, I prayed and prayed that you were safe, and then when Father began pretending that our Bertram was Clifford, I feared the worst had befallen you both. Truly his and Luka's fury – for I will not call that man Uncle ever again – if we ever called*

Bertram by his proper name, made us wonder whether they were both going mad. And then when Father himself nonetheless slipped up, and told the man from the government who came that Bertram was his son, you have never seen anything so terrifying as Luka's rage.

That was when we first heard him screaming about 'how could he claim he was Clifford's guardian, if his supposed father was still alive and living with him?' It is no wonder that my poor little brother has become such a dreamer, lost in his ancient Greek texts, for the real world must have seemed to have gone mad to him right from when he was tiny. We have tried so often to free him, but he is too scared to leave other than to go to his university library, where at least he gets some peace.

As long as I live, I will never believe that Father fell from his horse in the parkland. Edgar has since told me that he and Sydney had played all through that part of the park, and that he had never seen that rock before which supposedly crushed Father's skull in the fall. That and the way that Luka made everyone in the house look at Father's broken head, and told us all, 'that's what happens to people who do not behave', even at the time made me think that he did the foul deed and then tried to cover it up, but I am sure of it now. Sad to say, though, he got away with it.

"Golly!" Sarah gasped. "Well that's answered our suspicions of how Tarquin died!"

"Hasn't it just," Cleo agreed. "This has to be the first letter the girls dared exchange directly, though I'd presume that people like Sophia and Giulia quietly kept them informed of roughly what was going on."

"Hang on, though," Chris objected. "Until Olivia eloped, where would she have been where *anyone* could openly write to her? And who are we looking at here? Which Sydney is this and who was Edgar, again?"

Cleo again sketched out a short family tree for him.

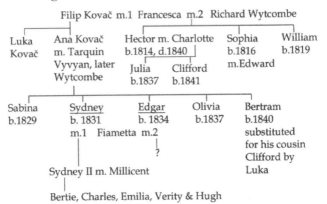

Filip Kovač m.1 Francesca m.2 Richard Wytcombe

| Luka Kovač | Ana Kovač m. Tarquin Vyvyan, later Wytcombe | Hector m. Charlotte b.1814, d.1840 | Sophia b.1816 m.Edward | William b.1819 |

Julia b.1837 · Clifford b.1841

| Sabina b.1829 | Sydney b. 1831 m.1 Fiametta m.2 | Edgar b. 1834 ? | Olivia b.1837 | Bertram b.1840 substituted for his cousin Clifford by Luka |

Sydney II m. Millicent

Bertie, Charles, Emilia, Verity & Hugh

"Ah! I'm with you now. So we're talking Bertie's grandfather's generation now, and Sophia was their half-aunt, and Julia their half cousin. Remind me where we are with those Italians, though. I think I've lost track of the generations over there too."

Sarah was nodding. "I've remembered that Guilia was Francesca's sister, but beyond that I'm getting blurry too."

"Hold on a tick, then," Cleo said, pulling the laptop over, and consulting her notes. A couple of minutes later, she turned her large pad around and showed them the tree she'd been working on while Sarah made them yet another drink to keep them going. "Here you go. This is the Italian side as best I can make out at the moment…"

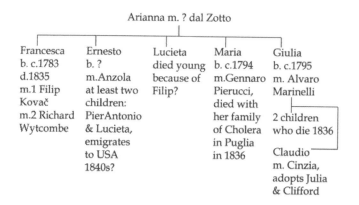

Arianna m. ? dal Zotto

Francesca	Ernesto	Lucieta	Maria	Giulia
b. c.1783	b. ?	died young	b. c.1794	b. c.1795
d.1835	m.Anzola	because of	m.Gennaro	m. Alvaro
m.1 Filip	at least two	Filip?	Pierucci,	Marinelli
Kovač	children:		died with	
m.2 Richard	PierAntonio		her family	2 children
Wytcombe	& Lucieta,		of Cholera	who die 1836
	emigrates		in Puglia	
	to USA		in 1836	Claudio
	1840s?			m. Cinzia,
				adopts Julia
				& Clifford

"Ah, I see," Chris said, "so actually Giulia was more Olivia's great-aunt than an actual one."

"Yes," Cleo agreed. "But I suspect that, as happens so often in families, it was easier to just call her aunt, especially as there was only one Giulia. If Lucieta had lived, for instance, then they'd have had to make more of a distinction between her and Ernesto's daughter."

Chris scratched his chin thoughtfully. "Still interesting that it's only at this stage that Olivia and Julia get to connect again, though, and my question still stands: how did Julia know where to write to her after all that time?"

"Maybe it'll be further on in this letter?" Cleo wondered, and read on,

> *And now I feel that I can pass on to you our side of the events which took place ten years ago. You know that Sydney used the army as a means of escape to get away from our father, who was eternally entwined in Luka's schemes. What I do not know if Aunt Sophia told you is that my next brother, Edgar, also escaped that way. Eighteen years*

ago, in 1847, our oldest sister Sabina died in childbirth, which may surprise you since you will never have heard of her marriage. We all suspected that she went willingly with our uncle, for they were two of a kind and she was always strange, never being a normal little girl as you and I were. It may sound heartless, but we felt it a blessing that the child died too, for what would it have been like, coming from such an unnatural union, and from two such perverted and wicked parents?

Certainly her death is the only time that I have ever seen that monster upset, as was Father, yet that was enough of a distraction for Edgar to be able run away. We had been writing to Sydney in secret with the help of the servants, and now he found a place with him in the army for Edgar. Then after Father was killed, the first time that Edgar was able to have any leave, he came for me, and I ran away with him. Dear Sydney then found me a place as a housemaid with the family of one of his senior officers, which was near Pershore, and that is how I met my Henry.

I had been with them some years at the point when Henry began courting me, and had eventually told them of our suffering at Luka's hands. So they knew that I would never get parental consent for any marriage, no matter how good, and by then the head of the house in day-to-day terms was the widowed mother, and she was full of sympathy for my predicament and supported our leaving together, as did Henry's parents. They would have all loved us to have a proper wedding, but Luka's infamy had travelled even that far, and they worried that having the banns read might allow enough time to bring him down upon me. But I wanted you to know the circumstances of my marriage, and to be assured that our seeming elopement was not some foolish flight of fancy – we were welcomed home with open arms, even by our local vicar!

But then my dear brother Sydney was killed in the Crimea. He died a hero's death, but that was little consolation. We were all devastated, as you can imagine, for only siblings who have suffered together as we did can be so close. And Edgar and I had been so glad to welcome Cinzia's cousin Fiametta when she and Sydney married, not least because with her being part of the wider family, we knew she was aware of the dangers of ever going near to Upper Moore – though mercifully there was no blood link between them, of course, to repeat Sabina's incestuous relationship. What none of us could have predicted was Sydney's death being announced in the local newspaper. Oh what a terrible twist of fate that was! For of course they got to hear of it at Upper Moore.

The next thing anyone knew, Cousin Frances and her husband – a fool of a man called Algernon Franks, who has been as potter's clay in Luka's hands – turned up at the barracks of the Welch Fusiliers to collect Fiametta and their baby Sydney. With Fiametta in her greatly distressed state, and of course no longer entitled to be with the other wives, the army handed them both over to Frances and Algernon, in the misguided belief that they would be safe with family. I do not blame them. If you had ever met those two, you would not think them capable of any wrong-doing, and as far as their own ability to scheme goes, you would be right. Neither of them was capable of a single thought which had not been put in their heads by Luka. Yet stupid though they were, they were still capable of great cruelty. With them both laid side by side in their graves now, I can only pray that they have been judged by God as fools, and that they did not act with the malicious intent of her father. Surely it is a judgement on them that Luka now has the raising of her young son, Mortimer, who was born in 1856, just a year after they separated our little Sydney from his mother.

Poor Fiametta was abandoned at a coaching inn not fifteen miles from where she had been living, while Frances and Algernon made off with baby Sydney, making out to other travellers that she was the deranged nurse who had stolen <u>their</u> child! Such audacity and wickedness on their part still takes my breath away, but they were such fools that they would not have given Fiametta's distress a moment's thought, even though I had hoped that becoming a mother herself might have changed that for Frances. God be praised that Fiametta heard the name Pershore being cried out for the next coach leaving, and that the lad hauling the bags knew of our farm, for he persuaded the coachman to let her on on the understanding of our paying her way. Once in Pershore, my dear brother-in-law who works at the coaching inn paid on our behalf, and she stayed safe with us for a while, though distressed to distraction at being separated from her son.

I beg you to please let Cinzia's aunt, and also William's Vedette, know that we did what we could for her daughter while she was with us, and that it was as Edgar and I fought to get her safely away, that she came to see Edgar as her salvation. If she was not in love with him when they married, they now have the deepest of feelings for one another, and we write as regularly as the distance between here and New York allows. I wish they had been able to at least visit you before they left, but by then Edgar was terrified of what might happen if Fiametta gave in to her maternal need to get back to Sydney, for at that stage we still hoped to one day free him and send him on to them. It grieves us as much as it must you that we may never see their children, but if they can live in safety over there, then we must accept the situation, for we would not have them back in England with us. I and my family are safe, for Luka had no interest in me as the surviving girl, but Edgar and Fiametta would not be – and especially not their sons.

As you no doubt know, Luka had already managed once to prevent Fiametta and Sydney taking their little son out of the country to come to you, by openly lying to the courts. He had clearly been paying someone at the barracks to spy for him, and *so knew that Sydney had come back from Italy with a new bride, and began scheming to pay him back for running away. Well Sydney may have escaped his revenge by dying, but poor Fiametta and the baby did not, and we would not have a repetition of that nightmare brought upon her and Edgar. Henry and I hope one day to travel to see them, but in the meantime we might soon be able to visit you,*

>   *Your dear cousin,*
>   *Olivia*

"Well, that's a parcel of news," Chris declared as Cleo finished reading and began drawing up the new set of connections, and Sarah gasped,

"Oh! That's what the connection to someone called Edgar was! I knew Archie's heir, David, had come from the States, but I'd no idea that the connection went that far back."

Chris smiled at his mother, but said, "You were right, Cleo, it sounds as though Sydney senior and Fiametta's second marriage ceremony *was* to convince a court that they were properly wed. How could Luka have found them, though?"

Yet Cleo had no doubts on that matter. "I think if I could find the relevant documents, you'd find that Sydney volunteered for the army, and once he was in, it was beyond even Luka to drag him out without paying out a substantial amount of money – money which presumably he didn't have. I bet he followed hot on Sydney's heels but found he was too late. Who knows, Sydney may have confided in a senior officer that he feared Luka had murdered his Uncle Hector, and so while that person lived, Fiametta would have been safe? In the meat-grinder of the Crimea, it would be odd if Sydney was the only member of his company who got killed, so if a senior protector died too, the subsequent person who shoved Fiametta into Frances' arms may barely have known her."

Chris accepted that, but added, "And how icky is it that Sabina was clearly sleeping with Luka? God, that bad blood just keeps on popping up generation after generation, doesn't it?"

However Cleo reminded him, "Don't forget, Sabina was only Filip's granddaughter, so she's an apple that didn't have far to fall from that rotten tree. It's more remarkable that with Sydney, Edgar, Olivia and the pseudo-Clifford all being his grandchildren too, that they all seem to have been decent human beings. And I think that that's a good indicator that it's not so much bad blood, as malevolent influence that keeps doing the damage. By the time you get to baby Sydney II in those letters, who will grow up to be the ghastly Sydney who fathers Bertie, there's only an eighth of Filip's DNA in him – that's science, not imagination. We each get half of our DNA from each parent. Fact.

"You might not think it in some cases, but we're all like that. The sibling variations you see come about because it's not the same fifty percent that gets handed down every time. So that fifty-fifty split can throw up an almost infinite number of combinations when you consider how complex DNA is, and that's why you sometimes look at two siblings and wonder whether or not they can even be related – they may well have two totally different parts of their parents."

"How fascinating, I never knew that," Sarah admitted, "at least not that it was so absolutely half and half."

Cleo smiled at her. "Well it is, and so every time you move another generation away from Filip, every time a new bloodline gets introduced into the family mix, it cannot do anything other than change those combinations – although when you double back as would have happened with Sabina and Luka's child, it's bad news. But you can see now why I think that Luka living so long was a dreadful blight on the family, because while he was there, he was grooming one or two in each new generation that came along. It's not some nasty quirk of fate that Bertie was such a shit towards Hugh, because the blame for that lies squarely at Luka's door for warping him, and Mortimer and Sydney II, from childhood. ...Here you are, this is the connections we've just read about as far as I can tell..."

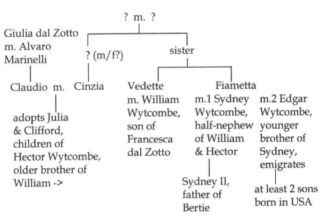

"...and have a glance back at this other tree, and you can see the connections on the English side."

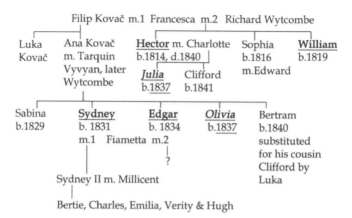

"See? Olivia and Julia – the letter writers are half-cousins. But the two brothers, Sydney and Edgar, are related via their wife to their younger half-uncle, William – who is likewise Olivia's half-uncle. And William is Julia's full uncle. But then William, Sydney and Edgar's children would have all shared another genetic link because of Vedette and Fiametta being full sisters."

"Oh my goodness!" Sarah gasped. "It's so much clearer when you see it like this. Good grief, they do keep getting intertwined, don't they?"

Cleo grimaced. "I think a lot of it has to do with not trusting anyone who isn't close to the family. The English ones knew that the Italians understood the danger in a way that nobody else would, and vice versa. Mind you, the Italian Catholic Church would have been having kittens over any further connections, because right up until 1917, it was actually illegal to marry within four degrees of separation – and they have less than that."

"So what does the next letter say?" Chris asked.

Cleo picked it up, but before reading it out reminded them, "Don't forget that this was found with Archie's papers, so he'd have only read exactly what was here. He wouldn't have had the horrible back-story to put it into context with like we have…"

Via San Lorenzo
Genoa
22nd October 1865

Dear Olivia,

You cannot imagine the relief and delight with which I received your letter. Truly, it is as if I had found my sister once more. Pietro was most alarmed to find me weeping over it, but now understands that it was mostly with joy.

You must know that we joined you in being distraught for poor Fiametta when she was with you. This was what we all feared might happen when she married Sydney, but they were so in love, and she would not be guided by us. Vedette was happily married to William, she kept telling us, so why should she not be happy with Sydney? And we could not make her see that William and Vedette were happy because they were, and are, safe here in Genoa, not living only a day's journey from the damnable Luka – and I do most solemnly pray that when his time comes, that he receives the full weight of God's judgement for his growing list of terrible sins.

"Wow!" Chris exclaimed. "Don't you hold back, girl! She really hates him, doesn't she!"

Cleo laughed. "It's being with the Italians for so long. They don't tend to be shy about saying what they feel. But you can understand it, can't you, especially as by now she must have been thinking that he'd done for both of her parents."

"Oh God, yes, of course!" Sarah breathed. "This is Hector and Charlotte's daughter whose letter we're reading, isn't it!"

"Certainly is," Cleo confirmed.

> *As for our own news, poor Grandpa Alvaro is lost without Grandma. It was a terrible thing that they lost their two daughters years ago when the Cholera took Great-aunt Maria and her family and them with her, and so he has had to bear such deep loss in his lifetime. Great-aunt Maria had only taken Papa's sisters with her to visit Gennaro's family, you know, because Grandma was having such a terrible pregnancy with the baby who was still-born, and thought to give her some rest. Praise be that Papa went to visit Grandpa Alvaro's sister, who is Vedette and Fiametta's mother and so on the other side of our family to you, and so he did not catch it, for had they lost him too, I do not know what they would have done.*
>
> *What you may not know is that despite the fears that Mama would not have children of her own, after we arrived she had a little girl, Ilaria. She is as much a true sister to me as ever she could be and is now a delightful young woman of twenty-three who is as determined to marry as her cousin Fiametta was. Please do not be alarmed when I tell you that the young man she is so in love with is Vedette's oldest son, Dante. Remember that she is not from our side of the family, so there*

is no problem with that. Dante and his younger brother, Virgil, are quite the young gentlemen, for William insisted that they go to school in England, but in the end found a boarding school for them in Scotland, where he knew they would not be traced. Not that we believe that Luka or his minions would have connected who Dante and Virgil Carrington were.

As for myself, I married Pietro four years ago and we now have a little girl, Maria. Life has been good to us here in Genoa, for the family business thrives and we are well provided for. Please write as often as you feel it is safe to do so, for I do not wish to lose you again.

> *Your affectionate cousin,*
> *Julia*

"My goodness," Sarah said, "yes, you can see why that would have foxed Archie if he had none of the background. Would he have realised that the mother and father she's referring to were Claudio and Cinzia, and not her real parents? I don't think he would, nor that the grandparents she's talking about were Francesca's *sister* and her husband, who of course weren't Julia's natural ones, either. I'm sure he would have assumed that William was one of Charlotte's Carrington nephews, not her son, William Wytcombe. And we know from the parish records that Charlotte had siblings, but that they moved from the area. It would be a perfectly reasonable mistake for him to make, as you said, Cleo."

"Yes, Mum," Chris agreed, "but Julia's made a mistake too, hasn't she? Cleo, can you sketch Mum another of those family trees? Because Ilaria and William's children were blood relatives, unless I'm horribly mistaken."

Cleo found a clean sheet and sketched the names in quickly.

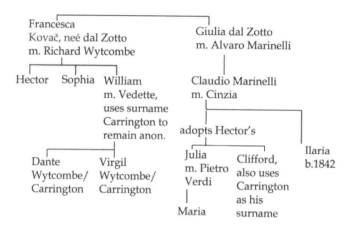

"See? William is Francesca's son, so his two lads are her grandsons. But Ilaria is Francesca's youngest sister Giulia's granddaughter via her dad, Claudio. Just because his surname is Marinelli, it doesn't make him any the less Giulia's son. And Chris is right, Julia has forgotten in all of those years of William calling himself a Carrington, that he's actually a Wytcombe by birth.

"But that's only the English side! Don't forget what I just showed you. Cinzia and Vedette are also full first cousins, and unlike Julia, who was Cinzia's adopted daughter, Illaria is her fully natural daughter, which means it really does matter on that side too. And that would mean that any marriage between Dante and Ilaria would at that stage have been completely illegal in Italy, and if the connections were known, probably frowned upon over here, even if it would have been allowed in the Church of

England. It would have been the same as in Italy if they'd wanted a Catholic marriage over here."

"Oh Lordy," Sarah sighed, "what a tangled web!"

"Web is about right," Chris sighed. "I think they spent so much time keeping secrets that they even started forgetting to tell their kids important stuff."

"There don't seem to be many of these letters," Sarah observed. "Did they not write so often after all?"

Cleo was scanning through them. "No, I think it's more that they only kept certain ones. What intrigues me more is how Julia's letters came to be here. You can understand Olivia's being kept by the Italian family, and if at some point she took them to what seems to have still been the family house in Verona, then that explains how Hugh found them. But who in this household knew Olivia well enough to hide the letters which had come to her and why? It's not as though she lived here as an adult."

"Yes, I was wondering that," Chris admitted. "Hmm, 1865... How close is that to when the wicked ones die?"

Cleo checked her data. "Well as we discovered, Luka lingered on until 1881, so that's sixteen years in the future for Olivia and Julia at this stage, though he'd have been sixty-five years old by then. They must have been thinking that he couldn't go on much longer. Good grief, it must have been torment for them as he hung on and hung on until he was eighty-one! Even if he wasn't very mobile, you get the feeling that he was lurking in the background all the while, scheming."

"And what about Mortimer Franks, Frances' son?" Chris wondered. "I can't remember if we told you this, Mum, but he keeps cropping up in the late Victorian family photo albums like some dreadful ghoul haunting the place."

Now Cleo added, "Sydney II lingered on until 1906, but the more we learn, the more I'm starting to see him as just some weak pawn in Luka's hands. But what intrigues me is, when did Hugh and his sisters get to go and visit Olivia? That can't have been while any of the key players were around, surely? Now Hugh was old enough to remember Olivia and what she'd talked about, so I think he must have been an older child at the point of those visits, so maybe after Sydney II died?"

She continued looking through her files. "As for Mortimer Franks, it's just occurred to me that his unfortunate daughter Janette was born the year after Luka died, because of course she was Luka's *great*-granddaughter. So it couldn't have been Luka who shoved Mortimer to marry her to Charles, can it? And there's only two years between Mortimer and Sydney II, so I wonder if he was the power behind Sydney, given that they grew up together? …Damn! I haven't found his death yet, because he's in the 1901 census but not in the 1911 one. I wonder if he was struggling to keep his grip over the family once he lost Sydney as his right-hand man?"

"Why do you say that?" Sarah asked.

"Because the obvious person for Mortimer to marry Janette to if he wanted to keep Upper Moore in the Kovač line was Bertie, surely? Yet we know that Bertie was a force to be reckoned with. So I think it's not unreasonable to then deduce that Mortimer had to turn his schemes to the more pliable second son, Charles. In which case, by then the younger three – Emilia, Verity and Hugh – might have found it a lot easier to go and see Olivia if Mortimer's attention was elsewhere."

Chris was looking thoughtful. "Didn't you say, Mum, that your dad always described Emilia as a tough old boot? So maybe she was the one who thought, 'I'm going to keep Olivia's letters, and to hell with the men of the family'? She was bang on the money with Bertie, wasn't she? So is it possible that she caught on so quickly to him because she was already primed by what Olivia had told her?"

"Good Heavens! Now that's a thought!" Sarah gasped. "In which case good old great-grandma, or whatever she is to me. …What other letters might she have kept then? What do the others say, Cleo?"

Chapter 27

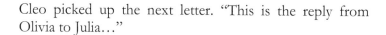

Cleo picked up the next letter. "This is the reply from Olivia to Julia…"

> *Lower Hopyard Farm*
> *Pershore*
> *17th November 1865*

Dearest Julia,

> *I write back to you with the greatest haste and only hope that I have reached you in time to prevent a terrible mistake. Ilaria and Dante <u>must not marry</u>! I can see how the mistake has come about, for you have all spent so long thinking of William as a Carrington that you have forgotten that he is not. William is Grandmother's son by Richard Wytcombe, and therefore his sons are her grandchildren, even if they have never known her any more than I did. They may not even be aware of William fleeing England to avoid Luka, but he is my blood relative through Grandmother, as are you. But if Ilaria is Aunt Giulia's granddaughter, then she too is connected by virtue of Grandmother and Aunt Giulia being sisters.*

> *And with you living in Genoa now, have you forgotten that there is a maternal connection too? Ilaria's mother and Dante's mother are cousins, though the family is back*

*in the Verona area, and it will bring the
wrath of the church down upon you if they
try to proceed with this marriage. I went and
spoke to the priest of our Catholic Church
here, and he has told me that you must
prevent the marriage at all costs.*

*It gives me no pleasure to send you this
news, and my heart breaks for the young
couple, for they can now be nothing more
than friends. I have no time to write more
just now, but pray that I have reached you
before they wed.*

> *Your distraught cousin,*
> *Olivia*

"Thank heavens Olivia was on the ball," Chris said
with relief. "Did she succeed?"

Cleo picked up the next letter. "Well it's one back
from Julia next…"

> *Via San Lorenzo*
> *Genoa*
> *6th January 1866*

Dear Olivia,

*Oh the ructions your letter has
caused, but I am beyond glad that you told us
in time. Ilaria has taken to her bed with
copious weeping, and refuses to be consoled;
while poor Dante has taken himself off after
Christmas back to Verona, declaring that he
cannot bear to be in the same city as Ilaria,
for his love is undiminished. Yet we all
understand now why that marriage cannot
take place. And you were right to think that
we have spent so long thinking of William as*

a Carrington that we had totally forgotten that he is a Wytcombe. Maybe if he had ever had any of his inheritance, which would have drawn him to England for business if nothing else, then it would have been different, but he has made his way in the family business over here. He and Vedette are also distraught, feeling that they should have remembered, but Vedette and Fiametta's mother died when they were so young that they think of a paternal aunt as more of a mother, though she too has long since passed away.

Therefore there was nobody on that side of the family to prompt us, and what I have not told you is that Grandma Giulia had had several strokes before she passed, so she could not tell us. What makes me weep is the memory of how agitated she became whenever we talked of the wedding, which we completely misread as excitement. She must have been alert enough inside to have made the connection, but could not get the words out.

I will write again once the dust settles and we can all take up our normal lives again. In the meantime I must go and help Mama console Ilaria.

> *Your loving cousin,*
> *Julia*

"Phew! So Olivia succeeded, that's a relief!" Sarah sighed. "But I'm beginning to get the hang of what you've been saying, Cleo, because thinking of Archie reading this, he still wouldn't have got beyond the obvious. He still wouldn't have twigged who Julia was, for a start off, or who she was calling mother, nor that she was actually Ilaria's second-cousin rather than her sister, as she implies."

And without thinking, Cleo added, "But if Emilia read this, then you can see why later on she would have been having a fit over her own daughter marrying a Carrington, can't you?"

A stunned silence followed.

Cleo was kicking herself for having let that slip quite so bluntly. She had been hoping to break the news more gently. For Chris and Sarah, the realisation that they had so far failed to make the obvious link was breath-taking, and it took a moment for either of them to speak.

"Does this mean that I'm more closely related to Archie than I thought?" Sarah finally managed to ask faintly.

Relieved that she wasn't immediately thinking of the inheritance, which would have taken some dancing around, Cleo felt able to answer honestly, "I think we can safely say that while you go back to the Wytcombes through the woman we now know was not your grandmother but your great-grandmother, Emilia; there's also a very strong probability that you have a connection through your dad's mother Lois' husband, too. If the Ernest Carrington whose son George married Lois, is the same Ernest Carrington who was the son of Clifford, who was born Clifford Wytcombe but became Clifford Carrington over in Italy, then yes, you are. Through that side of your father's family it would make you the great-great-great-great-grand-daughter of Francesca."

She took in Sarah's slightly glazed expression and began writing again.

Francesca Kovač-Wytcombe
|
Ana Kovač
m. Tarquin Vyvyan-Wytcombe

Hector m. Charlotte Carrington
|
Clifford Wytcombe, takes
his mother's surname m. ?

Sydney I m. Fiametta Conti
|
Sydney II m. Millicent
Powderham

Ernest Carrington m. ?

Emilia Wytcombe m. Frank Denby
|
Lois Denby m. George Carrington
|
Thomas Carrington/Denby m. Jane Osmond
|
Sarah Denby m. Jeffrey Palmer

"Let me take you back one generation at a time. Lois married George. As far as we know, he was the son of Ernest. Ernest was – as far as we can tell at this point – the son of Clifford who was born a Wytcombe and took the Carrington name for safety. Are you with me so far? …Good. So then Clifford was the baby boy who was born after his father Hector was murdered; and Hector was the son of Francesca and Richard. Therefore that makes George Carrington your grandfather; and his dad Ernest your great-grandfather. Then his dad, Clifford, was your great-great-grandfather, and Hector your great-great-great-grandfather. And of course Francesca was Hector's mum.

"Now, it's Francesca who is the common link in all of this. Because Emilia was the daughter of Sydney II, and she was your great-grandmother making him your great-great-grandfather. The line then goes back through his dad, Sydney I, to Ana; and as you know, she was Francesca's daughter by her first husband. That makes you Francesca's…" and she had to do a quick count back, "great-great-great-great-great-grandmother on that side. It's several generations back from you on both sides to

Francesca, but back to her via your father you definitely go!"

"Bloody hell!" Chris gulped. "*That* I did not see coming!" making Cleo feel that she had to confess,

"I've been having suspicions about this for a while now, but I didn't want to say anything to either of you because I would be the first to admit that I have no idea how far back a solicitor would go to find the 'true' heirs to the estate. If there was a title involved, I think they might investigate all of the various lines, but as there isn't, it might be that Archie's new will stands whoever that applies to. They might take the approach that going back all the way to the early nineteenth century for your connection is unreasonable, but on the other hand, you are linked back straight through a male line of succession.

"That runs: your dad Thomas, grandfather George, his father, Ernest. Then his dad is the real Clifford Wytcombe who goes to Italy and becomes Clifford Carrington. And of course he is the legitimate son of poor old Hector who got murdered, and he was Richard Wytcombe's oldest son and heir. So although I honestly wouldn't like to say more than that, let alone make any assumptions, in one sense you come more from the legitimate line than Archie did. But how far back anyone would take that legally is another matter altogether," and she gave Chris a pointed look to beg him not to now say that Archie had left everything to his mum.

Mercifully, he took the hint, and with great restraint asked instead, "So what about the next letters, then?"

Relieved to move back onto less personal ground, Cleo picked up the next one. "Hmm, it's another one from Julia to Olivia. I wonder whether the Italian family didn't hang onto the other letters going back that way, or at least that if they did they're mouldering in some hidden hidey-hole in Genoa, as you suggested, Chris? …Okay, so this is from a few years later on…"

Via al Cristo
Verona
10th September 1870

Dear Olivia,

I must ask for your help, for we desperately need to get a message to Aunt Sophia in Boston. In all the chaos of the last few months, I have somehow lost her address, but when I tell you what has gone on, you will understand how I could do that.

As you know, following the terrible break up between Ilaria and Dante, we really began to fear what it had done to both of them. With my brother Clifford only being a year older than Dante, and four more than Virgil, he has always been as an older brother to them, and so it seemed understandable that Virgil and Clifford should want to help him. And as I wrote to you two years ago, all three of them decided to head for America to seek their fortune there. I cannot blame them, for life has been very unsettled here for all of the last decade, what with the rebellions of Garibaldi and Victor Emmanuel, and we all knew that peace would not last, though we could not have predicted the war which broke out this July between France and Prussia. This was the reason why we felt we had to close the business in Genoa and return to Verona, for at least here we will hopefully not be in the path of the two armies.

When we got back here in January, we were all glad that the three younger men were far away, for my Pietro is not of any use in an army since his eyesight is so poor, and I have never been so glad that I have only daughters. However, Ilaria had been persuaded to marry a decent local young man called Ettore Bisozzi, and when she had a daughter, Lucia, within the year, we all hoped that she would settle. Oh how wrong we were!

We totally misunderstood why she was so keen to stay with Ettore in Genoa when we left. Far from being settled with him and his family, we now realise that instead it was a growing resentment towards us for splitting her and Dante which made her want to be away from us. Worse, the little minx must have been making poor Ettore's life a misery, because we had a distraught letter from his desperate mother. Ettore has gone to join the army after Ilaria had called him a coward in front of his friends, and made out that he was not the father of her child. You can only imagine his embarrassment and hurt! But within the week, Ettore's mother wrote, Ilaria vanished, taking baby Lucia with her. How we shall ever face his parents, I do not know, for they were quite rightly incensed by her actions, and demanded that if she was with us, that at least we send their granddaughter back to them, since they considered Ilaria an unfit mother. Sadly, given the way Ilaria has behaved, I can understand them thinking that dear Mama did not do such a good job of bringing up her, either, and that therefore Lucia was better off with them.

With all of the troubles in the west of this land, Papa did not dare risk travelling back to Genoa to see the Bisozzi family, but he wrote a deeply moving letter of apology, and explained that we knew nothing of this and have not seen Ilaria either. Yet not three weeks after that, a letter arrived from Ilaria herself. I know that Mama always treasured her particularly for being her own daughter, and not adopted like Clifford and myself, but where this spoilt and selfish young woman has sprung from I do not know. She spared Mama and Papa nothing in her vilification of them, and has declared that at the time of writing that she was boarding a ship bound for Boston. Where she has got the money to pay for her passage from I do not know, and Papa has had to humiliate himself by writing to the Bisozzi family again, asking whether she stole the money from them, and offering to pay restitution if she did. Truly, she has broken Mama and Papa's hearts, and for that I cannot forgive her.

But you see now why we need to get in touch with Aunt Sophia and Uncle Edward. If anyone can confirm that she has in fact turned up in Boston, it is them, though what anyone can do with her is beyond me. I think we are all now mostly concerned for the fate of baby Lucia, because more than Ilaria, now, Lucia is in our prayers.

Your distraught cousin,
Julia

"Blimey," Cleo gasped as she finished reading, "that was a turn up for the books, wasn't it?"

Chris huffed in disgust. "I think Ilaria sounds as though she was maybe always a bit scatty, and it was made worse by being spoiled. What a stupid girl to go wandering off when a war was breaking out! What on earth was she thinking?"

"It certainly wasn't love," Sarah said disapprovingly. "Love for her little girl ought to have made her stay put where she was safe! That's just obsession. I wonder if Dante had also married, and it was a case of if she couldn't have him then nobody could? Or was Dante the one who paid for her to travel?"

Cleo looked up at her with startled eyes from where she had scooped up the next letter. "Good grief, Sarah, that was a good guess! Listen to this…"

> *Via al Cristo*
> *Verona*
> *25th January 1871*
>
> *Dear Olivia,*
>
> *I do not know whether Aunt Sophia has written to you to tell you of our distressing news, but Ilaria reached Boston where she met Dante. They must both be mad, for he has now abandoned his wife, Marta, and their daughter Oriana, and has set out for Canada with Ilaria. The misery those two have caused their innocent partners is unforgivable, and now both Clifford and Virgil have joined us in resolving that they will not be welcomed back into the family.*
>
> *God be praised, Clifford is happily married to Delphina, and they have a son,*

Ernesto, named after Grandma's brother, though in America it seems he will be known as Ernest. He and Virgil, who is married to an Italian girl called Ysabel whom they met on the voyage, have set up a wine business such as we have here, and it is their hope that one day we shall be able to combine the two. So at least they are settled and may even return home one day. But it is to Virgil and Ysabel's credit that they have taken Marta and baby Oriana into their household, and Clifford is helping to pay towards their keep.

I cannot tell you how it shames Mama and Papa to hear this news, and William and Vedette are also mortified that their son should have behaved in this way. They are talking about bringing Marta and Oriana back to Verona to be cared for, though William is not in the best of health, so whether that will happen I do not know.

Yet I have other news of a very sad nature to pass on. Ettore Bisozzi has died in battle in France. I do not know whether to weep for his young life being so cut short, or to offer thanks to God that his misery is now over. God have mercy upon Ilaria, but it could be that Lucia is actually Dante's daughter, for she made out that Lucia arrived early and that may not be the truth. Only eight months elapsed after Ettore and Ilaria married before Lucia was born, so the poor lad may have been cuckolded even at his marriage. None of us have dared to reply to the letter from his father informing us of Ettore's death, for he made it quite plain that he blames us for that and he never wants to

hear from us ever again, and who can blame
him?
 I feel at the moment as though the whole
world has gone mad,
  Your loving cousin,
    Julia

"Dear me!" Sarah exclaimed. "To run off like that in those days? That must have been the kind of shame that they would never speak of ever again, especially in a Catholic country like Italy. I wonder if they ever even dared to speak of it in the confessional?"

"Possibly not," Cleo answered thoughtfully. "I suppose if you made the distinction between your own sin and someone else's, then it wasn't their sin to confess, was it? That might have been enough of an excuse for them not to say a word even to the local priest."

"I'm wondering why Olivia kept these letters?" Chris mused. "Do you think it might be that she wanted something with all the names on so that if any of these people turned up in the future, she would have something to jog her memory with? If we're struggling with all these people we've never met, so might she. It sounds as though she herself never travelled to Italy to meet them. And yet Dante and Ilaria had been acting crazy, so she might have wondered whether one or the other of them might eventually turn up in England?"

"I think you have a point," agreed Cleo. "The way this is reading, I don't think Julia and Olivia ever met up in person again."

"What's the war they were talking about?" Sarah asked her.

"Initially I think it's the fighting that went on during the unification of Italy. But later on it was probably the start of the Franco-Prussian War, and I only know that because we did Bismark and Kaiser Wilhelm in history at school, and they were both involved in that conflict. Certainly Genoa being in the north-west of Italy would have been a bit too close to the fighting for comfort, so I can see why they decamped back to Verona. In fact, that's probably when that letter of Olivia's got put into the secret hiding place with the others in their old home. I do hope we get to know where they went to next, though, because I can't help thinking that the house in Verona had been deserted by them well before the First World War. So something must have happened between about 1875 and 1910 to make them leave, and in the process maybe they just forgot about the old stuff."

What she wasn't saying was that there was something about Lucia that was ringing bells in the back of her mind, and that it probably wasn't going to be a good connection. Until she was far more sure, though, she wasn't going to say a thing. She'd dropped one bombshell in Sarah and Chris' lap this evening as it was, and they didn't need another one.

"Is that just one more letter in this batch?" she realised that Chris was asking her.

"Err…yes, it is." She turned the yellowing sheets of paper over in her hands. "Yes, more from Julia to Olivia. …Oh! This time it's from America!"

23ʳᵈ July 1882

Dear Olivia,

As you can see from the postage, we are in Boston with Aunt Sophia and Uncle Edward. After Mama died two years ago along with my own dear Pietro, and then Papa back in January, I found that I could no longer bear to remain in Verona. And so I have brought my girls over here to Boston, where I hope they will never have to worry about another war rolling over them. My dear brother Clifford lost his Delphina in a late pregnancy, and so he too wanted a change, all of which means that he and Ernest have travelled back to Verona to take over the family business alongside William, and we have come here. Virgil and Clifford had moved away from the wine business here into a general store, and with my girls all being quick with a needle and thread, there is a good opportunity for them to expand the haberdashery side of the business. However Clifford's heart was always in the wine business, and with William now in his sixties, he has welcomed a younger and more energetic man to work with him, especially as Ernest is determined to join them.

I am finding the change of scenery to be just what I needed to help me over my grief, but what has also helped has been a journey to New York to see Aunt Sophia and Uncle Edward. And I know that you have tried to explain things to me in your letters, but until I met them I had not appreciated fully who the younger Edward you mentioned was. So I was thrilled to realise that the man working alongside Uncle Edward is your own dear brother Edgar, who I vaguely remember, and that he had changed his surname to Fairfax so that the family name might continue, given that Uncle and Aunt have no sons to pass it on to. Nor had I fully appreciated that, with dear Fiametta having died in childbirth just as Delphina did, it has been Aunt Sophia who has brought up Edgar's sons, Edward and George. Young Edward is now a fine young man of twenty-two, and very much an asset as a clerk in the office, where he is learning and studying so that he too might one day practice law here. So Uncle can now proudly have his sign above the door proclaiming Edward Fairfax and Sons! George is now working in the family store in their brand new branch in New York alongside Virgil's oldest son Michele, and that is such good news all round.

I now also understand why you said that although the dreadful Luka is now hopefully burning in the fires of Hell, that it is a blessing that so many of the family are away from where his two acolytes, Mortimer and your nephew Sydney, might ever find them, and that they would not recognise their names should they ever come here or hear of them. That is a great relief to me also. And is it not strange that I have lived most of my life in either Verona or Genoa, and yet to be now in a place where everyone again speaks English, makes me feel as though I have come home? Yet for Clifford it is the exact opposite. He could never settle here, yet wrote as soon as he was back in Verona that he felt that he was back where he belonged.

Certainly I feel more optimistic for the future now. With my Sophia now a young woman of eighteen, Agnella now sixteen, and little Chiara soon to turn thirteen, I am now hoping that I might spend my old age blessed with grandchildren without the worry of them forming such strange attachments as Ilaria did. And of Ilaria we have never heard *any more, sad to say. Uncle Edward thinks that a girl calling herself Lucia Bisozzi may have been making enquiries about him a couple of years ago, but since she had a rather disreputable older man with her, he did not respond, believing that some scoundrel had heard Ilaria's story and was going to try and extort money out of him. Certainly they soon went away, and have never been seen again, so he believes that his suspicions were correct.*

As soon as I have found a home of our own, I will write to you and let you know. I will forever be grateful for the love and support you have given us,

Your loving cousin,

Julia

"Oh! How sweet was that!" Sarah gushed. "Oh bless her, she sounds so grateful, and how nice that Sophia did manage to create that refuge she talked about in her letters all those years before, and Julia finally managed to find some peace."

Chris smiled at his mother. "Yes, it is nice, but I was thinking again as you read those out, Cleo, that you're right: Archie wouldn't have known what to make of these letters. Would he have known that Edward Fairfax was married to his however-many-times-great-aunt Sophia, for instance?"

Cleo glanced at the various sketched out family trees she had laid out beside her by now. "Maybe no, because don't forget that Sophia was only his half-great-whatever-aunt," she corrected him. "It's going back a way once you get to him, and of course the one thing his parents and grandparents would never have talked much about was the fact that they came from Filip Kovač's line, not Richard Wytcombe's."

"God, yes, I'd forgotten that," Chris admitted. "So I wonder if he read these, but was as confused as hell as to why anyone had kept them? Knowing Archie, he would have had the wits to work out that they might be important, but I bet he never knew why."

And was that disreputable man who came with Lucia actually her father, Dante? Cleo silently wondered. *Did Edward see that Dante had fallen on hard times and was crawling back, expecting everyone to pick up the pieces? In which case Edward may have turned him away after all the harm he'd done in order to save the rest of the family more grief. Edward always comes across as a decent man. So did he offer Lucia a place with the family, but only if she'd leave her father? If so, more fool her for not taking up the offer. …Damn it, what am I missing about her?*

Chapter 28

"So… Last lot," Cleo declared, looking at the clock and being surprised to see that it was now coming up midnight. "These are much more modern and are between Clarissa and Verity." She began carefully unfolding them and then froze.

"What's wrong?" asked Chris.

"Well the top couple are, but there are others… Oh hell, I'm going to have to read you these as I come to them, because this is already feeling bloody spooky!"

Islington
London
15th November 1905

Dear Clarissa,

I was so delighted to meet you at yours and Bertie's wedding, and am so glad to welcome you into the family. My brother was in danger of becoming a crusty old bachelor, even though he was not as old as all that! I think it came of him being friends with those older army men who talk about their past glories all the time, almost as if he wished their experiences had been his. It was long overdue that Bertie started thinking about the future instead.

Now I hope you will take this in the spirit in which it is intended, but I want very much to pass a warning on to you as my newest sister: please be careful of our father and of Uncle Mortimer, though he is not a true uncle. You will be living at Upper Moore, and so I want you to be aware that you should <u>never</u> leave <u>any</u> child with either of those. Our father is a weak man who is forever under Uncle Mortimer's thumb, and Uncle is an evil, wicked man.

I am sure you will think it odd that a young lady such as myself should talk of such indelicate things, but my desperation to warn you makes me bold. I would not wish to revolt you with sordid details, but there is a reason why my dear brother Charles is so fragile, and it has everything to do with the unspeakable and unnatural things which Uncle Mortimer made him do as a child. Emilia and I were lucky, for Uncle Mortimer's strange tastes did not turn our way, but many was the night when Charles would return to the nursery weeping after being dragged off by that man, and though we were younger than him, we did our best to comfort him. I know Bertie does not believe these things happened, but he was lucky. Our mother managed to persuade Father that someone who was to take his place amongst the country gentlemen should have the schooling of one, and so Bertie was sent away just as Uncle was becoming interested in him.

There is so much more that I would tell you as we get to know one another better, but for the love of God, if you have a son soon, keep Uncle away from him!

Your fond sister,

Verity

"Yuk!" Chris growled. "Another bloody pervert! Jeez, Cleo, you were right, Luka must have groomed Mortimer, and while you have to feel sorry for the kid he once was, it does sound as though he didn't need much encouragement."

Cleo was also pulling a face in disgust. "And this is one of the times when I wish I wasn't right about that. Let's see what Clarissa's response was ...oh, and she was quick in replying to that letter!"

> *Upper Moore House,*
> *Bromyard*
> *27th November 1905*

Dear Verity,

> *I confess that I was shocked by your letter, but that was because your sister Emilia had come to see me and had a startlingly frank conversation with me on the same matter. She really is a most forceful woman! I freely admit that at the time I initially wondered whether it was some sibling jealousy, but having now had you come to me with a more subtle warning, I realise that I cannot ignore you both. Would you be willing to come and meet me when I travel up to London in a couple of weeks' time to purchase new curtains for the morning room? Or maybe I could call upon you then?*

> *Yours*
> *Clarissa*

"That's a bit abrupt," said Sarah. "Do you think she still didn't believe her?"

"Maybe it was more that she didn't want to speak too openly in a letter?" Cleo wondered. "Could it be that Sydney, sick as he undoubtedly was by that point, was going through the mail? Or maybe she spotted Mortimer doing it? She may have had to learn very fast to be secretive."

Islington,
London.
14th January 1906

Dear Clarissa,

I am so delighted that we were able to have such an open talk with one another when you came to visit. As we planned, this letter is going to Jessie the housemaid's home at Yew Tree Cottage, which she will bring in with her so that you do not have to explain your letters to anyone. Jessie will collect any letters you wish to send, and post them in Bromyard when she goes in on her day off. I would suggest that we occasionally write openly to one another at the main house, just to allay any of foul Mortimer's suspicions.

I wish I could say that I will grieve for my father when he passes, which from your description cannot be long now. But as I told you, seeing him allow Uncle Mortimer to beat our mother killed any respect I might once have had for him. Over the years we watched her fading away as all of her spirit was crushed into nothing, and for that I cannot forgive him. She was a kind and

> *loving mother to us all, but what broke her*
> *last reserves was seeing the way that Uncle*
> *Mortimer forced Charles into his marriage*
> *with Uncle's Janette. I think her inability to*
> *stop that was what made her finally give up*
> *the fight, for she was gone within the year.*

"Holy shit! Poor old Millicent!" exclaimed Chris. "To be beaten up and have to watch the resident pervert mauling your son. God, it was no wonder she ended up a broken woman."

Sarah, too, was looking aghast. "I can't imagine how she must have felt. To be so powerless to do anything to stop him…"

Cleo nodded. "And of course in those days the man was very much the master in his own house. I'm liking the sound of this Jessie, though. She sounds like a plucky woman if she'd risk the anger of her employer. I'll have to check whether Yew Tree Cottage was tied to the estate. I'm guessing not, and that by then she was just someone who came in from the nearby village, because the number of staff who actually lived in was probably already falling, especially in medium-sized country houses like this. Big places like Whitley Court were still in their heyday in Edwardian times, but others would have already had to start cutting costs."

She began scanning the next letter and then set it aside. "It's just about Clarissa getting pregnant, and then the next one is more of the same – interesting as a view on ladies of a certain class of the time, but not what we're looking at." In that way she quickly went through several of the letters, speed-reading them and setting them aside. "Ah! Now here we go! This is when Mortimer died in 1910…"

Upper Moore House,
Bromyard,
16ᵗʰ August 1910

Dear Verity,

  The Monster is gone! If I had ever needed confirmation of all that you have told me over the years, it was seeing the way that Charles and Janette wept at his funeral, not out of grief, but from relief. Therefore I am very glad that baby John was such a squealer that we were moved into the gardener's cottage once he arrived. In truth, I wish we could continue there, but it would not do now that Bertie is the master of the house.

  But oh my dear, you will not believe what I found when I was packing everything up from the main bedrooms – for The Monster would not allow Bertie and I to take over the master bedroom while he still lived, and Bertie would not gainsay him. And so Jessie, Gladys and I had a long few days packing up all of the old dresses and things, and putting them into cases to be stored, for they are now so outdated that we could not give them away. We tackled The Monster's things first, taking them out to Jackson the gardener, and with Bertie being away in London, the staff and I had a celebratory bonfire of all of his things. After that it felt as though a great cloud had lifted from the house, you know, and for once I wished that we were Catholic and could ask a priest to come around and say some prayers over the place to cleanse it.

But that is not what I must tell you! When we finally got to your mama's things, there, in amongst her small clothes, right at the back of the drawer were these letters I am sending you. They are love letters! After you were born, and your father and The Monster were so embroiled in their schemes, your mother had an affair! I cannot work out who this man was, but he seems to have come into the area rather than being from here. His name was Hugh or Hugo Marinelli, and he seems to have been a very distant cousin of your father's from America. As you will read, he came in secret when he could, but dearest Verity, I believe your brother Hugh is his child!

I am sending these to you, because I know that the very sight of them would send Bertie into one of his rages. I hope you will not take this amiss, but I often now wish that I had never met your brother. Where the charming man who wooed me went to, I do not know, but I fear that even though Bertie escaped the unnatural attentions of The Monster as a child, nonetheless they had enough time together for that man to have warped Bertie's true nature. Certainly once we came to live here, Bertie did nothing without consulting him first. I am with child again, but in later years Bertie's attentions have become much rougher, so that in truth I welcome this child as a reason to keep him from me.

Please write soon,

Clarissa

"Oh Lord, she does sound as though she was starting to get a bit desperate, doesn't she," Sarah said sympathetically.

"But what's this about love letters?" Chris asked eagerly. "Is that them, Cleo?"

She was holding a small handful of much more tiny folded papers, and as she sniffed them said, "Oh my goodness, you can still smell the lavender and rose perfume on them!"

Chris leaned in for a sniff, then asking, "Dare you unfold them? They seem pretty tightly packed."

Cleo tentatively tried to open a couple, but set them aside as needing more careful examination. One, however, would unfold and seemed to be the last one, making her wonder how many times Millicent had opened it herself, for the folds were almost falling apart now. There was no address, it just began,

> *My darling Millicent,*
>
> *I cannot tell you how I long for next week to come when we can be together forever. I must tell you now that I have told you a small fib, but only a small one. My name is not Hugo Marinelli. That is a family name connected to me, but it is not mine. I had to use it while in the area because if I had used my own name it would have been commented upon. You see I am really Hugh Wytcombe, for my father was Virgil Wytcombe, the son of William Wytcombe who was so vilely disinherited by that devil, Luka Kovač. Yet I care nothing for that.*
>
> *I first came to Upper Moore to see what kind of place it must be that it was talked*

about by my grandparents and their cousins with such loathing. I never expected to come across my perfect rose sitting all alone and unwanted in the garden. From the moment I saw you, I knew that I had to get you away to safety in Boston with the rest of the family. From the moment I saw you, any thought of the house or any money was gone. It was only you, only ever you.

I cannot wait to introduce you to my parents and the rest of the family over in America. The legal affairs which I came here, and to Italy, to conduct have now been wrapped up, and once the ship sails from Southampton, we need never set foot in England again. As far as anyone else will know, you will arrive in Boston as my wife, who was widowed when we met, and who has her son and two daughters with her. Oh my darling, I do hope that your two sweet girls will come to love me as much as I already love them, and your poor boy Charles will have a proper father in me, that I promise with all my heart. I will love your existing children as much as the child you are going to give me, I do most solemnly swear.

Meet me by the lichgate on Sunday evening when the men are in their cups, and I will take you to your new home where you will be loved and cherished for the rest of your life.

your ever loving and devoted Hugh.

The three of them sat in silence for a moment when Cleo had finished reading, everyone both shocked and moved.

After snuffling into a tissue for a moment, Sarah finally managed to say, "Well she clearly never went. I wonder what happened?"

"This is very tear-stained," Cleo observed. "There are patches where I can barely make out the words."

Chris got up and went into the kitchen, coming back with a whisky for himself and Cleo, and a large sherry for his mother. "I can't tell you why, but I have the nastiest feeling that Hugh never made it to that boat. Would you be able to see if he shows up anywhere on the records over here, Cleo? I know you said you wouldn't do any online searches tonight, but I don't think I can bear to go to bed and not know about this."

Cleo pulled her laptop up onto her knees and logged on. Her search didn't take long to find. "Oh shit! Hugo Marinelli, buried 18th September 1889, Worcester. Bloody hell! It looks like Mortimer and Sydney might have murdered him!"

"Could it have been Luka?" Chris wondered.

"No, Luka died in 1881, so eight years earlier – but I bet his influence was still bloody fresh with his two minions! I'll order a copy of that death certificate, but I don't think it's going to make pleasant reading."

Chris raised his glass, "Then here's to the memory of Hugo, or Hugh, whichever he was, for bringing a bit of love and romance into what must have been a bloody miserable life for Millicent. I hope he made her toes curl!"

"Chris!"

"Well I do, Mum! Poor bloody woman, it must have been damned near rape every time she got pregnant before that. Nobody deserves that. But damn, what a shock it must have been when the family in America realised he'd died, and where. And I wonder what that business was in Italy? Do we think that might have been the point when the house in Verona passed out of the family's hands?"

"It could be," Cleo admitted. "The last evidence we have is from Julia in 1882. I wonder if Clifford died, and by that time Ernest wanted somewhere smaller and more manageable than the big family villa? That address is right in the middle of Verona, you know, so it was probably quite expensive to run, and if he had vineyards out in the countryside, he might have decided that it was easier to just run the whole business from out there, especially if he wasn't getting a lot of time to spend in the town house."

Then Cleo suddenly gasped, making Chris ask,

"What? What have you found?"

Yet Cleo shook her head. "Not me. It's not what *I* found," And she very carefully spread the small folded love letters out. "Look at the hand writing! I think some of these were Millicent's letters back to Hugo or Hugh. *This* is what our soldier Hugh found when he said he'd found out something shocking about himself! I just thought I'd dropped this letter …and this one …and this one …from the others when I got all of the letters out. But I hadn't! I just know the look of paper from different eras enough to have known roughly when they came from, and so I assumed they'd come from out of one of the other envelopes in this lot, but they hadn't. These three were amongst *Hugh's* letters! She must have written to her lover when he was in Italy!"

"God, what a facer!" gasped Chris. "There's Hugh, lying all bandaged up and already having to face life without a leg, and then he goes and discovers that he's his mum's love child. No wonder he sounded rattled in his letter home. I wonder if he talked about this with Verity or Emilia?"

"He might have," Cleo conceded, "but given that they were getting a bit worried about his suspicions about Bertie …although…"

"Although what?" Chris prodded.

"Well…" Cleo began tentatively, "I think we're all thinking that Mortimer and Sydney II murdered Millicent's lover, don't we? Nobody else had any motive. So what if they knew exactly who he was?"

Sarah frowned. "But how? Surely Millicent would have been so careful?"

Cleo nodded. "Yes, *she* would, but you think about who she was taking away with her. Who was the one person who was missing?"

"Oh shit! Bertie!" Chris realised.

"Yes! Exactly! Now do you see Millicent taking all of her other children, and leaving one behind? I don't. Not after what had happened to Charles! So right at the end, she must have told the children that they were leaving – all of them! And at that point Bertie plain refused to go, so she was thinking she'd have to leave him or he'd kick up a racket when they left, but I bet she never dreamt that he'd actually tell his father."

Chris groaned and buried his face in his hands. "Noooo! Bertie betrayed her! Oh God, that *so* makes sense when you see it like that. He's the only one who could have, isn't he?"

"Oh, poor Millicent!" Sarah cried. "Oh fancy having to live knowing that your son brought about the death of the man you loved. No wonder the light just seemed to go out inside of her."

"But then doesn't that explain something else, too?" Cleo pressed them to see. "Charles was just ten at the time, but within nine years he's forcibly married to Mortimer's daughter. What's the betting that the beating Verity witnessed Mortimer giving her mother was to beat it out of her who her lover was? Can't you just imagine Mortimer being absolutely enraged by her infidelity to Sydney, but even worse than that, if he finally found out who Hugo was? I'm calling him Hugo, by the way to save confusion with World War One Hugh. Because can't you see that if Hugh is Hugo's son …and Hugo is William's grandson …then…"

Chris nearly choked on his Balvenie malt. "Jeez! *Hugh* was the rightful heir to Upper Moore if the other heirs from Hector couldn't be found! Oh no! …But if Bertie could betray his mother, and see the way that Mortimer reacted so violently …Oh God! And he might have then suddenly seen Hugh in a different light and not as his brother at all. …Oh crap, no! …Do you think that Bertie really did murder Hugh just to keep this place?"

But given that Hugh brought the necklace back, Cleo thought, *is it Hecate who's now in contact with the English family who has brought this run of bad luck on the family ever since?* And was suddenly glad that it was back safely tucked away in her laptop case.

Chapter 29

Believing that they now had the truth of the matter, yet wanting confirmation from the last few letters, they waited until Sarah had made them all a hot drink, and then sat down for the final stretch. Nobody had the heart to read Millicent's letters to her lover, even if they could have been safely unfolded after all this time, and neither could they face Hugo's letters back to her for both of the same reasons. Both just felt too tragic for words right now.

At first Cleo just read out bits from various later letters which confirmed that Bertie was becoming ever more brutal with Clarissa, until, that was, Emilia intervened.

"Listen to this!" Cleo gasped with a giggle. "It's Clarissa writing to Verity…

> *He was accusing me in the vilest of manners of infidelity, and that our next baby is not his… "*

"I think, by the way, that this must have been Catherine, the youngest, she was expecting at that stage, and you have to wonder if he knew that Hugh wasn't by his own father, even then, to suspect his wife like this a whole generation on…

> *But he forgot in his temper that your sister and her husband and family were visiting. Truly, Verity, I did not know that a woman could be so fierce! With Bertie in one of his tantrums, the servants were hiding*

down in the kitchen rather than coming to clear the dinner table, meaning the cutlery was still there. So as he was berating me and then raised his fist and punched me, Emilia came in like my avenging angel.

She seized the carving knife from off the table and told him that if he did not want to end up with his manhood on a plate, that he would desist right now. He was in such a rage that he raised his hand to her, but far from needing her husband to come and rescue her, though he was already helping me up off the floor, Emilia drew her own arm back and landed Bertie such a punch as to throw him back over the carver chair! I have never seen the like!

And not content with that, she marched around the fallen chair and put the carving knife to his throat! 'Do not ever raise your hand to me, brother,' she snarled – and it was a snarl, Verity! 'I will match you blow for blow, and you will come off worse,' she declared, and do you know, he went quite white. He was floundering around on the floor like a landed fish, and there was Emilia standing over him all icy fury. She told him that if she ever so much as found a bruise on me again, she would be taking me and the children away to live with her until he came to his senses.

He must have believed her, because the next morning he told the servants to move his things out of our bedroom, and he has moved into Hugh's old room over the morning room. Quite what will happen if Hugh needs to come home from the army, I

do not know, but for now, know that we are
living in the kind of peace we have not known
for years.

Cleo grinned at Sarah and Chris. "She goes on a bit more about finding schools for John and Horace, but isn't that an eye-opener? No wonder Emilia could say, 'I know your games, Bertie', because she truly did."

Sarah was agog, but Chris declared, "And no wonder she was able to survive in the Outback, too! My God, if you had to fight your corner every day like that as a kid, it's not surprising that she took no shit from anyone as an adult."

"I was thinking that," Cleo agreed. "And doesn't it then make sense of the way that Audrey was kept out of the loop of later letters? We wondered why, but if Clarissa and Verity saw Horace turning out to be a chip off Bertie and Sydney's blocks, then knowing this, you can imagine that they must have had substantial sympathy for her. By the look of things, the redoubtable Jessie carried on being Clarissa's messenger, but if there was nobody who could fulfil that role for Audrey if Horace had been encouraged to snoop by his father, then the other women may have cautioned her to never put anything into writing that he could use against her."

"Heavens!" Sarah gulped. "What a way to have to live your life?"

Cleo nodded, but said sadly, "Unfortunately that was the fate of far too many women in that era and before. It's easy to forget nowadays that in law women had far fewer rights than they do today. Even a century ago, domestic violence was completely ignored by the police unless it resulted in the wife's death, and even then I reckon it was damned hard to get a conviction if the man could make a decent case for having been 'provoked'. A man might get chastised by them for going home drunk and causing a disturbance, but it was more about him being a nuisance to the men who lived around him that was seen as the priority, rather than the fate of the poor souls living in his house."

"I'm awfully glad I was born when I was," Sarah said in a shocked voice.

However Cleo was quick to qualify her comments. "I don't mean that every woman was knocked black and blue – far from it! I just meant that when domestic violence *did* take place, there wasn't a lot done about it. If you were lucky, the husbands of the women around you would have a strong word with your husband if he overstepped the mark, but it was so much harder if you were from the upper classes like Clarissa. In inner-city Birmingham, for instance, for all that you might have been poverty-stricken and living in beyond dreadful conditions, there was a certain degree of sticking together, and so you had more chance of being helped out. There was a lot to be said for working-class morality!

"Yet even in this case, you get the impression that because Bertie was a step up the social ladder from Emilia's husband, Frank Denby, Frank would have been reluctant to cross Bertie in anything that might become public. On the other hand, Bertie would have looked a complete fool if he'd had to go to some magistrate, who most probably would have been one of his shooting and fishing buddies, and told him that he'd been flattened by his kid sister – it was all about perceptions in that sense."

As Sarah absorbed what Cleo had just said, Chris had got down on his knees beside Cleo where she was sitting on the floor, and was looking at the remaining letters.

"There are other handwritings in here!" he exclaimed in surprise.

"Yes there are," Cleo confirmed. "The envelope for this one is missing, but I think it might well be from Emilia to Clarissa from Australia, because unless I'm mistaken, that other handwriting is Hugh's."

Smothering a huge yawn, Chris tapped the next letter. "Come on, then, let's see what other secrets come to light!"

Cleo picked up the next letter. "Hmm… Nothing much in this one besides Clarissa confirming to Verity that Bertie has backed off substantially – which I think we're all relieved to hear. …Okay, this is now after poor Verity and her family died. Bless her, she seems to have been the most loved of all of the family, perhaps because she took on the role of peace-maker between all of the siblings. I won't read all of this out now, because we're all tired, but it was Verity dying that made Emilia finally commit to emigrating, and this letter here is her trying her hardest to get Hugh to leave and come with them. But this is his answer…"

Upper Moore House,
Bromyard.
18th November 1919

Dear Emilia

I understand all that you have said about me coming with you to Australia, and that there is nothing left here for me – unlike Charles, who has George to consider. And I do understand what you have said about Bertie never giving up Upper Moore. For my own part I have no aspirations to own it, and I would not dream of making any kind of statement to that effect which he might misconstrue. But I do feel a deep moral obligation towards the true heirs to the estate

*to at least find out if any of them are alive.
The chances of any of my generation having
escaped the horrors of the War seem slim,
especially in Italy, for I saw with my own
eyes the horrendous conditions in which the
Italian soldiers served. God knows that we
had much to endure, but compared to the dire
rations and kit that they had to deal with, we
lived in near luxury. So it may be that there
is genuinely nobody else left anyway. I have
told Bertie that I will let it drop, but once I
am up and about again, I intend to make
discreet inquires of my own. Clarissa and the
maids will be coming up to London to help
you to sort out Verity's house soon, for if
there are things that need to be stored, they
will have to come here now that you are
leaving, and God willing, I will be well
enough to travel with them and to see you
before you go.*

Your loving brother,
Hugh

"Good God!" Chris softly breathed. "He didn't know!
Hugh didn't make the connection that if he was his
mother's child by Hugo – as we're calling him – then he
was more the rightful heir than Bertie was!"

"I don't know about 'rightful'," Cleo cautioned.
"After all, he was, in effect, illegitimate. Millicent and
Hugo weren't married, don't forget, and even if Hugh
knew, he may have thought he came from a tainted line if
he didn't have the full family tree, as we have. But I do see
what you mean. Hugh at that point certainly hasn't made
the connection that if he comes from William's line, then
he's from the legitimate line, and his brother isn't. Rather

more important, though, is whether Bertie knew who Hugo was and had made the connection? Or at least as to who Hugh's father was. That could explain a lot about his attitude towards Hugh changing – maybe even back while Hugh was away in the army? And then if Hugh said much of the Italian connection, Bertie might have put two and two together faster than Hugh did as to whom was the rightful heir? No doubt Bertie was judging Hugh by his own warped morals, and assumed that since he would have tried to stake his claim over his brother, that Hugh would do the same. He probably never entertained the notion that Hugh wouldn't have wanted it."

She opened out the next letter. "…Aah, I wonder if Emilia and her family were temporarily staying at Verity's house before leaving? It might have made sense if they'd already sold their house, because this last letter to her has been bundled up with Verity's letters."

Upper Moor House
Bromyard
12th December 1919

Dear Emilia,

> *It was good to see you. I know that my condition was a shock to you, and so I hope you are now going to understand what I have to say. That train journey to London and back was more than I could cope with, even with Clarissa and the servants to help me on and off the train and the like, and I have had several days prostrate in my bed. I could not even summon the strength to put pen to paper until today, so I hope you can see that the long voyage to Australia would probably be the end of me. I am just not well enough yet to stand the strain.*

I have also given it much thought, as you begged me to, but I cannot see what sort of life a chap with one leg like me would have out there. Here I might live quietly on my army pension in one of the cottages. And eventually I hope I might find some form of employment in an office kind of way. But if I came with you, I would be nothing but a burden. I could no more attempt the physical work I once loved than develop wings and fly, and I have no desire to spend the rest of my days as the invalid indoors, who has to be waited on hand and foot by you and your girls – for if we were out in the wilds and with no servants, then my burden would fall on your family alone. Here I can hope for someone from the estate to call in and help me a few times a week, at least, and I have as good as been offered that help from Jessie's grown-up daughter and her son and his wife. So I hope you can appreciate that while my soul longs for the chance to go exploring a new land with you, my broken body will not allow it.

Please go and live a long and happy life on my behalf, and send me many letters telling me of what you have all been up to,

Your loving brother,
Hugh.

Chris shook his head in despair. "What a terrible waste of such a good man. He sounds like a thoroughly decent guy. And I guess he was right. Life for a cripple in the Outback in those days would have either killed him or left him a bed-ridden invalid. I can't help but wonder, though, whether he knew that Bertie was going to kill him, and that in his depressed state, and suffering from survivor's guilt as he undoubtedly was, that he almost welcomed it? I mean, that wouldn't be stretching things too far, would it?"

Cleo sighed. "Sadly, no it wouldn't. When you read what it was like for so many of those men who came home damaged, there was no support for them. Considering the percentage of suicides even amongst ex-service men and women these days, it wouldn't be surprising if Hugh hadn't felt like that before Bertie decided to help him on his way. And I reckon a lot would have depended on whether Hugh thought he could achieve his aim, and get Upper Moore back into the hands of its rightful owners.

"After all, Luka may have died nine years before Hugh was born, but he'd had the first sixteen years of his life with Sydney as his own father – or at least as far as the outside world was aware! And the other monster in the family, Mortimer, didn't die until Hugh was twenty. So on the one hand, with those two monsters now dead, he might have been quite optimistic at the start that he could change things; but then once he realised that Bertie was just another carbon copy of them, that might have substantially deepened his depression."

That made Sarah ask, "Do you think that Hugh went into the army to escape, like the first Sydney and his brother Edgar did?"

"It's a thought, isn't it?" Chris agreed. "He might have joined up very young as a cadet, or whatever the equivalent was back in those days."

However Cleo had the thought, "But we've just heard how Emilia stood up to Bertie, haven't we? Well that doesn't sound like the first time she'd done that. And she was a full eight years older than Hugh. So by the time he was, say, eight years old, and maybe of the age when Mortimer's paedo' instincts kicked in, she would have been a young woman of sixteen. Even Verity would have been thirteen, and Charles would have been already married to Janette, or very close to being. So there might have been a closing of the ranks of the sisters and Charles, to make sure that what happened to him didn't happen to Hugh.

"I know Charles has come across as terribly damaged, but if he was standing shoulder to shoulder with Emilia and Verity, and as an adult, he might have found the resolve to defy Mortimer. People often find the courage to stand up for someone they love when they can't or won't for themselves, so Charles wouldn't be abnormal in that respect. And that might have made the difference between Hugh going in as soon as he could, or waiting a couple of years and going in as an actual soldier – I think in those days you'd have been talking about sixteen or eighteen respectively.

"And if you compare ages, by around 1898 – if we're sticking with Hugh being a lad of around eight then – then Sydney would have been forty-four, and Mortimer forty-two. In those days, being in your forties made you definitely middle-aged. Remember those first photographs you ever showed me, Chris? Sydney was a whale of a man by then, so he might have been past physically holding onto anyone. So if it came to the crunch of Mortimer forcibly removing Hugh from the upstairs rooms which the children had, you could have been looking at him facing Charles, Janette, and Verity, with Emilia as the ringleader. And he'd have had to be careful about involving any of the servants, because by then, even allowing for late Victorian or Edwardian dual moral standards, buggering little boys wasn't something you wanted anyone to make public."

"I see what you're getting at," Chris said, "but what occurs to me, also, is that those two monstrous men might have believed that Millicent might find one last spark of resistance if Hugh was hurt. She could have gone down the route of Hugh being the only thing left to live for, and if he was gone, then she'd have had nothing to lose by making it clear who had killed her lover. God, Cleo, I'd love it if we could find out just what happened to him!"

"Well you might be in luck. It all depends on whether he died in Worcestershire or Herefordshire. If it was Worcester, then there's a very old newspaper archive we can access, which would undoubtedly give us the dirt on his murder."

Chris high-fived her. "Then here's to him having died across the county boundary, then!"

"Is that it, then?" Sarah asked. "Because I'm wilting. Even if there's more, I don't think I can stay awake another moment."

"No, that's pretty much it," Cleo confirmed, though she could see one last letter from Emilia to Clarissa. If that said what she feared it did, then it could wait until the morning. None of them needed to go to bed with the details of Hugh's murder lingering in their minds.

Realising that it was by now heading for one in the morning, they all gratefully went to their beds, and although Chris lingered enough to give Cleo a very long kiss goodnight, they were both wary of making their growing relationship too obvious to Sarah by him spending the night with her. But that meant that Cleo ended up lying in her bed alone, watching the moonlight glinting off Bruno II's glass eyes, and with her mind refusing to switch off.

Was it coincidental that once Hugh found the necklace, he became so adamant that Upper Moore be returned to its rightful owners, she wondered? *Hecate, did your influence arrive here with* him? *Were you the hidden force in all of this coming to light? And is that why these poor women of previous generations in England came to grief, yet Francesca and her family in Italy and Croatia effectively got away with the murder of their persecutor?*

The questions kept going around in her head, not letting her sleep. *I must find out exactly when Millicent died*, she found herself thinking over and over, until she had to put the bedside light on and make a note of it to remind herself. *She must have died before Verity for her to refer to it, and didn't she say something about that being before Clarissa became part of the family? I really must find out about her lover and make sure he was who he said he was,* she thought drowsily. *I do hope those death certificates hurry up and come. I really want to know what happened to these people. …Oh Lord, and there's Charles' death, too, isn't there? 1922 now seems too horribly close to the other deaths to be coincidental.*

And Hecate? If you're listening, could you find your way to making it clear whether Sarah and Chris are the rightful heirs? Because this keeping the details of where they might stand in all of this from them is driving me nuts! I don't want to give them false hope that they can not only stay here, but take over the whole place. Archie may have left it to them, but so much hangs on whether bloody Darcy D'Eath puts up a fight. If she drags them through the courts and wins, they can't afford legal fees, and they're both bright enough to know that. So I'm really worried that if that woman digs her heels in, Sarah at least will cave in rather than risk everything by standing up to her. At the moment Sarah can afford another house, so she won't put that at risk for a court case with less than a dead certainty of winning. So come on, Hecate, I need a hand here!

———⧸⧹———

Chapter 30

By the time they all crawled out of bed on Sunday morning, it was heading for midday, and so they decided to have a cooked brunch. As the sausages, bacon and eggs all sizzled on Sarah's Aga, Cleo got onto her laptop and began digging into the archives, fuelled by a steady supply of fresh coffee via Chris.

"Any joy?" he asked, as he brought her a plate of Sarah's idea of a full-English. Looking at it, Cleo thought that she might not need anything more to eat until late in the evening, because it was huge. Seeing her look of dismay at the piled sausages, bacon, tomatoes, scrambled eggs and toast, he leaned in and whispered, "I'll help you out with that if you need."

"Been missing your mum's home cooking?" Cleo teased him, having noticed that at every meal he fell on his food like a starving man. Then again, when she had hugged him she'd thought he was downright skinny, and it belatedly occurred to her that he might have been going short on everything to try and afford the airfare home. That endeared him to her even more. If he'd been sufficiently worried about Sarah that he'd been on half rations for a while, then that said a lot about how clearly he'd grasped the urgency of the situation with his father. *If only his brother had had half that empathy*, she thought in frustration, and covertly slid first one, and then a second and third sausage across the plate in his direction, once Sarah's back was turned.

"I've found Millicent's death," she announced triumphantly, brandishing a forkful of bacon as Sarah turned back around in order to distract her from seeing Chris licking his fingers. "You can't help but feel sorry for her. She died in February 1901. I wonder if she would have kept going if only she'd known that her lout of a husband would be dead within five years? Let's face it, for a man who hadn't lived a hard life, fifty-two was no age at all. Do you want to know what he died of?"

"Not really," Sarah said, with Chris adding,

"Having seen the state of him in the photos, I think we can pretty accurately guess that it would either have been a stroke or a heart-attack. Hell, he had to have been upwards of twenty-stone, and he didn't seem to be a particularly tall man. I'd be rather more interested to learn how Millicent died. I know I'm probably reading too much into this, but I can't help but wonder whether she was got rid of because when she died, Hugh, as a little lad of what…?"

"…Eleven," Cleo supplied.

"…wouldn't have been that hard to get rid of afterwards. Kids died young far more often in those days, didn't they?"

Cleo suddenly tutted sharply, making Chris look at her in surprise.

"Oh, I'm not tutting at you!" she hastily assured him. "I'm just thinking of all those bills for boarding schools up in the library. Damn! It would be really good to get our hands on them. You see, I'm remembering what you told me right at the start, Sarah, about how Archie's mum managed to prevent him from being sent to the school his forebears had gone to."

"Oh!" Sarah gasped. "Of course! If Bertie went there, then there's a good chance that they'd have sent Hugh too, because if they hadn't, the neighbours would have been asking why. Oh my goodness, the schemers got hoisted with their own petard, didn't they? The one thing they couldn't risk was anyone from the local big families getting suspicious about why the youngest son didn't follow the oldest. No! The oldest *two* – I was forgetting Charles!"

"I get what you mean now," Chris said with a grin. "You could just about excuse not sending Hugh if it had just been him and Bertie. Maybe made some excuse about Hugh being too delicate or some other crap. But once you bring poor Charles into the equation – who everyone hereabouts must have known was a bit off with the fairies, even if they didn't know why – then if they'd already sent *him* too, it would have looked *really* odd if they hadn't sent Hugh, who going by the letters and his army rank was bright and capable up until he got wounded. And Charles might have been very glad to go if it got him out of the house."

"I know it's probably very bad of me," Sarah confessed, "but I get a real buzz out of that thought – you know, that those two dreadful men tied themselves up in a knot which then kept them entangled as much as their victims." Then as if that had jogged her memory she looked at the clock and gasped, "Oh heavens, we've missed church!"

"We'll go to Evensong," Cleo offered, and dropped the hint Chris' way by adding, "your friends who you see in the morning service won't be there, but you can speak to Emma if you need to about the funeral on Wednesday."

Chris immediately pounced on Cleo's offer of a respite from the grilling they'd got last Sunday. "Yes, Mum, we can touch base with Emma, just to make sure everything's okay. I'm sure she'd be the first to understand that this week's been far from normal."

Seeing Sarah immediately relax, he turned and gave Cleo a conspiratorial wink of approval, then asked, "Who else are you looking for online, then?"

"I was just keying in another search for Hugo. We know he was buried in the graveyard of the parish church of St John's on the west side of Worcester, but that was most likely a pauper's burial. They wouldn't have known who he was, would they? And it just dawned on me that if his death was in any way suspicious, the powers that be of the time would have been more likely to give him a burial – where he could be exhumed for another autopsy – rather than cremation." She typed in several more words, and clicked the mouse a few times, then sighed.

"No success?" Chris asked.

Looking up, Cleo shook her head, but said, "No, I've found him alright. It's rather where he died that bothered me. Knightwick! That's far too close to the River Teme for my liking. I think tomorrow I might drive into Worcester to look at the local paper. Any hint of a man's body being found floating in the river would have made it into there, and I don't know why, but I got this sudden mental image of him being whacked over the head, and then taken to the river and thrown in." *Thank you for that hint, Hecate,* she mentally offered up, , wondering whether that prod had come because she was now keeping the necklace with her, but didn't say anything out loud. "If Hugo was unconscious when he went in, he could have drowned without ever waking up."

Chris shuddered. "Poor bastard! What a way to go! I don't suppose we can prove that they did it?"

Cleo shook her head. "Sad to say, very little chance at all. Back in those days they probably assumed that any damage to his head came from hitting it on stones or tree trunks in the river, and that stretch has some big old trees right on the riverbank. And as you know, it's also a river that rises very fast, because if you get torrential rain up in the Welsh mountains, then down here the Teme can come up several feet in just a few hours, and when it does it's really fast flowing; certainly fast enough to drown a man in. Sadly I can't find the weather conditions for that week or so, but I'd lay odds on it having been a soaking wet month, and the locals knowing that the river was treacherous just then. That would explain why nobody questioned a foreigner coming to grief there.

"What I'd rather focus on is proving that his son Hugh was murdered. If we can do that, then we can probably make a case for Hugo as at least collateral damage." She sighed. "I'm going to have to read that last letter. I couldn't face it last night, but it's got to be done," and she went and fetched it out of the lounge.

> *Alice Springs,*
> *Australia,*
> *February 25th 1921*

Dear Clarissa,

> *I am distraught beyond words at your news of Hugh. My dear little brother never was a match for Bertie in cunning and villainy! And while we had all become resigned to the fact that Hugh would never again be the bright and athletic lad we all once knew, I don't think either of us believes that he was that close to death's door either. This news of him passing so much blood has me deeply vexed, for before she died, Verity told me of a strange conversation she had with Hugh. He talked then of stomach cramps of a very violent nature, and that that was when he stopped eating anything Bertie brought to him. How terribly*

tragic, then, that he should have caught influenza this winter, and been laid so low that he was no longer able to be so discerning or alert.

But my worries are now for you and Charles. Clarissa, you must both leave Upper Moore! Go to the town house in London for your own safety. With all four children now away at school they at least are safe, and in the holidays they can as easily come to London as Bromyard; and with poor George now gone, Charles has nobody to worry about. Both of your reputations will remain intact if you are sharing your house with your widowed brother, so Bertie will not be able to ruin you with his lies.

And if you'll take my advice, once you are away from Bertie, look for another man who will watch over you and treat you more kindly than my boor of a brother has done. You have said that John loathes his father and is determined to make his own way in the army, and so as long as you can keep Horace away from him, your sons will have a chance to break away from the curse of our damned family. If you wish to run this far with the children, know that there will always be a home for you here in Australia with us,

My fondest wishes to you,
Emilia.

Sarah looked around from where she was making a cake, "I don't like those references to Charles, do you? How close is that to when he died, Cleo?"

"Too bloody close, is the short answer! Only a year and a bit later. God, I can't wait for the 1921 census to become available in 2021. We might find out from that whether he and Clarissa made it to London or not." Then she smacked her palm against her forehead. "God, I'm an idiot! I forgot …I'll look up his place of death again," and she clicked through to the file she had already saved. "Here we go, Islington! That's where Verity lived." She clicked on some more files, then added, "And that's where Clarissa died, too. It's no good, I'm going to have to order their death certificates, if only to satisfy my own curiosity. Wouldn't it be awful if they died the same way that Hugh had?"

Chris shook his head in dismay. "God! And to think that Archie died the same way! You'd almost think that Herself had read those letters, except that we know that she couldn't have."

"Oh no!" Cleo gulped. "Mrs W! She was so insistent that I didn't look into her family."

"Oh come on, Cleo," Sarah protested. "I can't stand her, but that's just ridiculous. She would hardly have married Archie if he was related to her."

"Wouldn't she?" Chris challenged her. "Come on, Mum. She was past the age when kids were likely, even if she was a generation younger than Archie. And she's bloody mercenary. Would she blanch at a few tumbles between the sheets with a man she silently despised if it got her what she wanted? I know you've always said that her hold over Archie was that he felt sorry for her, but even so…"

"But whose child could she be?" Sarah demanded. Then both of them turned around as they heard Cleo frantically keying searches in, using both laptops to access different archives at the same time.

Her, "Holy fucking hell!" was the warning that she had found something unpleasant, but she held up a warning finger for them to wait while she dug on. Fifteen minutes later she was sure of what she'd found.

"Chris, I think we need to look through that photo album again for around the 1860s."

He looked worried. "Oh crap, I'm not going to like this, am I?"

"No, I'm afraid not. You see Algernon Franks, the puppet who married Luka's daughter Frances, had a sister. A sister who then went on to marry Reginald D'Eath in 1858."

Sarah groaned, flopped down in a chair beside the kitchen table, and buried her head in her hands. "Noooo!" she softly moaned.

Cleo reached over and squeezed her arm reassuringly. "Well there's nothing wrong with your instincts, Sarah. You said that right from the start she made your flesh creep, and that you thought there was something wrong there. How right you were! It was the name of the farm that made me look twice. Do you remember when I was looking at Janette, and I told you that her father was a farmer at Lower Pencombe Farm? That was back before we realised who Mortimer Franks was. Well on the next census you see Reginald D'Eath and his wife Dorothy as tenant farmers, with Mortimer missing. …Here, let me start drawing that out for you…"

"Now we knew that Mortimer had his grubby boots under the table at Upper Moore by then, so of course I didn't look any harder at them. That meant I never tumbled to the fact that he was the D'Eaths' nephew via his father and Dorothy! But they also had a son, Thomas D'Eath, who was born in 1860. That makes him only four years younger than his cousin, the awful Mortimer.

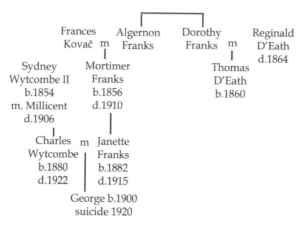

"Reginald D'Eath dies in 1864, so that's the end of any more children for Algernon's sister, Dorothy, but she carries on running the farm on her own – which I have to say was pretty unusual in those days. Farming was heavy labouring kind of work, so she would have had to employ men, and not many men were happy with having a woman boss, especially in a conservative rural community like this would have been. But if Algernon Franks was still the boss, even if he wasn't living there and was only Luka's puppet up at the big house, that would still have made it a very different thing, wouldn't it? When it was a family concern that was different – you could have a matriarch then, but not so much with just hired help.

"And of course the even worse Luka was still very much alive at that point. So we have to allow for him thinking that in young Thomas he's got a spare lad who he could always marry to one of the daughters – should it looked likely that he was going to run out of lads to shove at the estate. Of course that never happened, not least because there weren't any girls of the right age. Olivia was already married by the time Thomas was born, and Emilia and Verity were still an unknowable twenty years in the future. But I then picked up Thomas D'Eath – who I

found quickly because of his less than common surname –
on a ship heading for Boston in 1880, when he was
twenty.

"Now he could have just been escaping as others had
done, but I didn't like the coincidence of that being right
where Sophia and Edward Fairfax had gone to. That made
me wonder whether Luka, who still lived at that point, had
heard a whisper that that's where the last remaining child
of Richard Wytcombe was? Now I've just checked up, and
Sophia died in 1876 and Edward in 1878, so if Thomas
D'Eath had been sent their way with revenge in mind in
1880, he got there too late."

"Thank God for that!" exclaimed Sarah.

"Don't celebrate too soon," Cleo warned. "Thomas
must have been at least halfway bright, even if not enough
to realise that he should get away from Luka and Mortimer
and stay away. A bit over a year later, he comes back with
a new wife, a wife called Oriana. Now her surname is
Visconti, which turns out to have been Marta's maiden
name before she married Dante Wytcombe."

Chris practically choked on his coffee. "Oh the
bastard!" he gasped. "She was the kid Dante abandoned,
wasn't she?"

Cleo sighed sadly. "Yes she was, and that year Marta
had died in the spring, so you can't get away from the
obvious that Thomas singled out the most vulnerable
member of the family over there. Sophia's own daughters
were that much older and far more clued up in all
probability, if not already married; and so too would have
been Julia's. If Oriana had been brought up using the
surname Visconti – and to be fair, her poor mother must
have been so ashamed of being married to Dante – then
Oriana herself might not have realised what she was letting
herself in for. After all, she might have been forewarned

about anyone with the surname Wytcombe, but who would have know to warn her about a D'Eath?

"Of course, by the time they got back here, Luka was dead, but they go back to Lower Pencombe, and they appear on the 1891 census there. Now maybe Mortimer hadn't Luka's planning abilities, or he just got bored with running the farm, but although I'll have to check this through land transactions, I think they sold the farm. When you come to the 1901 census Oriana and Thomas are living in London; but the telling one is the 1911 census, because they've moved to just around the corner from Verity."

Chris and Sarah were too shocked to say anything, and so Cleo turned the one laptop around so that they could see, and brought up the relevant shot from Google Earth. "See here? That's Verity's house, the last one before the corner. But this one, whose garden runs right up to theirs at right-angles from the side street, that's where Thomas D'Eath and Oriana lived with their son …Sydney!"

"Oh that name's just too icky for words," Sarah gulped. "I feel quite queasy over this."

"When was he born?" Chris asked.

"1888. Your heart bleeds for Oriana, because she has a daughter within the year of them marrying, and then one in early 1883, one in late 1884, another in early 1886, and him in early 1888. After that she must have been exhausted because she has no more – either tha, or having finally had a son, Thomas lost interest in her. But you can almost see Thomas trying to match Sydney II for sons, and I can't help but wonder whether Mortimer and Sydney II had told him that if Millicent's sons died, then his son would inherit Upper Moore, in order to keep him on their side and compliant.

"I know that's really stretching things, and we'll never be able to prove it, but just remember that if they were in regular touch with Mortimer and Sydney Wytcombe II (as opposed to the infant Sydney d'Eath), then Thomas may have known all about what happened with Millicent and her lover Hugo. It could very well have made Thomas feel that he had been cheated of his chances if he knew just whose son Hugh Wytcombe was, and that despite him not being a legitimate heir, he still got brought up at Upper Moore. There Thomas was, having done his bit by going all the way to America to track down one of the female branches of the family and it's all for nothing."

Chris suddenly gasped, making Cleo and Sarah look to him.

"I've just had a horrible thought," he confessed. "Didn't we just find out that Clarissa and Charles went to what looks like Verity's old house in London? Well if *they* didn't know who Thomas D'Eath was – and they might well not if he was kept away from them by Mortimer and Sydney II – then they might never have known they were being spied upon."

That had Cleo checking her notes again and then giving a shudder. "Bloody hell! The D'Eath's must have moved there around the time that Verity and her family did, which was before the 1911 census. Before that they aren't so geographically close, though both of them are in Islington. God, it's like Mortimer's last bequest was to wish Thomas D'Eath onto the survivors!"

She brought up the Google Earth image on the laptop again. "Look! This is the street view of where the D'Eath's lived. But see those windows behind it beyond what has to be the garden? Those are the windows of Verity's house! So from the back of this house they must have practically been able to look in through the bloody windows! Certainly enough to get a good idea of how many people were living there at any time, and who they were."

Now Chris and Sarah shuddered too, with Chris adding, "Jeez, it's no wonder the ones who want to escape kept running to Italy, America or Australia. If they'd even caught the faintest whiff of being pursued all the way to London, they must have thought that nowhere in England was safe."

Sarah was also looking pale. "To think of it! Verity's children might even have played with them!"

However Cleo shook her head and scribbled further on the family tree.

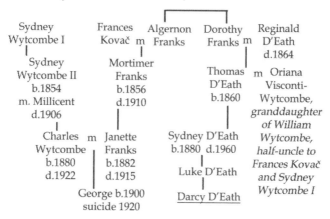

"No, not with Thomas' children, though his grandchildren maybe. *Sydney* D'Eath – that's Thomas and Oriana's son – was born in 1888, so he was only three years younger than Verity herself, but he in turn had three sons born in 1915, 1918 and 1921. The oldest two die in World War Two without leaving any kids behind, but this Sydney D'Eath lives on right up until 1966! That's within his granddaughter Darcy's lifetime. What doesn't help is that his youngest son, Luke – *brr*, how icky is that choice of name? – and his wife lived with him. So how many times do you think Herself heard the moans about how the family was diddled out of their inheritance? It's all rubbish, of course, because they never were in line to inherit a thing. But Sarah, did Archie ever say about his early days of meeting Darcy D'Eath, anything to the effect that it was such a coincidence that their families had known one another in London?"

For one awful moment Cleo thought Sarah was going to be physically sick, for the way she went white and had to take a lot of deep breaths was enough to know that words very close to that had indeed been spoken. Chris went and wrapped his arms around his mother.

"Poor old Archie," he said in a choked voice. "Poor bugger didn't stand a chance against her."

"No he didn't," Cleo said with such vehemence that it made the others turn to look at her, then were even more surprised by her fierce expression. "Don't you see it?" she asked them. "We've got a motive for murder!"

Chapter 31

For a moment Chris and Sarah were too stunned to respond, but that was just what Sarah needed to hear, and her colour began to come back. Chris went to the stock of Archie's malts and brought out a bottle.

"Cragganmore twenty-one year-old," he said reverently, pouring them each a tot. "I know it's a bit early in the day, but bloody hell, if we've got justice for Uncle Archie, then that's worth drinking to!"

"To Archie!" they chorused and clinked glasses.

Now, Cleo thought. *Now I can break the news I've been hanging onto.*

"Don't drain your glasses just yet," she said with a smile. "Because I have something else to tell you, but this time it's about your own family tree. You know we've talked a fair bit about whether the Ernest Carrington who was your great-grandfather, Sarah, was actually the son of Clifford Wytcombe, Hector's son? Well when we were reading those letters last night, one name wouldn't let me be. So in the end I had to come downstairs and check on it – that's why I was the last one up this morning. I confess that I wanted to do it while I was on my own, because if I was wrong, I didn't want to drop another bombshell on you."

"But you weren't?" Chris guessed.

"No I wasn't. You see, while I was checking up on the Carringtons, I saw the name of Ernest's wife. Ernest Carrington married Lucia Bisozzi." She saw that they recognised the name, but couldn't place it immediately.

"Do you remember Ilaria, the daughter of Claudio and Cinzia Marinelli? The one who was brought up with Julia and Clifford as her adopted sister and brother?"

Chris yelped as if she'd stuck a pin into him. "Yes! Ilaria married some guy called Bisozzi, didn't she! Then she cleared off to America to find Dante taking the baby with her. That Lucia?"

"*That* Lucia," Cleo confirmed. "On her marriage certificate she's down as Lucia Bisozzi, daughter of Ettore Bisozzi, deceased soldier, and born in Genoa in 1868. I can't believe that everything would line up that exactly for anyone else but her. Now it doesn't help in any way in the matter of who inherits Upper Moore. But that makes Lucia the great-granddaughter of Giulia, and Ernest the great-grandson of Francesca.

"So even if your great-gran' Emilia didn't twig who Ernest was, Sarah, I wonder whether she knew about Ilaria and Lucia? Don't forget those letters we read last night of Olivia's! Olivia might have been an old lady when Emilia, Verity and Hugh knew her, but she had the letters to prompt her memory. Now if Emilia was sharp enough to connect who those two were when her aunt was telling them about the family – because don't forget that by the time we're getting to 1906 onwards, Emilia isn't a kid but a grown married woman with her own daughters as babies who it might affect – and then remembered the names only a decade or so later, it starts to come together.

"Which possibly meant that she then saw her own daughter adding to the same family muddle of genes coming back together, and doesn't that make her outrage even more understandable? Without that, you could almost think she was over-reacting, given how far back the blood connection had to go, couldn't you? And clearly your dad did, Sarah, because he didn't know all the facts. After all, the common factor was Francesca and Guilia's parents, way back in the eighteenth century. But when you get a *third* link back to those same people, you can understand her being appalled!"

"Dear Lord!" Sarah gasped. "Thank Heavens for Mum's mongrel heritage! Who knows what we might have been like without it?"

"And there's one more thing," Cleo added. "In that first search I was only looking at the family connections, but while Ernest and George may have been trading in Verona, when I came to look a bit harder at them around the time of George's marriage, they were starting up a vineyard in Australia! Ernest and George were actually setting up business there. *That's* how George met Lois! It wasn't just a quick fling, they actually knew one another, because she went to be their secretary before she married George."

Sarah and Chris sat opened mouthed in astonishment as Cleo raised her glass again and said, "So here's to you, Sarah – the best connected of the remaining family going back to Richard Wytcombe!"

For a while they sat around the table, going over what Cleo had found and talking in general, but then Chris leaned back in his chair and said, "I want to find those school records, you know. That might prove that horrible Sydney II and Mortimer couldn't get their hands on little Hugh once his mum had died. After all, he was only eleven at the time, but if he was securely tucked up in some nice boarding school, they couldn't just whisk him away into the night without questions being asked, could they? You can't do anything today about the newspaper, Cleo, but we can do that. Shall we go and try to get into the house?"

They pulled on shoes and coats, and walked across the yard. However, knocking on the back door and the front door brought no response at all.

"I don't like this," Sarah sighed. "I may hate that bloody woman, but if she's choking on her own vomit having got blind drunk, I wouldn't want to just leave her to die in there alone, either."

"Let's go and see if we can force one of the French windows in the library," Chris suggested. "Being double doors, we might be able to push them enough to pop the latch and spring them open."

They duly made the climb up the soaking wet grass of the bank, and around to the short but sturdy oak bridges across the void at the back to the French windows. However, the equally solid old frames weren't moving, not even when Cleo and Chris both leaned on them.

"Well at least that shows that when Julia and Clifford got rescued the men got let in," Sarah sighed. "If we can't force them now when they're old, they wouldn't have budged back then."

Chris was squinting in through the panes of the three sets of doors, suddenly saying, "The key is still in this one! If I break the glass, we might get in."

"No," Cleo cautioned him. "Don't do that! You can't give her a reason to have a go at you for breaking and entering. We're going to have to call the police and let them do the breaking in – that way we're covered." She rolled her eyes in exasperation. "And to think that it's her own behaviour that means we daren't help her. What a way to live your life!"

They squelched back to the house and then Cleo called the police, being careful to use the non-emergency number. "I didn't ring 999," she explained to the responder, "because we've no proof that she is in danger. It's just that after all the bawling and shouting and threats that your colleagues responded to yesterday, it seems worrying quiet over there now, and we can't seem to get any sort of response. If she was at least telling us to sod off, it would be something, but the silence is starting to feel a bit ominous. She could be a heavy drinker, apparently, so she could have fallen or anything."

With the reassurance that someone would come out, all they could do now was wait. This part of the country wasn't blessed with many police anymore, and so it was seven o'clock by the time a police car pulled in.

"Sorry we couldn't get here earlier," PC Willis apologised as he walked across to them. "We had a drunken brawl to go out to – too much celebrating watching Chelsea winning against Tottenham over at the Red Lion! Bloody football matches; they're the bane of our lives!"

This time it was a burly younger man who was the PCSO who was with him, for which everyone was glad. Built like a rugby player, he was going to be far more effective at shoving doors. And so Cleo and Chris once again went through what they'd done and their concerns, and then led the two police around and up the bank to the library window, with Chris also taking a steel floor-board lifter from the cottage toolkit with him.

There was nothing for it but to break the pane of glass beside the key, but once it was turned, the old lock and bolt mechanism clicked perfectly, and they were able to get in. Once inside out of the freezing cold, PC Willis told Sarah, Chris and Cleo to stay there in the library, and he and Ben – as they now knew the PCSO was called – went to search the house, although they'd been told where it was most likely that they'd find Darcy D'Eath. The tread of their heavy shoes faded as they went towards the master bedroom, but then came back as they searched the other rooms on the first floor. When they set off up the stairs to the top floor, Sarah looked worriedly at Chris and Cleo and said,

"I don't like the sound of this. She never went up there. Why would she go now?"

Hecate! Cleo thought, but didn't dare say the name aloud. Had she at last found someone worthy of venting her revenge upon?

The sound of the PCSO's heavier footsteps running back down the stairs towards them had them all at the door to the landing, even as he got there.

"I'm going to call for an ambulance," he told them, "But you'd better go up. God knows what's happened to her, but she's frightened out of her wits and won't move. It's the room up above this one."

As he vanished off to get outside and pick up a signal on his radio, the three of them dashed up the old stairs. However, once out of earshot, Chris said,

"Bloody hell! Hugh's old living room! That's freaky. Why there?" and this time Cleo did say softly to him so that Sarah couldn't hear,

"Hecate! I told you – she's powerful and she doesn't like people who harm women and kids."

"But Herself is a woman – just!" Chris protested, as Sarah went in the door ahead of them.

"Maybe, but she comes from a long line of seriously wicked people, and she's most likely committed murder," Cleo hissed back. "And intent carries a lot of weight when you come to higher beings like that."

By now they had got into the old room to see Willis crouching before someone who was hardly recognisable as Darcy D'Eath. The immaculate makeup had run in streaks down her face, and been smudged into a patchwork of brownish-grey. The perfectly coiffed hair was sticking up in random spikes, and there was a strong smell of urine, speaking of her having wet herself in fear but still sitting in it.

It said a lot for Sarah that she now went and crouched down alongside Willis, saying in her most soothing voice, "Come on, love, you can't sit there like that. Let's get you up, shall we?"

Yet Mrs W shook her head vehemently, her eyes darting all around the room. "No! No, She might come!"

"Who?" Sarah asked gently. "There's nobody here but us. Nobody's been here with you. Did you take some of those pills you said you'd given up? Or have you been overdoing it on the slimming tablets again?"

Yet Mrs W's eyes suddenly fixed on a point just beyond Cleo's left shoulder and squealed. "*Her*! She's here! Look! She's... *Noooo*! No, I can't...! Oh God! Oh God! ...*Noooo*, stay away from me! Stay away!"

As she got more and more frantic, everyone else looked around to try and see what she was talking about. For Willis, Chris and Sarah, the room was absolutely empty, but for Cleo there once again loomed Hecate, spectral, classically beautiful, and yet terrible, saying 'Confess! Confess!' although whether Cleo was hearing words or thoughts, she couldn't have said. Yet behind the ancient goddess, almost as if they were crowding in to finally see someone getting justice, were a growing number of other, more human, ghostlike figures. Four of them were male, and Cleo was sure that the younger one in ghostly uniform was Hugh, and one of the older seeming ones Archie, going by the photos she had now seen of him; making her guess that the third and fourth might be the unfortunate Charles and his son George. But the others were all women, and going by the different apparel they were in, might well have been the generations going right back to Francesca and Giulia. Quite what the Italians were doing here, Cleo wasn't sure, but she guessed it might have much to do with the necklace having been moved to England – the same necklace which right now felt as if it was practically burning a hole in her pocket, and whose energy was an audible hum for Cleo if nobody else.

She was so absorbed in trying to guess who was who, that it made her jump when Chris whispered in her ear, "Cleo? Can *you* see something?"

Turning back to him, she was relieved to see that Sarah and Willis were focused on Mrs W, not herself, and so she was able to say softly to Chris. "Ghosts! The whole bloody family are queuing up in here behind Hecate!"

But then Mrs W must have realised that Cleo had seen them, for she pointed a wobbly finger at Cleo, screeching, "You! You brought them here! You brought them here to torment me!"

"I brought nothing," Cleo said firmly. "Whatever is plaguing you, it comes from your own conscience."

Make her tell them, the thought bore into her mind, and suddenly she knew that here was the chance to get Darcy D'Eath to come clean.

"My conscience is clear," she found herself saying, "but by the look of things yours isn't. What are you hiding, Mrs D'Eath-Wytcombe? What are you so worried someone is going to point the finger at *you* for?" and as she said the words, she felt the room go cold, and knew that Hecate had wrapped her form around herself, so that to Mrs W she became Hecate incarnate.

With a squeal of terror, for which only Cleo understood the reason, suddenly the words came tumbling out of Mrs W. How she had known about Upper Moore from long ago, and how her family had been cheated of it time and time again. How she had wormed her way into Archie's life, initially playing the grieving woman who had lost her soul-mate in an accident, so that she seemed more akin to him; and how she had vigorously suppressed her true nature in order to come across as caring and kind. She even confessed giving him Rohypnol, so that he woke up in bed beside her but with no memory of the night before, with her then making him believe that he'd spent a long and passionate night with her. Being a gentleman, Archie had felt no choice but to marry her after this had happened several times, she confessed, and the way that even in her confession Mrs W spoke of him with such derision had both Willis and Ben – who had returned by now – looking askance at her.

What had her practically spitting the words out was recounting how she had discovered that Penny had been the love of Archie's life, and that even having got her place as the lady of the house, it had turned out to be a hollow victory. Far from being weak and besotted with her, as she had believed he would be, Archie had instead only mourned Penny more when Mrs w had found it impossible to keep the act up any longer. Archie had loved and still wanted a woman that Darcy D'Eath could never be, yet rather than try to be more of that woman, she had only fought against him all the harder, seeing it as weakness to let her guard down and admit what sort of upbringing she had really had. But it was as she finally blurted out how she had feared that Archie was going to divorce her, forcing her to take action so that she would inherit while still his wife, that made Willis get up and begin taking rapid notes.

By the time she had confessed to the scenario, just as Sarah had told him she had feared it had happened, he was giving Sarah startled looks, but clearly wishing that someone had taken more notice of her fears back at the time. With Mrs W having given what amounted to a full confession in front of two police officers and three others, it was now obvious that whenever she was well enough, she was going to stand trial for murder. If that had Chris hugging Sarah tight as she wept with relief, it equally had Cleo thinking that now there could be no doubt that those two would inherit Upper Moore, and mouthing her silent thanks to Hecate, even as she and the ghosts faded.

The paramedics arrived, and with Mrs W heavily sedated, they got her into the ambulance and took her away, and it wasn't long before the police left too. With them having found Mrs W, there was nothing to be added in terms of the forced entry, and with Willis having attended only yesterday – though to Cleo it felt like a lifetime ago – Mrs W's state of mind was already known to the police, and little new to be added apart from the confession.

Left alone in the house, Sarah's first thought was to get a mop and bucket upstairs and clean the room, before the smell of urine became permanent. But after that, they were all too exhausted to do more, and so locking up the library – this time making sure that the key was out of the old doors – they left the house to the ghosts. What Sarah didn't know was that Cleo had slipped away across to her room, and as Sarah and Chris went back downstairs with the mop and bucket, she lit candles and incense in Hugh's room, and said a blessing. Already it felt to her as though a new air of peace had begun to pervade the place, and as she closed the door on the room, with the gentle scent of frankincense and myrrh beginning to fill it, and just the gentle light of the tea-lights throwing soft shadows, she was sure that the ghosts were beginning to fade.

The next morning they all drove into Worcester, and while Sarah and Chris went to see the new solicitors to bring them up to date on the weekend's happenings, Cleo went to the newspaper archives and searched for Hugo. Having the dates, it didn't take long to find him. To her relief, he had definitely been treated as a murder case, but with nobody seeming to have known him in the area, the police of the day had been unable to find a motive. That might all change now, though, she thought, and so made copies of the relevant articles before hurrying off to the solicitors to find Chris and Sarah. With there being no statute of limitations on crimes in the UK, had there been anyone alive still to prosecute, they might have got justice for Hugo too. And although Cleo wasn't naive enough to think that anything could be done now, what she hoped would be taken into account was that Darcy D'Eath's family had already been complicit in the murder of Hugh Wytcombe's father, and that this and the death of Hugh himself must have been known about for Darcy D'Eath to use the exact same method to get rid of Archie.

What Cleo didn't say was that she was hoping like mad that the death certificates for Charles and Clarissa would make it clear that Mrs W's grandfather, and possibly great-grandfather – the Sydney and Thomas D'Eaths she had found in her searches – might have been complicit in their murders too. Darcy D'Eath coming from a line of murderers with a vendetta against the Wytcombes, might well sway a jury who were hitherto undecided about her own guilt. And if it turned out that the methods had most likely been the same, that would be the perversely gruesome icing on the cake.

By the time they left the solicitors, it was clear that the bright young woman who was going to act on their behalf was relishing the prospect of this being a very newsworthy case, and one which might do her career some good. Certainly she was cautioning them not to speak to the press until after any court case, but hinted broadly that some papers would later pay well for a story like this. It was now that she also broke the news to Sarah that she was without doubt the new owner of Upper Moore House and its estate, and that was enough to reduce Sarah to floods of tears. Of all the things she had ever wanted, it had been to stay in the cottage which she loved, and to know that she could do that all by itself was an immense relief. But the other thing was the knowledge that she now had the money to be able to press for Aiden to be brought back to a British jail.

"Sell the Clarice Cliff," Cleo told her. "That alone will give you a nice pot of money to work with, and it will save you a fortune on insurance on the house. A big collection like that – even if it's not a coherent single service set – ought to go through one of the big London auction houses, because it'll attract international collectors and bump the price up."

However, nobody did anything about that for a while because two days later they had Jeff's funeral. Sarah was distraught, what with it coming on top of everything else, but by the end of the day, both Cleo and Chris thought it had been a cathartic experience for her. It was as if the last line had been drawn under all of the misery and misfortune in her life, and if she hadn't got Aiden back yet, at least she had lost the sensation of being quite so helpless about it all.

"I don't know what we'd have done without you," Chris told Cleo that night, as for the first time she shared his room. "You do realise that I'm not going to let you go, don't you? And we'd better go and get the rest of your stuff from that flat, because you're never going back there again!"

Some months later

"I think your idea for a workshop and retreat at the house is great!" Chris enthused as he and Cleo sent the last of Darcy D'Eath's ghastly modern furniture off in the house clearer's van. None of it had been worth much second-hand, despite having cost an arm and a leg new, and she was hardly going to need it, incarcerated in a secure psychiatric hospital as she was. It meant that there would be no public trial, but as Chris had said to Sarah when the news broke, if the papers then dug deep and found out about Aiden, making it seem as if he came from a family of murderers, it wasn't going to help his case any, and so it was probably a mercy it was never going to be brought into the spotlight. The dubious money from the sale of their story to a paper they could live without under those circumstances.

What had in part sent Mrs W down the psychiatric route had been the arrival of the various death certificates by the time her case had come up for review. Not only had Archie been exhumed and autopsied in the light of the discovery, but so too had Hugh, Charles and Clarissa. With all of them now being deemed to have died in a similar manner, it hadn't taken long for the coroners to decide that they had all died either by the same hand, or by two persons in collusion with one another. And with Darcy D'Eath having been virtually raised by her grandfather, she was perceived as having been perverted and warped by him since childhood. It didn't make her any less guilty of Archie's death, but it did mean that – in her current post-Hecate encountered state of near permanent terror – she was pronounced to be incapable of being brought to trial. That had Sarah immediately feeling sorry for her, but Chris and Cleo found it harder to be as forgiving, saying privately that it would have been easier to feel sorry for her upbringing if she hadn't murdered Archie.

They had also found that while Archie had left some money of his own, the way Darcy D'Eath had burned a hole in his investments in her short time as his widow, the house from this point onwards was going to have to earn its upkeep. They could afford a certain amount of restoration, but after that it was going to have to become economically viable. And that was the point when Cleo had had the idea of running residential sessions for small groups. Converting the top floor into a flat for her and Chris, and returning the first floor to its former grandeur, they would be able to have up to a dozen people staying as long as they were couples or prepared to share a room.

"There are so many people who want to know about their pasts," Cleo had explained to Sarah and Chris, "but they don't know where to start. Offer them a weekend in a beautiful house, with Joe's organic food and your wonderful cooking, Sarah, and we'll be full every time – especially if I advertise it abroad. Can you imagine how they'll feel doing workshops in that lovely library? It's like a step back into the past all by itself."

When they presented it to the bank manager, and he then sent them on to the bank's commercial expert, it became rapidly clear that this was going to be viable. So much so, that the bank was prepared to lend them money for the alterations needed to get the house back out of the mess that Horace had left it in. Central heating would be another must, but these days they could pick something which would be compatible with the old house, and if it could run off solar panels, then they would be offering a very eco-friendly option.

"We'll let your mum start off," Cleo also confided to Chris, "but then we'll get some young chefs in to start training up beside her. With Joe's daughter already on board as an additional housekeeper to help her, if we can keep the pressure off Sarah, that will be all to the good."

It also helped that Cleo had a good eye for appropriate antique furniture, and so while the builders were in, she and Chris were going to be busy scouring sales and second-hand shops for the new guest rooms. In no time at all, and on a very tight budget, they soon had the means to make the bedrooms feel authentic, even if the beds would be modern and comfortable.

One person who Cleo hadn't forgotten, though, was Angie. As soon as she could she invited her over to the house, and while her kids explored the grounds with Chris, she brought her up to date on what had happened. And by this time she had been able to track the American side of the family, and had confirmed that not only was Lucia who Cleo had thought she was, but also that, having shown the old letters to their current solicitors, they had confirmed that the murder of Hector ought, in the nineteenth century, have sent the solicitors of the time off in a search for an heir from Richard Wytcombe's line. That the now defunct company of solicitors of that era had endorsed Luka taking over Upper Moore House under the pretext of running it for his 'nephew', Clifford – or rather the pseudo Clifford who had been born as Ana's son, Bertram – was taken as a strong indicator that the solicitors had taken a bribe from Luka, for which in modern times they would have been struck off.

All of which had Angie hanging on Cleo's every word.

"I'm so sorry," Cleo apologised, when she had got to the end. "I was meant to be helping you out by getting the sale, and instead I ended up getting the house taken off the market permanently."

"Oh, don't worry," Angie said with a faint smile. "My bosses were actually grateful once they found out about Mrs W's arrest. I think they could see that if you hadn't exposed her, there was the potential for one hell of a mess if a sale had gone through. After all, even with just that new will, she was selling a house that wasn't hers to get rid of."

Cleo leaned across and gave her a hug. "Well I'm glad that worked out for you. However, I didn't just get you over here for that. Let me top up your glass, because you're going to want it. ...How do you fancy living in a cottage on the estate?"

"What?"

"Well the lodge house at the end of the old drive had been let out for ages, and one of the first things Mrs W did after Archie died was to give the tenants notice. They moved out at Christmas and it's been sitting empty since then. You'd want to come back around the big house to use the new drive to get in and out, because Sarah's right, you'd take your life in your hands these days trying to pull out of the old one. In fact, we're going to put some very solid gates across it to semi-permanently seal it off, so it would be safe for the kids. We can't afford to let you have it totally rent free, but we can charge you half of what you'd have to pay anywhere else."

Angie looked stunned for a moment, then a huge grin broke out. "We'd be neighbours! Fab!"

"Yes. So you'll come?"

"You try stopping me! Oh my God, Cleo! The kids would have this huge garden to play safely in, it's perfect!"

"Great, because you know you always said that you wanted to get back to your gardening?" Angie had trained as an RHS gardener before meeting James had sent her off down the estate agent route. "Well there's a superb arboretum here that needs a curator. So when I'm not running ancestry and archive courses, how would you fancy running a few gardening ones?"

The way Angie's eyes began shining told Cleo she'd say yes even before she spoke. She'd been longing for a way out of her cut-throat job for ages, and she wouldn't need asking a second time. But what Angie said was,

"Love it! What about the necklace? Do you still have it?"

"I do," Cleo confessed, "but I'm not sure how I feel about keeping it. It's gone quiet again now, and I'd rather it stayed that way. I'm just unsure whether a museum is the right place for it."

"And where's your statue of Hecate now? Sounds like I might have to revise my opinion of her."

"She's sitting on the uppermost terrace up behind the library," Cleo said with a grin. "Come and have a look. She's had daffodils around her feet in the spring, but I want your advice on a nice rambling rose for the summer, because in June next year there's going to be a ceremony held out there."

"You and Chris?" Angie gasped.

"Me and Chris," Cleo confirmed and found herself being wrapped in a hug as Angie whooped,

"I knew it! And I was the one who started it all!"

Author's Notes

I partly developed the idea for this story as I dug deep into my own family history, though I'm glad to report that I have no such ghosts lingering in my own past! So I, too, have dug into census records, ordered birth and death certificates, and drawn up family trees. An earlier inspiration came from a holiday to Croatia over a decade ago where I saw the 'red house' that I have made here into the dal Zotto home. Beautiful and yet dilapidated, I knew that there was a story to be written about it; I just had to wait until it surfaced. It wasn't in Rovinj, though, but another small town along that coast. However Rovinj really is a beautiful small coastal town, with the church of St Euphemia towering over it just as I have described, and the weight of its history as part of the Venetian Empire still lingers in its architecture and cuisine.

The idea of the necklace came somewhat later, and like Cleo, I wandered around the Etruscan museum in Rome, marvelling at the ancient finds and wondering about the people who must have used them. Hecate is very much an ancient goddess who looked after women, and like Cleo, I sometimes despair of those who feel the need to make her into some kind of ancient Goth with a very bad dark side. None of the ancient gods and goddesses are exactly pure, but equally, there are very few who are wholly demonic either.

And so on to the English side: there is no parish of Thornfield west of Bromyard. Hatfield has no parish church, and while Thornbury does have an old parish church, it dates from c.1300, not four hundred years earlier in the Anglo-Saxon period. I'm always conscious, when writing these books, that if I use real places, that somebody might take exception to the way I have portrayed their home, and so for those places with a darker history it is better to have somewhere wholly fictitious. Therefore there is no Upper Moore House, either, but there are some wonderful old houses of the same period in the wider Teme valley.

When it comes to Richard Wytcombe's exploits in the navy, all the ships are real vessels which were on active service at the time. And the same goes for the actions he gets involved in. 'Billy Ruffian', or the Bellepheron, was every bit the famous ship I have described, and there is an excellent book about it by David Cordingly for those who want to know more about life on board a Royal Navy ship in the Napoleonic era. Likewise, the various actions Richard takes part in were all part of the real ongoing naval campaigns in the Adriatic at that time.

The accounts of what Hugh went through in World War One come from my own family, though my grandfather never rose above the rank of private. He too went through the hell that was Passchendaele with the 12th Durham Light Infantry, and then went on with them to serve in the Italian Campaign. When I was researching my family history I was lucky enough to both find that the Durhams had been well documented by John Sheen, and that the regiment's war diaries had survived and been made available online through Ancestry, and so it was remarkably easy to write about them here. My grandfather never talked much about the crossing of the River Piave at the end of the war, which he was badly wounded at and which I have had Hugh take part in, but in its own way it was as much of a bloodbath as any of the actions on the Western Front, yet today it has been virtually forgotten about except by those who study the First World War.

And tactically, the same factors which made the Piave important in the First World War were also the reasons why it was important in the fight against Napoleon a century earlier. Although there are fewer firsthand accounts of that war from the point of the civilians caught up in it, the conundrum of whether they were better off staying in the Balkans and remaining ground under the Austro-Hungarian Empire, or fleeing to the less politically stable area of northern Italy is real. We think now of Italy as a unified country, but it took right up until 1870 before it ceased to be anything more than a confederation of individual states, and so the problems the family in this story faced, with the wars and civil unrest constantly washing over them, are not so imaginary.

In 2015 I went to northern Italy and stopped in the village of Selva, from where it was possible to take a trip to one of the few surviving sections of trenches from the War. Because the Dolomites are geologically so friable, most of the dugouts have been lost in landslips and avalanches, but one section amazingly survives and is worth going to see if you are visiting the area. It is an eerie experience walking those trenches, but even more so when you visit the small, local museums to the Italian soldiers who died in the mountains, and realise that they mostly came from the warmer southern provinces, and then look at how badly they were kitted out – it's not often that the British Army looks good in that war, but in comparison to what the poor Italian lads had, it does. And while we nowadays mostly think of Verona as the setting for Shakespeare's *Romeo and Juliet*, for an earlier generation of Allied soldiers, it was indeed the one place where they could fall back to from the front in the mountains with enough housing to accommodate them, and where the wounded could recuperate.

And finally, by the nineteenth century the Catholic Church had remained much stricter on the degrees of consanguinity that were permitted than the English churches had. So the issue of Ilaria and Dante marrying would have been bad enough in the Church's eyes had they only been connected in one of the ways, but to have more than one strand in common would have been beyond scandalous. And yet it is not so farfetched to think that a couple of generations on, the details of why they should not marry would have become blurred. Even nowadays, with all of the communication possibilities that exist for us, many people do not know much beyond their own grandparents, and more than a few not even that much. So with a family that had moved away from the main family base, it was not stretching reality too far to have had the wider family forgetting that they were too closely related to marry.

Thank you for taking the time to read this book.

I hope you would like to read other books like this, and the fastest way to do that is to sign up to my mailing list. I promise I won't bombard you with endless emails, but I would like to be able to let you know when any new books come out, or of any special offers I have on the existing ones.

Go to ljhutton.com to find the link or find me on Facebook

If you sign up, I will send the first in a fantasy series for free, but also other free goodies, some of which you won't get anywhere else!

Also, if you've enjoyed this book you personally (yes, *you*) can make a big difference to what happens next.

Reviews are one of the best ways to get other people to discover my books. I'm an independent author, so I don't have a publisher paying big bucks to spread the word or arrange huge promos in bookstore chains, there's just me and my computer.

But I have something that's actually better than all that corporate money – it's you, enthusiastic readers. Honest reviews help bring them to the attention of other readers (although if you think something needs fixing I would really like you to tell me first!). So if you've enjoyed this book, it would mean a great deal to me if you would spend a couple of minutes posting a review on the site where you purchased it.

About the Author

L. J. Hutton lives in Worcestershire and writes history, mystery and fantasy novels. If you would like to know more about any of these books you are very welcome to come and visit my online home at www.ljhutton.com

Alternatively, you can connect with me at Facebook

Also by L. J. Hutton

Time's Bloodied Gold

Standing stones built into an ancient church, a lost undercover detective and a dangerous gang trading treasures from the past. Can Bill Scathlock save his friend's life before his cover gets blown?

DI Bill Scathlock thought he'd seen the last of his troubled DS, Danny Sawaski, but he wasn't expecting him to disappear altogether! The Polish gang Danny was infiltrating are trafficking people to bring ancient artefacts to them, but those people aren't the usual victims, and neither is where they're coming from. With archaeologist friend Nick Robbins helping, Bill investigates, but why do people only appear at the old church, and who is the mad priest seen with the gang? With Danny's predicament getting ever more dangerous, the clock is ticking if Bill is to save him before he gets killed by the gang ...or arrested by his old colleagues!

The Rune House

A detective haunted by a past case, a house with a sinister secret, and a missing little girl! Can DI Ric Drake rescue her and find redemption along the way?

When DS Merlin 'Robbie' Roberts hears he's got a new colleague it's the last thing he wants, and especially when it's Ric Drake – infamous, recovering from a heart attack and refusing retirement. But when a modern missing child case links to one from Ric's past, and to a mysterious old house on the Welsh borders, they find a common cause. Do the ancient bodies discovered under a modern one hold the clue to both girls' fate, and does the house itself hold the key? As the links to the past keep getting stronger, Robbie and Drake must find a way to break the strange link before more children fall prey to Weord Manor's ancient lure.

The Room Within the Wall

A Roman shrine with a curse, a man accused of a murder he did not commit, and an archaeologist who holds the key to saving his life.

When archaeologist Pip comes across Cold Hunger Farm and the ancient Roman shrine to Attis embedded in its wall, it rakes up demons from her own past. Yet as she digs deeper into its records, shocking revelations come to light of heroic Georgian-era captain, Harry Green, accused of a vile and brutal murder – but who is the sinister woman manipulating his fiancée into making those claims?

464

She sounds frighteningly like someone Pip knew, so how did she get into the past, and can Pip follow her to put things right again and save Harry's life before he's hanged?

Printed in Great Britain
by Amazon

71241355R00279